red hill

ALSO BY JAMIE MCGUIRE

Beautiful Disaster

Walking Disaster

red hill

JAMIE McGUIRE

ATRIA PAPERBACK
New York London Toronto Sydney New Delhi

ATRIA PAPERBACK

A Division of Simon & Schuster, Inc.
1230 Avenue of the Americas
New York, NY 10020

First Atria Paperback edition October 2013

ATRIA PAPERBACK and colophon are trademarks of Simon & Schuster, Inc.

For information about special discounts for bulk purchases, please contact Simon & Schuster Special Sales at 1-866-506-1949 or business@simonandschuster.com.

The Simon & Schuster Speakers Bureau can bring authors to your live event. For more information or to book an event, contact the Simon & Schuster Speakers Bureau at 1-866-248-3049 or visit our website at www.simonspeakers.com.

Manufactured in the United States of America

10 9 8 7 6 5 4 3 2 1

Library of Congress Cataloging-in-Publication Data

McGuire, Jamie.
Red hill / Jamie McGuire.
pages cm.
1. Paranormal fiction. 2. End of the world—Fiction. 3. Fantasy fiction. I. Title.
PS3613.C4994R43 2013
813'.6—dc23 2013027649

ISBN 978-1-4767-5952-4
ISBN 978-1-4767-5953-1 (ebook)

To Harmony and her brains

Nom nom nom

red hill

Prologue

Scarlet

THE WARNING WAS SHORT—SAID ALMOST IN PASSING. "The cadavers were herded and destroyed." The radio hosts then made a few jokes, and that was the end of it. It took me a moment to process what the newswoman had said through the speakers of my Suburban: *Finally.* A scientist in Zurich had *finally* succeeded in creating something that—until then—had only been fictional. For years, against every code of ethics known to science, Elias Klein had tried and failed to reanimate a corpse. Once a leader amid the most intelligent in the world, he was now a laughing stock. But on that day, he would have been a criminal, if he weren't already dead.

At the time, I was watching my girls arguing in the backseat through the rearview mirror, and the two words that should have changed everything barely registered. Two words, had I not been reminding Halle to give her field trip permission slip to her teacher, would have made me drive away from the curb with my foot grinding the gas pedal to the floorboard.

Cadavers. Herded.

Instead, I was focused on saying for the third time that the girls' father, Andrew, would be picking them up from school that day. They would then drive an hour away to Anderson, the town we used to call home, and listen to Governor Bellmon speak to Andrew's fellow firefighters while the local paper took pictures. Andrew thought it would be fun for the girls, and I agreed with him—maybe for the first time since we divorced.

Although most times Andrew lacked sensitivity, he was a man of duty. He took our daughters, Jenna, who was just barely thirteen and far too beautiful (but equally dorky) for her own good, and Halle, who was seven, bowling, out to dinner, and the occasional movie, but it was only because he felt he should. To Andrew, spending time with his children was part of a job, but not one he enjoyed.

As Halle grabbed my head and jerked my face around to force sweet kisses on my cheeks, I pushed up her thick, black-rimmed glasses. Not savoring the moment, not realizing that so many things happening that day would create the perfect storm for separating us. Halle half jogged, half skipped down the walkway to the school entrance, singing loudly. She was the only human I knew who could be intolerably obnoxious and endearing at the same time.

A few speckles of water spattered on the windshield, and I leaned forward to get a better look at the cloud cover overhead. I should have sent Halle with an umbrella. Her light jacket wouldn't stand up to the early spring rain.

The next stop was the middle school. Jenna was absently discussing a reading assignment while texting the most recent boy of interest. I reminded her again as we pulled into the drop-off line that her father would pick her up at the regular spot, right after he picked up Halle.

"I heard you the first ten times," Jenna said, her voice slightly deeper than average for a girl her age. She looked at me with hollow brown eyes. She was present in body, but rarely in mind. Jenna had a wild imagination that was oh-so-random in the most wonderful way, but lately I couldn't get her to pay attention to anything other than her cell phone. I brought her into this world at just twenty. We practically grew up together, and I worried about her, if I'd done everything—or anything—right; but somehow she was turning out better than anyone could have imagined anyway.

"That was only the fourth time. Since you heard me, what did I say?"

Jenna sighed, peering down at her phone, expressionless. "Dad is picking us up. Regular spot."

"And be nice to the girlfriend. He said you were rude last time."

Jenna looked up at me. "That was the old girlfriend. I haven't been rude to the new one."

I frowned. "He just told me that a couple of weeks ago."

Jenna made a face. We didn't always have to say aloud what we were thinking, and I knew she was thinking the same thing I wanted to say, but wouldn't.

Andrew was a slut.

I sighed and turned to face forward, gripping the steering wheel so tightly my knuckles turned white. It somehow helped me to keep my mouth shut. I had made a promise to my children, silently, when I signed the divorce papers two years before: I would never bad-mouth Andrew to them. Even if he deserved it . . . and he often did.

"Love you," I said, watching Jenna push open the door with her shoulder. "See you Sunday evening."

"Yep," Jenna said.

"And don't slam the . . ."

A loud bang shook the Suburban as Jenna shoved the door closed.

". . . door." I sighed, and pulled away from the curb.

I took Maine Street to the hospital where I worked, still gripping the steering wheel tight and trying not to curse Andrew with every thought. Did he have to introduce every woman he slept with more than once to our daughters? I'd asked him, begged him, yelled at him not to, but that would be inconvenient, not letting his girl-of-the-week share weekends with his children. Never mind he had Monday through Friday with whoever. The kicker was that if the woman had children to distract Jenna and Halle, Andrew would use that opportunity to "talk" with her in the bedroom.

My blood boiled. Dutiful or not, he was an asshole when I was married to him, and an even bigger asshole now.

I whipped the Suburban into the last decent parking spot in the employee parking lot, hearing sirens as an ambulance pulled into the emergency drive and parked in the ambulance bay.

The rain began to pour. A groan escaped my lips, watching coworkers run inside, their scrubs soaked from just a short dash across the street to the side entrance. I was half a block away.

TGIF.

TGIF.

TGIF.

Just before I turned off the ignition, another report came over the radio, something about an epidemic in Europe. Looking back, everyone knew then what was going on, but it had been a running joke for so long that no one wanted to believe it was really happening. With all the television shows, comics, books, and movies about the undead, it shouldn't have been a surprise that somebody was finally both smart and crazy enough to try and make it a reality.

I know the world ended on a Friday. It was the last day I saw my children.

Chapter One

Scarlet

MY CHEST HEAVED AS THE THICK METAL DOOR CLOSED loudly behind me. I held out my arms to each side, letting water drip off my fingertips onto the white tile floor. My once royal-blue scrubs were now navy, heavily saturated with cold rainwater.

A squashing sound came from my sneakers when I took a step. *Ick.* Not much was worse than wet clothes and shoes, and it felt like I'd jumped into a swimming pool fully dressed. Even my panties were wet. We were only a few days into spring, and a cold front had come through. The rain felt like flying death spikes of ice.

Flying death spikes. *Snort.* Jenna's dramatic way of describing things was obviously rubbing off on me.

I slid my name badge through the card reader and waited until the small light at the top turned green and a high-pitched beep sounded, accompanied by the loud click of the lock release. I had to use all of my body weight to pull open the heavy door, and then I stepped into the main hallway.

Fellow coworkers flashed me understanding smiles that helped to relieve some of my humiliation. It was obvious who all had just arrived on shift, about the time the sky opened up and pissed on us.

Two steps at a time, I climbed the stairs to the surgical floor and snuck into the women's locker room, stripping down and changing into a pair of light-blue surgery scrubs. I held my sneakers under the hand dryer, but only for a few seconds. The other X-ray techs were waiting for me downstairs. We had an upper GI/small bowel follow-through at 8:00, and this week's radiologist was more than just a little grumpy when we made him run behind.

Sneakers still squishing, I rushed down the steps and back down the main hallway to Radiology, passing the ER double doors on my way. Chase, the security guard, waved at me as I passed.

"Hey, Scarlet," he said with a small, shy smile.

I only nodded, more concerned with getting the upper GI ready on time than with chitchat.

"You should talk to him," Christy said. She nodded in Chase's direction as I breezed by her and her piles of long, yellow ringlets.

I shook my head, walking into the exam room. The familiar sound of my feet sticking to the floor began an equally familiar beat. Whatever they cleaned the floor with was supposed to sanitize the worst bacteria known to man, but it left behind a sticky residue. Maybe to remind us it was there—or that the floor needed to be mopped again. I pulled bottles of barium contrast from the upper cabinet, and filled the remaining space with water. I replaced the cap, and then shook the bottle to mix the powder and water into a disgusting, slimy paste that smelled of bananas. "Don't start. I've already told you no. He looks fifteen."

"He's twenty-seven, and don't be a shrew. He's cute, and he's dying for you to talk to him."

Her mischievous smile was infuriatingly contagious. "He's a kid," I said. "Go get the patient."

Christy smiled and left the room, and I made a mental note of everything I'd set on the table for Dr. Hayes. God, he was cranky; particularly on Mondays, and even more so during shitty weather.

I was lucky enough to be somewhat on his good side. As a student, I had cleaned houses for the radiologists. It earned me decent money, and was perfect since I was in school forty hours a week at that time. The docs were hard asses in the hospital, but they helped me out more than anyone else while I was going through the divorce, letting me bring the girls to work, and giving me a little extra at Christmas and on birthdays.

Dr. Hayes paid me well to drive to his escape from the city, Red Hill Ranch, an hour and a half away in the middle-of-nowhere Kansas to clean his old farmhouse. It was a long drive, but it served its purpose: No cell service. No Internet. No traffic. No neighbors.

Finding the place on my own took a few tries until Halle made up a song with the directions. I could hear her tiny voice in my head, singing loudly and sweetly out the window.

West on Highway 11
On our way to heaven
North on Highway 123
123? 123!

Cross the border
That's an order!
Left at the white tower
So Mom can clean the doctor's shower
Left at the cemetery
Creepy . . . and scary!
First right!
That's right!
Red! Hill! Roooooooad!

After that, we could make it there, rain or shine. I'd even mentioned a few times that it would be the perfect hideaway in case of an apocalypse. Jenna and I were sort of post-apocalyptic junkies, always watching end-of-the-world marathons and preparation television shows. We never canned chicken or built an underground tank in the woods, but it was entertaining to see the lengths other people went to.

Dr. Hayes's ranch would make the safest place to survive. The cupboards and pantry were always stocked with food, and the basement would make any gun enthusiast proud. The gentle hills kept the farmhouse somewhat inconspicuous, and wheat fields bordered three sides. The road was about fifty yards from the north side of the house, and on the other side of the red dirt was another wheat field. Other than the large maple tree in the back, visibility was excellent. Good for watching sunsets, bad for anyone trying to sneak in undetected.

Christy opened the door and waited for the patient to enter. The young woman stepped just inside the door, thin, her eyes sunken and tired. She looked at least twenty pounds underweight.

"This is Dana Marks, date of birth twelve, nine, eighty-nine. Agreed?" Christy asked, turning to Dana.

Dana nodded, the thin skin on her neck stretching over her tendons as she did so. Her skin was a sickly gray, highlighting the purple under her eyes.

Christy handed the woman loose folds of thin blue fabric. "Just take this gown behind the curtain there, and undress down to your underpants. They don't have any rhinestones or anything, do they?"

Dana shook her head, seeming slightly amused, and then slowly made her way behind the curtain.

Christy picked up a film and walked to the X-ray table in the middle of the room, sliding it into the Bucky tray between the table surface and the controls. "You should at least say hi."

"Hi."

"Not me, dummy. To Chase."

"Are we still talking about him?"

Christy rolled her eyes. "Yes. He's cute, has a good job, has never been married, no kids. Did I mention cute? All that dark hair . . . and his eyes!"

"They're brown. Go ahead. I dare you to play up brown."

"They're not just brown. They're like a golden honey brown. You better jump on that now before you miss your chance. Do you know how many single women in this hospital are salivating over that?"

"I'm not worried about it."

Christy smiled and shook her head, and then her expression changed once her pager went off. She pulled it from her waistline and glanced down. "Crap. I have to move the C-arm from OR 2 for Dr. Pollard's case. Hey, I might have to leave a little early to take Kate to the orthodontist. Do you think you could do my three o'clock surgery? It's easy peasy."

"What is it?"

"Just a port. Basically C-arm babysitting."

The C-arm, named for its shape, showed the doctors where they were in the body in real time. Because the machine emitted radiation, it was our jobs as X-ray techs to stand there, push, pull, and push the button during surgery. That, and make sure the doctor didn't over-radiate the patient. I didn't mind running it, but the damn thing was heavy. Christy would have done the same for me, though, so I nodded. "Sure. Just give me the pager before you leave."

Christy grabbed a lead apron, and then left me to go upstairs. "You're awesome. I wrote Dana's history on the requisition sheet. See you later! Get Chase's number!"

Dana walked slowly from the bathroom, and I gestured for her to sit in a chair beside the table.

"Did your doctor explain this procedure to you?"

Dana shook her head. "Not really."

A few choice words crossed my mind. How a doctor could send a patient in for a procedure without an explanation was beyond me, and how a patient couldn't ask wasn't something I understood, either.

"I'll take a few X-rays of your abdomen, and then fetch the doctor. I'll come back, make the table vertical, and you'll stand and drink that cup of barium," I said, pointing to the cup behind me on the counter, "a sip at a time, at the doctor's discretion. He'll use fluoroscopy to watch the barium travel down your esophagus and into your stomach. Fluoro is basically an X-ray, but instead of a picture, we get a video in real time. When that's done, we'll start the small bowel follow-through. You'll drink the rest of the barium, and we'll take X-rays as it flows through your small bowel."

Dana eyed the cup. "Does it taste bad? I've been vomiting a lot. I can't keep anything down."

The requisition page with Christy's scribbles was lying on the counter next to the empty cups. I picked it up, looking for the answer to my next question. Dana had only been ill for two days. I glanced up at her, noting her appearance.

"Have you been sick like this before?" She shook her head in answer. "Traveled recently?" She shook her head again. "Any history of Crohn's disease? Anorexia? Bulimia?" I asked.

She held out her arm, palm up. There was a perfect bite mark in the middle of her forearm. Each tooth had broken the skin. Deep, red perforations dotted her arm in mirrored half-moons, but the bruised skin around the bites was still intact.

I met her eyes. "Dog?"

"A drunk," she said with a weak laugh. "I was at a party Tuesday night. We had just left, and some asshole wandering around outside just grabbed my arm and took a bite. He might have pulled a whole chunk off if my boyfriend hadn't hit him. Knocked him out long enough for us to find the car and leave. I saw on the news yesterday that he'd attacked other people, too. It was the same night, and the same apartment complex. Had to be him." She let her arm fall to her side, seeming exhausted. "Joey's in the waiting room . . . scared to death I have rabies. He just got back from his last tour in Afghanistan. He's seen everything, but he can't stand to hear me throw up." She laughed quietly to herself.

I offered a comforting smile. "Sounds like a keeper. Just hop up on the table there, and lay on your back."

Dana did as I asked, but needed assistance. Her bony hands were like ice.

"How much weight did you say you've lost?" I asked while situating her on the table, sure I had read Christy's history report wrong on the requisition.

Dana winced from the cold, hard table pressing against her pelvic bone and spine.

"Blanket?" I asked, already pulling the thick, white cotton from the warmer.

"Please." Dana hummed as I draped the blanket over her. "Thank you so much. I just can't seem to get warm."

"Abdominal pain?"

"Yes. A lot."

"Pounds lost?"

"Almost twenty."

"Since Tuesday?"

Dana raised her brows. "Believe me, I know. Especially since I was thin to begin with. You . . . don't think it's rabies . . . do you?" She tried to laugh off her remark, but I could hear the worry in her voice.

I smiled. "They don't send you in for an upper GI if they think it's rabies."

Dana sighed and looked at the ceiling. "Thank God."

Once I positioned Dana, centered the X-ray tube, and set my technique, I pressed the button and then took the film to the reader. My eyes were glued to the monitor, curious if she had a bowel obstruction, or if a foreign body was present.

"Whatcha got there, buddy?" David asked, standing behind me.

"Not sure. She's lost twenty pounds in two days."

"No way."

"Way."

"Poor kid," he said, genuine sympathy in his voice.

David watched with me as the image illuminated the screen. When Dana's abdomen film filled the screen, David and I both stared at it in shock.

David touched his fingers to his mouth. *"No way."*

I nodded slowly. "Way."

David shook his head. "I've never seen that. I mean, in a textbook, yes, but . . . man. Bad deal."

The image on the monitor was hypnotizing. I'd never seen someone present with that gas pattern, either. I couldn't even remember seeing it in a textbook.

"They've been talking a lot on the radio this morning about that virus in Germany. They say it's spreading all over. It looks like war on the television. People panicking in the streets. Scary stuff."

I frowned. "I heard that when I dropped off the girls this morning."

"You don't think the patient has it, do you? They're not really saying exactly what it is, but that," he said, gesturing to the monitor, "is impossible."

"You know as well as I do that we see new stuff all the time."

David stared at the image for a few seconds more, and then nodded, snapping out of his deep thought. "Hayes is ready when you are."

I grabbed a lead apron, slid my arms through the armholes, and then fastened the tie behind my back as I walked to the reading room to fetch Dr. Hayes.

As expected, he was sitting in his chair in front of his monitor in the dark, speaking quietly into his dictation mic. I waited patiently just outside the doorway for him to finish, and then he looked up at me.

"Dana Marks, twenty-three years old, presenting with abdominal pain and significant weight loss since Wednesday. Some hair loss. No history of abdominal disease or heart problems, no previous abdominal surgeries, no previous abdominal exams."

Dr. Hayes pulled up the image I'd just taken, and squinted his eyes for a moment. "How significant?"

"Nineteen pounds."

He looked only slightly impressed until the image appeared on the screen. He blanched. "Oh my God."

"I know."

"Where has she been?"

"She hasn't traveled recently, if that's what you mean. She did mention being attacked by a drunk after a party Tuesday night."

"This is profound. Do you see the ring of gas here?" he asked, pointing to the screen. His eyes brightened with recognition. "Portal venous gas. Look at the biliary tree outline. Remarkable." Dr. Hayes went from animated to somber in less than a second. "You don't see this very often, Scarlet. This patient isn't going to do well."

I swallowed back my heartbreak for Dana. She either had a severe infection or something else blocking or restricting the veins in her bowel. Her insides were basically dead and withering away. She might have four more days. They would probably attempt to take her to emergency surgery, but would likely just close her back up. "I know."

"Who's her doctor?"

"Vance."

"I'll call him. Cancel the UGI. She'll need a CT."

I nodded and then stood in the hall while Dr. Hayes spoke in a low voice, explaining his findings to Dr. Vance.

"All right. Let's get to it," the doctor said, standing from his chair. We both took a moment to separate ourselves from the grim future of the patient. Dr. Hayes followed me down the hall toward the exam room where Dana waited. "The girls doing okay?"

I nodded. "They're at their dad's this weekend. They're going to meet the governor."

"Oh," the doctor said, pretending to be impressed. He'd met the governor several times. "My girls are coming home this weekend, too."

I smiled, glad to hear it. Since Dr. Hayes's divorce, Miranda and Ashley didn't come home to visit nearly as much as he would have liked. They were both in college, both in serious relationships, and both mama's girls. Much to the doctor's dismay, any free time they had away from boyfriends and studying was usually spent with their mother.

He stopped, took a breath, held the exam-room door open, and then followed me inside. He hadn't given me time to set up the room before he came back, so I was glad the upper GI was cancelled.

David was shaking the bottles of barium.

"Thanks, David. We won't be needing those."

David nodded. Having seen the images before, he already knew why.

I helped Dana to a sitting position, and she stared at both of us, clearly wondering what was going on.

"Dana," Dr. Hayes began, "you say your problem began early Wednesday morning?"

"Yes," she said, her voice strained with increasing discomfort.

Dr. Hayes abruptly stopped, and then smiled at Dana, putting his hand on hers. "We're not going to do the upper GI today. Dr. Vance is going to schedule you a CT instead. We're going to have you get dressed and go back to the waiting room. They should be calling you before long. Do you have someone with you today?"

"Joey, my boyfriend."

"Good," the doctor said, patting her hand.

"Am I going to be okay?" she said, struggling to sit on her bony backside.

Dr. Hayes smiled in the way I imagined him smiling while speaking to his daughters. "We're going to take good care of you. Don't worry."

I helped Dana step to the floor. "Leave your gown on," I said, quickly grabbing another one and holding it behind her. "Slip this on behind you like a robe." She slipped her tiny arms through the holes, and then I helped her to the chair beside the cabinet. "Go ahead and put on your shoes. I'll be right back. Just try to relax."

"Yep," Dana said, trying to get comfortable.

I grabbed her requisition off the counter and followed the doctor to the workroom.

As soon as we were out of earshot, Dr. Hayes turned to me. "Try to talk to her some more. See if you can get something else out of her."

"I can try. All she mentioned out of the ordinary was the bite."

"You're sure it wasn't an animal?"

I shrugged. "She said it was some drunk guy. It looks infected."

Dr. Hayes looked at Dana's abnormal gas patterns on the monitor once more. "That's too bad. She seems like a sweet kid."

I nodded, somber. David and I traded glances, and then I took a breath, mentally preparing myself to carry such a heavy secret back into that room. Keeping her own death from her felt like a betrayal, even though we'd only just met.

My sneakers made a ripping noise as they pulled away from the floor. "Ready?" I asked with a bright smile.

Chapter Two

Scarlet

BY LUNCH, DANA HAD ALREADY BEEN IN AND OUT OF surgery. Christy told us they only opened her up long enough to see there was nothing they could do, before closing her back up. Now they were waiting for her to awaken so they could tell her she would never get better.

"Her boyfriend is still with her," Christy said. "Her parents are visiting relatives. They're not sure they'll get back in time."

"Oh, Jesus," I said, wincing. I couldn't imagine being away from either of my daughters in a situation like that, wondering if I would make it in time to see her alive one last time. I shook it off. Those of us in the medical field didn't have the luxury of thinking about our patients' personal lives. It became too close. Too real.

"Did you hear about that flu?" Christy said. "It's all over the news."

I shook my head. "I don't think it's a flu."

"They're saying it has to do with that scientist over in Europe. They say it's highly contagious."

"Who are *they*? *They* sound like troublemakers to me."

Christy smiled and rolled her eyes. "*They* also said it's breached our borders. California is reporting cases."

"Really?"

"That's what they say," she said. Her pager buzzed. "Damn, it's getting busy." She pushed a button and called upstairs, and then she was gone again.

Within the hour, the hospital was crowded and frantic. The ER was admitting patients at a hectic pace, keeping everyone in radiology busy. David called in another tech so he and I could cover the ER while everyone else attended to outpatients and inpatients.

Whatever it was, the whole town seemed to be going crazy. Car accidents, fights, and a fast-spreading virus had hit at the same time. On my sixth trip to the ER, I passed the radiology waiting room and saw a group of people crowded around the flat-screen television on the wall.

"David?" I said, signaling for him to join me in front of the waiting room. He looked in through the wall of glass, noting the only seated person was a man in a wheelchair.

"Yeah?"

"I have a bad feeling about this." I felt sick watching the updates on the screen. "They were talking about something like this on the radio this morning."

"Yeah. They were reporting the first cases here about half an hour ago."

I stared into his eyes. "I should leave to try to catch up to my girls. They're halfway to Anderson by now."

"As busy as we are, no way is Anita going to let you leave. Anyway, it's highly contagious, but disease control maintains that it's just a virus, Scarlet. I heard that those that got the flu shot are the ones affected."

That one sentence, even unsubstantiated, immediately set my mind at ease. I hadn't had a flu shot in three years because I always felt terrible afterward, and I'd never gotten one for the girls. Something about vaccinating for a virus that may or may not protect against whatever strain came through didn't sit well with me. We had enough shit in our bodies with hormones and chemicals in our foods and everyday pollutants. It didn't make sense to subject ourselves to more, even if the hospital encouraged it.

Just as David and I finished up our last batch of portable X-rays in the ER, Christy rounded the corner, looking worn.

"Has it been as busy down here as it's been up there?"

"Yes," David said. "Probably worse."

"Can you still do that port for me?" Christy said, her eyes begging.

I looked to David, and then back at Christy. "The way things are going, if I take that pager, I'll be stuck up there until quitting time. They really need me down here."

David looked at his watch. "Tasha comes in at three thirty. We can handle it until then."

"You sure?" I asked, slowly taking the pager from Christy.

David waved me away dismissively. "No problem. I'll take the pager from you when Tasha gets here so you can go home."

I clipped the pager to the waistband of my scrubs, and headed upstairs, waving good-bye to Christy.

She frowned, already feeling guilty. "Thank you very, very much!"

I passed Chase for the umpteenth time. As the hours

passed, he'd looked increasingly nervous. Everyone was. From the looks of things inside the ER, it seemed like all hell was breaking loose outside. I kept trying to sneak peeks at the television but once I finished one case, the pager would go off again to direct me to another.

Just as I had anticipated, once I arrived on the surgery floor, there would be no leaving until David relieved me at 3:30. Case after case, I was moving the C-arm from surgery suite to surgery suite, sometimes moving a second one in for whomever was called up for a surgery going on at the same time.

In one afternoon I saw a shattered femur, two broken arms, and a broken hip, and shared an elevator with a patient in a gurney accompanied by two nurses, all on their way to the roof. His veins were visibly dark through his skin, and he was covered in sweat. From what I could make of their nervous banter, the patient was being med-flighted out to amputate his hand.

My last case of the day was precarious at best, but I didn't want to have to call David up to relieve me. My girls were out of town with their father, and David had a pretty wife and two young sons to go home to. It didn't make sense for me to leave on time and for him to stay late, but I had already logged four hours of overtime for the week, and that was generally frowned upon by the brass.

I walked past the large woman in the gurney, looking nervous and upset. Her hand was bandaged, but a large area was saturated with blood. I remembered her from the ER, and wondered where her family was. They all had been with her downstairs.

Angie, the circulation nurse, swished by, situating her surgical cap. It was covered in rough sketches of hot-pink lipsticks and purses. As if to validate her choice of head cover, she pulled out a tube of lip gloss and swiped it across her lips. She smiled at me. "I hear Chase has been asking about you."

I looked down, instantly embarrassed. "Not you, too." Was everyone so bored that they had nothing better to do than fantasize about my non-love life? Was I that pathetic that a prospect for me was so exciting?

She winked at me as she passed. "Call him, or I'm going to steal him from you."

I smiled. "Promise?"

Angie rolled her eyes, but her expression immediately compressed. "Damn! Scarlet, I'm sorry, your mom is on line two."

"My mom?"

"They transferred her call up a couple of minutes before you came in."

I glanced at the phone, wondering what on earth she would be calling me at work about. We barely spoke at all, so it must have been important. Maybe about the girls. I nearly lunged for the phone.

"Hello?"

"Scarlet! Oh, thank God. Have you been watching the news?"

"A little. We've been slammed. From the few glimpses I've gotten, it looks bad. Did you see the reports of the panic at LAX? People were sick on some of the flights over. They think that's how it traveled here."

"I wouldn't worry too much about it. Nothing ever happens in the middle of the country."

"Why did you call, then?" I said, confused. "Are the girls okay?"

"The girls?" She made a noise with her throat. Even her

breath could be condescending. "Why would I be calling about the girls? My kitchen floor is pulling up in the corner by the refrigerator, and I was hoping you could ask Andrew to come fix it."

"He has the girls this weekend, Mother. I can't really talk right now. I'm in surgery."

"Yes, I know. Your life is so important."

I glanced at Angie, seeing that she and the surgical tech were nearly finished. "I'll ask him, but like I said, he has the girls."

"He has the girls a lot. Have you been going to the bars every weekend, or what?"

"No."

"So what else is more important than raising your children?"

"I have to go."

"Sensitive subject. You've never liked to be told you're doing something wrong."

"It's his weekend, Mother, like it is every other weekend."

"Well. Why does his weekend have to be the weekend I need help?"

"I really have to go."

"Did you at least send dresses with them so their daddy can take them to church? Since he's the only one who seems to care to teach them about the Lord."

"Good-bye, Mother." I hung up the phone and sighed just as Dr. Pollard came in.

"Afternoon, all. This shouldn't take long," he said. He held his hands in front of him, fingers pointing up, waiting for Angie to put gloves on them. "But by the looks of it we're all in for a long night, so I hope none of you had plans."

"Is that true?" Ally, the scrub tech, asked from behind her mask. "About LAX?"

"It happened at Dulles, too," Angie said.

I glanced at the clock, and then pulled my cell phone from the front pocket of my scrubs. I could be written up if someone felt like ratting me out for being on it, but an extra piece of paper in my file was worth it in this case. I pecked out the words *Call Me ASAP,* and then sent them on to Jenna's phone.

After a couple of minutes with no response, I dialed Andrew. It rang four times, then his voicemail took over.

I sighed. "It's Scarlet. Please call me at the hospital. I'm in surgery, but call me anyway so we can coordinate. I'm coming there as soon as I get off work."

Nathan

ANOTHER EIGHT-HOUR DAY THAT DIDN'T MEAN A DAMN thing. When I clocked out from the office, freedom should have been at the forefront of my mind, or should have at least brought a smile to my face, but it didn't. Knowing I had just wasted another day of my life was depressing. Tragic, even. Stuck at a desk job for an electric co-op that made no difference in the world, day in and day out, and then going home to a wife who hated me made for a miserable existence.

Aubrey hadn't always been a mean bitch. When we first got married, she had a sense of humor, she couldn't wait until it was bedtime so we could lie together and kiss and touch. She would initiate a blowjob because she wanted to please me, not because it was my birthday.

Seven years ago, she changed. We had Zoe, and my role switched from desirable, adoring husband to a source of constant disappointment. Aubrey's expectations of me were never met. If I tried to help, it was either too much, or it wasn't done the right way. If I tried to stay out of her way, I was a lazy bastard.

Aubrey quit her job to stay home with Zoe, so mine was the only source of income. Suddenly that wasn't enough, either. Because I didn't make what Aubrey felt was enough money, she expected me to give her a "baby break" the second I walked in the door. I wasn't allowed to talk to my wife. She would disappear into the den, sit at the computer, and talk to her Internet friends.

I'd entertain Zoe while emptying the dishwasher and prepping dinner. Asking for help was a sin, and interrupting the baby break just gave Aubrey one more reason to hate me, as if she didn't have enough already.

Once Zoe started kindergarten, I hoped it would get better, that Aubrey would start back to work, and she would feel like her old self again. But she just couldn't break free of her anger. She didn't seem to want to.

Zoe had just a few weeks left in second grade. I would pick her up from school, and we would both hope Aubrey would turn away from the computer just long enough to notice we were home.

On a good day, she would.

Today, though, she wouldn't. The Internet and radio had been abuzz since early morning with breaking news about an epidemic. A busy news day meant Aubrey's ass would be stationed firmly against the stained, faded blue fabric of her office chair. She would be talking about it with strangers in forums, with friends and distant family on social networks, and commenting on news websites. Theories. Debates. Somewhere along the way it had become a part of our marriage, and I had been edged out.

I waited in my eight-year-old sedan, first in a line of cars parked behind the elementary school. Zoe didn't like to be the last one picked up, so I made sure to go to her school right after work. Waiting forty minutes gave me enough time to decompress from work, and psych myself up for another busy night without help or acknowledgment from my wife.

The DJ's tone was more serious than it had been, so I turned up the volume. He was using a word I hadn't heard them use before: *pandemic*. The contagion had breached our shores. Panic had broken out in Dulles and LAX airports when passengers who'd fallen ill during their international flights began attacking the airline employees and paramedics helping them off the plane.

In the back of my head, I knew what was happening. The morning anchor had reported the arrest of a researcher somewhere in Europe, and while my thoughts kept returning to how impossible it was, I knew.

I looked into the rearview mirror, my appearance nearly unrecognizable to anyone that had known me in better days. The browns of my eyes were no longer bright and full of purpose like they once were. The skin beneath them was shaded with dark circles. Just fifteen years ago I was two hundred pounds of muscle and confidence; now I felt a little more broken down every day.

Aubrey and I met in high school. Back then she wanted to touch me and talk to me. Our story wasn't all that exciting: I was on the starting lineup of a small-town football team, and she was head cheerleader. We were both big fish in a small pond. My light-brown, shaggy hair moved when a breeze passed through the passenger side window. Aubrey used to love how long it was. Now all she did was bitch that I needed a haircut. Come to think of it, she bitched about everything when it came to me. I still went to the gym, and the women at work were at times a little forward, but Aubrey didn't see me anymore. I wasn't sure if it was being with her that sucked the life out of me, or the disappointments I'd suffered over the years. The further away I was from high school, the less making something of myself seemed possible.

An obnoxious buzzing noise on the radio caught my attention. I listened while a man's robotic voice came over the speakers of my car. "This is a red alert from the emergency broadcast system. Canton County sheriff's department reports a highly contagious virus arriving in our state has been confirmed. If at all possible, stay indoors. This is a red alert from the emergency broadcast system . . ."

Movement on the side of my rearview mirror caught my attention. A woman was sprinting from her car toward the door of the school. Another woman jumped from her minivan and, after a short pause, ran toward the school as well with her toddler in her arms.

They were mothers. Of course they wouldn't let the logical side of their brain talk them into hesitation. The world was going to hell, and they were going to get their children to safety . . . wherever that was.

I shoved the gearshift into park and opened my door. I walked quickly, but as frantic mothers ran past me, I broke into a run as well.

Inside the building, mothers were either carrying their children down the hall to the parking lot, or they were quickly pushing through the doors of their children's classrooms, not wasting time explaining to their teachers why they were leaving early.

I dodged frightened parents pulling their confused children along by the hand until I reached Zoe's classroom. The door cracked against the concrete wall as I yanked it open.

The children looked at me with wide eyes. None of them had been picked up yet.

"Mr. Oxford?" Mrs. Earl said. She was frozen in the center of her classroom, surrounded by mini desks and chairs, and mini people. They were patiently waiting for her to hand out the papers they were to take home. Papers that wouldn't matter a few hours from now.

"Sorry. I need Zoe." Zoe was staring at me, too, unaccustomed to people barging in. She looked so small, even in the miniature chair she sat in. Her light-brown hair was curled under just so, barely grazing her shoulders, just the way she liked it. The greens and browns of her irises were visible even half a classroom away. She looked so innocent and vulnerable sitting there; all the children did.

"Braden?" Melissa George burst through the door, nearly running me down. "Come on, baby," she said, holding her hand out to her son.

Braden glanced at Mrs. Earl, who nodded, and then the boy left his chair to join his mother. They left without a word.

"We have to go, too," I said, walking over to Zoe's desk.

"But my papers, Daddy."

"We'll get your papers later, honey."

Zoe leaned to the side, looking around me to her cubby. "My backpack."

I picked her up, trying to keep calm, wondering what the

world would look like outside the school, or if I would reach my car and feel like a fool.

"Mr. Oxford?" Mrs. Earl said again, this time meeting me at the door. She leaned into my ear, staring into my eyes at the same time. "What's going on?"

I looked around her classroom, to the watchful eyes of her young students. Pictures drawn clumsily in thick lines of crayon and bright educational posters hung haphazardly from the walls. The floor was littered with clippings from their artwork.

Every child in the room stared at me, waiting to hear why I'd decided to intrude. They would keep waiting. None of them could fathom the nightmare that awaited them just a few hours from now—if we had that much time—and I wasn't going to cause a panic.

"You need to get these kids home, Mrs. Earl. You need to get them to their parents, and then you need to run."

I didn't wait for her reaction. Instead I bolted down the congested hallway. A traffic jam seemed to be causing a bottleneck at the main exit, so I pushed a side door to the pre-K playground open with my shoulder, and with Zoe in my arms, hopped the fence.

"Daddy! You're not supposed to climb the fence!"

"I'm sorry, honey. Daddy's in a hurry. We have to pick up Mommy and . . ."

My words trailed off as I fastened Zoe into her seatbelt. I had no idea where we would go. Where could we hide from something like this?

"Can we go to the gas station and get a slushie?"

"Not today, baby," I said, kissing her forehead before slamming the door.

I tried not to run around the front. I tried, but the panic and adrenaline pushed me forward. The door slammed shut, and I tore out of the parking lot, unable to control the fear that if I slowed down even a little bit, something terrible would happen.

One hand on the steering wheel, and the other holding my cell phone to my ear, I drove home, ignoring traffic lights and speed limits and trying to be careful not to get nailed by other panicked drivers.

"Daddy!" Zoe yelled when I drove over a bump too fast. "What are you doing?"

"Sorry, Zoe. Daddy's in a hurry."

"Are we late?"

I wasn't sure how to answer that. "I hope not."

Zoe's expression signaled her disapproval. She always made an effort to parent Aubrey and me. Probably because Aubrey wasn't much of one, and it was clear on most days that I didn't know what the hell I was doing.

I pressed on the gas, trying to avoid the main roads home. Every time I tried to call Aubrey from my cell, I got a weird busy signal. I should have known when I got there that something was wrong. I should have immediately put the sedan in reverse and raced away, but the only thing going through my head was how I would convince Aubrey to leave her goddamned computer, what few things we would grab, and how much time I should allow to grab them. An errant thought ran through my head about how much time it would take the Internet to cease, and how ironic it was that a viral outbreak would save our marriage. There were so many *should haves* in that moment, but I ignored them all.

"Aubrey!" I yelled as I opened the door. The most logical

place to look was the den. The empty blue office chair was a surprise. So much so that I froze, staring at the space as if my vision would correct itself and she would eventually appear, her back to me, hunched over the desk while she moved just enough to maneuver the mouse.

"Where's Mommy?" Zoe asked, her voice sounding even smaller than usual.

A mixture of alarm and curiosity made me pause. Aubrey's ass had flowed over and cratered in the deteriorated cushion of that office chair for years. No noise in the kitchen, and the downstairs bathroom door was open, the room dark.

"Aubrey!" I yelled from the second step of the stairs, waiting for her to round the corner above me and descend each step more dramatically than the last. At any moment, she would breathe her signature sigh of annoyance and bitch at me for something—anything—but as I waited, it became obvious that she wouldn't.

"We're going to be very late," Zoe said, looking up at me.

I squeezed her hand, and then a white envelope in the middle of the dining table caught my eye. I pulled Zoe along with me, afraid to let her out of my sight for a second, and then picked up the envelope. It read "Nathan" on the front, in Aubrey's girly yet sloppy script.

"Are you serious?" I said, ripping open the envelope.

Nathan,

By the time you get this I'll be hours away. Your probably going to think I'm the most selfish person in the world, but being afraid of you thinking bad of me isn't enough for me to stay.

I'm unhappy and I've been unhappy for a long time.

I love Zoe, but I'm not a mother. You are the one that wanted to be a father. I knew you would be a good daddy, and I thought that you being a good daddy would make me a good mother, but it didn't. I can't do this anymore. There are so many things I want to do with my life and being a housewife isn't one of them.

I'm sorry if you hate me, but I've finally decided I can live with that. I'm sorry you have to explain this to Zoe. I'll call tomorrow when I'm settled and try to help her understand.

Aubrey

I let the folded paper fall to the table. She could never spell *you're* correctly. That was just one of a hundred things about Aubrey that bothered me but I never mentioned.

Zoe was looking up at me, waiting for me to explain or react, but I could do neither. Aubrey had left us. I came back for her lazy, cranky, miserable ass, and she fucking left us.

A scream outside startled Zoe enough for her to grip my leg, and reality hit about the same time that bullets came crashing through the kitchen windows. I ducked, and signaled Zoe to duck with me.

There would be no calling Aubrey's friends and relatives to find out where she was so I could beg her to come back. I had to get my daughter to safety. Aubrey might have picked a horrible first day for independence, but it was what she wanted, and I had a little girl to protect.

More screams. Car horns honking. Gunfire. *Jesus. Jesus, Jesus, Jesus.* It was here.

I opened the hallway closet and grabbed my baseball bat, and then walked over to my daughter, kneeling in front of her to meet her tear-glazed eyes. "Zoe, we're going to have to get back to the car. I need you to hold my hand, and no matter what you see or hear, don't let go of my hand, do you understand?"

Zoe's eyes filled with more tears, but she nodded quickly.

"Good girl," I said, kissing her on the forehead.

Chapter Three

Scarlet

"BIT OFF?" THE NURSE, JOANNE, ASKED, CAREFULLY prepping the patient's hand. "By a dog?"

"I don't know," Ally said, her voice muffled behind her mask. She was a new hire for the scrub tech team, just out of school. She was twenty, but the way her big eyes were staring at the patient's hand made her look all of twelve. "Some kind of animal."

"Her son," I said, waiting with my X-ray equipment for the surgeon to arrive. Joanne and Ally looked at the meaty, exposed knuckle. "I took the X-rays," I added. "She was pretty shaken, but she said her son bit off her thumb."

Angie walked through the door with tiny steps. Her scrub pants made a swishing sound as she busily finished different tasks around the room.

"Are you sure she said her son?" Ally asked, staring at the site of the missing digit with renewed interest.

"He's in the ER," Angie said. "I heard he's exhibiting signs of rabies. Several people are."

"You don't think this has anything to do with what's been on the news, do you?" Ally asked, nervous. "Could it have made it here already from Germany? Could it spread that fast?"

The room grew quiet then.

The anesthesiologist had been nervous from the beginning about putting Margaret Sisney under. Instead of playing on his cell phone like usual, he stood over her, focused on every rise of her chest. He looked away every few seconds to focus on the numbers on the monitor, and then returned his attention to Margaret. It was hard to tell with the rest of her under blue surgical sheets, but her face and neck were visibly bluish in color. "She's cyanotic," he explained. He adjusted several knobs, and then prepared a syringe.

"Dr. Ingram," the nurse said to the anesthesiologist. "The patient's fingernails."

Even through the orange-brown tint of the iodine scrub, Margaret's nails were blackening.

"Shit," Dr. Ingram said. His eyes bounced back and forth between the patient and the monitor. "This was a mistake. A big damn mistake!"

Margaret's thumb was on ice across the room, waiting to be reattached. It was cyanotic as well, and Dr. Ferber's call to take her to surgery when she wasn't quite stable in the ER was questionable, even to a newly graduated X-ray tech like me. I watched as her stats deteriorated, and moved my equipment to the far wall, knowing a Code Blue was imminent.

My pager vibrated against my skin, and I reached under my top to grab it from the waistline of my scrubs. "Shit. Angie, I've got to set up in OR Four, and then I'm off. I'll send David up here. He'll have the pager."

"It's probably going to be a while, anyway, if we do it at all," Angie said, opening packages and buzzing around the room.

I rushed to the end of the hall, pushing and pulling heavy X-ray equipment in front of and behind me. The moment I finished setting up for the next patient, the call came over the intercom system.

"Code Blue. OR Seven. Code Blue. OR Seven," a woman's voice droned, sounding calm and apathetic.

I picked up the phone that hung on the wall by the door, and called down to the department. "Hey, it's Scarlet. I set up OR Four, but looks like Seven's going to be a while, if at all. Tell David to meet me at the south elevator on one. He needs to work this code, and I need to give him the pager."

As I walked down the hall, nurses, doctors, and anesthesiologists rushed past me, making their way to Margaret Sisney. I pushed the button for the elevator, and yanked the surgical mask off my face. When the doors opened, I sighed at the sight of the crowd inside.

"We've got room, Scarlet," Lana from accounting said.

"I'll uh . . . I'll take the stairs," I said, pointing with a small gesture to my right.

I turned on my heels, pushed through the double doors of the OR, and then used my shoulder to help offset the weight of the heavy door that led to the stairwell.

"One, two, three, four, five, six . . . ," I counted quickly, jogging down one set, and then the other. When I pushed my way into the hallway of the first floor, David was already waiting at the elevator.

"Enjoy," I said, tossing him the pager.

"Thanks, buddy. Have a good one," he said.

The crowd I'd left behind in the elevator exited, walking as a unit down the hall, in tight formation, their voices low and nervous as they discussed the latest news on the outbreak.

"Code Gray. ER One. Code Gray. ER One," a woman said over the intercom system.

Anita, the radiology manager, stood in the middle of the radiology hall with her arms crossed. Within moments, men from maintenance and from every other department scurried through the open double doors of the emergency room.

"What does Code Gray mean, rookie?" Anita asked with a smirk.

"Er . . . hostile patient?" I said, half guessing.

"Good!" she said, patting me on the back. "We don't hear those very often."

"Code Gray. ER Six. Code Gray. ER Six," the woman's voice called over the intercom. Her voice was less indifferent this time.

Anita looked down the hall of our department. "Something's not right," she said, her voice low. Julian, the CT tech, stepped out into the hallway. Anita waved him to the emergency room. "Go on!"

Julian obeyed, the ever-present bored expression momentarily absent from his face. As he passed, Anita gestured to the women's locker room. "You better clock out before I change my mind."

"You don't have to tell me twice." The keypad beeped after I pushed in the code, and then a click sounded, signaling me to enter. I walked in, noticing I was alone. Normally the room was abuzz with women opening their lockers, pulling out their purses, laughing and chatting, or cursing about their day.

As I spun my combination lock to access my locker, another announcement came over the intercom.

"Code Blue, ER Three. Code Blue, ER Three. Code Gray in the ambulance bay. Code Gray in the ambulance bay."

I grabbed my purse and slammed the door, quickly making my way down the hall. The radiology waiting room was on my way, separated from the hall with a wall of glass. The few patients inside were still focused on the flat screen. A news anchor was reporting with a scowl, and a blinking warning scrolled across the bottom of the screen. Most of the words were too small to make out, but I could see one: PANDEMIC.

A sick feeling came over me, and I walked quickly, on the verge of breaking into a sprint for the employee exit. Just as I opened the door, I heard a scream, and then more. Women and men. I didn't look back.

Running across the intersection to my Suburban in the southwestern lot, I could hear tires squealing to a stop. A nurse from the third floor was fleeing the hospital in a panic. She was afraid, and wasn't paying attention to the traffic. The first car barely missed her, but a truck barreled around the corner and clipped her body with its front right side. The nurse was thrown forward, and her limp body rolled to the curb.

My training urged me to go to her and check for a pulse, but something inside of me refused to let my feet move anywhere but in the direction of the parking lot.

Angie, the circulation nurse from upstairs, appeared in the doorway of the employee exit. Her surgery scrubs were covered from neck to knees in blood, her eyes wide. She was more cautious, dodging the traffic as she crossed.

"Oh my God, is that Shelly?" Angie asked. She rushed to

the curb and crouched beside the woman lying lifeless. Angie placed her fingers on the nurse's neck, and then looked up at me, eyes wide. "She's dead."

I wasn't sure what expression was on my face, but Angie jerked her head forward to insist I respond. "Did you see who hit her?" she asked.

"I don't think it's going to matter," I said, taking a step back.

Angie stood, and looked around. A police cruiser raced toward downtown. Other employees of the hospital began to filter out of the door, racing to the parking lot.

"I can't believe this is happening," she whispered, pulling her scrub hat from her short blond hair.

"Your scrubs," I said. A dark red streak ran down the front of her green standard-issue surgery scrubs. Her neck and cheek were also splattered with crimson.

"Mrs. Sisney flat-lined, and then woke up," Angie said, her face red and glistening with sweat. "She attacked Dr. Inman. I'm not sure what happened after that. I left."

I nodded and then backed away from her, toward the parking lot. Toward my Suburban. "Go home, Angie. Get your daughter and get the hell out of town."

She nodded in reply, and then looked down at the blood. "I should probably just go back in. I don't know how contagious this is. Kate's with my dad. He'll keep her safe."

Her eyes left her blood-saturated clothes and met mine. They were glossed over, and I could see that she had already given up. I wanted to tell her to try, but when the faces of my own children came to mind, my legs sprinted to the parking lot.

I threw my purse into the passenger seat and then inserted the key into the Suburban's ignition, trying to keep calm. It was

Friday, and my daughters were already an hour away, at their dad's for the weekend. Each possible route flashed in my mind. Scenes from post-apocalyptic movies with vehicles lining every lane of highways for miles did, too.

I pulled out my cell phone from my pocket and dialed Andrew's number. It rang, and rang, and rang, and then a busy signal buzzed in my ear instead of his voicemail. "It just started," I said quietly, putting my phone in the cup holder. "I can still get to them."

I tossed my phone into my purse, gripped the steering wheel with one hand, and shoved the gear into reverse with the other.

A part of me felt silly. The logical side of my brain wanted to believe I was overreacting, but there was no music on the radio. Only breaking news about the pandemic, the rising death toll, and the ensuing panic.

The Suburban stopped abruptly, and I turned around, seeing Lisa Barnes, the employee-health nurse, gripping her steering wheel, her eyes bulging. I'd backed up while she was pulling out of her parking spot, and we'd crashed into each other. I pushed open my door, and ran over to her.

"Are you okay?" I said, hearing the subdued panic in my voice.

"Get out of my fucking way!" she screamed as she gripped her gearshift and threw it into reverse.

Just then a pickup truck barreled through the lot and slammed into my Suburban, taking it all the way to the street.

Standing still beside Lisa's sedan in shock was the only thing I was capable of in that moment. My brain refused to process the surreal scene in front of me until I caught a glimpse of a crowd of people pushing through the side entrance, and fanning out into the street, joining others who were from other parts of town, running for their lives, too.

Drew Davidson, the human resources director, stumbled and fell. He cried out in pain, and then looked around him, reaching out to those passing by, screaming for help. No one so much as paused.

A pair of wild eyes stood out from the mob. It was Mrs. Sisney. She was moving quickly, into the dispersing crowd. She crossed the road and finally caught up to Drew, who was still on the ground, reaching for his ankle.

I watched in horror as Mrs. Sisney charged Drew, leaping on top of him and grabbing at his expensive suit while opening her mouth wide. Drew was pushing back against her, but she was a large woman, and eventually her body weight helped to press Drew's arms down enough for her to take a bite of his shoulder.

Drew's cries attracted someone else—whom I recognized as Mrs. Sisney's son—and another woman in scrubs. They ambled over to Drew's flailing legs and began to feed.

Lisa's screams matched Drew's, and then the crumpled front end of her sedan flew past me and toward the road as she left me standing in the parking lot to witness the horror alone.

A loud boom sounded in the distance. It was then that I noticed several pillars of smoke in the sky, the newest in the area of the blast. Gunshots added to the noise, both close and far away. The chaos was confusing and happening so fast I didn't have time to be afraid.

Shiny silver keys lay fanned out on the grass a few feet in front of Drew. He'd just bought a Jeep Wrangler the month before. I had only paid attention because I'd just lamented over that Jeep in the showroom of the local Dodge dealership during lunch, and Drew had been sitting at our table. Not a week later, when arriving for my shift, I saw that Jeep in the parking lot, and Drew Davidson stepped out of it. He thanked me for the tip, and that marked the first and last time he'd ever spoken to me.

Taking even one step toward that scene was terrifying, but I found enough courage to scoop up his keys and run for the Jeep. My fingers pressed the keyless entry. I yanked the door open, praying that the gas tank wasn't close to being empty. Mrs. Sisney was still consuming the meat of Drew's neck and the others were slowly gnawing on Drew's now lifeless body. *He definitely wouldn't need his Jeep again,* I thought as I ripped out of the parking lot.

Speed limits and red lights were irrelevant. I glanced from one side to the other at each intersection, and then blew through them until I reached the main road out of town. Surely most people would head for the interstate, I thought, but I was wrong. Wrecks peppered the old two-lane highway toward Kellyville.

I kept the gas pedal pressed against the floorboard, trying to stay away from traffic jams and buy myself some time to think of what I should do. People, alive and dead, were running around. Gunshots could be heard from all parts of town as people shot reanimated corpses from their vehicles and porches.

A blinking sign signaled that I was entering a school zone. My stomach instantly felt sick. The children had been picked up more than an hour ago, thank God, but mine were so far away. If the pandemic had spread so quickly, the girls were probably terrified and running, too.

I had to get to them. My fingers tightened around the steering wheel. If it was the end of the world, I wanted to be holding my babies.

I turned up the volume on the radio, hoping for some clue about how to get out of town and to my children. Instead of reporting safety procedures or anything else helpful, the DJs were struggling to remain professional while one gruesome report after another came in about people being attacked, car accidents, and mayhem.

The one thing they weren't talking about was where the pandemic had originated. If either of the coasts had been struck first, it would have given me more time . . . and time was the only chance I had.

Chapter Four

Miranda

"WE'RE NOT GOING TO DIE," COOPER SAID. "TRY TO STAY CALM."

He had his arm wrapped around my older sister, Ashley, in the backseat, his eyes dancing as he watched the chaos surrounding my VW Bug. He leaned against Ashley when yet another person ran by and bumped the door.

"Damn it!" I said, frowning. "They're going to scratch the paint!"

Ashley watched me in disbelief, but I couldn't help but allow a little irrational anger to rise to the surface. My brand-new, shiny white Volkswagen barely had time to let the custom paint dry, and these assholes were rubbing up against it every time they passed.

"We're at a standstill," Bryce said, trying to see ahead. Bryce's tousled brown hair grazed the fabric of the Bug's convertible top. He'd wanted to drive his Dodge truck to my dad's ranch, but Daddy was a fan of Ford, and I wasn't going to listen to them discuss Rams versus F-150s all weekend. "If you let the top down, I can get a better look."

"Well that's just stupid," I said, my face scrunching in disgust.

My comment pulled Bryce's attention away from the frightened pedestrians outside. "What?"

I pointed over his shoulder. "There is a reason they're running. I'm not going to expose us to whatever that is."

Traffic had slowed down to about twenty-five miles per hour no more than ten miles after we merged onto the interstate to take our weekend road trip, and less than five miles later we were halted to zero miles per hour. That was half an hour before, and we still hadn't moved. Not even when people started getting out of their cars to make a run for it.

"Just drive, Miranda. Get us the hell out of here. I don't want to know what they're running from," Ashley said, fidgeting with her long, wavy hair. She was beautiful like my mother: tall, thin, and delicate. Her dirty-blond hair cascaded down each shoulder, reminding me of that girl from the *Blue Lagoon* movie. If Ashley didn't have a shirt on, it wouldn't matter. With a few well-placed dots of Elmer's glue, her tits would be completely obscured by her hair.

Growing up, I used to be jealous of her natural beauty. My five feet, five inches made me look dumpy next to her. I looked like my father: round face, dull brown eyes, and auburn hair . . . well, Daddy's was redd*ish* before it turned white. Bryce preferred to call me athletically built, but what did he know, he was six feet and six inches of meager man-child. His basketball coach worshipped him, but when we were together, his tallness only made my shortness seem more obvious.

"You know what they're running from," I said, gripping the steering wheel with both hands. Only those in denial weren't aware of what was happening.

News reports about a viral outbreak were the reason afternoon classes were canceled. Ashley had the bright idea to drive to Beaver Lake for the weekend and had invited her boyfriend, Stanley Cooper, to come along earlier in the week. Not wanting to be the odd man out, I asked Bryce, although once he knew about Cooper coming along, Bryce would have come whether I'd invited him or not. Especially once Daddy found out Mom was out of town and insisted we stay with him for the weekend. Bryce knew my relationship with my father hadn't been all that great lately, because Bryce knew everything about me. We had voluntarily tolerated each other since our sophomore year of high school. We traded off doing horrible and wonderful things for each other: He'd taken my virginity and helped me get through my parents' divorce, I'd wrecked his first truck and given him my virginity. Bryce was fiercely protective, and that is exactly how we ended up at the same college. His protection wasn't fueled by jealousy. It was more like he was protecting me from me. Bryce worked double duty as boyfriend and conscience, and I had never denied that I appreciated both.

Just like everyone else, we continued with our weekend plans, never truly believing something so frightening and dangerous would reach us all the way in the middle of the country. Nothing ever happened here. The worst thing that had happened to Ashley and me was our parents' divorce. Other than that, our lives had been fairly boring and worry free. It was a running joke with us. We would listen to our friends' stories of their brutal childhoods or how they were bullied in high school, how their father was a drunk or their mother was overbearing. Our mom and dad never fought in front of us. Their divorce was a complete surprise.

Another runner bumped the paint. I honked the horn. "Dick!"

"Miranda, maybe we should do what they're doing?" Bryce asked.

"The Bug is my birthday present. Dad special-ordered it, and he will never forgive me if I show up without it. And, the ranch is two hours away. We'll never make it on foot."

Ashley gripped my seat with her perfectly manicured fingers. "M . . . maybe we should go back?"

I rolled my eyes. "You act like you've never seen a zombie movie, Ashley. We can't survive in a city. Dad's ranch is the best place to go."

"Why do you keep saying that? It's not zombies, that's ridiculous!" she said.

"Viral outbreak. The infected are attacking and biting people. They said cadavers this morning. What do you think it is, Ash? Herpes?"

Ashley sat back in resignation, crossing her arms over her stomach. Cooper pulled her to him again. He wasn't fooling anyone. His wide blue eyes made it obvious that he was just as frightened as she was, but fear wasn't the only thing I saw.

"No, Coop," I said to the rearview mirror. "You're not getting out of this car."

"But my mom and my little sister. My dad's not around. They're alone. I should try to get to them."

I took a breath, trying not to think of my own mom. She was in Belize with my stepfather, Rick. That was why we'd made plans to visit my dad at his ranch in the first place. "They live in Texas, Coop. Let's get to the ranch, get some supplies, and then we'll go get them, okay?" I was lying. Cooper might have known it, too, but my dad's ranch was north, everybody was running north, and Cooper's mother and sister were south. Maybe one day he could try, but we'd all seen enough end-of-the-world flicks to know how this was going to go down: mass chaos and carnage until the population whittled down. That's when the walking dead would start leaving the cities to find a meal, but by then we'd be settled in and well educated in the art of zombicide. We had to survive the next few weeks first. The ranch would be the best place to do that.

A guy about our age bumped my door and then tripped and fell just out of sight. "Stay away!" I yelled, leaning forward to try to make eye contact with whoever decided to molest my three-day-old car.

Another running, screaming passerby knocked his hip against my side mirror. A woman trailed behind him, but stopped, and then crawled across my hood. I cussed again, shoving the gear into reverse. "We've got to get out of here. They're going to tear us apart." Just as I turned to get a handle on how far I could back up, from the corner of my eye I saw a flesh-colored struggle in the same spot the first man had fallen.

"Miranda?" Bryce said. "He's . . . he's got him."

I peered over my steering wheel, watching the second man trying to pull his arm out of the mouth of the first. A mixture of screaming and moans rose from their frantic wrestling match.

Bryce put both hands on his forehead just as the first man took a large bite of flesh and pulled away. Blood sprayed the biter's face, and meat and tendons trailed from his mouth to the arm of his prey.

Ashley's shrill scream filled my ear, and for a moment, a

buzzing noise accompanied a fainter version of what I'd just heard. I looked over at Bryce, and his face paled, his eyes saying everything he couldn't find words for.

I slammed my foot against the accelerator, only stopping when I felt the back of the Bug hit the car behind us. In the next moment, the gearshift was in drive, and I was maneuvering between a semi-truck and a minivan—both empty. The Bug tossed us up and down as it climbed across the asphalt to the shoulder.

"Don't stop!" Ashley said. "Keep going!"

We passed more people, unsure of who was running and who was chasing. I saw parents carrying their young children, and pulling along older ones by the hand. A couple of times people screamed at me to stop, begged me to help them, but stopping always meant dying in the movies, and I was barely eighteen. I wasn't sure how long we could survive, but I knew I wasn't dying on day one of the fucking zombie apocalypse.

Scarlet

IT WAS A RISK, TAKING THE OLD TWO-LANE HIGHWAY, but it was the quickest way to my children besides the interstate, and that would be suicide. The Jeep was part of a caravan of cars that had managed to make it out of the city. There were maybe ten or fifteen of us. The silver Toyota Camry in front of me had a forward-facing car seat in the back, and I hoped there was a child in it.

Mile after mile of farmland passed, and then someone at

the front slowed. We were coming up on a bridge, and for whatever reason, the car at the front was being cautious. Fear surged through every vein in my body. We couldn't stop. We had to keep going no matter what was ahead. I might have been in a Jeep, but it wouldn't cross the river. No matter what, I was going over that bridge.

I couldn't see why the car in front had slowed down until I reached the bridge. An old, glacier-blue Buick was stalled on the side of the road. The windows were rolled up, and a couple remained inside. A woman was staring blankly out the window, only moving when the man next to her tugged while he tore at her flesh with his teeth.

Instinctively, I thought to cover the eyes of my children. In the same moment I realized they weren't with me, and the panic and anxiety of getting to them, and wondering where they were and if they were scared or okay, became nearly too overwhelming for me to drive.

"I'm coming, babies," I said, swallowing the sob welling up in my throat.

One long stretch of highway north and another equally long stretch to the east would lead me to my girls. Two small towns stood between us. Their populations were only a few thousand, if that, but that was too many people to wade through if the dead were wandering the streets.

Most of the caravan turned west, toward more rural areas. It was the direction I would have headed if my girls were with me. West on Highway 11 was one of the roads we would've taken to get to Dr. Hayes's ranch.

Along with just two other vehicles, I turned the Jeep east, where each town's population was bigger than the last: Kellyville, Fairview, and then Anderson was on the other side of the interstate.

The stories of the families in the other two vehicles piqued my curiosity. Ahead of me was the Toyota with the car seat, behind me was a green seventies-ish pickup truck. Whether it held one person or a family I couldn't tell; the truck kept several car lengths back.

Five minutes from Kellyville, my hands began to tremble. I wondered if the other two drivers were as afraid as I was. Preparing for an outbreak like this was impossible, even when we'd been told for decades that it could happen, and were presented with hundreds of different methods of survival by the entertainment industry. Hoarding food, weapons, medicine. But none of that mattered if you were bitten . . . or eaten.

The Toyota sped up a bit as we entered Kellyville's city limits. My nerves were on edge, and my brow felt damp. At any second a quick turn or evasion maneuver might be necessary.

I wasn't sure what to expect, but the town appeared abandoned. No walking dead, no living humans. No running, no screaming. It gave me hope that maybe some way, somehow, the pandemic had stalled.

We left unscathed, just as we had come in, but it felt too easy. Something wasn't right. I turned up the volume on the radio, but the news was the same. Once in a while they would report that someone famous had been found dead or was killed because they'd succumbed to the sickness spreading, but even then the story was similar.

The DJ reported that the state capitol had been overrun just as we entered the west side of Fairview. A sick feeling came over me as we passed the high school. Bodies littered the football field, whole and in parts. I couldn't tell if it was students or adults, or a little of both. I tried not to look that close. A few corpses were ambling around, but nothing like I'd expected to see in a town overrun. Maybe they had gotten out.

The Toyota ahead of me slowed to a stop. I wasn't sure what to do. In the rearview mirror, the pickup stopped, too, maybe a hundred yards back. I waited for a moment, and then glanced around, hoping for an answer.

I had several all in one second.

The church on the corner was surrounded by reanimated corpses. Women, men . . . and children. Some with torn, bloody clothes, some I couldn't tell had been wounded at all, but I could see from the road that they all shared the same milky-white eyes. I shuttered at the sight, feeling more desperate to get going.

The dead were banging on the boarded windows and the doors. They moved sluggishly and clumsily, but fervently. They were hungry. A vertical trail of bright-red blood was on the west wall. Someone wounded had crawled to the upper level. The mob seemed to be drawn to it.

I understood then why the Toyota had stopped. There were people inside. They'd holed up in the church, and probably had nowhere to go.

"Don't be stupid," I said quietly. "Not with that baby in the car."

The Toyota horn beeped once, and then again, getting the attention of a few of the bloody corpses pounding on the front doors of the church. The horn beeped a couple more times, and then the driver's side door popped open, and a man stepped out, waving his arms.

"Hey!" he yelled to the corpses. "This way! Come over here!"

A few more turned in his direction, and then immediately stopped their plight to make a lumbering, slow journey to the road. Their shuffling caught the attention of more, and then a whole section of them broke away from the church to trudge in our direction.

"Shit," I said, my eyes darting between the corpses and the Toyota. I honked several times, too. "Get in the car. Get in the car!" I yelled the last words, banging my palms against the steering wheel.

The man jumped up and down a few more times.

"Get in, John! Get in!" his wife screamed, leaning over the console and grabbing for him.

John jumped back in, and pulled away quickly. I followed close behind, my heart thumping in my chest as I passed the approaching corpses safely.

A dozen or more appeared in my rearview mirror, and then I saw several people—alive people—dart across the street. The green pickup was still a block away from the church, waiting for something.

My heart never settled down after we left Fairview. I was just that much closer to my children, and closer to the obstacles I would likely face to get to them, closer to knowing if they were alive.

Tears streamed down my face as we approached the overpass that would bring us into the edge of my hometown. At first, it didn't faze me that there were army reserve vehicles of every shape and size parked at the mouth of the overpass. I was too distracted by the mess of vehicles on the interstate below.

"Jesus," I breathed.

It was as I had feared. Multiple-car pileups and stalled vehicles. Some people were standing outside of their cars and trucks, begging from the on-ramp for the soldiers to let them pass.

The Toyota stopped at what seemed like a checkpoint. John exited the car, and immediately something felt off. The soldiers were antsy, their eyes darting from each other, to the car, to John. Governor Bellmon was in town, so they were probably keeping Anderson quarantined, controlling who came in. Making sure no shuffling dead snuck by and threatened the man who might be the only living member of the state government, especially knowing the state capitol had been overrun.

John tried to shake one of the soldiers' hands, but the soldier only offered the barrel of his combat rifle. Adrenaline pumped faster and faster through my body, and every inch of me was on high alert. The soldiers were behaving erratically; nervous. John pointed past the soldier, and then to his family in the car. I could see he was becoming more and more agitated.

I looked down. There was a pickup truck upside down on the interstate below. It was full of bullet holes. To my left, a full-sized van, also covered in holes, was sitting about fifty yards off the shoulder in the grass. I put the Jeep in reverse.

"Just get in your car, John," I whispered.

When the soldier wouldn't budge, John took a step and shoved the soldier in the shoulder before returning to his car. I could see from thirty feet away it was just out of frustration. John probably had someone inside Anderson that he loved and wanted to get to—maybe an older child. In the end, the only thing any of us wanted was to be with our loved ones.

Thirty feet away was close enough to see the soldier give the order, to see them all point their automatic rifles at John's car, and light it up. But thirty feet away was too far to warn him.

As soon as John sat in his seat, the soldiers opened fire, filling every inch of the silver Toyota Camry with bullets. Instinctively, I stomped on the gas pedal, so hard that my chest was shoved into the steering wheel.

"No! Oh my God! No!" I screamed, yanking the gearshift into drive as I turned the wheel in the opposite direction. They weren't letting anyone in, and worse, the entrances were being guarded by scared young soldiers with automatic weapons. They had either been given orders to eliminate anyone who approached them, or they were operating without communication from their commanding officers. The latter seemed more likely—and more frightening.

I could barely see through my tears, quickly jerking the wheel north down a country road. How would I get to my girls? Were the soldiers gunning down everyone in town, too?

I forced my mind to stop wandering and focused on a solution. Getting inside the city limits was the goal. Anderson was my birthplace. I knew the ins and outs better than those soldiers. There had to be a way in.

On the northeast edge of town was a dirt road adjacent to a heavily wooded area. Those woods were nestled between the dirt road and the main road through town. The soldiers would likely patrol there, but on the other side was river, tall grass, and the old Blackwell Street Bridge. If I could get close enough to that wooded area, and then make it across the main highway, I just might be able to sneak across the bridge and follow Blackwell Street almost all the way to Andrew's house.

The only way to do that undetected would be to wait until

dark. The thought of walking around in the dark while those things were shuffling around created an instant sick feeling that came over me in waves, but no matter how terrifying it was, that was the only way to reach my children.

I drove three miles north of Anderson's eastern limits, and then cut east once I thought I was clear. The Jeep bounced over an overpass not nearly as wide as the soldiers', and then kicked up red dirt as I barreled toward my chosen point. Three miles was enough to stay out of sight of whoever might have been guarding the north entrance. I didn't even come across any shuffling things.

The Jeep slowed to a stop. For the first time, I realized that my purse hadn't made it with me to the Jeep—or my cell phone—and my stomach turned. The phone lines probably weren't working, but it made me feel sick not to have any way to even try to call Andrew . . . or anyone else. I looked around for shufflers, locked the doors, and then crawled into the back seat. I pulled up the piece of carpet hiding the tire iron. That and a small flashlight were the only things of use.

I waited in the driver's seat, ready to drive away at the first sight of a shuffler. My ears perked at every sound, and my muscles twitched every time a gust of wind rattled the leaves and grass around me. I hummed a random tune, picked at my fingernails, made sure my sneakers were double-knotted, and then talked to God.

As the sun set, the level of anxiety I was sustaining felt nearly unmanageable. My mind struggled not to revisit the moment John and his wife and baby were murdered. I also fought imagining whatever awful scenes I might stumble upon once I breached the streets of Anderson. The guarded entrances were both helpful and a hindrance. The armed guards, fearful and quick on the trigger, would at least keep the threat of shufflers to a minimum.

Darkness began to paint shadows across the woods, and with the rise of the half-moon came the fall in temperature. I rubbed my hands together, and then wrapped my arms around my ribs for warmth, wishing I had something heavier than a scrub jacket. Soon, I would be walking around in the dark, my ears and a tire iron my only weapon against anything hunting from the shadows, and the tire iron wasn't going to be much help. Anyone that hadn't been hiding under a rock could tell you that the only way to kill someone of the dead persuasion was to obliterate the brain stem. I needed a gun or at least something sharp enough to penetrate bone. Beating in the skull of a shuffler would take more time than I could spare.

It's incredible, the way the imagination can physically affect the body. My heart rate had doubled, and I was beginning to sweat. The more my fear crept up, the more I kept reminding myself that my girls needed me. They were probably scared to death, and no matter what happened or what state they were in, I wanted to be with them.

Nathan

ZOE INSTINCTIVELY KEPT HER HEAD DOWN, OR ELSE she was mimicking me, as we hurried to the car. Gunshots rang out two houses over, and I looked over to see my neighbor Lyle Edson shooting someone approaching his front porch in the face. An ambulance raced by, the back doors open and waving around as it fishtailed with lights and sirens blaring down the street.

"Daddy?" Zoe said. The fear in her voice was real. Something I wanted to shield her from until the world wouldn't let me anymore. I couldn't shield her from this; hell was raining down all around us.

My hands shook as I tried to shove the key in the door to unlock it.

"Daddy?" Zoe said again.

"Just a second, baby," I said, cursing at my trembling hands under my breath. Finally the key entered the slit and I turned it. In the same second, Zoe squeezed my hand.

"Daddy!"

I turned, seeing a police officer approach. He was shuffling slowly in our direction, his jaw relaxed, letting his mouth lie open. A low moan emanated from his throat. I picked up the bat that I'd propped against the car while trying to unlock the door, and then I stepped in front of Zoe.

"Stop right there," I said. The police officer kept walking. I held the bat in front of me.

"If you can understand what I'm saying, please stop. I am going to hit you with this bat if you come closer."

Zoe gripped the back of my pants, and I gripped the aluminum. "Close your eyes, Zoe."

My daughter's tiny hands left the fabric of my pants, and I pulled the bat back and to the side, in perfect position to swing. Before I could, a shot rang out. The police officer went down. I froze, and then saw Lyle Edson standing a few feet to my left.

"Thank you," I said with a nod.

"Better grab his sidearm and get that little girl outta here," Lyle said.

"You want to come?"

Lyle shook his head. "My wife's inside. She's been bit. I'm going to stay with her."

I nodded and then leaned down, unsnapping the officer's holster and removing his sidearm. I grabbed his radio, too, and then decided to take his whole belt.

Zoe opened the driver's side door and crawled over the console to her side. We both buckled our seatbelts, and I started the car. The gas tank showed three quarters left. I wasn't sure how close to safety we could get on three-quarters of a tank, but we had to leave town.

Zoe reached up to lock her door.

"Better lock the back door, too," I said, doing the same. I backed out of the drive and went in the same direction as the ambulance. I figured I should get away from whatever they were escaping from in such a hurry.

Chapter Five

Scarlet

THE LAST RAYS OF SUN UNCEREMONIOUSLY FELL BEHIND the horizon. Shaking with fear, I slowly stepped out of the Jeep. My tennis shoes, still a little wet from the morning rain, sunk into thick mud. Clutching the tire iron to my chest, I took a step into the woods. The night was quiet—so quiet that every movement I made seemed like a boom echoing through the trees.

Every sound made my body freeze. Could they see in the dark? Did they rely on smell like an animal? Only when I thought of my girls waiting for me did I find enough courage to take another step.

About an hour later, a dragging noise startled me enough to make me cling to a tree. I hugged it to me and closed my eyes, trying to listen for danger over the pounding in my heart and gasping breath.

Just when I thought I might hyperventilate, my eyes popped open wide to try to pull in enough light to penetrate the darkness. Something darker than the dark and about as tall as a man crossed from one tree to another, only twenty yards or so from me. I closed my eyes tight one last time, and then broke into a sprint, refusing to stop until I slipped in the culvert beside the main highway in and out of town.

My knees hit hard, and then my stomach, chest, and face shortly after. Face and palms down in the mud, I quickly tuned in to the sounds around me, and then flipped over, searching in a panic for whatever was hunting me.

My chest heaved as my lungs tried to keep up with the constant adrenaline pumping through my body. A scream welled up in my chest, but recognition choked back the noise. Drawing anyone's attention—alive or dead—could end my rescue mission before it started.

A man walked toward me, his arms out, trying to wave away the scream he could see was about to echo throughout the east side of Anderson.

The fear in his dark eyes was highlighted by the amount of white surrounding them. "Ssssh! I'm not going to hurt you!" he said in a loud whisper.

He slid in next to me, his clothes and skin already soiled with mud, spattered in some places, saturated in others. He looked like he'd been crawling on his belly through the woods for days.

I pressed my lips together to stifle a yelp, my entire body shaking involuntarily.

"I'm not going to hurt you," he said again, panting. He didn't need the mud. His skin was dark enough to keep him hidden, even if he was well over six feet tall. "I didn't mean to scare you. I'm just trying to get into town. Same as you."

I nodded, unable to form a proper response.

"My name's Tobin. You . . . you okay?"

I took a deep breath, trying to settle my nerves. "Scarlet."

Tobin took a quick scan of our surroundings. "Are you from Anderson?"

"I used to be."

Tobin nodded. "You got family in there, don't you?"

"My little girls," I said, feeling salty tears fill my eyes. For the first time since I'd left the Jeep, I felt cold. My body hadn't stopped shaking, and I was already exhausted.

Tobin pressed his lips together. "My sister and her kids live here. She ain't got nobody."

The knowledge that I wasn't totally alone gave me enough strength to focus on my plan. I pointed across the highway to another patch of woods. "Across the road is a valley that runs alongside the river. There's an old bridge maybe three blocks south of here."

Tobin frowned. "There are soldiers at every entrance, and they're walking the streets. Anderson is some type of military state now."

"The governor is in there somewhere. He was visiting today. My daughters were supposed to meet him."

Tobin shook his head. "That explains it, then. I'm not sure whether I should be glad or sick to my stomach. I mean . . . who gives a shit about his title when the whole world is going to hell, right?"

I laughed once without humor. "It's a good time to throw his rank around. At least he's not crawling through the mud."

Tobin offered a small smile. "We better get going. They could do another sweep of the woods soon."

"Another?"

Tobin looked at his mud-covered front and then back at

me. "A word of advice: If you see a dead person walking, run the other way. If you see a soldier, hide. They were shooting the bodies lying in the road earlier. Just making sure, I guess."

Tobin waited as I darted across the highway. My legs seemed to be moving in slow motion, but before I knew it, I was across the lit four lanes and hidden once again on the other side. A few seconds later, Tobin joined me.

I had never felt so much comfort from being around a complete stranger. That was just one more thing you didn't learn from the zombie movies.

Keeping to the overgrown foliage around the river, Tobin and I trudged through the mud to the looming Blackwell Street Bridge. An army truck passed over slowly, and we had to leap under the steel and asphalt to escape the spotlight they were shining on the river. I held my hands over my mouth. A body was floating facedown on the surface of the water, not two feet from where Tobin and I had walked just moments before. Shots rang out, the body convulsed as it was showered with bullets, and then the truck moved on, the spotlight parallel to its path.

Tobin reached out and touched my arm. "It's okay. They're gone. I need to take a piss, and then we'll keep going."

His words struck me as odd. I had to wait and take stock of my bodily functions, to figure out if I even had to take a bathroom break. All of a sudden, my bladder felt like it was going to burst, and it was all I could do to get my scrub pants untied and my panties around my ankles fast enough to keep from urinating all over myself.

Tobin met me at the edge of the water. It was dark, and it didn't seem like a good idea to swim, but we couldn't risk taking the bridge across, either.

"Did you think this far ahead?" Tobin asked, staring at the flowing river. The rain earlier had made the current stronger, and the water level higher.

"Not really, but we can't get caught on that bridge. They'll take one look at us and know we snuck in. They'll shoot us on sight."

"Agreed. You used to live here. What do you think we should do?"

"We can either try to find a shallower place downstream, try to cross here, or use the rope swing on the other side of the bridge."

"The rope swing?" Tobin said, dubious.

"There's been one on that tree over there as long as I can remember. They keep one there for the kids that live around here."

Tobin stared at me blankly.

I shrugged. "The city pool is on the other side of town."

Tobin blinked. "What kind of backward redneck village did my sister move to?"

Nathan

"LYLE SHOT A COP, DADDY."

"I saw that," I said, not knowing what else to say.

"What's happening?" Zoe said. "Why is everyone fighting?"

"Some of the people are sick," I said, turning on the police radio. "I think."

Reports were coming in that the virus had affected all

counties. After a while, the dispatcher stopped talking, so I turned up the car radio. Thirty-two of the forty-eight contiguous states reported casualties and illness. The East Coast reported that those who had chosen not to receive the flu vaccination were not showing symptoms as quickly as those who had. Some reports said that those who had had the flu shot didn't necessarily need to get bitten or attacked before they caught the virus. They would reanimate no matter how they died. I glanced over at Zoe. She had an egg allergy like I did. People with egg allergies were advised against the shot unless they stayed under the supervision of a doctor post-inoculation. Even though my allergy wasn't severe, Aubrey and I decided the benefit didn't outweigh the risk, for me or for Zoe. Well, I did . . . Aubrey left the decision to me. I let a small sigh of relief escape my lips. If I only did one thing right, I'm glad it was that.

All roads proved to be an obstacle course. If I wasn't jerking the wheel to the left, I was yanking it to the right, dodging people, other cars, and general debris left behind by the pandemonium. Aubrey used to always bitch about my driving, but we were almost out of town, and I'd yet to crash into anything. Even if it were a small miracle, even she couldn't complain about my driving skills now.

Zoe pointed ahead. We were on one of the few roads out of town that I thought would still be open. It was paved, but just a few miles ahead it would turn to dirt. Halfway between was a railroad crossing. A train was visible a little less than a half-mile away, and soon the lights would blink red, and the crossing rails would lower. There were cars behind me, and God knows what else. We couldn't get caught behind that train. The sedan's nearly bald tires wouldn't be able to forge through the wheat fields between us and the next road.

I pressed on the gas.

"Daddy, slow down!"

"I can't, Zoe. We can't wait for the train." I reached over and yanked up her seatbelt to be sure it was tight, and then I put both hands on the wheel. The crossing rails began their descent. The horn of the train wailed, drawn out and sad. I used to think that sound was romantic. Now it was what was keeping me from getting my daughter to someplace safe.

My foot ground against the gas pedal, slamming it to the floor.

"Daddy, no!"

The first crossing rail just grazed the paint on the top of the car, but we took the second rail out, easily snapping it in half. Zoe flipped around, covering her mouth. I looked in the rearview mirror. The wine-colored Lincoln Town Car behind us must have had the same idea, but was a second too slow. The train clipped its back bumper and sent it into a spin. The front end of the car whipped around, crashing into the train a few times before it was spit out a bit farther down into the wheat field. If they weren't badly hurt, they were going to have to walk.

"We should go back!"

I shook my head. "We're going to Uncle Skeeter and Aunt Jill's." Skeeter McGee was Aubrey's little brother. Aubrey's obvious disdain for me made Skeeter like me that much more. They lived in a tiny two-bedroom dump of a house just on this side of Fairview. The town was small. Small enough not to have to worry about a herd of the undead surrounding us.

Zoe's lips turned up in the tiniest hint of a grin. Skeeter and

Jill hadn't been married but a couple of years, and had no children. Skeeter was in love with Zoe like she was his own, and Jill was just as crazy about her.

One more reason to make a beeline for Fairview was that Skeeter was a hunting enthusiast, and had several pistols and hunting rifles with plenty of ammo. It would be the perfect place to hole up and wait out the end of the world.

The two-lane road didn't have the congestion I expected. A few times I had to steer around a two- or three-car pileup, most likely from the initial panic and worried drivers not paying attention, but for the most part the cars on the road were driving along at moderate speeds. Zoe pointed out her window when we arrived at Old Creek Bridge. A man was bent over, vomiting next to his '76 Buick LeSabre while his wife touched his back. Her expression was more than worry or fear; the residual lines on her face were deepened by resignation.

"Is he one of the sick people, Daddy?" Zoe asked as we drove slowly past them.

The woman looked up, hopelessness in her eyes, and then she helped her husband to the passenger side of their car.

"I don't know, baby."

"Maybe we should stop and help them."

"I don't think we can," I said, pulling my cell phone from my pocket. I tried to dial Skeeter's number to warn him we were coming, but all I heard was a busy signal. Of course the phone lines would be down.

We caught up to a short line of cars, one after another slowing as we approached and passed Kellyville. Not a single person could be seen. I didn't dare hope for the same in Fairview. As we approached the outskirts of town, it seemed quiet. At first,

I thought maybe we were faster than the sickness, but then the car in front slammed on its brakes as a woman ran across the road screaming, followed by a man covered in blood, much of it concentrated around his mouth. The woman had the most beautiful brunette hair I'd ever seen flowing behind her. She was running so fast, her hair was waving behind her head like a flag. Tires squealed against the asphalt, and a car in front led a frantic escape through town. The other vehicles chased it. I wasn't sure if any of them had meant to come here, but they definitely weren't going to stay.

I glanced over at Zoe. "There are sick people here, Zoe. When I say so, I want you to unbuckle your seat belt and I'm going to carry you inside."

Zoe nodded. She blinked a few times. I could tell she was nervous, but not because she was afraid to die. She wanted to make sure she did what I asked of her, and did it correctly. Zoe was always particular about procedures, especially when they were spoken and not just implied. Rules were formed very carefully in our house. They were something we couldn't take back. If there was an exception, we didn't enlighten Zoe, because she didn't understand the concept of an exception to the rule, and if we tried to explain it to her, she would get upset.

"Zoe?"

"Yes, Daddy?"

"It's time to unbuckle your seatbelt."

Zoe did as she was told as I made the first right and then pulled into Skeeter's driveway. Once the car came to a stop, I shoved the gear into park and pulled Zoe over to my side, and we ran quickly but quietly to Skeeter's back door. No one ever came to their front door, and if they did, Skeeter knew they were either a salesman or a cop, and Skeeter answered the door for neither.

I pounded on the storm door with the side of my fist, still holding Zoe by the waist with my other arm. The barrel of Jill's .22 became visible, as it pulled the curtain away just enough for her to get a good look at my face.

"It's us," I said, glancing behind me.

The lock clicked open and the doorknob turned, and then Jill opened the door wide, waving quickly for us to come in.

I set Zoe down. Her glitter sneakers slapped against the green-and-yellow diamond-patterned linoleum of the kitchen. I took a deep breath, trying to blow out all of the anxiety I'd just built up while attempting to get Zoe out of the car and inside the house alive, while Jill locked the door behind us and set her rifle down.

Jill slammed into me, wrapping her arms around my torso and squeezing so tight I was glad I'd taken a good breath beforehand.

"Oh my God, Nate! I'm so glad you came!" She let go of me and then bent down to hug Zoe. "Hi, sweet pea! Are you okay?" Zoe dipped her chin once, and Jill looked up to me, fear in her eyes. "Where's Aubrey?" When I didn't answer, she stood up and peeked out the window. She turned back to me. "Nate! Where is she?"

"She left me."

"What? When?"

I shrugged, unsure of what expression matched the conversation. "Today." Any other time I would have felt justified telling my sister-in-law the news, but at that moment I just felt stupid. With everything else going on, the end of my marriage seemed trivial.

Jill's almond-shaped eyes bounced between Zoe and me. Aubrey leaving wasn't exactly a surprise. She'd been depressed and unhappy for a long time. No matter what I tried or how many times I asked her to go to counseling—together or just her alone—Aubrey was no longer the woman I married, and we were all waiting for the woman who took her place to finally say she didn't belong in that life. We all pretended it would get better, but the unspoken truth is always louder than the stories we tell.

Still, for Jill any expression but a smile seemed out of place. She was a beautiful woman. Watching her clean a buck or a catfish with that porcelain skin and those long, delicate fingers had always been surreal to me. The fact that she could shoot a gun and bait a hook made her perfect for Skeeter, and he loved her as much as any man could love a woman. They'd been dating since high school, and neither seemed to mind that they'd never experienced anyone or anything else. Anywhere but Fairview, Jill would have never ended up with Skeeter, but here, in the middle of the middle, even with his blossoming beer gut and unkempt beard, Skeeter McGee only needed country-boy charm, working man's muscles, and a decent job to score the magnificence that was Jill.

Speaking of Skeeter . . . "Where is he?" I asked.

Jill put her hand up to the side of her face. "He left about half an hour ago. He went down the street to Barb's and Ms. Kay's to see if they needed help. They're getting old and their husbands have been gone for years. He shovels their driveways every winter, and fixes things when they need fixin'. He worries about them. With hell breaking loose outside, he wanted to try to bring them back here where he could take care of them." Jill unconsciously reached for Zoe's hand, the thought of the monsters outside reflecting in her eyes.

"Did he take a gun?"

Jill nodded. "His thirty aught six."

"He'll come back."

Chapter Six

Nathan

BEFORE THE SICKNESS CAME, WAITING WAS AN IRRITAtion. Now that the dead were walking amid the living, waiting felt like the violation of being robbed, the helplessness when you've lost something valuable like your keys or your wedding ring, and the unbearable dread that comes over you when your child falls just out of sight at the shopping mall, all rolled into one sickening ball of emotion.

Jill paced in the kitchen, her fingers in her mouth while she chewed off every last bit of fingernail her teeth could find. I checked the windows and the front door, making sure everything was secure. Zoe sat in the doorway connecting the kitchen to the living room, quietly picking at the hem of her long-sleeved T-shirt.

A familiar whistle sounded just outside the kitchen window, and then a shot rang out. Without looking, Jill scrambled to unlock the door, and Skeeter stumbled inside, out of breath and sweaty. He sat his rifle beside Jill's while she locked the door, and then they hugged and kissed like they hadn't seen each other in years.

Jill whimpered, and Skeeter held her face in his hands. "Don't cry, Jillybean. I told you I'd come back." He kissed her forehead, and then held his arms out wide to Zoe, crouching as much as his six-foot-three frame and 220 pounds would allow.

Zoe immediately popped up and ran to him, melting into his arms.

"Zoe!" he said, kissing the top of her head. "We've missed you!" He looked to me. "I think she's grown a foot!"

The conversation was typical, but typical conversation was unsettling during an apocalypse.

"Where's Aubrey, trying to boot up the computer?" he asked.

Jill looked to me, and I looked down at Zoe. "She wasn't home when we got there. She left a note."

Skeeter's expression was hard to decipher. I wasn't sure if he was confused or just trying to process what that meant.

Jill stood next to her husband. "Ms. Kay? Barb?"

Skeeter offered a contrived smile. "I got them both to the church. I came back to get you. They're boarding up the windows as we speak, and almost everyone brought supplies. Food and stuff. Guns. Ammo. It's a good holdout."

"Skeeter," I said. "It's not a good idea to get all those people in one place. It'll be like a buffet."

Skeeter's face fell a bit. "There's not that many people." He grabbed his gun with one hand and wrapped the other around Jill's waist, talking softly in her ear. "Get a few changes of clothes in a bag."

Jill squirmed. "I don't want to leave the house, Skeeter. Can't we just stay here?"

Skeeter lowered his voice even more. "They're breaking through the windows. We don't have anything to board ours up." He lowered his chin, waiting patiently for Jill to agree. Once she did, he continued, "We need to take as much food and water as we can carry. I'm going to get the weapons and ammo. Be quick, baby."

Jill nodded, and then disappeared to the other side of the house. Skeeter brushed past me into the living room and opened the closet door. He pulled out two oversized duffle bags and brought them to a brown safe sitting against the wall next to the television. It was taller than Zoe. Almost as tall as Jill. Skeeter turned the combination and quickly opened the heavy door, pulling out pistols two at a time and setting them into the bag. Once he emptied the safe of handguns, he began pulling out his rifles, scopes, and shotguns. He filled the other bag with ammo, hunting knives, a first-aid kit, and several boxes of matches.

I looked down at my brother-in-law, watching as he kneeled down on the floor to organize his survival bags. "Jesus, Skeeter, did you know this was going to happen?" I said, only half joking.

"Anyone that didn't think this was a possibility was in denial. With the technology out there, how long have people been talking about zombies? Since before we were born. I knew last fall when the reports about *human attacks* were on the news for a day or two, and then you didn't hear anything about it. I don't care how crazy bubble bath can make a person . . . there is no drug that can get me high enough to chew someone's face off."

"It was bath salts, Skeeter. They said the guy even admitted to it. It was in his system."

Skeeter looked up at me, dubious. "You still believe that, do ya?"

I crossed my arms and leaned against the doorjamb, trying to pretend his theory wasn't completely disturbing. Surely our government didn't know. This sickness couldn't have been here that long—months—without the government telling us until it got out of hand.

"They would have reported it in the news before now."

Skeeter paused and took a breath, still staring at the floor. "They did, Nate." He reloaded his thirty aught six and stood.

A crash sounded on the other side of the house, and Jill screamed.

The next events seemed to happen over a span of several minutes, but it was really only seconds. Skeeter scrambled up from the floor and tore through the living room to the bedroom. He yelled, and then shots rang out. They were loud. The emotional side of me thought about covering Zoe's sensitive ears, the logical side—which won—went into survival mode and I grabbed my daughter and raced through the kitchen to the back door, clawing at the dead bolt. Just as I pulled open the door, something dead and horrifying stood in our way.

Zoe screamed, and then another shot rang out, this one not far from my ear. All sound merged into a single, solid ringing noise. Skeeter had shot the . . . thing . . . in the face, and shoved past me with Jill on one arm and the survival bags on the other. He yelled something to me, but I couldn't hear him. The only thing I could hear was the ringing.

Skeeter finally pointed and motioned for me to follow. I

grabbed Zoe's hand and shut the door behind us, hoping whatever was coming through the bedroom window would have trouble with doorknobs.

Miranda

ONCE WE GOT TO THE RANCH, WE WOULD BE SAFE. THAT was what I kept telling Ashley while trying to keep the Bug from getting stuck—on or off the highway. Daddy would be there waiting for us. He was a crack shot, and Bryce had been hunting with him enough over the years that he was getting pretty good, too. I had teased my dad so many times about his ridiculous collections of firearms and ammunition. *No one needs this many. It's like a car collection. It's a waste,* I would say. But because of my dad's silly obsession we would have weapons, the kitchen cabinets and pantry would be well stocked, we would have well water, and Butch—my dad's bull. He didn't like anyone in the yard. Not even us. If we let him out, we'd have our own security system. Red Hill Ranch was the best place to ride this out.

All we had to do was make it there, and we were in like Flynn.

We'd all tried our cell phones. Different numbers. Even 911, but we all got the same busy signal, or out-of-range signal, as Bryce called it.

"The towers must be down," he said.

"Well, that's just great," Ashley said. "I can't get Internet, either!"

"Trust me," I said. "No one is checking your Facebook status right now."

"For the news," she snapped, irritated with my joke.

"I'm going to take this exit. Take a back way. The interstate isn't getting any better, and if I keep driving in the median and the shoulder I'll end up blowing a tire."

Bryce frowned. "We've only got another twenty miles until the Anderson exit. The interstate is the fastest way to your dad's."

"It used to be. Now we're bypassing hundreds of cars stuck or stalled and trying not to run anyone over." Ironically, just as I said that, an older man stepped out between cars. He leaped back just as I passed. I wasn't slowing down. Not even for the terrified people who were now on foot and crying out for us to save them.

"Miranda," Ashley said, her voice small. "They're not all sick. We can help them."

"Help them how, exactly? Give them a ride? We're in a Bug, Ashley, we don't have any room."

"Ash," Cooper said, trying his best soothing voice, "she's right. Everyone is afraid. If we stop, someone might take our vehicle from us."

"I'm taking this exit," I warned, glancing over at Bryce.

"Stay on the interstate!" Bryce barked, a hint of desperation in his voice.

He wasn't trying to be a jerk. I couldn't blame him; leaving the interstate was choosing something unknown. Anything unknown in this mess was downright terrifying. Staying on the same road as thousands of others who had the same goal of survival was less daunting somehow. We weren't alone in our terror, and passing all of these people with the only working car on the road was both scary and comforting. We had the advantage. We were the safest out here where no one was safe.

Against my better judgment, I passed the exit and continued on the shoulder, weaving between people, cars, and zombies, and hoping my tires would hold out for another twenty miles. I wasn't normally a pushover; as a matter of fact, most who knew me thought I could be fairly difficult. But the one person I was always able to depend on was Bryce, and in that moment, I needed to believe I wasn't the only one who could make a sensible decision.

Growing up, with my dad always working, and mom preoccupied with new ways to get his attention, I felt like the only grown-up in the house. Ashley leaned on Mom so much that there wasn't really an opportunity for me to be coddled. Ashley was so delicate. She had inherited that trait from my mother. Every obstacle was a tragedy, every struggle a death sentence. I could never understand why they were so susceptible to stress, and I eventually decided that my dad had accepted long ago that it was just part of his wife's personality. He thought it was better if we kept Mom and Ashley from getting even remotely overwhelmed. We let them believe that no matter what came along, together Dad and I had it under control. Dad would manage Mom. I would handle Ashley. Now that Mom was remarried, the endless reassurances and heroic displays of patience were Rick's responsibility—keeping Ashley's emotional meltdowns in check was still mine. I was better at it some days than others, but when our parents shocked us with the news of the divorce, it seemed right that Ashley had their attention. She was the one who needed them most.

When Bryce and I decided we were more than friends, it just felt natural—and a little bit of a relief—to rely on him. Most times I felt he was more my family than my parents, or even Ashley. But even so, it wasn't that romantic sort of love that Ashley and Cooper had. Ours was a friendship, first. We almost treated our relationship like a duty, and I liked it that way. I guess Bryce did, too.

"We can exit at Anderson," Bryce said, trying not to see the stranded people on the side of the road.

Chapter Seven

Scarlet

WE WALKED CAREFULLY ALONG THE RIVER ONCE AGAIN, this time on the other side of the bridge, making our way to a large, familiar tree. Just as I had said, there was a rope hanging from a thick branch. The rope was tattered and looked frail. We wouldn't know how frail until we were swinging above the cold river water. The streetlights on each side of the bridge fell just short of where we stood. Good for hiding from soldiers—bad for swimming. With just a half-moon above, the water wasn't just dirty, it was black like the night had settled inside of it. As if that wasn't frightening enough, shufflers didn't need to breathe, I imagined. That was probably why the soldiers were shooting at floating corpses, just to make sure they didn't reanimate and crawl onto the shore and into town.

I shivered.

"You're freezing," Tobin said, removing his jacket. "Take this." He held it out. I just watched him for a moment until he shook it once. It was covered in mud, but it was lined with wool. It would still help to fend off the cold. "Take it."

Tobin huffed, clearly annoyed with my hesitation, and then draped the jacket around my shoulders.

"Thank you," I said, hoping it was loud enough for him to hear. I slipped my arms into the sleeves, and then rolled them up so they didn't swallow my hands. I would need them for the trip across the night.

With Tobin's help, I crawled up the bark. The initial climb was tougher than I remembered. Back then climbing a tree was nothing. I hadn't climbed anything in years. Tobin's breath skipped while he struggled to keep his balance underneath me. I made it to the first branch, and then used the rest as a ladder until I reached the one just under the branch with the rope.

Tobin was breathing a bit harder than he had a few minutes before.

"Really?" I said. "I'm not that heavy."

"No, ma'am." He put his hands on his hips while he caught his breath. "You're not. I'm just out of shape, and it's been a long-ass day."

I nodded. "That it has. Have you ever done this before?"

Tobin shook his head. His short cornrows moved with the motion, making it a little easier to gauge his nonverbal responses in the dark.

"Just pull in the rope and get a good grip," I said, showing him as I spoke. The next part I couldn't act out. "Lean back, and then step off. Let your bodyweight take you across. When you see land below, let go. It's fairly easy from what I remember, but if you hesitate you'll end up swinging back, and either in the water or hanging above it. The point is *not* to end up in the water. At least not tonight."

"Okay. But, uh . . . how am I going to see land if it's dark?"

"It's not that dark."

"It's pretty dark."

"Listen for me. I'll tell you when."

Tobin nodded, and I leaned back. My heart began to pound as I silently prayed, to whatever god might still be watching over us, that the two dozen things that could go wrong didn't. "I want to raise my babies," I whispered. "Please help me get across." As I leaned forward, I stepped off the branch and held on tightly. Within seconds I was almost above the opposite shore. The only problem was the rope was at the end of its pendulum and was beginning to start its return. I let go, and my feet hit hard against the ground at the edge of the short cliff above the water.

Quietly as I could, I called to Tobin. "I'm over! Really lean back, it's farther than I thought!"

A second later, I heard another vehicle, and I kneeled down in the tall reeds. I glanced over to see where Tobin was, and at the same time, saw that he was coming my way on the rope.

"Drop!" I said as loudly as I could without the soldiers hearing.

Tobin made a clumsy departure from the rope and fell to his knees. The spotlight danced over the water, and then highlighted the swinging rope. Voices shouted to each other, and doors slammed. They were going to search the area.

I scrambled to my feet, bringing Tobin with me. "We have to go," I whispered. "C'mon!"

Tobin limped into the trees, and then we crawled on our bellies until we reached the border of where the streetlights touched the woods. A house stood maybe twenty yards away with a makeshift fence. I tried to remember who lived there, and if they had dogs. They probably did. Everyone in this town had a fucking dog. Most of them tied up outside so their owners could ignore them.

A muffled sound came from Tobin's throat.

"You hurt?" I asked.

"If I said I might've hurt my ankle when I fell, would you leave me here to die?"

"Yes."

"Then no, I'm fine."

I smiled and helped Tobin to his feet. "Where does your sister live?"

"I've never come into town from this way. I'm not sure how to get there from here."

"Do you know what street?"

"Padon. I think."

"East or West?"

"I'm not sure, I . . ."

I sighed. "Tell me how you get there from the other side of town, and I'll guess."

"Just come in on the main road, see," he said, talking with his hands, "and then turn right at that old armory, and then I go until I get to her street and take a left, and then I usually hit a stoplight right there. I'm not sure why there's a stoplight. Ain't no traffic in this damn town."

"Tobin . . ."

He nodded once. "Right. I'm sorry. I go through the light and pass a grocery store, and she's the second house on the right."

"Weird."

"Why?"

"That's right next to my grandparents' house."

"Really?"

"Yes. We're going to go straight down this street about five blocks and then hang a left. I'm going to drop you off at your sister's, check on my grandparents, and then I'm going to get my daughters."

"And then where are you going?"

"Red Hill Ranch."

Nathan

JILL WAS CRUMPLED AGAINST SKEETER, HOLDING HER bleeding, mangled arm up against her chest. She had it bent at the elbow, so I couldn't tell exactly how bad her injuries were. Glass had broken just before she screamed, so I hoped over and over that she had just been cut and not bitten. Everything we knew about the walking dead told us that a bite was fatal.

Zoe had a hard time keeping up with Skeeter's pace, so I pulled her up into my arms. Her little legs bounced as I chased Skeeter and Jill across the street and down the block to the First Baptist church. Its wooden exterior was in need of another coat of white paint. I couldn't imagine why it hadn't been done; the church was the size of Skeeter's house.

"Heads up!" Skeeter said, raising his rifle.

A woman was walking toward Zoe and me. I wasn't sure what to do. I was holding Zoe with both hands, and called out to Skeeter, running as fast as my legs could move. He stood still for a moment so he could let go of Jill long enough to aim and fire, and then he wrapped his arm around his wife again. I didn't wait to see if Skeeter had hit his target. I didn't have to. I'd never seen the man miss. After one more glance around, he took off into a sprint for the backside of the church.

Several of those things were following us, and the fear and adrenaline made me feel I could jump to the roof with Zoe in my arms if I had to.

Skeeter beat on the door with the side of his fist, and it immediately opened. A short man with white hair and matching complexion stepped to the side so we could file in, and then he shut it tight, and turned the bolt lock. Another man, bald and wearing a blue leisure suit, helped him pull a solid wood pulpit in front of the door before they turned to Skeeter.

Skeeter nodded his head to the short man. "Reverend Mathis." He looked to the other, and his eyebrows pulled in. "Where's Esther?" The man just looked to the floor, and it was then that I noticed a boy about eleven or twelve standing behind him.

Reverend Mathis put his hand on the man's shoulder. "Bob and Evan tried to get to her. They had to leave her behind."

Evan, the young boy behind Bob, sniffed and wiped his cheek, but kept his eyes on the floor. He was so still, as if moving would mean what was happening was real.

Skeeter offered a small smile. "You got your grandson here safe, Bob. Esther would be glad for that."

Someone was hammering away in the next room, the knocking echoing throughout the building.

A few people Skeeter and Jill seemed to be familiar with were gathered together, all wide-eyed and as frightened as we were. The room we stood in was obviously a kitchen, albeit a small one. Canary-yellow paint complemented the dated speckled countertops and metal cabinets. The seats and springs of the faucet were just one more thing that needed to be repaired in this place, made obvious by the steady drip of water from the spout. The only thing not some shade of yellow was the faded blue carpet; at least it was until Jill started bleeding all over it.

"Christ almighty, Jill, what happened to you?" a woman said, helping Skeeter to sit his wife in a folding chair.

Jill sniffed. "I was getting a few changes of clothes for me and Skeeter. I heard something outside, so I opened the curtain and Shawn Burgess was standing right next to the window. He didn't seem right, Doris." Tears fell down her cheek while Doris wrapped her arm with a damp towel. "Next thing I know, he's charging me like a bull. He broke through the window and less than a second later he had me on the ground."

"Shawn Burgess? Denise's son?" Doris said, looking to Skeeter. When Skeeter didn't respond, she pulled back the towel to reveal a large gouge in Jill's arm. I was expecting a set of bite marks, like a toddler might leave, but an entire section of her skin and muscle had been ripped away. "Oh my Lord, honey. You're going to need stitches."

"More like a skin graft," Evan said. He was staring at Jill's arm like it was on fire.

Doris shot a threatening look in his direction. "And a slew of antibiotics, I imagine. We're going to have to get to Dr. Brown's."

"Aunt Jill!" Zoe said, ducking under Jill's good arm. Jill hugged Zoe to her side and kissed her forehead.

The white-haired man spoke. "You think we'll get lucky and he'll come here with supplies?"

"No," Skeeter said. "I saw him chasing Jim Miller earlier when I brought Barb."

Skeeter watched Doris fuss over Jill's wound. A darkness had fallen over his face. He knew as well as I did that he was going to lose his wife today. Maybe tomorrow. If anything anyone had ever said about zombies was true, it wouldn't take long. By the subdued fear in Jill's eyes, she knew it, too.

Skeeter blinked. "Where is Barb and Ms. Kay?"

Doris nodded toward the doorway. "In the sanctuary. Prayin'. Gary and Eric are boarding up the windows."

"Good plan," Jill said. "They definitely don't have a problem with windows."

Skeeter kneeled in front of his wife. "I'm going to talk to the guys, Jillybean. Make sure they allow spaces for me to fit my rifles through. I'll be right back, and then we're going to get you fixed up." Jill nodded as Skeeter kissed her cheek.

"Can you stay here with Aunt Jill?" I said to Zoe. She leaned against Jill, the smallest tinge of sadness in her eyes. I wondered if she knew, but I wouldn't ask. Maybe she was just missing her mother.

I followed Skeeter into the sanctuary. It smelled like old people and mildew, and I began to wonder why in the hell Skeeter had thought this rickety building was our best option. Two men were working on opposite sides of the room, furiously nailing boards to the stained glass windows. There were three on each wall, and they had only one on each side left to cover. A hand flattened against the glass, making a clumsy attempt to get inside. I jumped, on edge from our desperate run to the church.

"They just started doing that," Eric said, gesturing to the window. "It's like they know we're in here."

When he started hammering again, shadows of the people outside darkened the glass portraits of Jesus and angels. They wanted to get inside, and I wondered how long it would be until they did.

"The noise is probably drawing them here," I said, running my fingers through my hair. Aubrey was always making snide comments about my shaggy hair and how bad I needed a haircut. I wondered if the world would ever calm down long enough for me to miss her bitching.

"Don't really have a choice. They'll have that glass broke before long." Skeeter walked over to two frail-looking women sitting next to each other on a wooden pew. "You ladies still doin' okay?" Skeeter said, putting a hand on the one woman's shoulder. She reached up and patted his hand, but did not stop her quiet prayer. Their mouths were moving, but I couldn't hear them.

"You think you could send one up for Jill?" Skeeter asked, his voice threatening to break.

One woman continued to pray as if she didn't hear, the other looked up. "Is she okay?"

"She's hurt. She's in the kitchen . . . all right for now."

"Jesus will take care of her."

I rolled my eyes. Jesus wasn't taking care of much of anything at the moment.

Skeeter started to return to the kitchen, but I motioned for him to join me in the corner of the room, away from listening ears.

"I know what you're going to say," he said. His eyebrows pulled together. "But don't."

I nodded, and then watched Skeeter return to his wife.

Chapter Eight

Nathan

I LOWERED MY CHIN TO PEEK FROM A SLIT IN THE BOARDS Gary had left for Skeeter. The sun was a little lower in the sky. Before too long, it would be dark. That thought scared me. We would need to sleep some time, but they wouldn't. Those things would be walking around, just on the other side of these walls, waiting to pull our flesh from our bones with their teeth.

Skeeter grabbed my shoulder; the sudden movement made me jump two inches off my chair.

"Whoa! It's just me, Nate. Calm down."

I settled back into my seat, trying to play off my fear. Watching a movie about zombies is one thing. Watching zombies outside your window was another. The movies didn't talk about that. Well . . . maybe they did, but they didn't drive home how terrifying each moment truly was. I tried not to think about tomorrow, or that we would still be fighting for our lives every day from now on. I glanced back at Zoe, and choked back the sadness welling up in my throat. I didn't want her to grow up in a world like this.

A combination of fear, anger, and utter depression fully engulfed me.

Skeeter squeezed my shoulder. I sat still, letting his fingers sink into my tense muscle. "It's going to be okay."

"Is it?" I asked, looking back out the window. "Is Jill?"

Skeeter sighed. "I don't know. I'm hoping the movies got it all wrong, and a bite is just a bite."

"What if it's not?"

"I don't know. I don't really wanna think about it."

I nodded, catching a glimpse of an elderly man shuffling by the window. His neck was half eaten away, and his dress shirt was saturated in blood. "We can't stay here. We're going to have to keep moving. Get into the country."

"Damn, brother, I thought I was in the country."

"I mean away from any town."

Skeeter took a moment to respond. "I know, but I can't move Jill. And we can't risk putting her in a car with Zoe until we know if she's going to get better."

I closed my eyes tight, trying to squint away the visual. Another one of those things ambled by. She was wearing a nametag and a long skirt. I couldn't read the nametag even if it was closer. It was covered in blood and what might be torn muscle lying over the top.

"Jesus Christ, that's Birdie," Skeeter said, disgusted. "She works at the bank."

A dog was barking at her, keeping just enough distance that it wasn't grabbed and eaten. Looking out at what could be seen through the boards, I watched whoever lumbered by, studying them, trying to notice whatever I could.

They were slow. Not as slow as I thought they might be,

but they were slow enough that if we had to head out on foot, as long as we didn't let one get too close, or get surrounded, we could make it. Some of them that had more extensive injuries moved slower than others. One guy's foot was completely gone, but he continued walking on a bloody stub. They weren't distracted by pain.

"I wonder if you can really only kill them by obliterating the brain," I thought aloud.

Skeeter raised his hunting rifle, situated it between the boards, and aimed. "I don't know. Let's find out." He picked out a target, and then breathed. "Sorry, Mr. Madison." Skeeter squeezed the trigger, and the fabric of Mr. Madison's shirt, in the spot where his heart would be, popped and sprayed open. Dark blood oozed from the wound, but Mr. Madison didn't seem to notice. "Okay. So that doesn't work." Skeeter squeezed the trigger again. This time a red dot immediately formed in the middle of Mr. Madison's temple and simultaneously seemed to burst, leaving a perfectly imperfect round wound. The man stopped midstep as his head jerked to the side, and then he fell onto his side.

I waited for a moment, watching for any signs of movement. Nothing. "You think we have to burn them, too?" I asked.

Skeeter frowned, his eyes darted over at me from over the sights of his rifle. "Now that's just silly."

"Skeeter, honey, I think Jill's not feeling well," Doris said. She was wringing her hands, clearly unnerved.

Skeeter hopped up and rushed into the kitchen. I followed behind, seeing Zoe sitting in the corner, watching her aunt Jill as she sat in her chair, crumpled over and heaving into a bucket.

"Zoe? Zoe, come here. Come sit in here for a bit." I motioned for Zoe to join me in the sanctuary. Zoe slid off her chair and walked toward me, and when she gripped my fingers, the strength in her tiny hand surprised me.

We sat together on a pew beside Gary, hoping the hammering would drown out some of the noise coming from the kitchen. Between the moaning noises Jill made while she vomited, she whimpered and cried for Skeeter to help her.

"She's sweating, Daddy," Zoe said, "a whole lot." Her eyes were heavy with worry. "Then her face went all wonky and she threw up on the floor. She said her whole body hurt like she had the flu."

I nodded. "Did that scare you?"

"It all scares me," she said. The skin around her eyes tightened, and I could see she was trying not to cry.

No one knew what would happen to Jill, but I had an idea of what might be happening, and I didn't want Zoe to witness it. Short of Skeeter moving Jill somewhere else, the only way to keep Zoe from witnessing her aunt's death was to take her away from the church. That meant taking her outside where it wasn't safe.

"I'm so sorry, honey. I wish I could make this all go away." I hugged Zoe to my chest, trying to buy some time before a solution came to mind.

Jill was sobbing now. She probably knew what was happening, too.

I cupped Zoe's little cherubic face in my hands, scanning the splash of freckles across her nose and light-brown hair. She'd kept the same simple shoulder-length hair cut since she was four. Her natural waves made it bouncy, but it seemed like her worry had weighed that down, too. "I'm going to try to help Uncle Skeeter. I want you to stay in here, okay? You're safe in here. I won't be gone long."

Zoe nodded quickly, glancing back to Gary and Eric as they pounded the last nails into the last board.

"Good girl," I said, kissing her forehead.

Skeeter was on one knee, both arms wrapped around his wife. She leaned against his chest, her face blotchy and glistening with sweat. Skeeter stared at the floor, whispering something to her, with the same hopelessness in his eyes as the woman we passed on the bridge. His young and healthy wife was dying in his arms, and they both knew it.

Doris filled a glass with water, and leaned down to hold it to Jill's lips. She took a few sips and then spit it out, leaning down to the bucket, emptying her stomach once more.

"We need the doctor," Doris said.

"The doctor's dead," Gary said, dropping the hammer on the table next to Jill. "So is his wife, and kids. They're all walking around out there with milky eyes and bite marks."

Jill sniffed once, and looked up at her husband. "Skeeter."

"No," he said, shaking his head, still staring at the floor.

"Skeeter, what if I hurt the people in here?"

"No."

"What if I hurt you?"

"No!"

"What if I kill Zoe?" she pleaded, tears streaming down her reddened cheeks. Her breath skipped, and she pulled Skeeter's face down so his eyes met hers. "Don't let me hurt that baby, Skeeter."

Skeeter's bottom lip quivered. "But what about *our* baby?"

I stood up straight, away from the doorjamb I was leaning on. "What?"

"What was that?" Doris said.

"Jill's pregnant," Skeeter said, his voice desperate. "Seven weeks. Dr. Brown just called her this morning."

I leaned down and grabbed my knees. I couldn't imagine the agony he was feeling. They didn't deserve this. They'd been trying to conceive since their wedding night, and now Skeeter would lose them both.

Jill touched her forehead to Skeeter's chin, and then looked up at him with a weak smile. "We'll be together, and we'll wait for you."

Skeeter broke down, burying his face into Jill's neck. "I can't do it, Jillybean," he sobbed.

The first window in the sanctuary crashed, and everyone but Skeeter froze. Sounds of searching hands on the wooden boards made my skin crawl. I leaned back to see Zoe, Barb, and Ms. Kay turned around in their seats, staring at the broken glass on the floor. The boards were holding, but I could still feel my heart pounding against my rib cage. Eric stood next to the broken glass, inspecting the board, and then he nodded, assuring us that they would hold.

"Wait. What are we talking about here?" Reverend Mathis said, bringing my attention back to the kitchen.

Doris was still wringing her hands. "I can't say I . . . we shouldn't be talking about this."

"It's okay," Jill said, cupping her hand over Skeeter's head until she had to bend over again and vomit into the bucket.

Another window broke.

I looked to Gary. "What is that hallway there?" I said, gesturing to the open doorway on the other side of the kitchen. There were two his and hers bathrooms, and then an open doorway leading down a dark hall. "We may need another exit."

"Just to the stairs."

That caught my attention. "What stairs? You boarded up windows but didn't secure the upper level?"

Gary shrugged. "I don't think they can climb."

"We're in the house of the Lord!" Doris said. "I'm not going to let this happen! We don't know what this is. Skeeter, Jill could get better!"

Bob spoke for the first time. His voice was deep and raspy. "We know exactly what this is."

Everyone turned in the direction of Bob's voice. He was sitting on a metal folding chair in the corner, where he'd been for the last hour. He'd perched his cane between his legs, resting his hands on the handle.

His gray mustache twitched when he spoke. "This is nothing less than a goddamn tragedy."

"Bob!" Doris said, pretending to be offended.

"Truth is, she's just going to end up like one of those things outside, only she'll be in here with us."

Glass crashed to the floor again, and this time a bone-chilling moan floated from the sanctuary into the kitchen.

Bob's eyes drifted to me, and then settled beside me about waist high. That was when I noticed Zoe standing just behind me. She stared at her aunt Jill, her beautiful hazel-green eyes filling with tears for the umpteenth time that day. I wondered if she would ever know happiness after today.

I kneeled beside my daughter, trying to think of something cathartic to say, but words wouldn't save Jill, and Jill being okay was the only thing that was going to make this hell somewhat tolerable for Zoe.

A heavy thud sounded above us, and we all looked to the ceiling. Skeeter kissed Jill's forehead, and then motioned for Doris to sit next to her as he grabbed his shotgun. Gary picked up his hammer. I gently pushed Zoe toward Reverend Mathis, and then followed my brother-in-law, Gary, and Eric through the doorway, and down the hall. Skeeter stopped at the bottom of the stairs, pointing his shotgun to the closed door at the top.

Gary flipped on the light. "Maybe someone crawled onto the roof to get away from them and made their way inside?"

We heard slow, clumsy footsteps, and then something was knocked over.

Eric took in a sharp breath. "They can't climb, can they? I've never heard of a zombie climbing."

"Why not? They used to be human. Humans can climb," Gary said, resituating the toothpick in his mouth and tightening his grip on the hammer.

I nervously ran my fingers through my hair. "We don't really know anything about them. Assuming is going to get us all killed. I say we get some boards, take them upstairs, try to communicate with whoever is in there, and if they don't answer, we board up the door."

"Simple enough," Skeeter said. His voice was low and smooth, and reminded me of the few times he'd invited me along on a deer hunt. That was his *in the woods* voice, like the guys in those hunting shows always used while they were narrating their victorious kill. He didn't pull his eyes away from the door, as if he were hunting whatever was on the other side.

"Skeeter?" Eric said. The nervousness contrasted with his large, burly frame. "We're almost out of boards."

Miranda

"NOW WHAT?" ASHLEY SAID. HER VOICE WAS INCREASingly whiny with each mile we drove.

I didn't want to be sitting still. I wanted to take the overly congested exit and then head west of the overpass, past the army, or reserves, or whoever those guys in green camo guarding the bridge into Anderson were, and be on my way to my dad's. A dozen or more guns were pointed in our direction, at us and everyone else caught in the mess of cars below the overpass. Three lines of cars and trucks were stopped on the northbound exit ramp by the men with guns. People were outside of their vehicles, yelling and pleading to pass.

I had maneuvered the Bug as close as I could to the ramp, but quickly ran out of room. There was no way to get through, and we were stuck on the shoulder of the interstate.

"What are they doing?" Cooper asked, still clutching Ashley to his side.

Bryce tried his phone again. When he heard yet another busy signal, he let the phone fall in his lap, and hit the door with the side of his fist.

"Hey!" I said. "She's gotten us this far! Be nice!"

A newer, red pickup truck approached the overpass on the Fairview side, slowed, and then came to a stop. A man got out, pointing toward Anderson. The army men shook their heads, motioning for him to turn back. He kept pointing to Anderson, but when more than a dozen semi-automatic rifles were turned in his direction, he got in his pickup and backed away.

"He came from Fairview. You think we should still go that way?" Cooper asked.

"It's the quickest way," Ashley said.

"So they're guarding Anderson," Bryce said, watching the scene transpire.

"Looks that way," I said.

"Then why are they on the Fairview side of the bridge? Wouldn't it make more sense to be on the Anderson side? Then they could guard the exit ramp, too."

I took a closer look. The soldiers were young, and from what I could tell, seemed antsy. "There is an armory in Anderson. You think they're really soldiers? Maybe they're just trying to protect their town?"

"The governor is in Anderson today," Ashley said.

We all turned, surprised she knew that interesting and pertinent tidbit of information.

"I listen to the radio in the mornings when I'm getting ready for class. They said it on the news. Governor Bellmon would be in Anderson today."

Bryce nodded. "There's no way he'd already have soldiers there. They must be random townspeople."

I looked at them again, and gasped. They weren't wearing fatigues. They were outfitted in Realtree and Mossy Oak. "Oh, Christ. Scared kids with AK-47s? Is the governor that stupid?"

"Maybe it wasn't him at all? Maybe they just took it upon themselves?" Cooper said.

"Either way," I said, turning to look out the back window.

I didn't see anything that would bite us, but it would only be a matter of time before they caught up. "We have to get going."

Just as I finished my sentence, the same red pickup from before came from the Fairview side at high speed, straight at the men with guns.

"Miranda!" Ashley screamed.

I gripped the steering wheel as they opened fire. The windshield of the truck broke, and then the truck veered off course, straight for our side of the bridge. It jumped over the side of the off-ramp, cartwheeled over three cars, and then came to a rest on its cab. The wheels were still spinning, making a terrible high-pitched whirring noise.

Everyone screamed, and those standing outside their cars crouched down for a second, waiting to see where the truck would go. For a while, everyone seemed confused, nervous, and unsure what to do, but once the shock of the earlier incident became secondary to the need to get home to their families, the yelling and pleading to pass continued.

"Maybe we could sneak by them on foot?" Cooper said.

Bryce shook his head. "We need a distraction."

As if it were scripted, a white full-sized van slowly approached the bridge. The gunmen were immediately on edge. The people standing outside of their cars yelled louder, and a few of them attempted to throw shoes and anything they could get their hands on at the gunmen, but none of it made it to the bridge.

"Oh, man. Get back in your car," Bryce said.

The driver had gotten out, and was arguing with the gunmen. He then grabbed one of the gunmen's rifles. I wasn't sure who shot the first bullet, but once a gun went off, they all opened fire. The man from the van convulsed while his body was punctured by bullets. When he hit the ground, the gunmen targeted his vehicle, too.

"Oh my God! Oh my God!" Ashley cried.

The gunfire didn't stop. The men with guns were agitated and angry, and the yelling from below drew their attention. The people standing outside of their vehicles on the ramp were suddenly prey, and they all began to scream and run. Following the running families, the men let their gunfire spread to everyone else trapped in the gridlock below.

"Jesus Christ!" Bryce yelled. "Get us out of here, Miranda! Go! Go!"

I yanked on the gearshift and backed into the car behind me, and then spun the wheel, shoving the gearshift into drive. After a few near misses and even more sideswipes, we were under the bridge. I didn't stop, hoping the psychopaths above would be too busy with the poor people on the south side to see that I was going to take the on-ramp on the other side and floor it toward Fairview.

"What are you doing?" Ashley said. "Hide under the bridge!"

"We'll get stuck there!" Bryce said, knowing I was too focused on getting us the hell out of there to respond. "Keep going, Miranda! Don't stop!"

We cleared the bridge and flipped a U-turn to catch the southbound on-ramp. The Bug caught air more than once on its climb to the top—sometimes on the asphalt, sometimes not—and finally made it to the road.

Cooper patted my seat ardently. "They're not even paying attention! Keep going!"

We rode in silence for the next mile, but the second we were out of range Ashley began to sniff and whimper. We had left behind a massacre. Children were among the victims on the interstate.

"Has the whole world gone crazy?" Ashley cried.

Bryce and Cooper were sniffing, too. Before long hot tears were burning down my cheeks. Moments later, we were all sobbing.

Bryce wiped his nose on his shirt, and then took my right hand. "You saved our lives, Miranda."

I squeezed his hand, unable to speak. I took a long, broken breath, and tried to concentrate on the road. We would be coming up on Fairview soon.

Chapter Nine

Nathan

ERIC RETURNED QUICKLY CARRYING SEVERAL BOARDS IN his arms. "I found these in the shed. I took as many as I could carry because they're really starting to gather around the church. I don't think anyone should go outside anymore."

"They must know we're in here," I said. "It's just a matter of time before they get in."

Gary pulled the toothpick from his mouth, frustrated. "But Eric just said we can't leave."

"He said he didn't think we *should*," I said, looking to Skeeter. "Doesn't mean we can't. It isn't safe here."

He ignored our discussion, and began climbing the stairs, never taking his eyes off the door.

We all followed. The silent hopes to find nothing were louder than the stairs that creaked in a slow symphony beneath our feet.

Gary gripped the doorknob and pulled, using his body weight as leverage. None of us could be sure if the walking dead had enough coordination to climb or even twist a doorknob, but just one mistake meant death. I didn't want to take any chances, and neither did these men.

Skeeter lifted his fist, and knocked his knuckles against the door. "Hello? It's Skeeter McGee. Anyone in there?"

The footsteps that we'd heard before had been silent for several minutes.

Skeeter tried again. "I have a gun, and I'm prepared to shoot. Identify yourself."

Nothing.

"Let's board it up," Eric said, repositioning the wood in his arms.

Skeeter held up a hand, signaling for Eric to wait, and then he held his ear against the door. His eyes targeted me, and then he shook his head. "I don't hear anything. Don't tell me those things know how to hide. I'm going in."

Skeeter put his hand over Gary's, and I grabbed his arm. "What are you doing? What if there's several in there? What if they overpower us and get downstairs?"

Skeeter smiled with his mouth and frowned with his eyes. "I ain't gonna let that happen. Just like I ain't gonna leave those things walking above us. If we're going to ride this out in this church, it's got to be secure."

I sighed, and let go of his arm. "All right. Gary?"

Gary reluctantly released the doorknob, and Skeeter went in. I checked behind the door, and then my eyes scanned the large, empty classroom before they touched on what Skeeter had already seen.

A young woman, early twenties, was lying next to a fallen end table and an open window. Blood marked her trail. Her arm had been chewed on, in several spots down to the bone.

"Christ almighty, that's Annabelle Stephens!" Eric said, rushing to her side. He looked up at us after touching her neck. There wasn't a spot on her from her chin down that wasn't saturated in blood.

We heard a whimper from the corner, and Skeeter immediately trained his shotgun in that direction. I grabbed the barrel and slowly pushed it down, seeing a little boy, alone and huddled into a ball.

Skeeter lowered his weapon. "Hey there, little man."

Gary let out a breath, glancing at Eric while he covered Annabelle's face and chest with the only thing he could find: a small rug. "That's Craig and Amy Nicholson's boy."

Skeeter kneeled down, put his gun on the floor behind him, and held out his arms. "I went to school with Amy. You must be Connor. C'mere, buddy. I know you're scared, but you're safe here."

Connor shook his head quickly. He held his knees against his chest, and his chin was resting on his knees as he rocked back and forth.

"Is Annabelle his aunt?" I asked.

Skeeter shook his head. "Annabelle's the first grade teacher at the elementary school."

"She saved me," Connor whispered, "from my mom." His breath caught, and then he let out a sob.

Skeeter scooped him up into his arms. "Sssh, buddy. You're safe now. You're safe, I promise."

Skeeter walked to the window, opened it further, and then stepped out onto the roof. I followed him. From what I could see, the entire church was surrounded.

"A lot of them followed us here," Connor said.

Skeeter nodded, noticing the drag marks along the roof and the windowsill, and the trail of blood on the sidewalk leading up to the church. "Annabelle bled out. We'll probably have them coming from all over town."

"At least we know they can't climb," I said, pointing to the group lifting their arms and scratching at the church's outside walls.

Connor sniffed. "Annabelle was already on the roof. She saw me running and climbed back down."

Skeeter gave Connor a squeeze. "She was a sweet lady."

Connor peaked over Skeeter's shoulder at the rug covering Annabelle, and then shut his eyes tight.

"We *can't* stay here," I said.

"We can't leave. Give it a couple of days, Nate. They'll move on."

"What if they don't? We'll be trapped here."

Skeeter sighed, pulling the toothpick out of his mouth with his free hand and throwing it down to the growing crowd of undead below. "I can't move Jill."

My eyebrows pushed together. "What if she gets worse? What if she turns into one of those things?"

Skeeter looked down, and then back at me, resolute. "You should go. Get Zoe some place safe. She shouldn't be here when Jill . . . but, I can't leave, brother. I wouldn't have anything to live for, anyway."

My stomach dropped, and goose bumps formed on my arms. Skeeter was going to die in this church, with his wife.

"I've gotta get Zoe out of here."

"I know."

Skeeter crawled back inside carefully with Connor still in

his arms. He walked past Eric and Gary, but stopped in the doorway. "Board up the door."

"But," Eric said, pointing to the sheet, "they can't climb, and Annabelle's dead."

"In case she comes back as one of them," I said, nodding to the window.

Gary frowned. "Maybe we should roll her off the roof. She'll start stinkin' before long."

"No!" Connor cried.

Skeeter patted his back. "The smell might help cover ours. Leave her be. Board the door."

Gary and Eric nodded, and Skeeter and I walked back downstairs to the kitchen, joining Bob and Evan, Reverend Mathis, and Doris. They had made Jill a pallet on the floor with a rolled-up dish towel for a pillow.

"Oh my Lord in Heaven! Connor Nicholson! Are you all right, sweetheart?" Doris said, taking him from Skeeter.

Connor hugged Doris tight, wildly sobbing all over again. They obviously knew each other, but I wasn't sure how.

Doris blanched, looking up at Skeeter. "Where is Amy?"

"She's outside. Annabelle Stephens helped him up to the roof."

"Well . . . ?" she said, looking past Skeeter. "Where is she?"

Skeeter shook his head. "Upstairs. She didn't make it."

About that time the hammering began. Doris held Connor while he cried. Reverend Mathis went to the sanctuary to check on Barb and Ms. Kay, and Skeeter sat on the floor next to his wife. Jill was unconscious, her bloodshot eyes barely visible between the two thin slits of her eyelids. She was nearly panting, and a thin sheen of sweat covered her paling skin.

Zoe was standing in the doorway, her eyes fixed on her aunt Jill. I kneeled beside my daughter and pulled her against my side. There wasn't really anything I could say; no point in asking if she was all right. None of us were.

Skeeter bent down to speak soft, comforting words to Jill. Unable to watch, I walked into the sanctuary. Broken glass lined the carpet next to all three walls. The townspeople of Fairview were clawing and batting at the boards Eric and Gary had nailed across the windows. The boards wouldn't last forever, just like the small amounts of food Skeeter and a few others had thought to bring along with them.

Reverend Mathis was praying with Barb and Ms. Kay, but paused to watch me approach the windows. I peeked through, trying to gauge how far my car was from the church. I didn't see any of the sick around Skeeter's house, or even between there and the church, but that didn't mean there weren't any. Still, the hardest part would be walking out the door.

I walked into the kitchen, pulling my car keys from my pocket. "I'm going to make a run for it with Zoe. I have a car down the block. We've got two, maybe three empty seats, but we're going to need a diversion to get outside."

"But I don't wanna leave Aunt Jill, Daddy," Zoe said.

Doris shook her head. "I'm not going out there."

Bob frowned. "Why don't you just stay here? It's as safe as anywhere."

I covered Zoe's ears and spoke softly. "Because Annabelle left a trail of blood leading to the church, and it's smeared on the west wall. Skeeter and I were just on the roof. The church is surrounded, and more are coming. Who knows when they'll go away, or if they ever will?"

Skeeter nodded. "You'll need a gun. Something light but with a lot of stopping power. Grab the AR out of my bag there. The two twenty-three. Don't forget the clips. I'll cover you."

A long, camouflage duffle bag holding nearly every gun Skeeter owned was tucked under the church's kitchen table. I crouched down to pull the nylon across the worn linoleum, and found a squat-barreled rifle that was smaller, but looked just as ferocious as anything else in the bag. "I've never shot a semiautomatic rifle, Skeeter. I'm not sure I can handle this."

Skeeter laughed once, but he couldn't quite smile. "Zoe could handle it. And you should let her practice when y'all get somewhere safe. Just in case."

The thought of something happening to me, and Zoe then being left alone made my world stop. She was so little, and if we left Skeeter and Jill, I would be all she had. "Maybe we should stay?" I said, my gaze floating to the sanctuary. The things outside were still trying to get in, pulling and banging against the boards.

Skeeter looked at his wife, and then back at me. "No. You shouldn't." I pulled a 9mm from the bag and a box of ammo. "Can I take this, too?" Skeeter's eyes touched on Zoe for just a moment. He knew why I wanted it. I couldn't leave her alone to fend for herself.

"Of course, brother."

I nodded in thanks, and then stood. "But we still need a distraction."

Doris set Connor in the chair that Jill was in. "Maybe we'll get lucky and someone will pass through town. Will they follow a car?"

Zoe tugged on my pant leg. "I don't want to go outside, Daddy."

I leaned down, looking her in the eyes. "I know you don't. It's scary out there, isn't it?"

Zoe nodded.

"But this isn't the safest place for us. We have to find somewhere else."

Zoe's lips formed a hard line, and a tiny indentation appeared between her eyebrows, but she didn't argue.

"You should take Connor and Evan," Skeeter said.

Evan looked to Bob with fear in his eyes. Connor shook his head and hid behind Doris.

Doris shook her head, too. "I can't stop him from taking his daughter, Skeeter, but I won't let him take these boys outside with those things."

"Connor," Skeeter said. "I think you should go with Nathan. We're going to work to keep those things out but I'm not sure that you'll be safe here, little man."

I could barely see Connor's head shake in protest as he stood behind Doris. I wasn't going to force him, and really, I couldn't blame him after what he'd just been through.

"Bob?" Skeeter said. "You sure you don't want to give Evan a chance?"

Evan stared at Bob, his eyes pleading to stay. Bob patted the boy's shoulder, and then shook his head.

Barb located a plastic grocery sack, and I put a few boxes of bullets and five bottles of water inside, and then stuffed the 9mm in the waist of my pants. If someone were to tell me the day before that I would be doing anything close to this, I would have laughed them out of the office. I'd been hunting and shooting with Skeeter a handful of times, but owning a gun was not a priority for me, and I wasn't opposed to gun control.

Now that the undead had taken over the earth, I imagined any member of the NRA was doing better than most.

Just as I hooked the handles of the sack in the crook of my elbow, the sound of salvation echoed through the church: a car horn.

Scarlet

MOST HOUSES WERE DARK, LETTING THE STREETLIGHTS cast ominous shadows over everything. The army was on patrol, and Tobin and I had to leap behind bushes or into the shadows once in a while, slowing down our pace. In addition Tobin's injured ankle slowed us down. I wondered if anyone was still in their homes, or if the army had taken them all somewhere. That thought was pushed out by sheer will; that would mean my girls would be in a place nearly impossible to reach, with murderous armed guards.

Refusing to believe that, I pulled Tobin along, pushing back when his limp forced more of his bodyweight on me. I tried to encourage him through the pain. His ankle was swollen, and getting more so by the minute. The walking wasn't helping. He needed ibuprofen and an ice pack at the very least.

"It's not far now," I said.

Tobin had been holding his breath with each step for the last three or four blocks, but he didn't complain.

"You think she's there?" he said.

"I hope so."

"Doesn't look like anyone's home. Is there a public shelter around here? Maybe they were all moved there?"

"It's possible. Maybe the hospital, or the elementary school. It has an old fallout shelter."

"She has a little boy, did I tell you that?"

I smiled up at him. "You said she was a single mom. What's her name?"

"Tavia. And my nephew's name is Tobin."

"Wow. Namesake."

"Yeah," he said, beaming with pride even though his face was dripping with sweat. "He's a good kid, too. Athletic. Polite. She's done a helluva job. I don't think I've ever told her that."

"You will," I said, praying it was true.

An army Humvee turned the corner, and I pulled Tobin to the dark side of the closest house. A small pop came from Tobin's ankle. He grimaced and let out a small grunt.

Tobin tried to keep his labored breathing quiet. "They're armed, too. I don't get it. Why would . . . why would they be patrolling the streets if they're just trying to keep—what do you call 'em?"

"Shufflers."

"Yeah, shufflers. Why patrol inside the city limits if they're just trying to keep shufflers out? Maybe they're looking for survivors? Maybe they're just gathering people to take to a shelter?"

"I don't know that we should walk out and ask them for help," I said, pulling him along once the Humvee passed.

"A black man can get shot sneaking around in the dark, that's what I know."

I offered a half smile. "C'mon. We're almost there."

Tobin's limp became more pronounced. A block away from Tavia's, he was in agony. He moaned and groaned through the pain; every step was torture.

"If you don't quit making that noise, someone is going to think you're a shuffler and shoot us from their window."

"I'm sorry," Tobin said, genuinely regretful.

"I'm kidding. You want to rest?"

He shook his head. "No. You need to get to your girls." He looked at his sister's house, just three houses away. "I wish I could return the favor. I wish I could help you find them." His large hand that was cupped over my shoulder squeezed gently into my skin, and I hugged him back.

We stopped at Tavia's front steps. Her house had a screened porch and a rickety screen door. Tobin's voice was barely over a whisper. "Tavia! It's Tobin! You in there?" He paused, waiting for a response. "Tavia!"

I pointed to my grandparents'. "I'll be right next door. Holler if you need me."

Tobin laughed. "You've done enough. Thank you, Scarlet."

I nodded to him, and then crossed the yard to my grandparents' drive. The grass was just beginning to turn green, and it was half soft, half crunchy under my shoes. My footsteps sounded loud amid the quiet night. Muffled noises Tobin was making next door were barely audible, but I felt like my every breath was picked up by a megaphone.

I pulled on the screen door, and it whined as it opened. I turned the knob, half expecting it to be locked, but it wasn't. I walked in, trying to see through the darkness. "Mema?" My voice was as soft and nonthreatening as I could manage. My grandparents were getting older. If they weren't obsessed with the news, they could have been completely oblivious to the outbreak. "Mema, it's me, Scarlet." I crossed the living room to the hall, and turned toward their bedroom. Pictures of our family lined the walls, and I stopped in front of one 8 x 10, noticing it was a picture of Andrew and me with the girls in happier days. No, that was a lie. We were never happy.

When I called my mother to tell her I was leaving Andrew, she scolded me. "You don't know how good you have it, Scarlet," she would say. "He's not an alcoholic like your father. He's not on that dope. He doesn't beat you."

"He doesn't love me," I told her. "He's never home. He's always working. And when he is home, all he does is yell at me and the kids. He acts like he hates us."

"Maybe if you were easier to live with he would want to be home."

Standing in the hall, in front of that picture, I held my fist to my heart in an effort to stave off that years-old hurt. When I chose to leave him, he had the support of his family—and mine. To them, it was a badge of honor to wear his ring. But he was an angry, sometimes cruel man. Of course, I was no doormat, but refusing to let him bully our children only led to louder arguments. The yelling. Christ, the yelling. Our former home was full of words and noise and tears. No, he wasn't a drunk, or an addict, nor did he beat me, but living in misery is not so different.

I stayed as long as I did to protect the girls. The only person that stood between them and Andrew during one of his rages was me. When he would chase Jenna up the stairs and scream in her face, I would chase after him. I would hold him back, out of her room. His anger would be redirected at me so Jenna wouldn't have to be afraid in her own home.

But he didn't beat me. No, he did not.

Sometimes I wished that he had, so at least that was something I could offer my mother. A tangible sacrifice to lay at her feet so she could see that selfishness or something as shallow as boredom didn't influence my decision. She might allow me that excuse instead of taking Andrew's side and commiserating with him about what a horrible person I was to live with, and how they had that in common.

Our home was so quiet now, and the slamming doors and screaming were replaced with laughter and yes, persistent arguing between the girls. But in the next hour they would be snuggling on the couch. Their home was a safe haven. I owed that to them after what Andrew and I had put them through.

I put my hand on the knob and turned, unsure of what to expect. Mema, my mother's mother, was refreshingly neutral. She simply nodded when I told her my marriage had ended, and said that Jesus loved me, and to keep the girls in church. Nothing else really mattered to her.

The door moved slowly. Part of me braced for something to jump out from the shadows, and the other prepared my heart to see something awful. But when the door opened to reveal their tiny bedroom, with their four-post bed and dated wallpaper, I let out the breath I'd been holding. The bed was made. They hadn't been in it, yet.

Just as quickly as the relief washed over me, it left. They would've been in bed by now. They weren't home. That meant they had been collected, and if it was by the soldiers, the girls were more than likely not at Andrew's, either. A sob caught in my throat. I refused to cry until there was something to cry about.

The picture in the hall grabbed my attention. The Jeep waiting for me on the outskirts of town didn't have the same wallet-size photo of my daughters that the Suburban did. It didn't have their drawings and school papers littering the floorboard. I reached up and grabbed the frame, and then threw it on the ground, letting it crash. Quickly pulling the picture from beneath the shards of glass, I folded it twice, and slid it snugly into my bra. Every photo album we had was sitting in a hutch cabinet at home. Their baby pictures, snapshots of birthdays and of them playing outside. It was all left behind. The picture poking into my skin might be all I had left.

I bolted from the house and let the screen door slam as I ran into the street. Tobin was standing on Tavia's steps, holding himself up with her door.

I stared at him, and he stared back. She wasn't home, either, and neither was little Tobin. "I'll try to come back and get you."

Tobin offered a small, understanding smile. "No you won't. And you shouldn't, anyway. I'd just slow you down."

I watched him for a moment, seeing no judgment in his eyes. "My grandparents have a lot of meds in their bathroom. Ibuprofen, painkillers, Ex-Lax. The door is open. You're welcome to it."

Tobin managed a small laugh. "Thank you. I hope you find your girls."

"I will," I said, turning and breaking into a sprint. The next block was Main Street. It was well lit, the main road of Anderson, and boasted the only four stoplights in town. A four lane with room to spare on each side for parking, the road was wide, and didn't offer much in the way of cover. I had so much momentum going when the streetlamp on the corner revealed my presence like an escaped convict, I just kept going, hoping I was lucky enough that no one would see. I flew across the street and the sidewalk, and cut across the funeral parlor's back parking lot, shooting down the alley. A broken chair was right around the corner, and before I even thought to jump, my legs were already pushing me up and over.

My tennis shoes and scrubs were wet and weighed down with mud, but knowing my girls were just a few miles away, my legs carried me like I was weightless.

Tobin called to me from blocks away. "Go, Scarlet! You will find them! You will! Go!"

My legs ran faster than they ever had before, even in high school when I attempted track and wanted to please my mother so much that I ran until my lungs felt they would burst. Still, I was always the slowest, always the one left behind. But not that night. That night, I could fly.

The old railroad station came into view, and I skipped over the rails, and then surged past the remnants of the brick and mortar that displayed the word ANDERSON. The letters were dirty and rusted like my hometown had become. I glanced back just once before crossing the street. Even though sweat poured into my eyes, and my lungs could barely keep up, I wouldn't stop. Three more blocks to my babies. They would be there. They would.

I cut down an alleyway, getting a second wind when I felt the familiar gravel crunch under my feet. A dog barked, and I smiled. Not a single dog could be heard on the other side of town. The soldiers hadn't reached this side yet. Jenna and Halle would be waiting for me and I would take them into my arms and squeeze them so tight that nothing else would matter. The craziness outside the city limits would disappear.

I reached the end of the alley, across from Andrew's house. His detached garage and drive were directly in front of me, but his white Tahoe was absent. My chest heaved, and my guts lurched, purging the rattled remnants in my stomach.

Chapter Ten

Nathan

"THAT'S YOU, BROTHER, LET'S GO!" SKEETER SAID, RUNning to a window. His head moved in every direction as he tried to get a good look. "Two cars! Right out front!"

Someone outside yelled, and I could see a large group of the dead peel off the wall and amble toward the street.

I ran to the door and pressed my ear against the door. No scratching, no rubbing noises. No moans.

"Zoe?" I called.

Zoe jogged to my side. I positioned her behind me and grabbed the knob.

"Wait!" Zoe cried, looking at her aunt Jill, who was lying lifeless on the floor, aside from her eyes. They were forcing themselves open, bloodshot and weeping, but alert.

"Zoe, we have to go," I said, holding her wrist.

"I love you!" Zoe cried. She was just a child, but she knew that she wouldn't see her aunt again. "I love you, Aunt Jill!" Tears streamed down Zoe's cheeks as she reached out to her aunt, pulling against my grip.

Jill wore a faint smile. The veins had become more visible under her skin: blue, slithering lines, branching off and covering her like the virus spreading through her body. A single tear slipped down Jill's cheek and dripped to the blanket beneath her.

Skeeter rushed to Zoe, pulling her into his arms. "Don't cry, lil' bit." He placed his thumb under her chin and lifted her eyes to his. "I'm going to take care of Jillybean, mmkay? You know how much Uncle Skeeter loves Aunt Jill, don'tcha?"

Zoe nodded, and her eyebrows pulled together.

Skeeter smiled and hugged her to him once more. "We love you, Zoe. Listen to your Daddy. He's going to take good care of you. Be quiet, now." Zoe's fingers pressed into Skeeter's shoulders. Skeeter let her go and stood. "Go, Nate. Go now."

I nodded, put my car keys in my mouth, shoved the clip into the AR, cocked it, and opened the door. I leaned out to take a quick look. It was clear. I nodded to Zoe, and then nodded to Skeeter. He winked at me, and I ran, tugging Zoe along with me.

Crossing the street, I saw a black Jeep Wrangler speeding away toward Anderson. I didn't wait to see if those things would follow.

I let go of Zoe's hand and pulled the keys from my mouth. "Zoe, keep up!" I said, holding the key out in front of me so I could shove it in the lock as soon as we got to the car. I didn't want to do anything stupid like drop the keys, so I made sure to hold it securely between my fingers.

When we reached the car, I remembered I hadn't had time to lock it before, so I just opened the door and reached back to grab Zoe. Something rounded the corner of the house, but I didn't pay attention to what it was or how many, I just picked up my daughter and nearly tossed her into the passenger side. And then I did exactly what I said I wouldn't do. I dropped the fucking keys.

They slid under the car, out of sight.

"Daddy!" Zoe cried.

My focus shifted to the man walking toward me. I raised the AR and pulled the trigger and missed. I pulled the trigger again, this time hitting this ragged, bloody predator in the neck. The wound didn't faze him. Suddenly the left side of his skull exploded, and he fell to the ground, midstep. Skeeter stood on the other side of the street, with his hunting rifle in his hand. He held up his fist, extending his index finger, pinky, and thumb. I returned the gesture and jumped in the car, backing out of his drive and turning west onto the highway.

Miranda

FIFTEEN MINUTES EAST, I PULLED THE BUG OVER TO the shoulder of the road. Mascara was burning my eyes, and it was getting harder to see. Bryce was still looking out the window. I reached back, squeezing when I felt Ashley's hand in mine.

She was my older sister, but Daddy had always said I was the strong one. Ashley didn't give me a choice. When our parents split, Ashley became a different person, like a sweater you put in the wash and it never fits or looks the same. She wasn't the giggly, carefree girl I grew up with. Instead she was sensitive, overly emotional and cynical. When she leaned up to show me her eyes, her blond hair fell forward, the long, stringy strands hovering over her lap. She was still sobbing, most of her face blotchy and wet.

"What if there's soldiers waiting at Fairview, too?" Cooper said, stuttering over his words.

Ashley's voice surged, in a half hum, half groan. "I want to go home, Miranda. I want to see Mom!"

"Fairview won't have soldiers. The only reason Anderson had those idiots with guns is because of the armory," Bryce snapped. He was clearly more than annoyed with Ashley. As if the loud sobbing wasn't stressful enough.

"What do we do?" Ashley said. "It's going to be dark soon. I don't think we should be out at night."

I looked to Bryce. "She has a point."

He didn't necessarily agree, but he didn't argue. I pulled back onto the road and drove a few more miles until we came upon an old farmhouse. I turned into the drive, nearly taking out the formerly white, rusted mailbox.

The Bug's new brakes squeaked to a stop. We all stared at the house, waiting for someone to open the door, or greet us, or try to eat us. I reached for the door handle, but Bryce grabbed my arm.

"I'll go," he said. He pushed open the passenger door and slowly walked up to the side of the house.

I glanced around. There were no vehicles, but there was a barn. Maybe they had parked there, and it only appeared deserted. Two cars traveling west on Highway 11 caught my eye: a silver car and a black, four-door Jeep Wrangler. For half a second, I focused on the child in a car seat. She was passing by in slow motion, holding up a teddy bear, oblivious that the world had gone to shit around her.

"Oh my God," I said, turning to watch them drive past. "Oh my God!"

"What?" Ashley cried, instantly panicked.

"They're headed straight for Anderson. They're going to be killed by those crazies on the bridge!" I opened my door and stepped out.

"Bryce, let's go! We have to stop them!"

"We can't save everyone that heads that way," Ashley said, gripping my headrest.

"But there's a . . . there's a baby in the car! Bryce!"

Bryce turned to me with a frown, holding his finger to his mouth.

"But . . . ," I said, watching them drive out of sight. And then they were gone. I sat back in the Bug and shut my door. "That's on us," I said, my eyes meeting Ashley's in the rearview mirror.

"Hurry up, Bryce," Cooper whispered, mostly to himself.

Bryce took one look inside and turned on his heels, jumped off the small, concrete porch, and sprinted to the Bug. He slammed the door and pointed to the road. "Go," he said, out of breath.

"What did you see?"

"Go! Go!" he yelled, pointing.

I stomped on the gas and pulled back onto the highway. "What?" I said, safely back on the road. "What did you see?"

Bryce shook his head.

"We should turn around."

"No."

"Try to warn that family about the bridge."

"No."

"Didn't you hear me, Bryce? There was a baby in the car! We should turn around!"

"There was a baby inside that house, too!" he yelled. He took a few deep breaths to calm himself, and then spoke again. "Trust me. If they're killed on that bridge, they're better off."

I watched Bryce for a moment, and then returned my focus to the road. All color had left his face, and sweat had formed along his hairline.

"What did you see?" I said quietly.

He looked out the window. "You don't want to know. I wish I could unsee it."

The next miles were quiet as we made our way to Fairview, but it wasn't hard to tell when we'd reached the city limit. More infected roamed the streets than I had anticipated, alone and in groups. We were almost through town when I slammed on my brakes.

"What?" Bryce said loudly, slamming his palm against the dash.

A woman was running down the street barefoot, carrying a little girl in one arm, and pulling along a boy, maybe nine or ten, with the other. She wore a red dress with white polka dots, and her hair had mostly fallen from her low, dark ponytail.

"Bryce," I said.

"I see them."

The woman stopped at the corner church, and helped the boy climb up on top of the air-conditioning unit, bravely passing a large group of infected. She heaved the boy onto her shoulders, and then pushed him up, allowing him to climb onto the roof, and then held up the little girl. He pulled her up safely, but she was reaching for the woman, crying and drawing the attention of the mob of bloody horrors pounding against the front of the church. Several of the dead ones broke away and ambled in the woman's direction. She was struggling to climb, but the boy waited, bent over and holding his knees, encouraging her.

It was then that I saw a trail of blood running up the side of the white wood of the church. Someone else had already gone in that way. Someone that was probably infected.

"We've got to help them," I said, determined this time.

"Look," Cooper said, his hand stretching between my and Bryce's seats. He pointed to the church. "The windows are boarded! There's people in there!"

Bryce looked to me. "It seems like a good place to wait out the night."

I watched as the woman barely made it to the roof before the dead reached the unit she'd been standing on.

I let out the breath I'd unconsciously been holding. "Okay, but how do we get in? How do we get them to let *us* in?"

"They're not very fast," Cooper said, gesturing to the woman on the roof. "She ran right past them."

"I'm not going out there with those things walking around!" Ashley wailed. "No way!"

I looked around the Bug, making sure we'd have no surprises, and then noted the position of the sun. "We can't make it to the ranch before dark. There are already people inside there. They probably have guns, and water—"

"And a bathroom," Cooper muttered.

Bryce nodded. "We have none of those. We're going in there.

We just have to find a way to distract them long enough to get inside."

"You guys get out here. I'll drive past them and lure them away, ditch the Bug, hide, and then double back."

Bryce shook his head. "I'll do it."

"Look!" Ashley said.

The woman was trying to open the window, but was having trouble. Suddenly it opened, and she held back her children, shielding them for a moment until she recognized whoever was standing on the other side. A tall, scruffy man ducked through the window, and helped the mother and children inside. He walked over to the edge and took a look at the frantic pack below. They were clamoring over each other, trying to get at the people on the roof.

"Look at them. They can't climb," I said, surprised.

Bryce stepped out of the Bug and waved his arms. "Hey!" he yelled.

"What the hell are you doing? What if he shoots at us?" Cooper said.

"Help us!" Bryce said, ignoring Cooper.

The man on the roof signaled for us to come around to the backside of the church, and then pointed at his gun.

"He's going to cover us. Let's go. Let's go!" Bryce said, getting back in.

Without hesitation, I slammed my foot against the accelerator, and the Bug surged forward. Within moments, we were bouncing across the street and into the church lawn. The man held up his hand, palm out, and then turned to point, directing us.

I parked the Bug in the back of the church, and then jumped

out, pulling up my seat for Ashley. "Go. Go!" I said, watching every undead thing on the side of the church turn in our direction and begin their approach.

The back door of the church opened, revealing the man from the roof. He turned the bolt lock as soon as the last of us was inside. The room was full of scared people, the mother and her children, another woman, two other little boys, and five men: the man that saved us, two middle-aged men, and two older men.

"Thank you so much," I said to the man who let us in. "We needed a place to stay for the night."

"Skeeter McGee," he said, holding out his hand. I shook it, and he nodded to Cooper, Bryce, and Ashley, and then turned to one of the middle-aged men. "Gary, we're going to have to nail the boards back up on the door upstairs. Just one board this time."

Gary nodded, and then turned, disappearing down a dark hall. His footsteps echoed back into the kitchen, and then the hammering started.

Everyone in the room traded glances, and then Skeeter tended to a woman on the floor. She looked near death, and a white, foamlike drool was dripping from the side of her mouth to the blanket she was lying on.

"Was Annabelle . . . ?" the older woman said.

"Not yet," Skeeter answered.

"That's good news. Maybe Jill won't come back as one of those things. Or maybe she'll get better. We just don't know, Skeeter. Please don't do anything rash."

"You don't have to bullshit me, Doris," he told her. He ran his large fingers through Jill's damp, blond hair, and whispered something in her ear.

Doris looked at us. "Bless your hearts. You from Anderson?"

"We go to the university in Greenville. My father has a ranch northwest of here. We didn't really want to travel after dark."

Doris nodded with understanding. "Can't say I blame you. You kids want some water?" she asked, already making her way to the refrigerator. She handed us all bottles of water, and we wasted no time tipping our bottles back.

"Your father has a ranch close to here?" Skeeter asked.

Ashley smiled. "Red Hill Ranch."

Skeeter nodded. "I've hunted over there. That'll be a good place for you."

GARY RETURNED FROM THE HALLWAY, HAMMER IN HAND.

Everyone settled in as best they could. Doris comforted the mother and her children, Skeeter alternated between checking on his wife and checking the windows in the other room. They all gasped and traded glances when a new person was seen ambling around outside with the rest. Fairview was a tiny town. It made sense that they all knew each other. I wondered who the woman on the floor was to Skeeter, and what her life was like before she was bitten. Even with her sweaty, bluish skin, and the dark around her eyes, it was obvious that she was beautiful.

The man they called Bob pointed to the next room. "The sanctuary is in there. Plenty of places to sit."

"Thank you," I said, accepting his invitation.

Two more women, quite a bit older, were seated in pews. I chose one in the front and sat nearest the center aisle, farthest away from the broken windows. Even if they were boarded, hearing the dead ones trying to get in was unnerving.

Bryce sat on one side of me, Ashley on the other. Cooper sat beside my sister, and took her hand in his. We all let out a collective sigh of relief.

I let my head rest against Bryce's shoulder, and he rested his head against mine. After everything we'd seen, and everything we'd been through, I didn't think I would be able to sleep, but the longer I sat on the hard, cold, wooden pew, the more comfortable I became—and the harder it was to keep my eyes open. I shifted, prompting Bryce to turn his head slightly to kiss my temple.

"It's okay. Go to sleep. We're safe now."

"It's never going to be safe again," I whispered, trying not to let the words trigger more tears.

"Safe enough to get some rest," he whispered back. "Now close your eyes, Miranda. We've got a long day tomorrow."

"Once we get to Red Hill, we'll be all right, right?"

"Your dad is probably there now, scared to death, wondering where you are. He's going to be so happy to see you and your sister. We'll be far away from everything, with a stocked pantry and your dad's crazy gun collection. We're going to be just fine."

With his words, I let my eyes close and the heaviness of sleep engulf me.

Chapter Eleven

Scarlet

THE HOUSES SURROUNDING ANDREW'S WERE DARK AND abandoned like the others. I walked across the street, devoid of cars and people. The incline of Andrew's driveway made me feel like I was trudging up a steep mountain face after the stretch I'd just sprinted. Careful not to let my shoes crunch too loudly against the gravel beneath them, I took gentle steps and paused at the gate. It whined as I pushed through it, and I slowly walked the ten steps or so to Andrew's back door. I'd only traveled this patch of earth a handful of times since Andrew had moved in.

After the divorce, he could no longer afford the two-story fixer-upper we'd purchased in the next town over and moved to the converted two-bedroom, former duplex. It was literally on the wrong side of the tracks, nestled deep in the west side of Anderson, where a meth-lab raid was not uncommon.

Andrew was humbled by the move and the divorce, and he surprised us all during his visitation weekends. Slowly the yelling stopped. The bullying was replaced with short bursts of mild annoyance or long sighs. I wasn't sure if being away from the girls for most of the month helped to quell his rages, or if it was my absence that offered him peace.

I climbed the two steps to Andrew's back door, and tapped on the Plexiglas on the top half of the door. A curtain hid the inside from view. I tapped again, then tried to turn the knob. It was locked.

My heart pounded so hard in anticipation that I could feel it in my throat.

The windows on each side of the house and the one beside the front door were locked, too. I slapped the dining room window with my hand. "Andrew! Jenna! Halle? It's Mommy! Are you here?"

Nothing.

I pressed my ear to the glass and listened. The silence triggered tears, and my bottom lip quivered. I leaned in harder, the coldness of the window offsetting the burning sensation the pressure ignited throughout my ear. My eyes clenched shut as I silently begged someone inside to relieve my fears.

Finally, I pulled away from the window, looking down the street. A tear welled up and broke free, sliding down my cheek. I wiped it, and as I did, my elbow bumped into the glass. Without a second thought, I reared back and let my elbow make contact with the glass a second time, the corner of my bones an extension of all the frustration and fear pulsing through my body. The window shattered. It wasn't as loud as I thought it would be. Large chunks broke off, some falling inside the dining room, and some at my feet.

"Andrew?" I whispered loudly.

After pulling myself inside, I searched every room, every

closet, every corner of the house. Something wasn't right, though. The girls' jackets weren't crumpled on the floor, their drawers weren't cracked open, and none of Halle's drawings were scattered on the table. They had never come home. They must have been at the town meeting with the governor when the outbreak happened. They could be trapped inside a shelter with the governor, or Andrew could have run with them. They could be anywhere.

"Goddamnit," I said, louder than I'd spoken in hours. "Goddamnit!" I screamed. I picked up Andrew's dining room chair and launched it across the room, and then lost my balance, falling to my knees. "No," I cried, crumpling into a ball on the floor. I saw their little faces, innocent and frightened, wondering where I was and if I was safe, just as I was wondering about them. I couldn't do this if I wasn't with them. I needed to see Jenna roll her eyes at me again, and for Halle to interrupt me. They needed me to tell them that everything would be okay. We couldn't survive the end of the world without each other. I didn't want to. Sobs built up and released with such ferocity that my entire body shook. Certainly someone would hear me, my screaming and bawling was probably the only sound that could be heard in the entire godforsaken town.

"I'm so sorry," I said, letting the guilt and despair wash over me. I leaned over and let my forehead and arms rest against the carpet; my hands clasped together above my head. Before long, extreme exhaustion pulled and tugged on my consciousness like I'd never felt before. The sobbing quieted, and within moments, I fell into a vast sea of darkness. The depths surrounded me on all sides, and eventually I was swallowed up by it, warm and calm.

Tornado sirens. Odd. I didn't remember the meteorologist mentioning a storm that morning. It wasn't a test. They tested at noon every Thursday, and today was . . . I wasn't sure what day it was.

The first thing I noticed when my eyes peeled open was baseboard, and the way the carpet was newer closer to the wall than farther out where people walked. I used to notice those things when I was a child, when I spent more time on the floor: playing, watching television, being bored. I spent so much of my childhood on the floor. As an adult, I couldn't remember the last time I had this view. But the carpet between my fingers wasn't mine.

My eyes burned. Tears had washed all of my mascara in and out of my eyes, leaving them dry and on fire. The second I remembered why I'd been crying, my head popped up, and I took a quick glance around the dark room. The tornado sirens were blaring. They could be malfunctioning, or there had been a breach.

On my hands and knees, I quickly made my way to Andrew's front door. The streets were still empty, but the sirens continued to wail. The church in Fairview crossed my mind, and I prayed the sirens would stop. The noise would draw every shuffler for miles.

I pulled open the wooden door, and pressed the side of my face against the glass of the storm door. My breath blew moist, visible air in quickly disappearing puffs, clouding my view. When I saw the first person running down the street, intermittently exposed by the street lamps, the breaths became a single gasp.

She was older, maybe in her fifties, but she was alive. Even from a block away, I could see the horror in her eyes. A few seconds later two men—one holding a child—and a woman appeared before they slipped into darkness again. Then five more, and then a dozen. Men, women, and children. At least fifty had passed before I spotted the first shuffler. I could only make him out because he happened to take someone down just under the street lamp. Not long after, several more shufflers became part of the crowd. The screaming slowly built from one or two intermittent cries to full-blown panic. The crowd seemed to spread out, but they were all coming from the same place; from wherever they were held with the governor, maybe. It seemed like the entire town was in the street, running for their lives. My eyes squinted, desperately searching for Andrew and the girls, hoping they would turn down his street from the main road any minute, but as the river of people thinned out, I began to lose hope.

Tears threatened to moisten my eyes once again, but instead I let anger take control. The helplessness I felt at not being able to get to my children sent me into a rage. I ran to Andrew's bedroom and searched his closet. He kept a hunting rifle and a 9mm. Just in case he happened to come back here, I left the rifle and grabbed a backpack from the back, filling it with ammo. My movements were clumsy, both from the adrenaline pumping through my body, and because I hadn't held a gun since before my divorce. I took a few cans of food. The can opener was in the silverware drawer, but I left it, hopeful that Andrew would remember to pack it if he wasn't already on the road. I also took a plastic reusable water bottle.

Not until I made my way to the laundry room did I come across anything really useful: a flashlight, some batteries, a large screwdriver, and a folding knife.

I grabbed one more item, zipped the backpack, and then returned to the front room. I pulled some frames off the wall, and then shook the can in my hand. The aerosol hissed as I pressed my index finger on the trigger, my arm swaying with the silent music of my good-bye as it formed large, conspicuous black words.

RED HILL
I'LL WAIT
♥∞MOM

I watched the paint drip from the letters, hoping that it was enough; that in the middle of this hell my children would remember the name of Dr. Hayes's ranch, and tell their father how to get there. If Andrew was in that crowd running from the town hall, he would bring them here.

I let the can drop to the floor, and then looked out the glass column of the front door again, seeing slower, shuffling dead ambling down the main road, following the scent of the living. Andrew had gotten our daughters out somehow, before the breach. I had to believe that, and I had to trust that my next decision was the right one.

I gripped the straps of the pack at my shoulders and rushed out of the house, stupidly letting the screen door slam behind me. I paused, slowly turning to see a few of the shufflers to the west automatically turn toward the noise. I ran east toward my grandparents' house, maybe even faster than before, knowing that before long, the sun would rise, and there would be no more shadows to hide behind.

Nathan

"ZOE, TRY TO SLOW YOUR BREATHING," I SAID. ZOE WAS nearly panting, struggling to wrap her head around everything she'd seen, including telling her aunt Jill good-bye for the last time. I reached over and held her small hand in mine. "We're going to be okay, honey. We'll find someplace safe."

"I thought the church was safe," she said softly.

"Not safe enough. We need a place to stay for a long time. In the country, away from all the sick people."

"Where is that?"

I paused, careful not to lie to her. "I'll find it. Don't worry."

Zoe sat up tall and lifted her chin, seeing the green pickup truck idling in the road the same time I did. I let go of Zoe's hand and raised mine to shield her eyes just as the man raised his gun to a woman lying in the road, in a puddle of vomit and blood. A pool of dark red was spilling from her beneath her soiled dress, too, almost like she was having a miscarriage, but I knew that wasn't where the blood was coming from. She was emaciated, her skin a grayish tone except for the lines of red that drained from her eyes, ears, and nose.

A shot was fired to her head, but the woman didn't move. As we passed, the man was blank-faced, scooping her up tenderly into his arms. He carried her into the cab of his truck, shutting the door behind him.

I lowered my hand, and placed it back on the wheel. Ten and two. "You have your seatbelt on?"

"Yes, Daddy." Zoe was struggling to keep it together.

I wanted to pull over and hold her, to allow her time to transition to our new life of running for our lives and surviving, but we would never have enough time. If it was anything like the movies, life would be lived between near-death experiences.

"Good girl."

Shades of pinks and purples bruised the sky, signaling the beginnings of a sunset. Without any houses in sight, or even a barn, I wasn't sure if I should worry about shelter, or be comforted that we weren't likely to run into a large group of those things—at least for a while.

Zoe was playing with the hem of her lavender dress, humming so softly I could barely make out what it was. Something by Justin Bieber, by the sounds of it. The corners of my mouth turned up. The radio had been silent since we started our journey. I wondered if we would ever hear music again.

Chapter Twelve

Nathan

LESS THAN A HALF HOUR DOWN THE ROAD, I NOTICED A small sign that read HIGHWAY 123. Another small two-lane, it ran all the way to Kansas. It was less than an hour away, and if I remembered correctly from my and Skeeter's last hunting trip, there was only one small town between where we were and the state line. Beyond that was nothing but farmland and ranch land for miles. Maybe we could find an abandoned farmhouse in the middle of nowhere where we could set up camp. Maybe we would get lucky and it wouldn't be abandoned, and the occupants, old or new, would let us stay.

My mind was drifting when I turned onto the highway, so it must have been instinct, or at least a choice on a subconscious level. Either way, Zoe and I were headed north.

"We're not going back to get my papers, are we?" Zoe said. She didn't try to hide her disappointment.

"I'm sorry, honey. I don't think it's safe."

"So I'm not going to school tomorrow?"

"No."

"Won't you get arrested if you don't take me to school?"

"Not if everyone else stays home from school, too."

That answer seemed to appease Zoe for the moment, but I knew she would only form a list of more questions to ask at a later time. The end of everything was hard for everyone. Especially children. Even more so for children like Zoe that didn't handle change well. My daughter had required a routine since birth. Rules and boundaries were her safe haven. I wasn't sure how I could provide that for her now.

I watched Zoe's head bounce subtly with the tune in her head. Once in a while the splash of freckles across her nose would move when she scrunched her nose to sniff.

"You're not getting a cold, are you?"

Zoe shook her head, willing to let me make small talk. "I don't think so. I wash my hands a lot."

I nodded. "That's good . . . ," I trailed off, noticing something ahead. At first, I thought it might have been a car stalled in the road, but then I saw movement. A lot of movement, fluid and slow. When we came closer, I saw a herd of those things surrounding a vehicle. The car alarm was bleating, and the dead seemed to be agitated by the noise. They were wildly trying to get inside the vehicle. I couldn't see whether anyone was trapped within. I didn't want to.

"Daddy?"

"Hang on, Zoe," I said, turning the wheel off the highway and into the town. The first houses were within a block of the highway. I drove faster than I should have, but I was hoping to get around the herd and make it back onto 123 without losing much time. The sun would set soon, and I didn't want us to be near those things in the dark. Every road I turned down led me either down another road that was too close to the herd, or to another group walking toward the herd.

After the third U-turn, a yellow light on the dashboard, accompanied by a chime, nearly sent me into a panic. We were low on fuel, the sun was going down, and I wasn't familiar enough with this town to find a safe place for me and Zoe for the night. For the first time since I'd left the church, I was afraid that I'd made the wrong decision.

We came up on a dead end, and I pressed on the brakes, seeing a gas can on the front porch of the only house on that end of the road. The last two blocks had been a gravel road, and I didn't see much around. Most of the townspeople were congregated in the middle of the highway.

"Zoe, I'm going to get that gas can over there, and then put some in the car so we can drive the rest of the way."

"The rest of the way to where?"

"I'll be right back, honey. Don't get out of the car, okay?"

Zoe nodded, and I took a quick glance around before getting out. I walked to the porch quickly, hoping with every step there was actual gasoline inside that red plastic container. I climbed the steps and bent over, but when I placed my hand on the handle, the door opened, and the distinct sound of a shotgun being cocked made me freeze in place.

I closed my eyes. "Please don't. My little girl is watching." After a short pause, and the realization that I wasn't dead yet, I looked up. An old man was at the opposite end of the shotgun. Sweaty, dirty, and in an oversized pair of blue and white striped overalls, he pulled the gun away from my temple. "You lettin' your kid watch you steal?"

"I wasn't trying to steal," I said, standing up slowly, keeping my hands up and away from my body. The goal was to be as nonthreatening as possible. "The gas light in my car just dinged. It's getting dark. We're just trying to find someplace safe for the night."

The man squinted his eyes and scratched his white five o'clock shadow, and then lowered his gun. "Get your girl. Bring her inside. Better hurry. One or two pass by here ever so often."

A part of me wanted to grab Zoe and bring her into his home without a second thought. The other part remembered he'd just held a gun to my head. A woman poked her head out from behind the door, and then stepped out onto the porch. She was a bitty thing, her short gray hair styled a lot like Zoe's.

"Oh, good Lord, Walter. Let these poor people come in."

"I asked them in, honey. He's just standing there."

She pushed down his gun. "Well put your gun away, silly!" She held out her hand. "I'm Joy."

"Nathan Oxford. My daughter Zoe is in the car. Nice to meet you."

Walter frowned. "That's great, son, but you best get your baby and come inside."

I nodded and took a long step off the porch, turning off my car and coaxing Zoe outside. She'd seen Walter pull the gun on me, and wasn't sure this was a good idea, either. We followed Joy inside, and Walter locked up behind us.

Joy wiped her hands on her trousers and paused in the center of the living room. The house was immaculate, but the carpet was at least thirty years old, and it smelled like it. "We're going to sleep downstairs in the basement. Walter is going to nail the door shut for the night."

"What if they get in the house?" I said quietly.

Walter held his gun at his side. "We've got food and water down there. Joy was just bringing more. They don't seem to notice the house, though. They're all attracted to something on the other side of town."

"There's a car with a security system going off on the highway. They're all crowded around that."

Walter frowned, deep in thought. "So they're attracted to sound. We'll just keep quiet. They won't have a reason to mess around here. I'll lock the doors. I don't think they'll try to get in through the windows unless we draw attention to ourselves."

It made me nervous to think we wouldn't have an exit strategy, but it was better than nothing, and safer than sleeping upstairs.

Zoe and I helped Joy bring food and water downstairs to the basement. It was finished, with a couch and a couple of recliners facing a flat-screen television.

Walter laughed once. "Joy bought that for me for Christmas last year. All you can see on it now is snow."

Zoe and I snuggled up on a yellow and brown plaid couch while Walter nailed the basement door shut, and then nailed a two-by-four across the middle section. Joy covered us with a blanket, also straight out of the 1970s, and in record time, Zoe was relaxed and sleeping in my arms. I was afraid she wouldn't be able to sleep because we were in a strange place, but she was exhausted. I rested my cheek against her hair. The light-brown strands were stringy and tangled, making me think of all the comforts of home we no longer had. Simple things, like a brush.

"You sure have a pretty girl there," Joy whispered, smiling. "My daughter Darla lives in Midland. You ever been to Midland?"

I shook my head.

"We were actually packing to go see them this weekend. We were going to leave yesterday, but I wanted to make sure I had someone to water my flowers before we left." She sighed, and her eyes filled with tears. "I might never see her again, or my grandbabies. Because of the goddamn flowers."

"You could see her again."

"You think so?" she said, cautious hope in her voice.

I smiled and kissed Zoe's temple, and then leaned my head back against the cushion. "Thank you. For letting us stay here tonight."

"You can stay as long as you like," Joy whispered, glancing up at her husband still busy securing the door. "Who knows when this is all sorted out . . . or if it will ever be."

Miranda

EVEN WHEN MY EYES OPENED, IT WAS STILL DARK. THE scratching and padding by the dead ones outside had stopped, and Bryce was awake, staring straight ahead. I sat up and tried to stretch the knots out of my back.

"Did you sleep?" I asked quietly.

Bryce shook his head, and then looked over at me with a smile. "I might have dozed off for a few minutes. I'm glad you did, though." He leaned over and touched his lips to mine for the first time in twenty-four hours. "You were incredible yesterday. I didn't know you knew how to drive like that."

I wrapped my arms around my middle to ward off the early-morning chill. Bryce cradled me to his side. He wasn't the most muscular guy at school, but he was athletically built, and his sweet smile made staying mad at him impossible. His dark hair was about two months overdue for a haircut, and when he leaned over to kiss me, some of it fell forward into his eyes. He used his fingers to comb it away, refusing to do the incredibly annoying head jerk most guys did to get their hair out of their eyes.

They look like they're having a seizure, he used to say. I didn't like it, either, but I would ignore it if it meant I could see his blue eyes. Bryce's smile was amazing, and he was nothing less than noble, but his eyes were my favorite part about him. I think I fell in love with them before I fell in love with him.

Ashley and Cooper were cuddled together. With just a cardigan, white tee, and baby blue fashion scarf, she wasn't any more prepared to be without heat than I was in my cotton T-shirt and light jacket. The guys didn't show it if they were cold.

"What is that noise?" Cooper asked, turning his right ear in the direction of the kitchen. His eyes bounced around as he listened.

Bryce grabbed my hand and stood, leading me to the doorway of the kitchen. It was dark in there, too, but there were a few candles around the room. The small flames provided just enough light for us to see Skeeter McGee on his knees, weeping over the woman lying on the floor. He was trying to keep quiet. If it wasn't for him sucking in a breath every now and then, I might not have known.

"Oh my God!" Ashley said.

Bryce shushed her, and returned his attention to Skeeter. "Is she . . . ?"

Doris brought a blanket from the hall and spread it over the top of the woman. "God bless you, Jill. May the Lord open his arms wide for you and keep you."

We all stood there and watched in uncomfortable silence while Skeeter sobbed quietly for another twenty minutes or so. After a while he caught his breath, and then wiped his face. "So I guess uh . . . I guess we better bury her."

Doris shifted, nervous. "How are we going to do that with those things out there?"

An older man with white hair spoke. "We can't just throw her outside, Doris, and she can't stay in here."

Doris fidgeted, finally putting her fingers to her mouth. "I'm . . . I'm so sorry, Skeeter, but I can't go out there."

"I'll go," Bryce said. Skeeter looked up at him with wet eyes. "I'll help you. We'll need someone watching our backs, and maybe a distraction, but I'll help you dig."

I crossed my arms, trying to keep the words I was about to say from falling out of my mouth, but they came anyway. "I'll help, too. I'll distract them."

"You can be the lookout," Bryce said. "Coop was in track. He can be the distraction."

"What?" Cooper said, eyes wide. "Me?"

Ashley grabbed on to him. "No," she frowned, desperation in her voice. "We're not sending him out there as bait."

Cooper wrapped both arms around Ashley, his eyes falling on Skeeter. "I appreciate you helping us out back there, man, but going outside in the dark is an unnecessary risk. What if they get inside and we're all out there digging a hole? There are women and children in here."

"I'm buryin' my wife," Skeeter said, standing. He was just as tall as Bryce, and a lot more intimidating. "I'm not asking anyone for help."

"I know you're not," Bryce said. "Let's take a minute and think of a plan so that everyone is safe."

Skeeter wiped his face again and nodded. The white-haired man went over to the woman's body and began to quietly pray.

"It should be light before long," I said. "Let's put together a plan, and when the sun comes up, we'll bury Jill."

Skeeter nodded. "Thank you."

The youngest and oldest of us were fast asleep while we planned Jill's funeral. The church's cemetery wasn't fifty yards away. Skeeter wanted to bury her there. Already my heart was pounding, thinking about standing in the morning fog, in a cemetery, watching for zombies. It didn't get any more Hollywood horror story than that.

"I'm going to bury her by her grandpa," Skeeter said. "He was laid to rest on the north side."

Bryce nodded. "Okay, so Eric and Gary get on the roof and get them away from the back door. Coop can run out and get them to follow him around until we're finished."

"How long do you think that'll take?" Cooper asked, swallowing hard. "To dig a grave, I mean."

Bryce shrugged. "As long as it takes. We'll work fast as we can."

Ashley sighed. "This isn't a good idea."

"I'll keep an eye out while you're digging," I said. "Cooper will run around like lost zombie bait . . ."

"I'll say a few words," the reverend said, straightening his tie. He looked more nervous than Ashley. "And then we're getting the hell back inside."

"Not before," Skeeter took in a quick breath, "not before I make sure she doesn't come back, and we cover her with dirt."

I nodded. It was a plan. A simple plan. There was no way it was going to work, but at least we had one.

Chapter Thirteen

Scarlet

THE BACKGROUND NOISE OF MY ESCAPE FROM ANDERSON was intermittent gunfire as the patrols were likely panicking with the herd of undead roaming the streets. I had retraced my steps back to Tavia's, planning on persuading Tobin to come with me to the doctor's ranch.

Just as I crossed the intersection into my grandparents' front lawn and the streetlight was behind me, I saw a dark form lying on the ground. "Tobin?" I said quietly. I still held out hope that it wasn't my friend until I saw the cornrows poking out in every direction.

"Tobin?" I said, approaching carefully. He was lying on his side, facing away. I prepared myself to run if he moved toward me. I wasn't sure what he was.

I glanced at Tavia's house, noting the spray of bullet holes that had penetrated the siding, the windows, and the storm door. I leaned down, seeing that Tobin's lifeless body was in the same tattered condition.

I choked back tears and vomit. The same bastards that had

gunned down the family on the bridge had done the same to Tobin. I didn't want to leave him in the yard, but what could I do? Just then a diesel engine gunned several blocks away. "I'm sorry, friend," I said. Running once again as fast as I could, I raced back the way we came, not knowing which I dreaded more: getting caught, or escaping through the woods alone in the darkness.

Back through town, I had to chance running across the bridge and then down the road. It seemed safer than traveling through the tall grass by the river. The engines of the soldiers' trucks couldn't be heard, so I darted back across the highway and through the woods to my vehicle. I slammed the door and locked it, taking one quick glance around before bawling uncontrollably. I hadn't prepared myself for what it might be like to leave Anderson without my children, or seeing Tobin's body full of holes, or surviving something that made me feel an unbelievable amount of fear.

The headlights of the Jeep burned through the night as I flew down Highway 11. Less than half an hour after I turned north onto Highway 123, the high-pitched wail of a car alarm could be heard. The noise peaked and fell quickly, like the ray guns in the old science-fiction movies my mother used to watch.

I'm trying to watch a movie, Scarlet. Can't you find something else to do other than to bug me all day? Can I never have time to myself? Go away! my mother would say.

My desperate, tiny, eight-year-old voice replayed perfectly in my ear. *You've been working all day.*

I'm trying to watch TV!

I'm lonely! I would cry softly. I didn't want her to hear me. I wanted her to see me.

She would raise the remote in her hand and turn up the volume, a disgusted look on her face. *Lost in Space* might have been the one piece of happiness she had, between working three part-time jobs and raising me alone. My needing her attention appeared to have ruined her life.

You make me sick, Scarlet. You're just like your father. One of the most selfish people I've ever met, she would say, nearly ruining mine.

The words were an afterthought, an outlet for her residual anger, but they burned through my clothes and charred my skin, leaving a brand so inexorable, it wore me even as I fought to survive the end of the world. Was I selfish for leaving Anderson? Should I have stayed and waited for them? Would that choice sentence me to a life without ever seeing their sweet faces again?

The Jeep's headlights lit up dozens of shufflers. Like a herd of sheep, they meandered about in the middle of the road. I winced at the sight of children among them. Some with visible bites on their carotids. Some with mouthfuls of their skin and muscle missing; all covered in the blood of their former selves. Jenna's and Halle's faces flashed in my mind, and then were projected onto the faces of those children. Tears sizzled down my cheeks.

I slammed on the brake and gripped the steering wheel. If I chose to drive through them and was forced to stop, they could surround the Jeep. On one side was a grassy knoll. A rock with the town's name, Shallot, carved into the stone sat at the crest of the small, gentle hill. The sun had begun to rise, so I could just barely see the shadows of more shufflers crossing the sign and making their way down to the road toward the noisy car. Noise attracted them.

The left side was field. Acres upon acres of wheat field, still saturated from the downpour the previous morning. If I wanted to make it to the ranch, I had two choices: drive through the herd, up that knoll and hope if I hit one of those things it didn't crash through the windshield, or risk getting trapped in the muddy field.

Courage came slowly. Each beat of my heart felt like an explosion as my hand rested against the center of the steering wheel, preparing to press down. I took a breath, and then honked the horn once. Dozens of dead slowly craned their necks in my direction. The explosions in my chest turned into the cadence of a thousand tiny sprinters. Even sitting still, I began to pant with fear. After a short pause, they began to hobble and limp toward the Jeep. Again, I honked and waited. Despite the shufflers being less than twenty yards away, I pressed the heel of my palm against the center of the steering wheel, holding it there, until every last one of those fuckers were moaning and reaching out for the meal seeming so eager to be had. My fear kept my hand down, waiting, hoping they would move faster so I could drive past them and in the opposite direction of their new path.

When the shufflers were just over an arm length away, I jerked the wheel to the left and headed toward the wheat field.

"Don't get stuck. *Don't* get stuck," I repeated. My hands jerked the wheel right to make a large circle around the herd, and panicked when the Jeep struggled in the mud. "C'mon!" I yelled, my fingers digging into the padding of the steering wheel.

The Jeep weaved back and forth, fishtailing and threatening to lose control, but the mud tires clawed through the rain-swollen soil, and back onto the road. After turning into the skid more than once, the Jeep straightened out, and I was screaming in victory, barreling toward the white tower.

The sun had just peaked over the horizon when I saw the water tower looming above the trees. With Halle's sweet singing in my mind, I turned the wheel, never so happy to hit dirt road. By the time I turned left at the cemetery, the night sky had cowered from the clear, bright blue sky. The storm clouds from the day before had moved on. If the world hadn't gone to shit, it might have been considered a beautiful day. The Jeep took the right at the first mile section hard, but I couldn't slow down. The closer I came to sanctuary, the more afraid I was. My foot was grinding the gas pedal to the floorboard, but the Jeep's engine just growled louder instead of going faster. Maybe five minutes had passed since seeing the white tower, but it seemed to be taking an eternity.

Turning into the drive, my foot instinctively pulled away from the accelerator. Dr. Hayes's truck was in the yard, and a silver Mercedes was parked next to it. He'd made it home.

I didn't even bother to shut the Jeep door. The second my feet touched the ground, I broke into a sprint, only stopping until my hands hit the door.

"Dr. Hayes? It's me! Scarlet!" The side of my fist pounded against the wooden frame of the screen door. "Dr. Hayes? It's Scarlet! I'm not sick . . . please . . . *please* let me in."

With every passing second, my relief and excitement turned to disappointment. He was a radiologist, for Christ's sake, he had more than one beat-up pickup. Dr. Hayes and his girlfriend, Leah, only stayed there on his off week. The radiologists worked two weeks on, one week off, and they all had a farm or ranch they ran away to during those seven precious days. Leah was an attorney and lived two hours north. They usually had me clean the weekend before they met in the middle—the farmhouse. It was her Mercedes in the yard. They'd probably met here and then took the doctor's car somewhere else. To get his daughters, maybe.

The light on the barn flickered and then turned off. I had nowhere else to go. I had to get inside.

I pulled open the door slowly, wincing at the loud creaking sound it made. The doorknob twisted and with caution, I pushed it open and listened. "Dr. Hayes?" I said softly, half hoping he wouldn't hear me, and half hoping he would.

The house seemed untouched. When I'd checked every room and decided no one was home, I wandered to the back porch and hoisted myself onto the dryer, wondering what I needed to do to secure the house. Should I board up the windows? It wasn't my house to alter, but even if Dr. Hayes made it back here with Miranda and Ashley, he might be glad some of the work had been done. My eyes drifted to the floor, and relief and fear hit almost simultaneously. There were muddy footprints in front of the door that led to the side patio. I hopped down off the dryer and looked out the Plexiglas that took up the top half of the door. Something was splattered on the concrete. Something sticky with chunks of something else—definitely vomit. The footprints led inside and to my right, down the stairs, and into the basement.

I'd cleaned the basement many times before. It was used for storage, was carpeted, painted, and not at all scary, but in that moment I was terrified to walk down those stairs.

I stared at the trail of mud and whatever else, and then

finally took the first step. It complained under my foot, and I squeezed my eyes tight, hoping nothing jumped out at me as punishment for making a sound. When nothing happened, my eyes popped open, and I immediately searched for a weapon. The closest thing was a hammer sitting in a hand-held, red toolbox lying open on the floor. I quickly picked it up, making sure I had a good grip, and then descended the stairs, preparing myself for whatever might be down there.

If he's alive, don't hit him. Don't just swing. Don't just react. Those thoughts were on loop, getting louder with every step, which made it difficult to listen for anything that might signal I might actually *need* to swing in reaction.

The door opened, and I bent forward to look inside, immediately seeing a pair of legs lying flat on the floor. They were Leah's, and even though I couldn't see all of her, I could tell she was face down. After a quick glance to both sides, I stepped in, following the trail. Dr. Hayes was sitting back against the wall, a large wound in his neck, and a single gunshot hole in his temple. One of his many handguns was at his side, next to his open, lifeless hand. Leah also had a head wound, similar to Dr. Hayes's, but her chin and chest were covered in blood, and the missing piece from Dr. Hayes's neck was peeking from her mouth.

Blood was sprayed in several directions: on the open gun safe in the corner, the wall, and floor. From what I could tell, Dr. Hayes had come to the basement to get a gun for protection, but Leah had apparently caught him in the act, and attacked him. She must have turned quick. He must have been running from her. I imagined that he knew he was infected, so after shooting her, he'd killed himself. It made sense.

Suddenly I felt very alone. It hadn't crossed my mind that the ranch would be devoid of anybody else. His daughters weren't here. Leah was dead. Would the rest of his family try to make it to this safe haven? Miranda and Ashley were supposed to visit this weekend. Maybe they were already on their way. If not, maybe they would have the same idea I had and come here anyway with their mother. The ranch was obviously the best place to be, and even though they didn't visit as often, Dr. Hayes, like every girl's father, was their protector. It made sense for them to try to make it here. That was my hope, anyway.

Dr. Hayes was just smiling about his daughters visiting the morning before. I couldn't believe he was sitting in a pool of his own blood just a few feet from me. It was so surreal, I couldn't find an emotion to attach to the situation. I couldn't pull my eyes away from the gruesome scene until it finally dawned on me that if the girls did reach the ranch, they could see their father like this.

"Damnit," I said. My mind went on an inexplicable memory search for every time I'd seen the doctor eat a donut. He was a stout man, and I had no idea how I was going to pull him up the stairs.

I walked over to the mess and picked up the pistol off the floor. The safety was off. With my foot, I nudged Leah's hip, pointing the gun at the back of her head. A rather large exit wound was visible, but I didn't want any surprises. She rocked forward, and then didn't move again, prompting me to click on the gun's safety feature.

Satisfied they weren't going to attack me, I walked upstairs—gun in hand—through the house to the front porch. I stood on the wood deck, taking stock of my surroundings, trying to decide what I should do first.

A sudden wave of exhaustion came over me, and I sat on the steps so hard that I hurt my ass. I'd made it. We had said this was the place to come if an apocalypse happened. It happened, and I was here. Without my girls.

I shook off the thought, refusing to shed another tear. They were on their way here, and I had to get this place ready for them. There was definitely plenty of work to do, but I knew I would collapse soon, and certain precautions needed to be taken so I could fall asleep safely. There were old boards in the barn, but the bull was in there, too. Securing the windows and the perimeter and burying Leah and the doctor would have to be done before I could sleep. All of that would likely take all day. I stood up and took a deep breath, wondering how much more I could push my body before it just couldn't go any longer.

I walked around the back to the shed and found a shovel, and then found a nice spot under the big maple tree on the south side of the house, and began to dig.

Nathan

MY EYES BULGED AND I BLINKED, TRYING TO CLEAR them so I could figure out where we were. I'd just had the mother of all nightmares, and Zoe was still in my arms asleep, but I could tell from the musty smell that we weren't home.

When the room finally came into focus, feelings of both relief and dread came over me. The dread overpowered the relief without effort. We were running for our lives. Jill was either dead or would be soon, my wife was gone, and Zoe and I were on the run.

To my right were the old couple, Walter and Joy. Walter was asleep in his recliner, snoring. He would suck air in through his nose, and then blow it out from his mouth, the air building up until it escaped from his lips. Joy was awake, watching me with a smile.

"He's always done that," she said quietly. "Used to drive me nuts. Now it's relaxing."

I sat up, careful not to wake Zoe. The sun lit up the room from the small rectangular windows near the ceiling. The television was on, but muted.

"I don't think the news is going to come back on, but at least we still have electricity."

I nodded, folding my arms across my chest. "Wonder if you'll get a bill?"

Joy laughed once. "I doubt it. I saw my postman walk by yesterday afternoon."

That struck me as funny, even though it was morbid as hell, and I couldn't stop the laughter that bubbled to the service. Joy began to giggle, too. We were trying not to wake Walter and Zoe, so our laughter consisted of breathing and shuddering. Joy's eyes began to water, and then she stood. "I'm going to make a cup of coffee. Want one?"

I nodded. "I better go with you."

I made sure Zoe was still snugly tucked into the blanket, and then I followed Joy upstairs. She started a pot in silence, and I checked outside. There were no broken windows or open doors, and I didn't see any of the sick, either. I stepped onto the porch. In the distance, I could barely make out the sound of the alarm from the highway. It was still going off. Skeeter, Jill, and even Aubrey crossed my mind: where they were, if they were safe, if they got any rest the night before. Other people from my life flooded my thoughts as well. My boss, who was a huge asshole, but his wife and children were very sweet; my cousin Brandon and his six kids; our neighbors; Mrs. Grace, my second grade teacher. It was possible that almost everyone I'd ever known was dead. Or . . . a version of dead.

Joy was just pouring the steaming, dark coffee into a mug when I returned to the kitchen. "I meant what I said last night," she said, encouraging me to sit. "You and Zoe are welcome here for as long as you like."

I added creamer and sugar to my cup and swirled it around with a spoon. "I appreciate that. But don't you think it's dangerous to try to see this through in town? We just came from Fairview. We were inside the church with several other people. The sick were trying to tear it apart. I left with Zoe because it's only a matter of time before they got in."

"I couldn't imagine leaving here. I don't know where we'd go."

"Do you know anyone with some land near here? Out of the way? That's what I was hoping we would come across."

Joy thought for a minute. Instead of answering, she took a sip of coffee. Her eyes were kind, the light blue in her irises even more pronounced bordered by her silver hair, but they also gave her away. She was holding something back. I didn't know these people, but if I had a chance of learning whatever it was that she was keeping from me, it was in that moment, while I had Joy alone.

"I understand. You don't know me or Zoe. I didn't mean to pry."

Joy frowned, clearly conflicted. "Oh, it's not that, Nathan. I'm just not sure."

"Sure of what?"

The basement door opened. "Your little girl is awake, Nathan. I tried talking to her, but I think she's confused. You might get down there before she gets too upset," Walter said. "Bring her up for some breakfast. We'll try to keep her mind off things."

I nodded with an appreciative smile, and then left the table, hoping that wasn't my only chance.

Chapter Fourteen

Scarlet

THE FRIDGE HAD AN ENTIRE CASE OF BOTTLED WATER inside. I took the first bottle, unscrewed the lid, and chugged it. Just two days before it would have taken an entire morning at work for me to finish that amount, but I felt like I hadn't had anything to drink in weeks. I opened another, and sucked the water down until only a quarter was left in the bottle.

It had taken me most of the morning to dig one hole, I still had one more to dig, and a dozen other things to do before I could rest. It had been more than twenty-four hours since I'd slept. I was physically, mentally, and emotionally exhausted.

I trudged back to the backyard, staring at the bodies of Dr. Hayes and his girlfriend, Leah, lying side by side. Dragging him up the stairs was almost the hardest thing I'd ever done, second only to giving birth. At the halfway point on the stairs, I paused to rest and nearly let him go. The only thing that kept me going was weighing the alternative: to dismember him and carry the smaller bits upstairs. Easier, yes, but a whole hell of a lot messier.

I leaned against the tree, feeling lightheaded. My body was screaming for rest. Before I was passed out and vulnerable outside, my sense of self-preservation told me to retreat inside the house. With only one objective in mind, I stumbled into the laundry room, descended the stairs, and shut myself in the basement, pulling the old loveseat against the door with the last bit of my energy. My body collapsed onto the scratchy cushions, and before I could have another thought, I lost consciousness.

WHEN I FIRST PEELED MY EYES OPEN, I SAW TAN, SOILED carpet and the adjacent wall going in and out of focus. Everything was devoid of sound, even the air. My line of sight followed the carpet until the chunky remnants from the tussle with the doctor and Leah came into view.

It was then that my heart broke into a million pieces. I wasn't sure what time it was, or what day it was, but I knew I was in hell. My children were somewhere else where I couldn't protect them, and I was alone. It took longer that time to recover from mourning my situation, but I gave myself adequate time to cry, and then I went to the doctor's gun safe. It was one of many, but it was the only one open. A rifle stood out to me, and fit well in my hands, so it accompanied me upstairs.

The position of the sun confused me at first. It was higher in the eastern sky than it was when I decided to rest. *It's not possible,* I thought. But that I had slept the rest of my first day at the ranch and through the entire night was the only explanation.

The doctor's bloody shirt was damp with dew. The thought of being out for so long was disturbing, and a flood of emotions came over me. What had the girls been doing the day before and all night? Irrational feelings like the fear that they wouldn't survive if I hadn't worried about them every minute of every hour crept into my mind.

Unable to process any more, I rolled Leah into her grave, and grabbed the shovel to fill the hole. As I covered her with dirt, my hands began to burn and complain from the digging the day before. Leah lay face down, slowly disappearing beneath the soil. Once I filled one hole, I began to dig another. I was sure to make Dr. Hayes's hole a little wider, and a little deeper. I dug until the clay was too difficult, and then I rolled him into his hole, too. His leg managed to prop, so I had to bend it so he would lie right.

By noon, I had said a few words about my friends, made myself a sandwich, and found rope, twine, and Leah's stash of recycled cans. The plan was to line the perimeter with the cans so if any shufflers crossed the cans, the noise would be a warning. Not foolproof, but it kept me busy.

Two days passed before I saw the first shuffler. He was only wearing a robe, stumbling down the road unaccompanied. The barrel of my gun followed him until he was out of sight. Shooting him crossed my mind, but because I'd seen the shufflers react to the car alarm in Shallot, I was afraid the noise would attract more. I let him pass, praying my cowardice wasn't freeing him to attack someone else down the road.

Every day I watched the road for the girls. To pass the time I cleaned, rearranged, reorganized, and wrote down how the food and water should be rationed. The girls were coming, and I had to make sure there were plenty of supplies for them when they arrived, especially the mac and cheese for Halle, and the double butter popcorn for Jenna.

Day four was depressing. A part of me wanted to believe the

girls would come straight to the ranch, but with each passing day it became obvious that wasn't going to happen. I wasn't sure why they hadn't come. Refusing to entertain the worst scenario, I told myself Andrew was taking his time to keep our children safe. Still, the waiting was agonizing. Before the outbreak, there was never enough time. Now, the days dragged on, and I felt more and more alone, wondering if I was the only person left alive. That led to more uneasy thoughts: If Christy leaving early had helped her and her daughter Kate find someplace safe, if David and his family were okay, if David had made it out of the hospital at all. If he was working Mrs. Sisney's code and she was attacking people outside . . . I shuddered, shaking the likely scene from my mind, only to think of other, less settling things. My mother was home alone, and so was my neighbor, Mrs. Chebesky. I wanted to call them to see if they were all right. I'd tried the doctor's landline the first evening and every day after, but an automated response turned into weird, incessant beeps, and then there was no dial tone at all.

The next day, I saw another shuffler. Part of me wanted to use her for target practice, but again I was afraid the noise would attract others. I hid inside the house and she passed, across the neighboring field, without event.

A sense of pride swelled inside of me that my theory had been right. The doctor's ranch was the perfect place to survive the end of the world. But it wasn't surviving unless my girls were there with me. So I watched the road, sometimes looking so hard I could almost see them.

But on Thursday morning, it wasn't on the road that I saw someone. It was over the hill.

Nathan

"DADDY!" ZOE SAID, HALF AFRAID, HALF ANGRY. SHE WAS using her scolding voice, the one she used to parent Aubrey and me when we were breaking a rule. "You left me!" she said, her eyes already puffy and wet from tears. "You left me!"

"I didn't leave," I said, rushing to my knees in front of her on the couch. I kept my voice calm and soothing. "I was just upstairs talking to Miss Joy."

It was irresponsible of me to let Zoe wake up alone in a strange place. My daughter was sensitive to many things—fabric, noise, situations—and our routine had kept her calm for the most part. A year had almost passed since Zoe's last "episode," as her school counselor called them, but I could always tell when she was working up to one.

Knowing we needed to be quiet to survive, Zoe couldn't release an overstimulation like she used to. I refused to make it a rule, though. Not before she found another outlet. "Zoe," I said, letting my voice slide over the back of my tongue. Aubrey didn't have the patience for this, but she also didn't have a butter voice, as she called it. Zoe responded much better to the silky smooth tone I used for these moments.

Zoe balled up her fist and hit my shoulder. It didn't hurt. She didn't mean for it to, she was just releasing the overwhelming emotions she couldn't process any other way. "Never leave me!"

"I wouldn't. I would never leave you. I'm sorry you were afraid when you woke up. That's my fault."

She used her other hand to hit my chest. "I was! I was afraid!"

"That's it," I said, encouraging her. "Use your words."

Zoe took a deep breath, always a good sign. "I was having a bad dream! I didn't know where I was! I thought you were dead!"

I nodded. Her eyes were wild and her body trembled, a signal that she wasn't quite on the down slope, but she was peaking.

"Never again!"

"You know I can't make promises, Zoe."

"No, you promise!" she screamed.

I nodded. "What I can promise is to never leave without telling you again. You'll always know where I am. Deal?"

Zoe took in a staggering breath, and then breathed out. She blinked a few times, and then her eyes relaxed. I held out my arms for her to hug me. She wouldn't have allowed me to before she was ready, anyway. I'd learned over the years to just offer and wait.

When her tiny body was nuzzled up against mine, I wrapped my arms around her. "I'm sorry, baby. I'm here. You're safe and loved. Safe and loved."

Zoe melted against me and whimpered. It was exhausting and frightening for her when she lost control, and if she hadn't just woke up, she probably would have lied down for a nap. I wiped her eyes and took her hand.

"Miss Joy made breakfast."

I led her up the stairs, unable to ignore the looks from Walter and Joy. I had become accustomed to them. People who happened to be around during an episode were usually either annoyed or sympathetic, with no in-between. A woman at the mall once approached Aubrey to advise us that Zoe just needed a good spanking. It seemed like everyone who didn't understand always knew how to parent Zoe better than we did. Even if they didn't say it, they let us know with their expressions. Zoe never seemed to notice. I hoped she never would.

"Here you go, Zoe. I hope you like cinnamon rolls."

"Oh, I do," Zoe said, her eyes big and her smile wide. She followed the plate until it was in front of her, and didn't hesitate to pick one up with both hands and shove it into her mouth.

Joy smiled. "I didn't figure she'd want a fork."

"Nope," I said. "I can't thank you enough."

"Daddy? Where's Mommy?" Zoe asked through a mouthful of bread.

"She's uh . . ." I stuttered, looking to Joy. "She went on a trip."

"Is she coming back? How will she find us?"

My mouth pulled to the side. "I don't know, baby."

Zoe looked down at her cinnamon roll, clearly trying to process the news.

A small dog began to yap. Just a few times at first, and then consistently. Joy smiled. "That's Princess. She belongs to the Carsons next door. I've been feeding her and letting her out in the backyard. Would you like to help me feed Princess, Zoe?"

Zoe nodded emphatically, shoving the rest of the cinnamon roll in her mouth as she pushed her chair away from the table. The chair screeched against the floor as she did so, and I closed one eye tight, recoiling from the noise.

Walter smiled. "This floor has survived three grandchildren, two of 'em boys. I think it can stand up to Zoe."

We spent the rest of the day talking and watching the road. After she and Zoe returned from feeding Princess, Joy found a few board games and some cards, and played Go Fish with

Zoe. It was quiet, but once in a while, someone from Shallot would shuffle by, their eyes milky white, and always with a wound. I wondered if people that had been bitten were slowly turning and making their way out to the road.

Walter and I returned to the porch to sit in twin wooden rockers after the last dead person wandered by. Joy brought us sandwiches and apple slices. I thanked her, wondering when my next chance would come to ask her about what she didn't say that morning.

"That was Jesse Biggins," Walter said, biting off a piece of apple. He shook his head. "He's a big hunter. Has quite a few guns at his place. Maybe we should visit?"

"Does he have any family?"

Walter shook his head. "His wife died several years back. His kids moved to the city. It'd be a worth a try."

I nodded. "Maybe we should hit a couple of places for supplies?"

"We just have the one general store. Not much a store, really, but it's all we got. I don't know who else isn't sick. Maybe everything is already gone."

"How many people live here? Just a ballpark figure."

Walter breathed from his nose while he thought. "A hundred. That's a generous number."

"Gauging from the group on the road, I'd say less than half are left."

Walter nodded and his eyes fell. "That's what I was afraid of."

After I spoke to Zoe at length about where we were going and why, and exactly what time we would return, Walter and I decided to set out on foot carrying several empty bags and two gas cans. Joy stood behind Zoe with her hands on her shoulders as Zoe waved good-bye. The store was only a few blocks away, and Jesse's house a few more, so we assumed it would be a quick trip.

Just as I suspected, the general store was nearly stocked full of supplies, but empty of anyone else. Keeping the sick's attraction to noise in mind, Walter and I brought our guns—his shotgun and my semi-automatic—as a last resort. Walter had a couple of hatchets in his shed, and we both carried one with us for protection.

Walter went straight to the coffee aisle. I put as many bottles of water in my bag as I could carry and some nonperishable foods. Matches, every lighter they had, flashlights, batteries, pantyhose, and maxi pads.

Walter gave me a look.

"The hose are good for tie-offs, filters, you name it. The pads stick to you, and they're absorbent. Good for wounds."

Walter nodded. "I thought maybe you were a cross dresser," he said, and then picked up a couple of first-aid kits. "I'm not that creative. I'll stick to these."

I smiled. My bags were nearly full, and we hadn't been to Jesse's. "Maybe we should head back to the house? Drop these off and then get the guns, or make the trip tomorrow."

"It's just up the street there. Let's just get it over with."

"Famous last words. Have you ever seen a zombie movie? What you said would be a clear signal that something bad was going to happen if the characters continued on. My mind is made up. We're going back."

Walter's eyebrows pulled together, but he smiled. The bell over the door sounded, and Walter's smile went away. We acknowledged to each other the sound of something dragging, slow and clumsy, across the tile floor. I pointed to the back, mouthing the word *exit.*

Walter nodded quickly, and I followed him through double swinging doors to a storage room. I kept my hatchet ready, and he did the same. We escaped through the back door without even seeing what else had visited the store.

"Do you think it knew we were in there?" Walter said, walking more quickly than he had before.

"Maybe it smelled us?"

"You, maybe. I've showered."

I laughed once, and tried to keep pace with the old man.

Miranda

MY EYELIDS WERE HEAVY. EVEN THOUGH WE WERE PREPARING to carry Skeeter's wife outside amid dozens of dead just waiting to bite us, time seemed to have stopped. The faucet was leaking, letting one drop at a time fall into the sink, creating an irritating beat inside the silence.

Bryce and Skeeter were discussing strategy while the reverend and the other men listened intently. Ashley was busy trying to talk Cooper out of baiting the dead ones away from the church, and the women were trying to keep the children warm and comfortable on their pallets in the hallway so they would sleep through it all.

Jill had been rolled in a couple of plastic tablecloths once Skeeter was finally okay with it. It bothered him at first to see her covered, complaining that she couldn't breathe. He knew as well as we did that she was gone, but his mind was still getting used to it. No one blamed him, waiting patiently until he was ready.

I was sitting in a metal folding chair at the table with my chin resting on the heel of my hand. It was ridiculous, but the only thing running through my head was how stupid it was that I didn't get more sleep the night before the apocalypse. I'd stayed up late cramming for a test that I didn't even get to take because the school let out early due to the pandemic. Now I had double and triple integrals running in my brain. I would never have used them before. Now I *definitely* wouldn't need them. The thought about how much time I'd wasted studying for shit that no longer mattered made me angry.

I could have been backpacking across Europe. Now there was a very real chance I might never see it.

"Miranda?"

I sat up, blinking. "Yeah?"

"You ready? The sun is coming up. It will be light enough in a couple of minutes for us to move Jill."

"Yeah. I'm ready. Just waiting on you." I stood, watching the reverend fidget and take big enough breaths that, to him, made him look something other than nervous.

Before I made it the few steps across the room to help Bryce and Skeeter with Jill, a quiet moan reverberated upstairs. Every pair of eyes in the room slowly moved upward to stare at something they couldn't see on the other side of the ceiling. In the next moment there was a loud bang like someone had fallen.

Gary looked to Skeeter. "I told you. It's Annabelle."

Skeeter glanced down at the sheet covering Jill, and then

grabbed a gun from his duffle bag. It looked pretty mean. Something my dad would love. "We need to take care of Jill, first."

The mother, April, wrapped her arms around her middle. "You're just going to leave us in here alone with that thing walking around upstairs? What if she gets through the door?"

"It's boarded," Gary said.

"My husband boarded the windows of our house. Notice he's not here," April said, her voice raising an octave.

"All right," he said quietly. "We put Annabelle down, and then I'll take care of Jill before we take her outside. They were bit about the same time, and she'll hate me if I let her hurt anyone."

"Not in the church! Reverend, tell them!" Doris said.

Reverend Mathis nodded to Doris. "We can't take the risk of trying to get Annabelle outside, but Skeeter . . . maybe you could wait to put Jill to a final rest until we get outside."

"If they were bitten at the same time," Bryce began, but Doris cut him off.

"Poor Annabelle," she said, tears spilling over her cheeks.

Skeeter took the safety off his rifle. "Let's get it done."

Bryce kissed the corner of my mouth quickly before following Skeeter, Gary, and Eric upstairs. At some point during the discussion, Evan woke up and lumbered into the kitchen from the hallway. It didn't take him long to figure out something wasn't right, and he clung to Bob's arm.

"What's going on, Grandpa?"

Bob rested his hand on Evan's shoulder. "Annabelle woke up."

"Woke up?"

"She's like one of those things outside now."

The dread the rest of us felt played out on Evan's face. At that point we'd all seen the dead walking, but to witness someone's death and then watch—or hear—them reanimate was something entirely different. A person could go from someone you trusted and loved to an animal waiting to eat you alive. I didn't know Annabelle and had never seen her, but hearing the story of how she'd made it to safety and then didn't hesitate to risk everything to save Connor, she must have been a sweet soul. Hearing her clumsy footsteps upstairs as the sickness told her braindead body to move to find food was unbelievable. Annabelle sacrificed her life to save Connor, and the creature she'd become wouldn't hesitate to strip his flesh from the bone.

The sounds of the board being stripped from the doorjamb traveled down the hallway.

"I still don't want you to go, Cooper," Ashley said. "You don't have to."

"I know. I don't want to go, either."

"Then don't."

I sighed, irritated with the repeated conversation. "They didn't have to let us stay here. We can do this one thing for them."

"This one thing?" Ashley said. She usually didn't confront me, so her tone was a surprise. "This one thing could get him killed."

"Cooper hasn't lost a race in three years, Ashley. He can run forever. Have some faith."

Ashley frowned. "No."

"Bryce and I are going out there. If Cooper doesn't lead them away, we could be killed."

"That's your choice."

"God, you're a spoiled brat."

"Well you're a bitch! Who died and made you team captain?"

"Uh . . . Ashley," Cooper said.

"Team captain? This isn't cheer camp, Ashley! It's common knowledge in a situation like this, no one can survive alone. We have to work together. Quit being stupid."

"Miranda?" Cooper said.

"Shut up, Cooper!" Ashley and I said in unison.

"Jesus Christ in heaven," Doris said, holding her hand to her chest.

It was then that I heard the distinct crunching of plastic, and a scratchy moan coming from the tablecloths covering Jill. Evan stumbled back, flattening himself against the wall. Bob stepped in front of him protectively; the rest of us stood watching in confusion and amazement.

No matter how many times I told myself it was true, seeing someone I knew to be dead moving around was unbelievable. I couldn't move. I couldn't call out to Bryce. I could only watch as Jill slowly wriggled out of the tablecloth. Her milky eyes glanced around the room, and then she awkwardly attempted to stand.

"Whoa, shit," Cooper said, pulling Ashley behind him.

"What do we do?" Doris said.

Evan let out a cry and then moved to the door, frantically clawing at the doorknob.

"No! They're outside the door!" The words came from my mouth in slow motion. When I started the sentence, Evan had already reached for the bolt lock and in the next second the door was open. He poked out his head and the next moment he stood up straight, pushing the door closed. Something was pushing back, and the familiar moans accompanied arms of various sizes reaching inside.

Skeeter's rifle went off upstairs, making the grayish arms reaching in even more desperate.

"Evan!" Bob said, rushing to help him. They struggled together to get the door closed, but there were so many on the other side pushing against it. They knew we were inside, and they were hungry.

April ran into the hallway to wake up the children, making Jill take notice. She took a step in the direction of the hallway until Ms. Kay stepped around the corner.

Before Ms. Kay could react, Jill charged and tackled her to the floor. The old woman's screams sent us all into a panic, but the only way out was up. Bob planted his feet on the ground.

"Go, Evan! I'll hold the door, you go!"

"No!" Evan said.

Instinctively, I grabbed Evan's shirt and dragged him into the hallway, following April and her children up the stairs. Doris, Ashley, and Cooper were trailing behind. Bob yelled and then cried out in pain. His screams were matched by Ms. Kay's, and quickly after, Barb's.

Skeeter opened the door at the top of the stairs, and Cooper shut it behind us.

"What the hell?" Skeeter said.

"Jill!" Doris cried. "And the back door is open! They're all coming in!"

Skeeter's expression metamorphosed from confusion to determination. "The biters out front will follow the rest to the back. Y'all can get down off the roof and out of here. I've got to take care of Jill."

Cooper grabbed Skeeter's shirt. "The whole downstairs is full. You can't go down there!"

Skeeter furrowed his brow. "I made a promise to my wife. I'm going to keep it."

Bryce opened the window, helping April and her kids to the roof while he spoke. "Skeeter, Coop's right. Jill wouldn't want you to get yourself killed."

Skeeter cocked his rifle. "My two favorite things—my wife and my guns—are downstairs, boys. I'm going."

Skeeter opened the door and immediately started shooting his gun. Eric locked the door behind him, and Gary helped him to move a file cabinet in front of the door. What was left of Annabelle was lying on the floor beside the window. We all had to step over her to get outside.

Just as Skeeter said, most of the dead ones had followed the rest to the back to get inside the church. Gary and Eric hopped down first, and Bryce and Cooper helped everyone off the roof before jumping down themselves. The whole process took less than a minute, and Skeeter's rifle was still blasting inside the church.

The sun had broken completely free of the horizon, and I watched the last living citizens of Fairview spread in different directions. My group jumped into the Bug and I drove away, my heart beating so fast it could have taken flight and beaten us to the ranch.

"Way-way-wait!" Bryce said, pointing to the oncoming lane. "Slow down!"

Everything inside of me wanted to do the exact opposite, but I pressed my foot on the brake, next to a green pickup truck. A guy about our age was sitting inside.

I rolled down my window. "What are you doing? This town is crawling with those things!" He didn't respond. "Hey. Hey!"

He looked up.

"Have you been bit?"

He shook his head, and then leaned against his window to look down at the mess on the road. There was a girl in a hospital gown, skin and bones, lying on the street, a large bullet hole in her skull, parts of her brain spilled out onto the pavement.

He rolled down his window, too. His eyes were swollen. He'd been crying, probably over the girl in the street. "I'm out of gas."

I glanced around. We couldn't leave him here to die. "Get in."

Chapter Fifteen

Nathan

JOY SLOWLY KNEELED ON THE FLOOR TO HELP WALTER with his boots. He was sweaty from the near jogging he did on the return trip. She grunted each time she pulled, until she finally had them both off.

Walter sat back in his chair. "Can I get a glass of water, dear? I'm parched."

"Yes," Joy said, curious. "You look like you were chased back."

Zoe watched us from the other side of the room, glancing out the sliding glass door once in a while. After Joy's comment, Zoe's eyes seemed to scan every blade of grass outside. The door looked over the patio, and into a room on the other side of the house. The bedroom opened to the backyard with a sliding glass door, too, but was concealed by the ugliest curtains I'd ever seen.

"It's okay, Zoe. They're all still on the highway."

Joy sat two glasses of water on the kitchen table, and then she put her hands on her hips. "Well? I think we've been patient enough, right, Zoe?"

Zoe turned away from the glass just long enough to nod, and then returned to her watch.

Walter cleared his throat, and then gestured to our bags. "We got some supplies. It was getting late and sugar britches over there wouldn't leave without his pantyhose."

Joy frowned in confusion, and then waited for me to explain.

"They're good for lots of things. I'm not going to wear them. Well, actually, I might, if it gets cold. Good insulation."

Joy and Walter were content to watch me talk myself into humiliation.

"What?" I said. "I was a Boy Scout."

Walter laughed once. "And all this time they've been worried about the gays infiltrating their organization, and they're teaching lulu things like that."

"I think my leader was a closet survivalist, too. I learned a lot from him."

"Pantyhose?" Walter said in disbelief, his voice going up an octave.

I shrugged. "You don't worry about what you're wearing if you're warm."

"Then I'll be toasty all winter," Joy said. Her expression immediately softened when she turned to Zoe. "Come on, peanut. I bet Princess is getting mighty hungry."

Zoe nodded and followed her outside.

Walter and I moved to the front porch, sitting in the rocking chairs and discussing our next move. We decided we would try again for Jesse's the next day. We also needed to fill the gas cans. Walter didn't seem to be in a hurry, even though I reminded him we would be leaving before long. He pretended he didn't hear me.

* * *

THE NEXT DAY WE WALKED THE DISTANCE TO JESSE'S house. Walter was right: Jesse had more guns than Skeeter. We took as many as we could carry, along with the appropriate ammunition, and then made the trek back to Walter's. We made that trip every day for three days. The basement began to look like an arsenal. I put several rifles and a few handguns in my car, reminding Walter again that Zoe and I weren't staying.

The days were beginning to get longer, and it panicked me when I had to think twice about what day it was. The only reason time mattered was to avoid getting caught outside at night. Weekends were irrelevant. Every day was about survival. Living with Walter and Joy, though, even with the occasional infected stumbling by, the apocalypse wasn't so bad. Still, I had to take Zoe somewhere out of the way, and I still hadn't carved out a quiet moment with Joy to see if she knew of a place we could settle.

"You don't believe me, do you?" I whispered.

Walter and I were watching an infected walk by. We'd learned over the last few days that if we stayed still and quiet, they kept walking.

Walter didn't respond until the infected passed, and then he shook his head. "You need to get more sleep. You're not making any damn sense."

"I'm going to start making trips out of town. Scout the area. See if I can find some acreage with a house."

"You have a house right here, you fool," Walter grumbled.

Joy occupied the space inside the open front door, and looked over to Walter with a knowing smile. Walter shook his head so slightly that if he hadn't paired it with a glance in my direction,

I would have questioned whether I'd seen it. They were in disagreement about something.

Joy walked over to stand behind Walter, patted him reassuringly, and then spoke. "You asked about a place out of the way."

"Yes," I said. My posture straightened instinctively, eager to hear what she would say next.

"There is a doctor that comes to the store here sometimes. He buys things in bulk. I've only spoken to him once. He seems like a reasonable man, not what you might expect from a big city doctor. I know he has two girls, and he lives northeast of here. He's several miles out, so it might be isolated enough to be safe for you and Zoe."

Walter frowned at his wife.

"I would never force my way in, Walter. I hope you know that. I have to find the safest place to raise Zoe, though."

Joy smiled. "It's not that. He likes having you two here. He doesn't want you to leave."

Walter crossed his arms over his chest and settled into his chair, unhappy.

"Is this true?" Antagonizing Walter was probably not a good idea, but it was also too fun to pass up.

"Go to hell." He frowned.

Joy let out a cackle, and she shook her head. "Oh, you stubborn man," she said, rubbing his shoulder.

Walter stood up quickly, his rifle in his hand.

I aimed at nothing in reaction. "What is it?"

Walter squinted over the rifle's sights. "Kids."

Miranda

THE SUN HAD POURED A BRIGHT LIGHT OVER US AND everything else by the time we'd made the north turn on Highway 123. My hands were shaking, knowing we were that much closer to my dad's ranch. I imagined his reaction when he saw the Bug pull into the yard, and what it would feel like for his arms to wrap around me, strong and warm; his cheeks wet from worried and happy tears.

I wasn't sure why I blamed him for the divorce. Mom was the one that had decided she didn't want to be married to his profession anymore. It broke Dad's heart when she said it was over, and for whatever reason my loyalties were with my mom. She seemed more fragile, and less capable to be on her own. I wasn't sure what Dad could have done differently. Quit his job? Thrown away years of education? What else would he do? It wasn't until I began my second semester of college that I realized it wasn't just parties and friends. It was hours of studying and worrying and writing papers that would never pass through any other hands than a professor's. But, I blamed him. I punished him with my absence.

Tears welled up in my eyes as I pressed on the brake to bring the Bug to a slow stop about a hundred yards from a large herd of dead ones. The car alarm confused me. It was grating to the ears, and yet I'd been so engulfed in my thoughts of my dad, the sound and even the headlights blinking on and off, visible through the dozens of ambling bodies, didn't register until we were nearly on top of them.

"What do you want to do?" Bryce asked quietly.

"Turn off your lights," the guy we'd picked up said, his voice tired and sad. He hadn't told us his name, and no one had bothered to ask. We had more important things to worry about, I guess, but still it seemed strange. It was another reminder that in just a few days the environment had changed us.

A few days ago, Ashley would have been giggly and bubbly and the first thing she would have done is asked the guy his name. She didn't even seem to notice he was in the car, even though she was sitting half on his lap, half on Cooper's.

I reached up to turn the headlamp knob, and we idled. The wheat field on the right was still damp from rain. A vehicle had cut huge ruts into the soil, really deep in some spots. On the right was a grassy hill. I wondered for a moment why the person who made the ruts had chosen the wheat field. Then, the road leading into the tiny town of Shallot caught my eye. Ashley and I had passed this town and that wheat field so many times without a second thought. Now, the wheat field was dangerous, and the town a frightening unknown. The hill hid parts of the town from view, and the wheat field ruts led me to believe the person before us wanted as far away from that hill as possible.

The dashboard pinged, and I looked down. The gas gauge was a centimeter to the right of the red line.

"Of course," Ashley said. "How could we possibly star in a horror movie without something catalyzing like that happening?"

"Catalyzing?" Cooper said with a smile.

"Shut up," she replied, barely acknowledging his playful teasing.

The truth was, Ashley had done significantly better on her SATs than I had. She'd always been a straight A student, even taking college courses in high school. She'd inherited our dad's intelligence, but my mom's inability to handle any amount of stress. She was an emotional ball of nerves and tears. Cooper once told me that his mother was the same way, and that's why he was one of the few guys in school that didn't find her high-maintenance. One late, drunken night when everyone else had passed out, Cooper shared with me that he actually found her neediness and constant need for assurance comforting, which was just . . . odd, and maybe a little co-dependent, but they *were* perfect for each other. Cooper understood Ashley, and made her happy like no one else could. They clung to each other because they believed it, too.

I don't know. I guess it was sweet. Even weird people deserved to be happy.

"Well"—I breathed, hating what I was about to say—"look on the bright side. There is a gas station in Shallot."

"But we're so close," Ashley said. "Let's just drive around and go home."

"We can't make it home."

One of the dead ones seemed to notice the Bug, and she took a slow step toward us. She was young, and her long, blond hair might have been as beautiful as Ashley's if it wasn't ratted and covered in blood and . . . other things. Her movement drew the attention of another dead one, and then another. Soon, several were walking slowly but with purpose. Their eyes were milky and lifeless, but their mouths were open. Some of their upper lips were quivering, like a growling dog. The blonde reached out to me, and a low but excited moan pushed from her throat.

I pulled back on the gearshift and pushed the gas pedal to

the floor. A few days ago, I had parked the Bug in the middle of nowhere to avoid door dings, and now I was driving it like a go-kart. I whipped us back and away from the approaching dead ones, and then followed the road on the right into Shallot, praying that there wasn't another herd behind the hill, and we wouldn't be boxed in.

"Whoa!" Bryce said, as I cut across a median. Everyone's head but mine hit the ceiling.

"Sorry!" I said, grabbing the wheel with one hand over the other quickly as I turned to keep control.

"Ease back, babe," Bryce said. "We're okay."

The town was vacant, and I sighed in relief to see a grocery store ahead, with a gas station directly behind it. I pulled around to the station, and we all climbed from the Bug, stretching and taking a moment to breathe.

I was relieved that even in the early hours of the morning, it was warmer than the day before. The previous day's rain had brought with it a cold front, and I was worried Ashley and I would be miserably cold before we made it to Dad's. For just a second, I thought about pulling out my cell phone to check the forecast, but then I realized I hadn't had service since yesterday. None of us had.

Bryce walked around us with his eyes to the ground, checking the tires.

"Did I break her?" I asked.

"No, but you have to be more careful."

"I was scared. I wasn't sure what was behind the hill. Did you see those ruts in the field?"

"Yeah," he said simply, his eyes moving from the tires to our surroundings. Once he was satisfied that we weren't in immediate danger, he noticed my struggle with the gas pump. "Not working?"

I glared at the nozzle plugged into the Bug. "I was all excited because this thing is ancient. It doesn't even have a place to run a credit card."

"I'll run in. Maybe there's a switch to trip."

He gave me a quick peck on the lips and jogged across the small lot to the station. He pushed open the door and jumped over the counter. He searched the register and surrounding area with a focused frown, and before I could register a thought, my legs broke out into a sprint toward the station.

"Bryce!" Our eyes met, and I was sure his reactive expression matched mine. He turned to face the dead one that had walked up behind him.

Just as I opened the door, the word *no* erupted out of me. Bryce pressed his forearm against the man's chest to keep the snapping teeth at bay, and then reached across the counter to a pen that was attached to the cash register with twine. He yanked it away from its anchor, and in the next moment stabbed the man in the face. The man kept coming at him, so he stabbed him again; this time the pen went through the corner of its eye, and he collapsed against Bryce.

Movement on my left caught my eye, and dead ones, two females, one adult and one child, were slowly shuffling toward me. She was obese, her skirt dragging the floor around her ankles, and she was covered in dark, dried blood and dirt. The skin on her face and her lips were all gone. She'd been chewed on before she'd come back. I couldn't see a wound on the girl, but her eyes were milky white like the woman's.

"Bryce!" I screamed.

He pushed the man off of him and jumped back over the counter, yanking my arm as he pushed the door open and pulled me toward the Bug.

"Go! Get in!" Bryce swung his free arm around wildly as he commanded everyone standing around the Bug.

Everyone scrambled to get inside the car but me. I stood on the driver's side with the door open, watching the dead ones claw at the glass on the double doors of the station.

"Miranda!" Ashley screamed.

"Look at them," I said softly, my voice calm and full of wonder.

They couldn't get out. Even though the doors would open a little when they pushed against it, they weren't coordinated enough to continue pushing and walk. The doors would come back against them, so they clawed at the glass like it was a wall.

The woman's swollen belly bumped the door, and I recoiled, realizing she wasn't fat, but heavily pregnant.

I sat in the seat and closed the door, still breathing heavily. "Did you find a switch?"

Bryce shook his head. "We can't make it to your dad's?"

"I don't think we should try. We might get stranded."

"It's too dangerous to go on foot. We need to figure out how to get inside and turn on that pump."

"I have this," the guy we picked up said. He held up a handgun.

I frowned. "Did you see those things around that car earlier? They're attracted to noise."

He didn't flinch. "We could search the houses for something quieter. Baseball bats, scissors, kitchen knives. Bryce took that one down with a pen."

"That could take days," I said.

He shrugged. "You got somewhere to be?"

"Yeah, I do, actually."

"Not until you get gas in this car, you don't."

I turned to face forward in a huff. He was right, but I didn't like his smart-ass comment. I glared at him in the rearview mirror. He was tall and looked ridiculous sitting in the back, his knees nearly as tall as his head. His dark eyes were deep set, and his face was still sprayed with that girl's blood. Combined with his buzz cut and muscles, he looked like a serial killer, and I'd let him in my car. For all we knew, he could have killed that girl before she turned.

"What is your name, anyway?"

"Joey."

"What's with the haircut, Joey?"

"I just got back from Afghanistan."

"Oh," I said. My response was more acidic than I'd intended. I was trying not to show my surprise, or sudden admiration.

"Dude," Cooper said. He wasn't holding back the fact that he was impressed. Cooper shook Joey's hand. "Appreciate you, man. And I suddenly feel much safer."

"Don't," he said. "I only have what's left in this clip."

"Still," Cooper said. "You're a badass."

I wasn't sure if Bryce was as impressed with Joey as Cooper was and just trying to hide it like me, or if he wasn't impressed at all. I caught him rolling his eyes at Cooper's words, and I elbowed him. We exchanged smiles. It wasn't uncommon for us to know what the other was thinking. We'd been together so long and had spent so much time together it wouldn't surprise me if Bryce knew what I was thinking before I did. That was probably why marriage wouldn't be on the table until well after we both graduated. We were accused frequently of acting like an old married couple.

"No one move," I said, watching a dead one pass slowly across my rearview mirror. It was heading to the highway.

We all sat like statues. The females in the station were still pawing at the doors, and I hoped they didn't draw the new dead one's attention. He was dragging a broken ankle, even slower than was typical. Ashley began to turn to look, but Cooper stopped her, just as Bryce stopped himself from telling her no.

The dead one passed. Rattled, we stepped back out onto the cracked concrete. The sun was getting higher in the sky . . . and hotter. I peeled off my jacket and tied the arms around my waist into a double knot. There were only a few straggler clouds that broke up the blue sky. It was bluer than it had been in a long time, or maybe it had just been a long time since I'd noticed. A gentle wind blew the leaves on the trees, making it sound like lazy waves pulling away from the sand.

As beautiful and calm as it was in this tiny town, being outside was a risk, and the absence of cars on the road or even the occasional stray dog made even a perfect day fearsome.

Several gunshots rang out in the distance, echoing and bouncing so many times we didn't know which direction they came from. It was too far away to be in town, but everyone but Joey looked around, uneasy and unsure how to react.

"Let's get the shit we need, and get out of here," I said.

Everyone agreed with a nod, and we set off toward the grocery store, more cautious knowing there were still dead citizens of Shallot making their way to the noisy car on the highway.

Joey walked with both hands on his gun, holding it in front of his body while he walked sideways like you'd see in a movie. It was kind of sexy, but I still thought he was an arrogant asshole. My mother liked to share what she learned while drowning in the dating pool, and the one thing she said over and over was that it took a certain personality to be a soldier, a cop, or a firefighter. None of which I was attracted to, but for whatever reason, watching Joey move like an action hero made something inside of me squeal like a fan girl.

Cooper had emptied his duffle bag and was carrying it with one hand, and holding Ashley's hand with the other. We all stopped just outside the door, fidgeting and nervous. I hated not knowing what to expect, especially when something that wanted to eat us alive could be inside, and I imagined everyone else had the same thoughts.

Joey glanced down at Cooper's duffle bag. "Water, weapons and ammo, food. In that order."

We all nodded.

Joey crouched down, and Cooper did the same. He looked like a little boy trying to emulate his favorite super hero. He stepped his foot inside the nylon handles and dragged the bag along with him.

What are you doing? Joey mouthed, immediately reacting to the noise the duffle bag made as it slid across the floor with each step Cooper took.

Cooper held up his hands. *Hands free,* he mouthed back.

Joey rolled his eyes and shook his head. Cooper looked like a scolded puppy, stepping back out of the duffle bag's handle before picking it back up. A few moments later, we heard a noise come from the back.

Four pairs of eyes grew wide, and Ashley immediately attached herself to Cooper's side. Joey disappeared down one of the short aisles. We all stood around, not sure what to do.

Joey returned, his posture more relaxed, and his gun at his side. "Must have been an animal. I didn't find anything."

"Let's get to work," Bryce said. He took a miniature basket, the perfect size for that miniature store, and I followed him as he made his way up and down the aisles. He grabbed water bottles, canned goods, Ramen noodles—which was a staple for us as college students, anyway—a couple of large screwdrivers, various sizes of knives, a meat tenderizer mallet, an umbrella, and a few brooms.

"You gonna clean someone's house?" I teased.

Bryce unscrewed the bristle end and then picked up a knife. "Spear."

I nodded and smiled. "Impressive."

He winked at me, and then we met everyone else at the front of the store.

Joey had several boxes of condoms, a first-aid kit, matches, a box of trash bags, and four bottles of water in his arms.

Bryce saw the condoms and was instantly defensive. "Seriously?"

Joey wasn't fazed. "Each one can hold up to two liters of water. Seriously."

Bryce's shoulders relaxed, and then he looked to me. "We can just wheel this to the Bug. I'm sure no one will say anything."

"Funny," I said.

As we returned to the car and practiced our Tetris skills loading it up with our finds, the boys began talking about searching the houses and garages for gas cans. Joey suggested that if we had to, we could syphon gas from one of the vehicles.

"Depending on what we find and how quickly, we're talking about spending a few nights here."

"No," Ashley said. "Miranda, tell them. We need to get to Dad's."

I looked to Bryce. "Dad is probably worried sick about us."

Joey didn't wait for Bryce to answer. "We're not going anywhere until we get gas, and I think we can all agree that we need more than just a tank full. Let's be smart about this. We have resources here. Let's use them before we move on."

Bryce made a face. "When we found you, you'd run out of gas."

"Exactly," Joey said. "Learn from my mistake. It's no fun being stuck in a car with those things trying to get in, and this car is a convertible. It won't protect us."

"Those things can't even work a swinging door," Bryce snapped.

"You wanna risk it?" Joey said.

Bryce looked at me, and then back to Joey, shaking his head. "No."

"It's settled, then. We search until we can fill the tank and as much extra as we can. You guys can break up into groups if you don't want to let the girls search alone."

"I'll go by myself," I said.

"No," Bryce responded instantly.

"I'm not helpless. I can handle a gun."

Bryce reached for my fingers. "Maybe I don't want to go by myself." He used his most charming smile, the one I could never resist. I nodded, and his hand squeezed mine.

Joey rubbed his neck. "First thing's first. We need to set up camp. The ideal place would be away from other houses. On the outskirts of town, maybe."

"Okay. That's like two blocks away," Ashley said.

"Let's walk. We'll find something," I said.

Joey kept talking as we walked. "Several exits. Good visibility."

"Now you're just being picky," I said.

Joey smiled at me. I tried not to, but I smiled back.

Ashley was right. It only took about twenty minutes to find a location that fit Joey's description. It was a yellow house on the end of a long line of houses, but it had a large field in front of and behind it, and there were two lots between it and the next house. It also had a fenced-in backyard and the small windows running along the ground screamed basement.

We climbed the steps to the porch, and I knocked. Everyone looked at me like I was crazy. "What?"

"Let me clear it first, drop off what we have, and then we can go back for the rest."

Bryce held his arm out to his side, gesturing for Joey to go in. I made a face at him. Joey was just trying to keep us safe, and Bryce was being kind of a dick about it.

Joey was inside for quite a while. Just when I thought about mentioning that we should go in and check on him, he appeared in the doorway.

"It's clear."

"You have blood on you," Cooper said. "I mean, more than before."

Joey pulled up his shirt to wipe his face. A full set of abs was revealed for just a second before he let his shirt fall back down into place. "Well . . . it's clear now."

"I didn't hear your gun," Bryce said.

"I used a fork."

Cooper nodded, an impressed smile flashing across his face. "Well played."

Chapter Sixteen

Nathan

"KIDS?" I ASKED.

"The corner house. Three . . . no, make that four. Two boys and two girls. Teenagers, by the looks of 'em. They're alive."

I lowered my gun and motioned for Zoe to stay in the house. "Then we should probably introduce ourselves."

As I crossed the street and walked down the block, I tried to keep my posture relaxed, and my gun down. I could only see one kid, one of the boys, his dark hair wiry. He was a ball of testosterone and muscles like I was at that age.

I stopped on the street corner and held up my hand. "Hey there. We're friendly. No need to worry."

The boy didn't speak, he just watched me. Another girl, blond, pale, and exceedingly beautiful, took a step out from behind him, her eyes fluttering between her people and me and Walter.

Walter walked up beside me and stopped.

"Are they from Shallot?" I asked.

"Nope."

"Uh," I began. "You guys okay?"

Another girl stepped out. This one was shorter, with long, auburn hair. Her brown eyes looked right through me. "We can't get the pumps at the gas station to work."

"You're out of gas?" I asked.

The kids looked at each other. They were either really smart and didn't want me stealing their ride, or they were too scared to speak. I didn't think for a second the latter was the case for the redhead. I doubted she'd ever hesitated to speak what was on her mind in her life.

Walter's screen door slammed and I turned to see Zoe standing next to Joy. She clearly wanted to leave the safety of the porch to be closer to me, but Joy kept a gentle hand on Zoe's shoulder. I couldn't hear what she'd said, but it seemed to calm my daughter.

I turned back to the kids. "You guys just passing through, then?"

"Yes, but like I said, we need gas. The pumps at the gas station aren't working," Red said. "Do either of you know anything about it?"

I took mental notes of everyone in their group. The tallest one had a nice face. The second tallest looked like he'd had some military training. I could tell by the tall kid's shoes and his hands that he was a rich kid, but his eyes said he was a good kid. The other boy looked like a jock, possibly a frat boy. He watched the soldier and the redhead a lot. The soldier was the one to watch for sure, although the other two could definitely do some damage. Even with all the muscle and manpower, it was the redhead that seemed to be the boss. Oddly, she seemed to be the most trusting out of the five.

I looked to Walter. "I need to fill up myself." I looked to the group. "I'm traveling with my daughter, Zoe," I said, gesturing to the porch. "We're leaving soon. I'm looking for a place out of the way. Someplace safe."

One of the boys smiled at Zoe and waved. I stared him down, and he immediately righted his posture. "I have a little sister about her age," he explained.

"This is pretty out of the way. Where are you all headed?" I asked.

They all looked at each other again. They had a destination in mind. It must have been good if they were protecting it.

"We can help ya with the gas," Walter said, "in exchange for helping Nathan and Zoe to a safer place. You have my word that he's a good man. I don't really want them to leave, to be honest, but he's right. They need to be farther away from those things."

They all watched us, especially Red and the soldier.

"We'll think about it," she said, turning and leading the rest away.

They left us, walking two by two except for the soldier, who brought up the rear. The redhead was with the tallest, and the blonde was with the jock. I wondered where the soldier fit, and then when I saw them all crowd into a Volkswagen Bug, I *really* wondered where he fit.

Walter and I returned to the porch to join Joy and Zoe. I sat on a rocking chair, and Zoe sat on my lap, watching the kids talk around their vehicle.

"They seem nice," she said simply.

"I think so. I don't really know them."

"They're strangers?"

"I suppose so."

"We're not supposed to talk to strangers."

"No, kids aren't supposed to talk to strangers."

Zoe turned to me, her brows pulled in. "But what if the strangers are kids?"

I kissed her cheek and pulled her against my chest, rocking her and ignoring that her heels were digging into my shins. Her hair was starting to smell less like shampoo and more like sweaty skin. I imagined I didn't smell so great, either.

"Joy?" I said.

"Yes, dear?"

"May we use your facilities? I'd like to make a good impression on this doctor."

Joy chuckled. "I doubt he's dressed for church, either, if you know what I mean."

"That's true."

Joy shook her head and made a face. "Lord have mercy, I am so rude. Of course, Nathan. There is a shower in the bathroom in the hall. I'll get you some towels."

I nodded. "Thank you."

THE BLONDE SAT ON THE BOTTOM STEP OF WALTER'S porch, disinterested, and the rest of them stood before us. Having so many eyes on us was a bit intimidating, even if they were just kids. I looked down at a stain on my Oxford shirt. Now that Zoe and I were freshly showered, our clothes smelled horrible, and felt heavy with dirt and sweat. Joy had offered to wash them, but I was afraid they wouldn't be dry in time and the kids would be antsy to get going and leave us behind.

The redhead spoke first. "I'm Miranda Hayes. That's my sister, Ashley," she said, nodding to the blonde on the steps. "Our father is Dr. Hayes. He lives about nine miles north, up the road, there, and then back west. It's perfect for you and Zoe. If you help us fill up our tank, and a few gas cans, you can follow us. I can't promise you that my dad will let you stay, though."

"No deal," I said, my eyes narrowing.

"He'll probably let you," Ashley said, finally looking up at us. "He won't turn away your little girl."

"But we don't know how many people he's helped already. I expect he will, but I can't promise. Understand?"

"What about the guys with you? How will you get him to let them stay?"

"We have an open invitation," the jock said. "Well, except him."

He was talking about the soldier. They must have picked him up along the way. I decided that if they had done that, they must think the father is open to more guests. "I'll take my chances."

"It's getting late," Walter said. "Meet us at the station in the morning. You got a watch?"

The soldier nodded.

"Eight a.m."

Miranda

"HOME SWEET HOME," ASHLEY SAID. SHE WAS HOLDING an empty gas can, looking up at the two-story building just four blocks from the general store.

"Not really," Cooper said, shrugging his shoulders to redistribute the weight of his bulging backpack.

I shook my head. Why did guys insist on stuffing everything they needed for a weekend in a small bag? As if it wasn't manly to appear to need more than one set of clean clothes?

The house wasn't anything special. The windows were darkened by dirty screens. The chipped paint—on both the house and the concrete porch—admitted years of negligence. One small, apologetic spot of soil in the front begged any visitors to believe all wasn't lost. Even though the rest of the house might have been too much for the owner to keep up with, that two-by-two plot of ground was adorned with every color of pansy in existence. Not a single weed in the bunch. Every blade of grass was carefully trimmed at the borders of the square of flowers, and fresh soil had been added not long before.

The home was at the end of a dead-end road. Continuing on was possible, but only through tall prairie grass and about a hundred head of cattle. Only one other house was two lots away, across the street and on the opposite corner. We'd pushed the furniture against any entrances the first night and used wooden planks from the privacy fence down the road to board the windows, and then slept in the basement, each of us taking watch every two hours. Well, except Joey. He never seemed to sleep.

The first morning we secured the windows and doors, but we still slept in the basement. We pulled the mattresses downstairs. Especially after seeing Nathan and the old man walking down the street a few days before with their guns and reappearing with at least fifteen more, it just felt safer. When we saw them return the next day, we watched where they went, waited until they left the redbrick house on the next block, and then searched it ourselves. It didn't take long to find out why they were making the trip. The house was full of nearly every gun imaginable. More than my dad's collection. More than any collection I'd ever seen—and my dad had dragged me to more than one of his fellow gun enthusiasts' houses. We took a few pieces and ammo ourselves, and quickly returned to our safe house. When we saw the duo visit the redbrick house again, we followed them home to the other side of town. It was less than a twenty-minute walk. That's when they spotted us, and when we made the deal to show Nathan to my dad's ranch in return for helping us with the gas pump.

I followed Ashley up the steps, and then stopped when Joey's arms appeared in front of us.

"Hold up. Let me clear it first."

We waited, Ashley biting her nails, and me kicking at the welcome mat as if it were perfectly normal that the soldier we'd just met was searching our temporary home for any curious dead ones.

Sensing Bryce's irritation, I turned. He was chewing on the inside of his cheek, making that face. The one that distorted his beautiful green eyes and made them glow and change into beady, unfamiliar pools of emerald.

"What?" I asked.

Bryce began to say something, but Joey poked his head from the door with a trace of a smile. "Clear."

We unpacked our newest treasures, ranging from more packs of condoms to cans of corn. Bryce walked into the back bedroom and sat on the box springs, making fists and then stretching his fingers, and then repeating the process.

"Tell me," I said, knowing if he kept another thought to himself, he might burst.

Bryce stood up, took a step, and swiped at the door, making it slam and my shoulders shoot up to my ears.

"I take it you're upset?"

"Who is that guy?" Bryce said, pointing to the closed door. "We pick him up from his shitty pickup and the girl he killed in the street, and suddenly G.I. Joe is running the fucking show?"

"Is that what you think he's doing?" I asked calmly.

Bryce was only blowing off steam. He got that way any time he'd been under stress for any length of time, like when his dad left his mom for Danielle the nail tech for a few weeks before he figured out he was already married to the best woman he could find. He also yelled at me over the phone much like he was yelling in that bedroom the time Cooper's little sister got really sick and Bryce agreed to drive him home from school. By the end of the phone call he was sobbing, barely able to describe how hard it was to watch Cooper and his family so worried and sad.

Bryce trusted me to love him anyway, even at his worst, just like I did when I was snapping at my dad for things out of his control. Dad always listened patiently, and then no matter what I said or with how much anger I said it, he responded with words of unconditional love. After he and Mom split, that was one trust I didn't make him earn back, and he took the responsibility of that trust very seriously. That wasn't the only thing I pretended I hadn't learned from him.

"Wait," Bryce said, mimicking Joey's deep voice and holding out his arm. He had the most ridiculous, smug look on his face, a thousand percent more arrogant than Joey's. "Clear." Bryce rolled his eyes.

"He just got back from a tour in Afghanistan. They talk like that, don't they?"

"Who *cares?*" Bryce seethed. "He keeps telling us what to do. I'm fucking sick of it. We somehow managed before he came along."

"True," I said, nodding.

"We don't need him. We should leave him here. He probably knows how to hotwire a car. There are dozens here to choose from." When I didn't respond, Bryce's eyebrows pulled together, and he ducked his head to make eye contact. "What are you trying to say? You want him with us?"

Bryce and I had been together so long, I didn't have to say everything. It was one of the many things I appreciated about him.

"He's a soldier. It makes sense to keep him around, don't you think?" With his intimidating size and piercing glare, Joey's looks alone were enough to scare off any living person who might want to harm us, and his particular skill set made him an asset against the dead ones. Bryce was taller than Joey, but his biceps didn't bulge from his sleeves the way Joey's did. Come to think of it, all of Joey's muscles seemed to bulge from his clothes.

"No! I don't!" he said, incredulous. His anger helped my thoughts break free of the chiseled parts of Joey's body—which were all of them.

Bryce paced, and after several minutes, his breathing slowed, and he stopped fidgeting. "You . . . do you really think we need him?"

I shrugged. "Not if you don't. But, he's a good shot. And he's smart. And I'd rather have him ducking into a house first than you."

Bryce glanced up at me from under his brow, fighting a smile. "I love you, you know that?"

I wrapped my arms around his waist as he towered over me. "You should. I'm fairly awesome. Or so I've been told."

He laughed once. "That was probably me. Actually I'm sure it was me. I'm your biggest fan."

"My tallest fan," I said with a smile, reaching up on the balls of my feet to kiss him as he leaned down. His soft lips touched mine, reminding me of better days. Normal days.

Bryce pulled me over to the box springs, and we lay together on the bumpy springs and wood covered by a thin layer of fabric. He unzipped my jacket, and I kissed him, silently agreeing to his equally silent request.

"We might as well christen the zombie apocalypse," he whispered in my ear.

"You're so romantic," I said, watching him with a smile as he pulled my jeans down over my hips and knees, and finally my ankles.

Bryce stood at my feet, unbuckling his belt and then unbuttoning his jeans. He used the toes on his right foot to pull off his left sneaker, and then repeated the action on the other side before kicking it aside. He pulled his cream henley over his head and tossed it on top of a growing pile of his clothing.

I reached down to the sides of my panties and lifted my hips and pushed down the fabric at the same time. It had stopped being romantic for him to undress me over a year ago, and that was one thing that hadn't changed in the last few days. My feet fluttered back and forth a few times before my panties catapulted to a dark corner of the room, and then Bryce reached down to pull off my socks at the same time. We were smiling, relaxed and comfortable; our sexcapades had graduated from trying to be sexy or feeling uneasy long before that evening.

After pushing down his jeans and stepping out of them, he lowered himself on top of me, kissing the corner of my mouth. To my surprise, he kept kissing me without advancing to any other part of my body. Just before I asked him if everything was okay, his head slumped and he buried his face in my neck.

"I can't."

"You . . . can't?"

He fell onto his back next to me on the mattress, staring at the ceiling. "I think I'm too stressed. Or tired. Or both."

"Oh. *Oh.*" I shouldn't have been so surprised. Sometimes before a basketball game he couldn't get it up, either. The end of the world definitely qualified as a source of anxiety. I guess knowing it had been over a week made me assume he would be beyond capable. "It's okay," I said, snuggling closer to his chest. "I like just being like this, too."

Bryce took a deep breath and blew it out, making my hair tickle my face. "We're going to be at your dad's tomorrow. We may never have sex again. It's not okay."

I giggled. "We've been sneaky before."

Bryce wrapped both of his arms around me, and kissed my temple. "I wouldn't want to be anywhere else, you know. I'm glad it happened this way."

"Yeah?"

"I might have gone crazy worrying about you otherwise."

I closed my eyes and listened to Bryce's breath as he inhaled and exhaled. He fidgeted more than usual, still restless for any number of reasons. I fantasized again about the look on Dad's face as we pulled up into the drive, and wondered what his reaction would be to Nathan and Zoe. He wouldn't turn Zoe away, but desperate times made people do weird things.

"Bullshit!" Cooper said from the living room.

Bryce and I stood up quickly and got dressed, both awkwardly reentering the world, feeling like everyone knew what we were supposed to be doing but weren't. My fingers knotted in my hair as I twisted it up into a messy bun and sat on the floor with my sister. She sat next to Cooper, and Joey was standing by the window, peeking intermittently through the crack.

Joey managed a small, amused smile. "No, I'm completely serious."

"About what?" I asked, noting that Bryce already wore an unimpressed expression.

Cooper crossed his ankles and leaned back against the couch and Ashley simultaneously. "He's telling us war stories."

"It's classified," Joey joked.

"Picnic?" I asked, noting the small, empty bags of potato chips on the floor, along with a few empty cans of soda.

"What we need is popcorn," Ashley said. "Joey is quite the storyteller."

Joey made an airy sound with his lips in protest, and then glanced out the window.

"Anything out there?" Bryce asked.

Joey nodded. "One crossed the intersection earlier. Probably just turned and is making her way to the highway."

I shuddered. Whoever she was must have been bitten, otherwise she would have already been on the highway. "I wonder why it's different."

"What's different?" Joey asked.

"How long it takes them to turn. For some it takes days. Some just hours."

Ashley chewed on her thumbnail. "Jill didn't die right away after she was attacked, right?"

"But she got really sick," I pointed out.

"Maybe they . . . reanimate after a certain amount of time after they die," she said. "How long had Jill been dead?"

I shrugged my shoulders. "What about that woman upstairs? Anabeth? Ana . . . something."

"Annabelle," Cooper said, staring at the floor.

"It's different for everybody," Joey said, all joking stolen from his tone. "They said on the radio just before they stopped broadcasting that it had to do with the flu vaccine. Those who had it were turning more quickly."

"What about the girl you were with?" Bryce asked.

"She's dead," Joey said, matter-of-fact.

Bryce didn't push the subject. Instead, he went to the food stash and picked through it until he found what he was looking for. After a few minutes, he brought over twin peanut-butter sandwiches and two lukewarm cans of Sprite.

"I love you," I said, biting into the sandwich. I hadn't realized how hungry I was until a whiff of peanut butter hit my nose as I was bringing the sandwich to my mouth.

"Enjoy it," Bryce said between bites. "Who knows if we'll eat bread again after this loaf is gone."

"That's depressing," Ashley said. "But not as depressing as chocolate."

Cooper made a face. "Just wait until we run out of toilet paper."

We all traded glances.

"This sucks," Ashley said, and we all agreed.

• • •

JOEY AND I SAT IN THE MIDDLE OF THE FLOOR, A FEW feet away from one another. The house we'd been staying in might have been the first one built in Shallot. It was older than the rest, and creaked and moaned like a grandmother complaining about her aging joints. The former occupants were definitely grandparents, easily deduced from nearly every surface and wall space covered in mismatched frames. Protected behind a slate of glass were their loved ones, frozen at each age, still alive and smiling. Some of the photos were decades old, some new. They surrounded us, a bright and cheerful wall holding out the hell outside.

The gold sofa's arms were worn, matching the rest of the house. The seat cushions were sunk in from years of visits from friends and family. I sat on the floor because it felt wrong to sit on their furniture. The house didn't belong to me, even if the owners were lumbering aimlessly on the highway, forgetting all about anything that mattered to them before.

I wasn't sure which old couple in the pictures were the owners of the home, but I liked them. The home they left behind made me feel safe, the love they left behind hopeful. The strangers in the pictures were fighting their own battle to survive like we were, and probably making their way to each other, too. At least that was what I wanted to believe.

The wind picked up, moving the house just enough for the moaning to begin again. It was eerie, like the groans of the dead ones when they noticed prey and got excited about the prospect of feeding. Other than that, the night was quiet. Even Joey's movements seemed to be absent of sound.

Bryce had fallen asleep downstairs several hours before. I'd tried to relax beside him, but my eyes were wide in the dark as I listened and assessed every sound the old house made. I finally peeled the covers away and climbed the stairs of the basement, joining Joey in the living room.

He had stood dutifully beside his favorite crack in the boards, his eyes straining to see in the dark. I bumped into a side table and gasped, prompting him to ask if I was okay and a subsequent offering of shared light in the middle of the room.

"Sorry," he said, sitting across from me. "I'm not sure yet if they're attracted to light."

I shrugged, even though it was pointless. He probably couldn't see the gesture. I still didn't feel the need to voice my answer, possibly from spending so much time with Bryce, who already knew my next thought.

We sat there for some time without speaking, neither one of us uncomfortable with the silence. I was listening for any sounds that might mean trouble, and I assumed he was doing the same.

His hair was just starting to grow out from that weird military buzz cut. The dim light gave me an excuse to study his face; his prominent chin with a faint indentation in the middle, and his upper lip that was a little on the thin side. His eyes were deep set and a little buggy, but it didn't make him unattractive. I wasn't sure there was anything about him that was unattractive. It all sort of fit him and made him that much better, kind of the way imperfections give a house character.

The wind hissed through the trees, and a low rumble sounded in the distance.

"Shit. Is that thunder?"

Joey nodded, pointing a few times with his handgun. "It's going to go south of us, I think."

I opened a can of cashews and popped one into my mouth. "I can't stop wondering where my mom is. If she's okay. I wonder if she'll ever get back here."

"Where is she?"

"She and my stepdad went to Belize."

"Oh."

"Do you wonder about your parents?"

"Yeah."

"Your high school friends?"

"I've been away a long time. I joined right out of high school. You lose touch."

Talking to him was so frustrating. He didn't offer any extra information at all. "Aren't you worried about them? Your parents?"

"My mom is the daughter of a war widow, and then became one. If anyone can survive this, she can."

"You really think she made it?"

"We're from North Carolina, and the coasts were the first to get hit. I talked to her while Dana was in surgery. She was reporting all kinds of crazy shit going down, but she was at her neighbor's house, and he's a hardass former marine. I believe he's keeping her safe. I have to."

"Is everyone you know military?"

He chuckled and shook his head. "Not everyone. I lived in Jacksonville. Right next to Camp Lejeune, which happens to be the largest marine base on the East Coast. I'd say Mom has a good chance."

I smiled. "I'd say you're right. So you're a marine, then? I'm going to go out on a limb and say you're not air force."

He smiled. "What makes you say that?"

"I don't know. When I think air force, I think lanky pilot with glasses. You look like a jarhead to me."

"Oh yeah?"

"If you don't want to answer, just say so."

"I'm just enjoying the commentary. I am air force, actually. I'm a PJ."

"PJ. I'm assuming you don't mean of the pajama variety."

He chuckled quietly. "No. Of the pararescue variety."

"Oh."

" 'Oh.' You say that like you know what it is."

"I have an idea," I said, maybe a little more defensive than I would have liked.

"Okay," Joey said, holding up his hands. "Most people don't. Well, some people don't."

"*Some people*. Like females, you mean."

"Yes, that's what I mean."

I rolled my eyes. "Oh. You're one of *those* guys."

He shook his head. "I'm not. Don't peg me like that. I have a lot of respect for—"

"The girl that was in your truck?" I said, watching for his reaction.

"Dana." His eyebrows pulled together and he picked at his boots. "I'd just got back, and our friends threw a welcome-home party. It was stupid. I should have just . . . I should have just stayed home with her. Enjoyed her. She was the only one I wanted to see, anyway."

"She was yours."

He nodded and his mouth pulled to the side, and then he looked up quickly and sniffed. "Yeah. She was attacked after the party. She got really sick."

"Is that why she was in the hospital gown?"

"She had an appointment for some kind of exam. It came back bad. She'd lost like twenty pounds in a couple of days, so I knew . . . I knew that she . . . they took her straight to surgery. I was going to wait for her as long as it took, you know. I would have," he said, nodding, "but she was gone for less than an hour. They'd just opened her up and then closed. Her insides were dead. There was nothing they could do." I watched as the memory replayed in his mind, and then his face compressed, his pain filled the room, barely leaving room to breathe. "Not long after she woke up the hospital went crazy. Those things were running around attacking people, and after the phone call with my mom, I knew what was happening. I didn't know what else to do. I just scooped Dana up and ran. The goddamn truck ran out of gas just outside of Fairview, and so I held her. She was in and out a lot, but when she finally came to . . . she was in a lot of pain. They'd stapled her up. It was a pretty shoddy job. They figured in a few hours she wouldn't care. I'd watched a lot of people come back as those things while I held Dana in the truck, so when she went . . . when she went, I knew I'd have to put her down. My Glock was under the seat."

He pressed the barrel of his gun to his temple, clearly trying to push the thought from his mind.

"That's horrible."

His eyes jumped up from the floor, instantly pulling away from the horrible nightmare in his head. "I've been on two tours. I've seen limbs blown off, bones protruding . . . smashed, I've seen the incomplete bodies of children brought in and out of my helo. I've seen intestines on the outside of a man's body more than once. I've seen eyeballs hanging from their sockets.

I've seen grown men bawling and begging for their moms to save them from the death they knew was just minutes away. I've *seen* horrible. The woman I wanted to spend the rest of my life with died in my arms, and then again when I put a bullet in her brain. That was fucking gruesome."

I stared at Joey, speechless. Every word he'd just uttered and every visual that came with them sizzled as they were branded to my brain. I wanted to cry, or throw up, or run away. But instead I threw my entire body at the stranger across from me and pulled him against my chest. My fingers gripped at his T-shirt, hoping the tighter I held him, the less pain he would feel. His chin dug into the tender part between my collarbone and the muscle of my shoulder, but the pain meant nothing next to his. After his initial shock, he held me, too, and then his entire body shook as he mourned the loss of so many things. When his grip became too tight, I just kept hanging on, letting him do what was needed to finally grieve.

When he let go, he simply nodded in thanks and stood, walking over to the window to resume his post.

The space between us was suddenly thick and full of energy, but not the good kind. That moment, however innocent, was far more intimate than it should have been, and neither one of us realized it until the moment had passed. Being in his presence was suddenly unbearably awkward. "I'm, uh . . . going to head to bed," I said, whispering so low I doubted Joey could hear. That statement suddenly sounded inappropriate, too, and I cringed, hoping he didn't think it was an invitation.

I turned and pushed myself off the floor, bumping into a figure standing in the doorway. I gasped, but then relaxed, recognizing Bryce. The relief didn't last long when I saw the expression on his face. He wasn't even looking at me. Instead, he was busy boring a hole into the back of Joey's head.

"C'mon. Let's go to bed," I said, pulling Bryce with me downstairs.

His fingers were tense, as if he were holding onto a hot coal instead of my hand. He lay in bed next to me, but because he had nowhere else to go—not because he wanted to. He didn't have to say it, the betrayal he felt radiated from him like heat on a blacktop road. I had no idea what time it was, but starting a discussion that would likely lead to an argument in the middle-ish of the night wasn't appealing to me, so I closed my eyes and prayed the creaking walls wouldn't keep me awake. No matter what I said, convincing Bryce that such an intimate embrace wasn't what it seemed would be difficult when he'd calmed down and impossible when he was that angry. He had shared with me just hours before his disdain for the man I'd just had so tightly in my arms. I wondered in that moment if Bryce would have rather been outside in the dark with the dead ones than lying next to me.

Chapter Seventeen

Nathan

"GOOD MORNIN'," WALTER SAID, GREETING THE KIDS with rifle in hand.

Miranda worked to produce a smile, seeming tired and cranky. "This is my boyfriend, Bryce. That's Cooper."

I nodded to them.

"Now that the pleasantries are over," Walter said, gesturing to the station, "looks like we have a situation."

It was obvious why they'd had trouble. Two infected were inside the station, pushing excitedly against the double glass doors. One of them was a young girl, not much older than Zoe.

"Yeah," Cooper said, rubbing the back of his neck nervously. "We've run into them before."

"It should be just the two," Bryce said. "Unless more wandered inside. I put down a male. He should still be lying by the cash register."

Walter motioned for the boys to follow him. "Better let us take care of this, Nate. I don't want you to think about this every time you look at Zoe."

Regardless of the coward I might have looked like, I turned my back and tried not to listen as Walter and the boys eliminated the infected inside the gas station. Miranda kept an eye on the situation, but Ashley did as I did and looked the other way.

"Clear," the soldier said. The jargon and tone confirmed my suspicions.

I stayed with the girls while Walter helped them look for a switch to turn on the pump. The owner's resistance to new technology was fortunate. I wasn't sure we could have got it to work if it had been one of the newer ones.

"Okay!" Walter said. "Pull up the lever, and listen for it!"

"For what?" Miranda said.

I pulled up the lever, and the pump buzzed. "For that."

With a big grin, Miranda began pumping the gas, and Ashley opened the trunk and pulled out three large gas cans.

"We're in business!" Miranda said to her boyfriend.

He jogged to her side, and then interlaced his fingers on top of his head when he saw for himself. "Oh, thank God."

"I'll go get my car and fill it up, too, and then we can be on our way. You can pull up to the house and wait once you're finished here. Load up what you can."

Miranda nodded. "Will do."

They were all bouncing and smiling, excited that we would be leaving soon. Once I made the quick walk to Walter's house, I waved to Joy and Zoe, and then hopped into my car, which was still parked in the middle of the dead end.

"I'm going to fill up with gas, and then I'll be right back to get you."

Zoe smiled.

"I'll pack you a few things," Joy said. She was smiling, too, but her eyes were heavy with sadness.

Bryce was just topping off the last gas can when I pulled up. I'd passed Walter on the way. He didn't look up. I imagined he was probably sad, too, and the responsibility of surviving alone was weighing on him. Guilt burned my insides, but not enough to sway my decision. They could come with us, or we could ask the doctor's permission and then come back for them. Things weren't so bad in Shallot that they couldn't survive for another day or two. At least as long as the infected were still ambling around on the highway instead of in town.

Bryce put the last of the gas cans in the trunk, and then they crowded into the Bug. Ashley was hunched over in the backseat, sitting on both Cooper and the soldier. It looked uncomfortable as hell.

Miranda smiled. "We'll meet you at Walter's."

"Does one or two of you want to ride with me? Looks kind of cramped in there."

Miranda looked to the boy in the passenger seat, and then to those behind her. "Yeah, I bet Joey could fit better in your car."

Joey lifted his hand. "Joey."

"Nice to meet you," I said with a nod.

They pulled out of the lot onto the street, and I pulled up the lever on the pump, waiting for the noise to click on. It didn't. I jogged into the station, and toggled what I thought was the switch, but I wasn't in there when Walter had showed the boys, so I wasn't sure which it was.

I had barely crossed the parking lot and stepped into the street when I saw an infected just a block away making her way to the highway. I turned on my heels and ran back to my car, reaching inside to pull out the bag of guns Skeeter had given me.

Skeeter. As I made my way back, I thought about my brother and sister-in-law. They were both likely dead by that point. Aubrey probably was, too. Aubrey and Skeeter's parents had been gone for several years, but knowing they were all gone made the situation even sadder. Zoe was the only one left.

When I approached the porch, Walter smirked. "You forget something?" he said, nodding to my car that still sat at the pump.

I laughed once, glad for the distraction. Walter and Joy were good people. Changing their minds about joining us at the doctor's place was still a possibility. Once I got Zoe settled in, I was determined to come back for them.

"The pump didn't come on."

"No?" Walter said. "I can head back down there to see what the problem is."

"Do you mind?"

Walter descended the porch steps, taking care to use the railing. "Not like I've got anything better to do, son."

Miranda had parked in front of Walter's house, and then she and her group lingered around the Volkswagen, discussing their next move. Joy and Zoe had just come back out to the porch, Zoe with a small packed bag hung over her shoulder. Walter and I had barely stepped out into the street when gunshots rang out. We'd heard them in the distance every day, but this time they were closer. Much closer. Soon after, an engine revving echoed through the quiet streets, and then a car came careening down the main street from the highway, fishtailing out of control.

"Daddy!" Zoe yelled, just as the car T-boned mine, both crashing into the pumps.

A huge explosion accompanied by a big boom immediately took the place of the gas station. As soon as the ball of fire traveled up into the atmosphere, the charred vehicles were visible only for a moment before thick, black smoke and even more fire shot from where the pumps once were.

"What do we do?" Joy said through the hands that covered her mouth.

The kids were still standing next to their car in shock, and my hands were on my head, my fingers knotted in my hair. "No. *No*!" I yelled the second time, in complete disbelief. I knew my car was gone, but with each passing second, the comprehension of everything that being without a car meant became more real. We were trapped, unable to travel on foot, and worse, every infected lingering on the highway would be enticed back into town by the explosion.

Just as that thought entered my head, I saw the first infected. One after another they stumbled down the street, until the irregular pattern turned into groups, and then an army of undead, moving as one unit, toward the street.

"Nathan?" Miranda said, her expression frozen in fear at the sight. She reached inside of her car and pulled out a rifle. The others did the same before slowly retreating to the porch, keeping their eyes on the dirty, bloody parade.

"Move slow," Walter warned quietly as he and I backed away from the street to the house. "Don't draw their attention over here."

The kids were at least smart enough not to make any sudden movements. I glanced up at Zoe, who was watching with a blank face like it was something she'd seen a hundred times before. As a knee-jerk reaction, I thought about discussing her lack of reaction at Zoe's next therapy session, but there would be no more counselors, or evaluations, or IEP plans.

It seemed that once we realized Zoe was not like other children our lives had been consumed with meetings and doctor's appointments, care plans and behavior management. Life was difficult enough for those of us that could process stress and overstimulation normally. Even when we had what seemed like limitless tools to help Zoe head off or navigate the meltdowns, life would never be easy for her. A different panic emerged, one that we couldn't run away from: Those things we took for granted were no longer available. The recognition of that truth made a wave of dread wash over me. Zoe thrived on routine, and she was without treatment during this decimation of everything familiar. A plague that could last months, or years . . . or forever. Zoe would have to survive both.

"We could wait this out downstairs," Walter said, pulling me back to the current problem. The break in his voice signaled that not even he believed his words.

I gripped the bag in my hand, thankful I'd taken it from the car. "We can't stay here, Walter. With all of those things in town, it's not safe."

Joy's eyes left me and settled on her husband, resigned. "Maybe it never was."

Walter's lips turned into a hard line. "Goddamnit. God damn those things."

We all retreated inside the house. Joy scrambled around to pack, and the boys stood next to the windows to keep watch. Miranda and Ashley helped Joy put as much food as they could carry into bags, and then we met in the kitchen.

"I don't . . . have a lot of room in my car," Miranda said.

"My Taurus is in the garage," Walter said, grabbing a set of keys hanging from a nail on the wall. The key ring was made of multi-color plastic that spelled ORLANDO.

"Okay, Zoe and I will ride with Walter and Joy. Problem solved."

Miranda nodded nervously.

"They're starting to fan out!" Bryce said.

A muffled, high-pitched yapping came from next door, and we all froze.

Joy blanched. "Dear Jesus, it's Princess."

Bryce and Cooper leaned against the windows to get a better look. Princess continued to bark excitedly at the horrifying procession. It didn't take long for the first of them to notice the barking and veer away from the others.

"We can't wait," Bryce said. "We have to go now before any more come down this dead end."

Miranda nodded, and then looked to me. "He's right, Nate. It's time to go."

"But what about Princess?" Zoe asked.

Joy leaned down to Zoe with tears in her eyes. "We'll come back for her, sweetie."

Walter held out his hand to his wife, and we followed them to the garage. Miranda and Joey lifted the garage door while Ashley and Bryce loaded Joy's bags into the trunk. Zoe and I settled into the backseat of the Taurus and waited for Walter to start the car. After a few seconds, the engine made a sickly whirring sound and then Walter turned to me.

"Walter?" I said.

"I . . . I don't know. I just changed the oil and filter thinking we were headed to see Darla."

"Try it again," I said, trying to keep my voice calm.

"They're coming!" Ashley cried.

"Shit. Shit!" Cooper yelled, pulling Ashley toward the house.

Walter tried the ignition again, but this time the Taurus's engine wouldn't even turn over. "M-maybe it's the uh . . . alternator. I had trouble with it last year . . ."

"We don't have time to figure it out, let's go!" I said, opening the door and pulling Zoe with me.

Bryce and Joey were already fighting with a few infected by the time we made it inside. A shot was fired off, and then they were inside with us.

Cooper had a look of bewilderment on his face. "I'm sorry," he said, a gun in his hand. "It almost bit Joey."

I rushed to the window. More were filing down the street. Princess's barks were at an even higher pitch as the infected climbed up onto her porch and pawed at the window where she stood. Bryce and Miranda pulled the refrigerator in front of the door in the kitchen that led to the garage. A dozen or more infected were on and around the porch, pounding on the front door and windows. The glass broke, and I threw Zoe over my shoulder. "The bedrooms! Go out the back!"

When we reached the bedroom, the kids were pulling the dresser in front of the bedroom door, and Joy was pulling a long, wooden stake from the bottom of the sliding door. She stood up and immediately panicked.

"Walter? Walter!" she screamed.

Walter was standing at the other patio door, trying his damnedest to slide open the glass. He had somehow gone one way when we went the other, and, unlike us, he had no one with him to barricade the bedroom door while he tried to escape to the backyard. A group of infected appeared behind him. His eyes grew wide as they tore into him, but he kept trying to claw at the door, realizing too late that he'd failed to remove the wooden block they'd placed there for protection.

Joy was right behind me, and her loud screams for her husband made my right ear buzz. The infected mashed him against the glass, biting into him. He screamed, and the sound, although muffled, made the hairs on the back of my neck stand on end.

"Walter!" Joy bawled, tears streaming down her face. She clawed at the glass, and then yanked the door open. She ran to the adjacent door, working in a panic to free her husband.

"Joy! Joy! Joy!" Zoe bawled, reaching for her friend. Her words bounced as each of my feet hit the ground. I held on to my daughter tight, afraid she would wriggle free.

Joey opened the back fence gate, and led the kids to the Bug.

I watched them squeeze in, and then Bryce shut the door.

It was then that I recognized our fate. "Please, take her," I said, standing at the passenger door.

Miranda started the car.

Bryce looked past us to what was sure to be a mob of infected headed in our direction. "We don't have room. I'm sorry."

"Daddy, no!" Zoe screamed. She balled up her fists, gripping my shirt in her tiny hands so tightly that her arms shook.

"Please!" I said, staring straight into Miranda's eyes. "I have no way to get her out of here. She's small. She'll fit."

Miranda looked to Bryce. He shook his head. "Let's go, Miranda. Go! Go!"

She pulled the gear into drive, and then Cooper shoved Bryce forward and reached for the handle. As soon as he reached it, he pulled the door open and jumped out.

"What are you doing?" Ashley cried.

"She can have my seat," Cooper said to Bryce.

"Coop, no," Bryce said, his eyes widening at whatever was happening behind us. "We don't have time for this, let's go!"

Cooper tore Zoe from my grip with one hand and pulled Bryce's seat forward with the other, pushing Zoe into the seat. She was fighting him, but Joey grabbed hold of her. Cooper shut the door.

"I can help Nathan get to Red Hill."

"It's ten miles from here, Coop! No!" Ashley said, squeezing between the front seats to reach for him.

"Daddy!" Zoe said, leaning away from Joey.

"I'll see you soon, honey. It's okay. Daddy will see you soon."

Cooper touched my shoulder. "I know the way, Zoe. I promise I'll get him there, okay? Don't worry."

"We have to go!" Bryce said. "For any of us to have a chance, we have to go right now, Miranda!"

Miranda's face crumpled, distorted from guilt. "Run fast, Coop."

Cooper nodded and winked at Ashley. "I can make ten miles in an hour, baby. No problem."

"Don't leave him, Miranda, please!" Ashley begged, reaching out for him. "No, please! Please! *No*!" her screams trailed as they pulled away.

Cooper raised his gun and shot behind me. I turned, seeing an infected fall to the ground.

"I was all-state four years in high school. I was the man to beat in college. I hope you can run, Nathan, because I made Zoe a promise."

I nodded. "So did I."

Chapter Eighteen

Scarlet

THE MOTHS AND LIGHTNING BUGS WERE BOUNCING AND gliding over the top of the prairie grass not far from me. I sat on the top step of the wooden deck that doubled as a front porch, waving away the mosquitos buzzing in my ears. The crest of the red dirt road that Jenna and Halle might be walking toward was bright, lit by the setting sun. There were so many variables for them to make it to the safety of Red Hill. What if Andrew hadn't made it back to the house to see my spray-painted message on the wall? What if the girls were too upset to know what it meant? What if they had forgotten Halle's song? Carrying those questions with me all day and night weighed down on me and made it too easy for exhaustion to set in, but I kept busy with getting the house cleaned and ready for the girls' arrival.

With wooden stakes and fishing line that I'd found in the barn, I'd strung a primitive alarm system around the perimeter. The dirt was still soft enough from the previous night's rain that it was fairly easy to shove the stakes into the ground. In just half a day, I'd bounced along the ground, winding the string around the stakes, poking holes in the cans, and stringing them on the line before moving a few feet down to start the process all over again. The line was far enough from the house that if I was awoken in the night, I would have time to get a weapon and defend myself. Stringing the line was easy; it was trying not to lie awake, waiting for something to rattle the cans, that was hard.

Six days after the world ended, the lines hadn't jingled once. The few shufflers that had come close always stayed to the road for whatever reason. Maybe they'd already come upon other houses and had learned that a building didn't necessarily mean a meal. If I stayed quiet, most didn't bother me.

I sat on the porch, aware that a beautiful sunset was visible from the backside of the house, but when I wasn't checking the wooden slats I'd nailed to the windows, eating, sleeping, or practicing with Dr. Hayes's guns, I was watching that red dirt road, waiting for Andrew's white Tahoe to fly over in a hurry to reach their destination, or for my babies' heads to rise above the hill, higher with each step. I imagined that moment a hundred times a day: They would be worn and filthy, but very much alive. I didn't even mind that their arrival would mean living with Andrew again. If it meant having my babies, I welcomed it.

Every night my hopes were dashed and my heart was broken. I never gave up until it was too dark for safe travel. But about this time was when the tears came. I picked at the small stick in my hand, fighting the desperation and helplessness that overwhelmed me.

Earlier that day, I thought I'd heard thunder, but the sound echoed from the east, and the storm clouds were off to the west. At first I thought I'd imagined the noise, but then a tall pillar of smoke rose slowly, high above the tree line. I prayed to God that whatever it was, it had nothing to do with Jenna and Halle.

When I heard the noise coming from beyond the hill directly in front of the house, I trusted my ears. A voice yelled intermittently. Then, another began to answer back. My eyes narrowed, and then my heart leapt seeing two heads bobbing just above the tall prairie grass. When two men became visible, I stood. When the herd of shufflers following behind them appeared just as they cleared the hill, I cursed under my breath and retreated inside the house.

"Help us!" one of the men yelled. I grabbed Dr. Hayes's hunting rifle, and peered through the scope. The first of the men was younger, maybe late teens or early twenties. The other was a head taller, but older, maybe in his midthirties like me, his shaggy dark-blond hair bouncing as he ran. He was wearing a suit and loosened tie, the younger was in a T-shirt and jeans with boots on. The boots didn't slow him down. He had probably been running for miles and still managed to keep an exhausting pace. The older man wasn't far behind him, puffing and drenched in sweat.

I cocked the rifle and aimed at the closest shuffler. "Goddamn it," I said, knowing the noise would carry, and might attract shufflers from the next two towns. I pulled the trigger, and took the damn thing out. The men—without slowing—covered their heads and ducked. The shufflers' pace was between a walk and a jog. The older man was at least fifteen feet ahead of the fastest shufflers, but they were leading them directly to the ranch.

"Don't shoot us! It's me!" the young man said, waving his arms in the air.

What the hell is he talking about? I assumed he was just scared and talking nonsense. I reloaded and then shot at the next shuffler in line. I'd missed my target. My heart began to hammer against my rib cage. I had brought a box of ammo to the porch with me, but at least thirty shufflers had followed those men over the crest of the hill. A few weeks on the gun range four years ago didn't exactly make me a marksman.

The younger man tripped over the fishing line, but as he worked to get it off, he just became more tangled. The other man checked behind him to get a glimpse of the shufflers before stooping down and trying to help.

"You've got to be kidding me!" I said, steadying the rifle against my shoulder and looking through the scope. I tried not to rush, but half a dozen shufflers would be on top of them in five seconds. I pulled the trigger and felt the gun recoil against my bone. The first went down, I missed the second but hit him with a third shot, and the next two seemed to walk right into my sights. Before I needed to shoot a sixth time, the kid was free and they were sprinting toward the house.

"Where's the Bug?" the young man asked, confused by the sight of me.

I jerked my head back to the house. "I'll explain later. There are rifles on the sofa. Grab one and get your ass back out here. They're going to be knocking on the front door in a minute." I peeked through the sights and continued to shoot. Soon, there were two more sources of gunfire, one on each side of me.

By the time they hit the fishing line, the herd looked more like a small group. The loud booming of our rifles seemed to fall into a rhythm. Later I would consider us fortunate that both men at least knew how to shoot a gun. It wasn't something I'd thought to ask in the moment.

We kept shooting until they'd all fallen. I watched the shufflers for a moment, making sure all of them were downed. After a full minute with no movement, I met the eyes of the bewildered men on each side of me. I backed up to the door and pointed my gun in their general direction, just in case they realized I was alone and could rob me—or worse.

"My name is Stanley Cooper. I'm Ashley's boyfriend. Have you seen her? Have they been here?" Before I could answer, the kid began to panic, rubbing the back of his neck and looking around. "They're not here, Nate. They didn't make it."

Recognizing the situation, Nate glanced at my gun for a fraction of a second before staring down the road. His eyes narrowed, focusing on the crest of the red dirt with the same desperate, hopeful expression on his face that I'd had for the last six days.

"Okay, so we head down the road and look for them," Nate said.

"Wait," I said, letting the end of the rifle drop a bit. "Ashley Hayes?"

"Yes!" Stanley said. "Have you seen her?"

"No."

His face fell as the last bit of hope I'd given him disappeared. "They should be here by now!"

"It's almost dark," I said. "You shouldn't leave. They're out more at night. Getting snuck up on is a good way to get killed."

Stanley interlocked his fingers on top of his head, and after a short moment of deliberation, looked to Nate. "I'm goin'."

Nate nodded, and then looked at me. "Do you have any flashlights we could borrow?"

I nodded, went inside to the kitchen, grabbed a flashlight from under the sink, and then got another from the bedroom, returning to the porch. They both snapped the flashlights from my hands.

Nate took a deep breath. He was exhausted, but for whatever reason, he was just as anxious to find Ashley. "We'll bring back the guns."

I didn't answer, knowing I shouldn't say what I truly believed: They wouldn't make it back. Wandering around in the dark was a death wish. I narrowed my eyes, glancing down the road to where they were headed. Barely visible in the dim light, a cloud of red dust puffed just above the road. "Wait. Wait! Look!" I said, pointing to the road.

Nate and Stanley had just left the porch to start their run when they eyed a white Bug catch air over the hill. It jerked into the drive as if it were being chased, bouncing over every pothole before sliding to a stop.

Stanley ran over to one side of the car, Nate on the other. The driver was Miranda, Ashley's sister, and her boyfriend, Bryce, stepped out from the passenger side. I'd only seen him once before. I'd never met Stanley, and as I watched him pull Ashley from the backseat, I wondered if he was a new boyfriend. I remembered Dr. Hayes calling Ashley's boyfriend by a different name.

Ashley was nearly hysterical, wailing and clawing at Stanley's shirt. Her eyes were swollen and red, long soaked from the tears she'd wept while they were apart. Nate leaned down and pulled a tiny girl from the backseat. She wrapped her arms and legs around him as best she could as he held her, silently weeping, clearly emotionally exhausted. My chest burned at the sight of her. She was about Halle's size, and I knew immediately that she belonged to Nate. Seeing them reunite made the need to see my daughters unbearable.

Another man, a head taller than everyone but Bryce, climbed from the backseat. He scanned the house with wary eyes, making me feel on edge. He was different than the others. He moved differently, and his eyes took in everything.

"Where've you been?" Stanley said.

Miranda's face turned instantly annoyed. "She made us wait at the corner by the water tower. I finally got her to agree to let us leave at dark."

Stanley's head jerked to look at Ashley. "I told you I would meet you here," he scolded. "It made more sense for us to cut across. Why would you wait at the road? Are you nuts?"

More tears spilled down Ashley's red cheeks.

Miranda raised an eyebrow. "That's what I told her. We could have been here with Dad and not listening to Zoe freak out for the last four hours!"

Nate hugged his daughter tighter.

The man with no name smirked. He towered over most of the others. Just the sight of him made my fingers grasp my rifle tighter. His chest bulged from his white T-shirt, which was speckled with blood. The red stains were spattered down his jeans, too, varying from specks to large splotches. "Are you just getting here?" He clearly wasn't impressed with their time.

Stanley nodded to the top of the hill and the mess of bodies in the yard. "It's not a straight shot, and we had company. We ran into hills, and a creek. It was rough going. We tried leading the ones that caught up to us away from the house, but then ran into more. And Nathan had to rest a few times."

Oh. His name was *Nathan*. That fit him better, anyway.

"Where are you guys coming from?" I asked.

Nathan paused from whispering things into his daughter's ear. "Shallot. It's about ten miles straight across."

I glanced around, grabbed the flashlight from Nathan, and jogged out to the fishing line. The shufflers had pulled it loose and a few sections were lying on the ground. I pulled the line from the some of the shufflers' decaying ankles and then re-wrapped it around the stakes, pulling them taut.

Pulling the downed shufflers into the field and burning them crossed my mind, but it was nearly dark. Resigned to leave it until the next day, I joined the others inside the house.

Miranda met me at the door. "Where is my dad?"

I glanced at Ashley. The sisters had already been through hell, and I hated to make it worse. I just shook my head a little, unable to say the words.

Miranda lowered her chin. "What?"

"When I got here, he was . . . Leah had . . . I buried them. By the tree."

Miranda turned on her heels, ran through the living room and kitchen into the laundry room, and pushed out the storm door. Bryce followed her. I walked over to the window and peered between the wooden slats. Miranda fell on her knees and covered her face; Bryce began to touch her face, but then acted like he couldn't decide where to place his hand, finally settling on his neck. He paced back and forth, offering words of comfort.

Ashley was sniffing and crying quietly, most likely already cried out for the day.

"She should come back in," I said softly. "It's not safe out there."

"Thank you," Nathan said. His voice was so smooth and calming. "For helping us. That was pretty impressive."

"You're welcome," I said. "I'm glad everyone made it here safely."

Nathan walked away, twisting his upper body and whispering something into his daughter's ear. His shaggy hair was opposite his gray suit and boring tie. He glanced back at me, and I looked away, realizing at the same time he did that I was still staring. It had been a while since I'd felt anything but fear. Next to the nightmare we were all living, embarrassment didn't seem so bad.

I looked at Nathan again from the corners of my eyes, trying not to get caught. The girl's eyes were getting heavy, and I found myself curious about their situation: Where was her mother? Did they find themselves together much like Andrew found himself now with the girls?

"He's nice," Stanley whispered. His voice was tired and sad, but the corners of his mouth were turned up ever so slightly. "If you were wondering."

"I wasn't," I said, shaking my head and dropping my eyes to the ground.

Nathan

FOUR HOURS OF WORRYING AND BEING IN AN UNFAMILiar situation had exhausted Zoe in every way anyone could be exhausted, and while I was watching the woman with the fiery red hair and staggering blue eyes break it to Miranda and Ashley that their father was dead, I noticed a pair of French doors right off the living room and peeked in, seeing a king-size bed that took up most of the room around it. There were piles of clothes everywhere, and opened dresser drawers. Odd, because the rest of the house was immaculate.

Zoe didn't flinch when I peeled back the covers and let her sink into the pillow-top mattress. The luxurious down pillow and high thread count of the sheets didn't match the farmhouse. As I thought about the custom-made tree-trunk coffee table in the living room, and the seventy-inch flat screen, I decided that wasn't true. There were a few oddly placed expensive items peppered inside the old, outdated house. That puzzled me, much like the tiny woman with a huge set of balls holding the rifle in the living room.

I waited to be sure Zoe was sound asleep, and then stepped into the living room, listening to Ashley weep quietly on Cooper's shoulder. She was asking the mystery woman how her father died and about a woman named Leah. The answers were vague, I assumed on purpose. The details didn't really matter, only that two girls had lost their father, and everything they expected to find here was gone with him.

Cooper held Ashley as she shook and moaned, rubbing at her face and raking her back in frustration as she bounced between devastation and anger. Finally, she met the woman's eyes.

"Why are you here, Scarlet?"

Scarlet sighed, and then scratched her head. "It seemed like the safest place, and I knew there was a chance my girls would come here."

Ashley sat up as Scarlet sat down on the couch. She seemed to be suddenly exhausted, as if saying the words out loud took the last bit of energy she had.

Ashley sniffed and wiped her nose with the sleeve of her jacket. "Why aren't they with you?"

I braced myself for what she might say.

Scarlet fidgeted, clearly trying not to break down. Ashley obviously knew her, but from what I could gather from the bit of conversation I'd caught earlier, their father's significant other was buried outside with him. The woman sitting on the couch didn't seem to be family, so I wondered how she would know about this place, so far removed from everything.

"Scarlet?" Ashley prodded. "Where are your girls?"

"They're coming."

"Here?" Ashley said, sounding surprised. "How do you know?"

"Because I left them a message. On Andrew's wall."

The conversation made less sense as it went along, and Ashley didn't seem to understand, either. Agitated, Scarlet stood up and disappeared into the back of the house. Ashley and Cooper traded glances, and then we all looked to the side door leading to wherever the father was buried. Bryce was leading Miranda inside the house, shutting the wooden door. The bottom half was wood, the top half Plexiglas.

"We're going to need to board that up," I said. "Tonight."

Joey nodded and stood up from the corner. I'd almost forgotten he was here, he'd been so quiet. "I'll help you."

Bryce jerked his head toward the door, careful not to take his arms from around Miranda. "There should be some leftover wood in the barn. Be careful. There's a bull out there."

As Joey passed Miranda, she watched him walk by, and I assumed by the way her eyes fell to the floor that something wasn't right. I had been conditioned by Aubrey for years to detect a problem and buffer it before it got too far out of control. These people were still strangers, but I had a very real fear that if the delicate fibers of our group broke down, Joey, my daughter, and I would be the first to go. The others seemed to know each other. We were the outsiders, and I needed to ensure my and Zoe's place here.

With the flashlight Scarlet had given me, I shined the light around in the darkness until it highlighted the side of the barn. I could already hear the grunts and movements of the bull. Fortunately the boards were in a different part of the barn than where the animal was corralled.

"Let's get this and get back in," I said. "We don't want anything sneaking up on us out here."

Joey nodded and lifted a stack of boards up into his arms with a grunt. I picked a stack as well, and we made our way back to the house. Scarlet brought a small, red, carry toolbox and set it on top of the dryer. "I didn't board this because there aren't many nails left."

"We'll make do," I said, pulling the hammer out of the box. As I hit the nail head and watched it slide easily through the board to the wood on the other side, I thought of Gary and Eric from the church in Fairview, and wondered if they were alive. And then I thought of Skeeter, and of Jill, and their unborn baby. I hadn't had much time to mourn them, so I took out my anger and pain on each nail as I buried it into the boards.

The last nail was used to secure the second board horizontally across the center of the Plexiglas. It wasn't enough, but it would keep something out long enough to give us time to react.

We left the stack of wood in the laundry room, and returned to the living room, where Miranda and Ashley were comforting each other. Scarlet had rejoined the group, sitting in the same spot she couldn't stand to be in less than half an hour before. I wondered about her daughters and why they weren't with her, but didn't want to upset her again by asking. I followed her eyes to a frame on the wall across the room. A creased picture of Scarlet, a man, and two girls was inside.

Beyond the walls of the farmhouse was blackness only a place far away from city lights could provide. Even the moon had hidden away behind thick clouds. Scarlet stood up and busied herself with pulling hanging dark sheets across the wooden slats, and then brought a box of matches to light a few candles around the room. We sat in silence for what seemed like forever, and then a low rumble echoed from miles away.

"Thunder," Ashley said, looking around.

"I noticed some pretty dark blue clouds back there," Scarlet said, pointing her thumb to the east. "The wind is blowing west."

"It won't miss us this time," Joey said.

Scarlet glanced at the soldier, and a light of recognition touched her eyes. Joey met her stare, seeming hopeful that she might say something. Scarlet was the first to look away. The awkwardness between everyone was bugging the shit out of me.

"So are you guys family?" I said to Miranda, motioning to Scarlet.

Miranda shook her head. "Scarlet works with my dad . . . *worked* with my dad."

Scarlet nodded and smiled. "I'm an X-ray tech. Miranda's dad is Dr. Hayes."

"*Was* Dr. Hayes," Miranda corrected, staring at the flame dancing above the candle on the coffee table.

"Stop it," Ashley hissed.

"I've been so mean to him," Miranda said, holding her shaking hand to her mouth. "I'll never get to tell him I'm sorry. I'll never get to talk to him again."

Bryce squeezed her to his side. His eyes were moist, too, and it was apparent that the boys were close with the doctor as well. "He knew you were having a tough time with the divorce. He knew you loved him."

"Did he?"

Ashley lost her battle to hold in a sob. She kneeled in front of Miranda and then rested her head on her sister's knees.

Scarlet nodded. "He knew, Miranda. I promise, he did."

Miranda and Ashley cried together again, with Bryce and Cooper on each side.

"Did everyone that Dr. Hayes worked with know where he lived?" I asked. The more they talked, the more confused I became.

Scarlet seemed to be amused by my nosey question. "I cleaned for him when I was in X-ray school." Her eyes glistened. "He was very kind to me. They both were."

"Both?"

"Wes and Leah," Scarlet said.

Ashley leaned against Cooper, thinking fondly of the two. "Leah was my dad's girlfriend. She was very sweet."

"She was," Cooper nodded.

Ashley shook her head slowly. "I can't believe she's gone.

That they're gone." She looked to her sister. "I hate this. I want to wake up and this all be a bad dream." She began to rock back and forth a bit, struggling with the new reality we all faced. "I don't want this."

"None of us do," Miranda snapped. She sighed, realizing she was too harsh. "We've had a long day. Bryce and I will take my room; Ashley and Coop have their own. Scarlet, I guess you've been sleeping in dad's room?"

Scarlet nodded. "Yes, but the girl is in there. I'll take the couch."

"You sure?" I said.

Scarlet offered a small smile, and then looked to Joey. "There is a couch downstairs in the basement, but it might not be big enough for you. I can switch with you if you'd like."

Joey shook his head. "The basement sounds good to me. I'll make a pallet if I have to."

"I'll show you the linen closet," Scarlet said, standing. That prompted everyone else to stand, and Scarlet laughed once without humor. "I'm glad you all made it," she said, her voice breaking. "I was afraid I was the only one left."

Scarlet could clearly take care of herself, and wasn't the slightest bit fragile, but something about the way her voice broke made me want to pull her into my arms and hold her. She and Joey walked away, and the distance created lessened my urge to comfort her. I shook my head and silently scolded myself. I'd just met her, and she probably didn't need anyone to make her feel better, anyway, not that there was any way for someone to feel better about being separated from their children in days like these.

I went into the doctor's bedroom and closed the French

doors behind me, sliding quietly under the covers beside Zoe. Even as I thought about the horrors of the last few days, warmth washed over me, comforted by the knowledge that this was the safest place to raise my little girl. At least until someone found a cure for the sickness that had taken so much from everyone under that roof. Knowing we weren't alone and that we were still waiting for others was the most comforting. That was a hope I would help Scarlet hang on to.

Chapter Nineteen

Miranda

I'D IMAGINED SO MANY TIMES IN THE LAST WEEK WHAT it would feel like to finally lie down in my bed, to feel the safety of the walls that my dad's house provided, but even under a familiar comforter, my head resting on a pillow I'd picked out myself, I didn't feel at home. I felt sick, displaced, and afraid.

Bryce was lying behind me, his body outlining mine. My body was nearly in a ball, but Bryce made sure to surround me with his warmth and love, as if it would keep reality away.

"I can't remember the last thing I said to him, but I don't think it was anything nice," I whispered.

"He was excited that you were coming. If you weren't nice to him, he obviously didn't notice."

"I wanted to hug him." I sniffed, turning my head so the sleeve of my zipup hoodie could catch more tears. "Getting here and being safe meant him being here to protect us. I don't know where my mom is, and my dad is dead. Leah's dead. I have no one."

Bryce propped his head up with his hand. "You have Ashley, and you have me."

Those words should have offered more comfort than they did. I lay there until the rain began to patter on the roof and Bryce's breathing turned deep, and rhythmic. The lightning cast quick flashes and shadows on the wall, including my own as I quietly snuck to the door and into the living room.

Scarlet was asleep on the couch, a rifle nestled in her arms like a child. She'd always been kind to us, and her little girls were so sweet. Once when Dad made Ashley and I help him burn brush, Jenna and Halle helped, too, entertaining us so much that by the time we were finished, it barely seemed like we'd started.

I crept over to the front door and twisted the knob.

"I wouldn't," Scarlet whispered in the dark.

I jumped, and then when my nerves stopped trying to jump out of my skin, I sat on the rocking chair adjacent to the couch Scarlet was resting on.

"That was smart. The cans, I mean. I would have never thought of it."

She didn't raise her head, and if she hadn't spoken to me moments before, I would have thought she was still asleep. Lightning lit up the room for a second, and I caught sight of a tear dripping from her nose.

"They're probably worried about you, too," I said. Trying to comfort someone else made me feel better. It kept my mind off the fact that I was probably an orphan.

"I worry about them being outside in this weather," Scarlet said, sitting up. "I worry that Andrew was hurt or killed and they're alone."

"Worrying won't help them."

"I know," she said quietly. "You shouldn't go outside. I've watched out the window at night. Sometimes I catch glimpses of shufflers in the fields. They're not that fast, and not that smart. Getting caught off guard is how they get you. That, or getting caught in a big group of them like on the highway."

"By Shallot?"

Scarlet nodded.

"We've been staying there. In Shallot. They were all on the highway, but now they're in town."

"You sure about that?"

"Someone ran their car into the gas station. Blew up. Drew them all back in."

Scarlet's eyebrows pulled in, and she closed her eyes. "Was it a white Tahoe?"

"Huh?"

"The car that hit the station. Was it a white Tahoe?"

"No. Is that what your ex drives?"

Scarlet opened her eyes and sighed.

"So they're with him."

After a short pause, Scarlet rested her elbows on her knees. "I hope so. Andrew picked them up from school. By the time I got off work and everything went to shit, they were in Anderson."

I waited, watching her eyes search the darkness for something.

"I tried to get to them," she said. Her breath caught sharply. "I snuck into town. They weren't home. The town was overrun. I didn't know what to do." Her voice broke, and she covered her mouth with a trembling hand. "So I left them a message to come here. I'm not sure it was the right decision . . . to leave. Did I abandon them?"

"I saw you," I said. Scarlet's head jerked up to meet my eyes. "In that Jeep. I saw you heading toward Fairview on the highway. You got past them?"

"Past who?" Scarlet asked.

"The kids with the guns. On the bridge."

"Yeah," she said quietly, looking down. "I got past them."

"You're lucky," I said. "We were stuck under the overpass. They opened fire on everyone."

Scarlet offered a small, tired smile. "I guess you were lucky, too."

"Who shot at you?" A deep voice said. I turned to see Joey standing in the dark kitchen.

"Jesus, you scared the shit out of me," Scarlet said, blowing out a quick breath.

"Men—kids, actually—at the Anderson bridge had guns, shooting at anyone trying to get in," I said, watching Joey sit on the carpet next to me.

"Good thing we ran out of gas. We were headed to Anderson. Dana's dad lived there."

"Small world," Scarlet said, her smile fading.

Joey sighed. "Even smaller now."

We sat in silence for a while, listening to the thunder rumble and the lightning crack across the sky. The sky opened up and rain poured down, drenching the farmhouse until it moved slowly toward Shallot and then Fairview. I thought of the dead ones, if they even noticed the storm, and of the small children in Shallot with the milky eyes that just a few days ago might have been terrified of thunder and lightning. They were now ambling outside, impervious to the rain, the wind, and the monsters walking alongside them.

"Dana liked storms," Joey said. "She would have wanted to go outside and dance in the rain."

"Dana is your wife?" Scarlet said.

"She was going to be."

"You lost her," Scarlet said, more a statement than a question.

"A couple of times."

Scarlet's eyebrows pulled together. I thought about explaining, but it wasn't my story to tell.

"You saw my father?" I asked.

"I saw him at work," she said. "He was really excited about you girls coming here for the weekend. It was all he talked about."

Tears burned my eyes again.

Scarlet continued, "We were busy, so I didn't get to talk to him much. Mostly just that morning . . ." Scarlet seemed to get lost in a thought, and then she looked up. "Joey?"

"Yeah?"

"You said your girlfriend's name was Dana?" Joey nodded and Scarlet shook her head. "Was she at the hospital Friday?"

Joey nodded.

"I met her!" Scarlet said. She smiled and touched her chest. "I did her exam! She met Miranda's dad!"

Scarlet's smile seemed so out of place for the discussion, but I was waiting for Joey's reaction. At first, he just stared back at her blank-faced, and then a small smile turned up the corners of his mouth. "She was beautiful."

Scarlet nodded emphatically. "Oh my God, she was. Crazy about you, too. You being there was so comforting to her."

Joey nodded. Even in the dim light, I could see his eyes fill with tears.

Scarlet yawned. "Wow. Crazy how we all ended up here," she said. She lay on the couch, and used her bent arm as a pillow.

Joey and I stood; that was our cue. Joey walked a few steps toward the laundry room, and then stopped and turned. "I don't sleep much. You're welcome to hang out downstairs with me, if you want."

I knew I shouldn't. I looked to Scarlet for judgment or guidance, but her eyes were already closed. "Okay," I said, following him downstairs. I'd been up and down that stairway so many times since my father had bought that ranch, but this time was different. My blood rose to the surface of my cheeks, and burned hotter with every step. When we walked into the vast space of the finished basement, Joey raised his arms.

"Welcome to my place."

I smiled. "Technically, it's my place."

Joey sat on the floor, and I sat on the loveseat. I glanced to each side of me, amused that Scarlet had to guess if he would fit. His legs from thighs down would have hung off the end.

We spent hours talking about how long my father had owned the ranch, how Ashley and I spent our summers there, and the stupid predicaments we would get into, like the time she lost her shoe in the mud because we snuck out in the middle of the night to meet Bryce and his friends so they could drive us to the Diversion Dam for Matt Painter's kegger.

It felt good to laugh and remember things that didn't mean anything at the time. Any good memories were everything now.

Joey's eyes began to redden and droop, and I was finally feeling the effects of exhaustion myself, so I stood and headed for the stairs. Something stopped me, and I turned.

"Joey?"

"Yeah?"

"Why did it make you so happy to know that Scarlet did Dana's exam? Wasn't she really sick then?"

Joey nodded. "Yeah, but . . . I don't know. Talking to someone else who knew Dana when she was alive makes her real, you know? It's easy to forget that our lives before weren't a dream. This isn't the reality, how we're meant to live, or who we are. The people we were seven days ago . . . that is who we are, and Scarlet remembering Dana when she was alive makes that true."

I shook my head. I still didn't understand.

Joey shrugged. "It feels good to know she lives in someone else's memory, too."

I offered a small smile, and shoved my hands in the pockets of my hoodie. "Goodnight."

Nathan

MY EYES PEELED OPEN, AND IT TOOK A MOMENT FOR ME to recall where I was and why. Simultaneously, I remembered that Zoe was supposed to be asleep next to me, and realized that her side of the bed was empty. In a panic, I scrambled over the bed and ran through the French doors to the living room. Zoe was sitting at the head of the dining room table, chomping away on Frosted Mini-Wheats and chatting Scarlet's ear off.

Scarlet was sitting in the chair next to Zoe, her chin resting in her hand, listening intently to every word my daughter uttered. Zoe and Scarlet mirrored each other's happiness in that moment, and I got a little choked up at the sight of them. Zoe's sweet smile had returned, and Scarlet's fiery red hair glowed in the morning sun that poured through cracks in the wooden slats on the window. I wasn't sure I'd seen anything more beautiful.

Once Scarlet caught a glimpse of me, she pushed away from the table and went outside. Zoe took another bite, and I winked at her before joining Scarlet on the porch. She was staring down the dirt road, longing for her daughters, I imagined.

"My daughter Halle isn't much older than Zoe," she said, covering her mouth with a few of her fingers. Her pink nail polish was nearly completely chipped away, but her fingers were still elegant.

"How old is the other one? You have two, right?"

Scarlet cast a curious glance in my direction.

"The picture on the wall."

"Just the two," she said with a guarded smile. "Jenna is thirteen." I laughed once, and Scarlet nodded. "Boy, is she ever."

"I can't imagine."

"You will," she said. Her smile faded. "They were supposed to meet me here if something happened. They were with their father when . . . I couldn't get to them."

"They know their way?"

She nodded. "Halle made up a song. She makes up a song for everything. It used to drive me crazy. I try to remember some of them, but I can't," she whispered the last bit. "Having all of Halle's artwork from school all over my Suburban was maddening. I remember getting on her case for it so many times. I wish to God I had just one piece of that now. That picture is all I have of them."

Her blue eyes glistened, and I fought the urge to wrap my arms around her. Before that thought was complete, her soft, red hair was under my chin, and her hands were interlocked at the small of my back. It took me a moment to realize what was happening, but then I rested my cheek against her hair and squeezed her tight. She wept quietly in my arms, and I waited patiently until she stopped shaking.

She let go first, and wiped her eyes. "I'm sorry. That was probably a weird thing to do."

"Nothing is weird anymore," I said with a half-smile.

She laughed, for maybe the first time since this all started. It sounded like music and sunshine. "That's true." Her eyes wandered back to the crest of the hill, and we waited in silence for a while until Zoe called for me. I left her alone to tend to my daughter. After an hour, Zoe tugged on my slacks.

"Is she going to stay out there all day?"

"I don't know," I said. Scarlet hadn't moved. She watched the road like she was expecting her children to come over the hill at any moment.

Minutes later, Scarlet tore herself away and came back in, immediately checking the nails in the slats, and then finding things to organize or clean.

Miranda and Bryce emerged from their bedroom. Miranda's eyes were swollen. It looked like she'd been crying again. Bryce was holding her hand, and squeezed it once before letting go to make them some breakfast.

"We should be careful what we consume," Joey said. "We'll probably have to go back to Shallot eventually for supplies."

"Not for a while," Bryce said, opening the cabinet. It was stocked full. "There is a pantry, too. A big one."

"What about the water situation?" Joey asked.

"Well," Ashley said, following Cooper out of her room. They were more affectionate toward one another than Bryce and Miranda. They reached out to touch each other recurrently, like a dolphin rising to the surface for air.

"Well what?" Joey said.

Ashley smiled. "Water well."

"Is it electric?" Joey asked.

"The pump is," Scarlet said. "Why?"

"How much longer will we have electricity, and what will we do for water when we don't?" Joey said matter-of-factly.

Everyone traded glances. I felt the same way. It hadn't occurred to me that it was only a matter of time before we were without power.

Ashley looked to Joey. "How much longer do you think we have?"

"It depends on if the operators and utilities had enough warning to take measures to keep things running for a while," I said. "I'm pretty sure this area is run by a hydroelectric power station, otherwise we would have been off by now."

"How do you know all of that?" Miranda asked.

"It's what I do," I said. "Or what I used to do. If operators had time to isolate key portions of the grid to reduce connections, and then terminate power delivery altogether to areas prone to potential drains, a hydro plant could easily function for weeks or months. In theory, they have an unlimited fuel supply, assuming normal rainfall. We'd basically be waiting for an essential component to fail or wear out."

"So we should prepare," Joey said. "We have food, we have weapons, but they won't mean anything if we don't have water."

"Should we find containers and start filling them?" Cooper asked.

Joey nodded. "That will work for a while, but we'll eventually need something more long-term. We need some kind of a water filtration system."

Ashley sat at the table. "How much longer is this going to go on? It's not permanent . . . is it? They'll fix it."

"Who's they?" Joey asked.

"The government," Cooper said.

Joey shook his head. "We shouldn't assume this is temporary. We should take measures now to . . ."

"I'd just like to know who the fuck died and left you running the show," Bryce said, cutting Joey off.

"Bryce . . . ," Miranda said.

"Okay," I said, holding up my hands. "We're all tired and stressed. I'm sure with the storm last night not many of us got much rest. Bryce, you've got a point. We need to work together and come up with a plan. Joey, you seem like you know what you're talking about. You've had training?"

"He just got back from Afghanistan," Miranda said. Her input only agitated Bryce more.

"Okay, then," I said, trying to avoid a scene. "Joey, why don't you look around and see what you can come up with? We'll need to fashion some sort of water-holding cistern, and we'll need to go into town for a hand-pumped water filter, replacement filters, and some purification tablets if we can find them."

"That's asking a lot," Miranda said. "You would find all of

that at a large camping outlet. The closest one I can think of is over two hours away."

"I used to watch those preparation shows on TV," Scarlet said. "They showed someone pouring water through sand once, and then putting cloth at the bottom. Sand is a really good filtration system. There is charcoal out back. We just need a large jug or barrel, gravel, sand, and charcoal and put some cloth at the mouth. Turn it upside down and voila! Water filter . . . that is, in theory."

"That's a pretty good theory," I said with a small smile. She smiled back.

"It's still a theory," Bryce grumbled.

Joey glanced over at Bryce, his jaws working, and then nodded, leaving out the side door.

Miranda glared at Bryce, and then continued making her cereal.

Bryce held out his hands. "What?"

I noticed Scarlet had quietly excused herself to the porch, standing in the same place she had that morning, staring at the road. She wore a man's T-shirt that swallowed her and a pair of navy scrub pants.

"Now I know why the bedroom is a mess," I teased. "You raided the doctor's wardrobe."

Scarlet looked down at her haphazard appearance and absently pulled a lock of stray hair behind her ear and then smoothed the rest. "Just the one T-shirt," she said. "I actually didn't ransack his room. It was like that. I was going to clean it—I actually needed to after I'd cleaned everything else and ran out of things to do—but I decided it was his room, and for some reason I had to leave it the way it was. Maybe for the girls."

"His girls?"

She nodded to confirm, but soon her eyebrows pulled together and I realized too late my casual question for clarification reminded her of who she was waiting for.

"I can't imagine waiting for Zoe, wondering if she was okay, or if she was coming at all."

Scarlet laughed once. "You're not helping."

"But you have to believe that they're coming."

She closed her eyes and a tear slipped from beneath one of her eyelids. "I do." She looked at me. "Trust me, I believe it. Andrew was a terrible husband, and to be honest, he wasn't that great of a father, but what he lacked in compassion and patience, he more than made up for in efficiency and sense. He's smart. Quick witted, you know? He could think on his feet. If anyone can get my girls here, to me, it's him."

"I'm sure you're right."

She looked down her feet for a moment, fighting a hopeful smile, and then stared back at the road. We stood together in silence, watching the road together, until Zoe called for me. She was playing with small plastic horses, and Cooper was standing over her with a proud smile.

"They were Ashley's."

I nodded. "That was very kind of you."

"She reminds me a lot of my little sister." Cooper looked up at me. "Ashley was majoring in early childhood education. She's good at it. I bet she could work with Zoe a little every day."

Ashley walked by, on her way somewhere, and reached out for Cooper. Without looking back, he reached his hand behind him, and their fingertips grazed as she walked by. I wasn't even sure how he knew she was coming.

"I can," she said as she walked through the dining room to the back hallway. Her bedroom was back there somewhere, so I assumed that's where she was headed.

"That will be so good for her. You have no idea. I can't thank you enough." I said the words to Cooper, even though it was for Ashley. Speaking to one was like speaking to both.

It was odd watching them interact and move about, orbiting each other, like an old couple who'd been married fifty years or more. If reincarnation was possible, these kids had to have found their way to each other again, many times over.

After an hour, Scarlet returned inside. She smiled at Zoe. "Do you have horses?" she asked.

Zoe held up a tiny horse in each hand. "Just these."

Scarlet nodded her head, her expression absent of condescension. "Better than that bull out there, that's for sure."

"Butch?" Cooper said. "He's not a bad guy. He's just sick of being cooped up in that pen. You've been feeding him, haven't you?"

"He has hay," Scarlet said, "and water. I'm worried he's going to attract shufflers, though."

"Attract what?" Cooper said, chuckling.

Scarlet glanced at me, and then back at Cooper, clearly taken off guard by the question. "Shufflers. I can't call them *zombies,*" she said, rolling her eyes at the word. "Zombies are from Hollywood. Zombies aren't real. Those things need a name that's real."

"Yeah, but shufflers?" Cooper said, making a face.

"They shuffle!" Scarlet said, mildly defensive.

The conversation had drawn the attention of the rest of the group, and everyone else was congregating in the living room, too.

"I've been calling them sick, or infected," I said.

"Those things," Ashley said. Everyone craned their neck in her direction. She shrugged. "That's what I call them: *those things*."

Miranda crossed her arms. "I can't call them zombies, either. I call them dead ones."

"Biters," Joey said.

"I like biters," Miranda said, nodding.

"Well, I like shufflers. They shuffle," Scarlet said.

Joey laughed once without humor. "They also bite."

Scarlet frowned, but everyone seemed to be amused with the conversation.

"I think we should call them cows," Zoe said, still playing with her horses. "They sound like cows."

I laughed. "They groan."

"Hmmm . . . ," Zoe said, thinking very hard. "What about ted? It rhymes with dead. 'Oh, no! There is a ted! Hide! Run, Cooper! Shoot the ted, Scarlet!' " She made all sorts of faces while she acted out the different scenarios in which we might yell *ted*. Everyone was smiling, everyone but Scarlet.

"Why me? Why do I have to shoot the ted?" Scarlet asked.

"Because you're the best shot," Zoe said.

"I like you," Scarlet said, smiling only with her eyes.

"I like you, too," Zoe replied.

Scarlet lifted her arms and let them fall to her thighs. "All right, I'm sold on ted. Anyone disagree?"

Everyone shook their heads.

"Good choice, Zoe," Cooper said.

Zoe smiled wider than I'd seen in years, and in that moment, it was easy to believe everything was going to be okay.

Chapter Twenty

Nathan

ZOE HAD BEEN SPENDING A LOT OF TIME OUTSIDE ON the porch before and after her studies with Ashley. Scarlet may have inspired her, I couldn't be sure. When Zoe was asked what she was doing, she would barely explain.

"Waiting," she would say. She alternated between examining her fingers as they rested in her lap and squinting to see beyond the hill.

I'd learned not to ask what she was waiting for. She wouldn't tell me. I worried that she was missing her mother, but if Aubrey wasn't who or what she was waiting for, I didn't want to upset Zoe by bringing it to her attention. I worried that being safe wasn't enough for my daughter. Then again, she seemed happy and hadn't had an episode in over a week, so maybe I was so used to having something to worry about with her that I was overthinking things.

"Zoe?" I said, joining her on the porch. She'd been waiting quietly for nearly half an hour, and Ashley was waiting for her at the table. "Miss Ashley has made up some multiplication flash cards for you to try."

"I don't really like math," she said.

I smiled. "I don't really like math, either, but sometimes we have to do things that aren't fun."

Her expression was thoughtful. "We have to do that a lot."

"Some days more than others. Are you ready?"

Zoe shook her head. That took me off guard. Zoe had never flat-out told me no before. I wasn't sure how to react.

"Why not?"

She pointed at the road. I turned, seeing a man and a girl just clearing the hill. At first I was startled, but then I realized they weren't sick.

"Is that Scarlet's family?" Zoe asked.

"No. I mean, it doesn't look like them." The man was very tall and lanky, with his bald spot obvious from and vulnerable to the morning sun. His arms were abnormally long, and the closer they came, the longer they seemed to be.

"Scarlet!" I called, wanting to mentally slap myself the second I yelled her name. Just like I feared, she came running out the door, already breathing hard from hope and anticipation.

"Is it them?" she asked, just as they came running for the farmhouse.

"Oh, God, no, I'm sorry," I said, feeling like a complete ass.

Scarlet kept her eyes on the pair, swallowing loud as they approached. Her whole body tensed and leaned in such a way that it looked like her heart was breaking on the outside of her body.

I reached out and grabbed her hand, unsure of what else to do.

"Hey," the man said, holding the girl's hand loosely in his. His head, lips, and nose were badly sunburned, his eyes were sunken, and his cheekbones had just begun to protrude. The girl didn't seem as affected by the elements or hunger as he did, but she didn't lift her eyes from the ground. Even though she was tethered to the man by the hand, she didn't stand close to him.

"I'm Kevin. This is my daughter, Elleny," he said, breathing hard through his smiling lips.

"Hi, Elleny," Scarlet said, her smooth mom voice automatic and natural.

When Elleny didn't acknowledge her, Kevin shrugged. "She's been through a lot."

Scarlet tilted her head. "How old are you, Elleny?"

"She's fourteen," Kevin said. "Is this your place?"

Scarlet looked at Kevin, and then at me. He was a little weird, but Scarlet and I both knew we wouldn't turn away a child. "Pretty much. There's water and food inside," she said, gesturing toward the door. "But you'll have to leave your weapon outside." Scarlet looked down to the fire poker in his right hand.

Kevin wasted no time, laying down the poker and pulling Elleny along with him.

Scarlet showed them around the kitchen while I got Zoe situated at the table with Ashley.

"Who is that?" Ashley whispered.

"Survivors," I said. "A father and daughter."

Ashley made a face. I knew what she was thinking. Kevin looked like a skeleton, and Elleny was nearly plump, the baby fat still bulging her cheeks just enough to make her look younger than fourteen. Her green eyes and chestnut hair were opposite Kevin's ice-blue eyes. Her round features stood out from his boney face and pointy nose.

"Zoe doesn't look like me, either."

"Yes she does," Ashley said, smiling down at my daughter, who smiled back.

Ashley and Zoe worked on her times tables and read for about half an hour, and then they worked on an old puzzle of Ashley's, putting together all fifty of the United States. Once they were finished, Zoe returned to the porch again.

"So what do you think?" I said to Scarlet. She was cleaning out the refrigerator, throwing away uneaten food.

"This is a goddamn waste, that's what I think."

"About Kevin."

"I told him they could sleep in the doctor's bed until we get things figured out. He didn't say if they're staying or going on. I figured you and Zoe could sleep downstairs for now. I didn't really want them down there with all the weapons and supplies. Oh, unless you think that will bother Zoe?"

"No, no. I'll explain it to her. She'll have plenty of time to prepare." I looked into the living room and saw Elleny sitting alone on the couch. I walked toward the porch to start the process of preparing Zoe for the move, and saw Kevin sitting next to my daughter, side by side, on the top step. He had his arm planted on the porch, a bit behind her.

"Zoe," I said, opening the door quickly. "I need you inside for a minute. We need to talk."

Kevin immediately pulled away his hand, but his expression was calm and relaxed. "You got a cute little girl there."

I nodded, holding the door open for Zoe to pass, and then

brought her to Ashley's door and knocked. Ashley opened it and allowed us inside, even though I could tell she was surprised.

"Zoe," I said, kneeling in front of her. "First, we don't know Kevin, yet, so until I say otherwise, what is he?"

"A stranger," she said confidently.

"And what is the rule about strangers?"

"We don't talk to them."

I nodded. "Good girl."

"I told Kevin the rule, but he said he was a nice man, and he had met you, so he wasn't a stranger."

This made my stomach turn, although I reasoned that Kevin had a daughter of his own, so maybe he just knew how to talk to children. "Meeting someone and knowing them are different. Until I say it's okay, I don't want you to be alone with Kevin. Deal?"

"Deal," Zoe said.

Ashley and Cooper were standing next to us in a silent exchange. They would look at each other after certain points of my and Zoe's serious talk, never speaking, but having a conversation, nevertheless.

"Next, I need to tell you that to make room for Kevin and Elleny, you and I are going to move downstairs."

Zoe made a face, but I was prepared. "I like our room."

"I do, too. This is just for a little while, and then we can have our room back."

The skin between Zoe's eyebrows creased.

Ashley kneeled beside us. "Zoe, how about you and I bring your things downstairs and I'll help you decorate it just the way you want?"

Zoe thought about this for a while, and then nodded. She

still wasn't happy with the move, but her already agreeing, and without a fight, was momentous. I couldn't hide my appreciation to Ashley, and when we stood, I reached out with one hand and pulled her against my side, pressing my cheek against her hair in a half hug.

Ashley took Zoe to gather her things, and Cooper and I went into the living room where Kevin and Elleny were sharing a sandwich.

"You can make another sandwich," I said. Kevin was so thin; I couldn't imagine why he wouldn't. Maybe he thought he might overstay his welcome if they ate too much right away.

"We share everything, don't we?" he said, lovingly patting Elleny's thigh.

Elleny didn't speak or react. She just sat next to him, chewing the bite he'd just given her. I wondered if she'd lost her mother or someone else that had made her shut down so completely. Scarlet had been trying to get through to her since they arrived, but Elleny stayed in her own world, blocking everything and everyone out.

That, I somewhat understood. What I didn't understand was Kevin's dismissal of her behavior.

Elleny stayed quiet through dinner, although she ate more than she had earlier, having her own plate to herself. She ate slowly, though, making sure to savor every bite. No one discussed anything that we normally discussed. Somehow everyone knew to protect our house, our secrets, and our family from strangers. Even from a waif of a man and his strange little girl.

Kevin was the first to finish. "Man, I am tired. About what time do you all turn in around here?"

"It depends," Scarlet said. "You can go ahead."

Kevin put his hand on Elleny's. "You ready for bed?"

She took another bite.

He patted her hand. "Come on, now. I think you've had enough. Time for bed."

She scooped up more rice. "I'm still really hungry," she said, her voice just a breath.

Kevin became annoyed. "You're not that hungry. I'm tired. Let's go to bed."

Scarlet leaned her elbows on the table. "I realize you don't know us, but Nathan and I are parents. We wouldn't let anything happen to Elleny. Once she's finished, we'll send her that way."

Kevin's coolness left him for just a moment. "I'll wait." Elleny took another slow bite, and we all tried not to give in to the ensuing awkwardness.

After another ten minutes, Kevin stood and pulled Elleny up by the arm with him. "You're finished. Let's go."

Elleny went with him, but reluctantly. "I'm . . . still . . . ," she said, but he shushed her before she could finish.

They disappeared into the bedroom. Kevin shut the French doors and we all stood up to clean up after dinner.

"That was weird," Joey said, turning on the faucet.

We all agreed, and tried our best to continue as usual, even with our strange houseguests. Scarlet was scrubbing the plates and pans as if she were trying to work off nervous energy. At one point, the dish she'd just finished crashed into the others. She put the sides of her fists on the counter, took a breath, and then began again.

"Slow down, would ya?" Joey said as he rinsed and dried. "I can't keep up."

"Sorry," Scarlet said, still scrubbing with subdued fury.

"What's up?" I said, walking up behind her. My chin was just above her shoulder, but she didn't seem to mind.

"I don't know."

"You know."

"There's something off."

"I agree."

I walked Zoe downstairs and pulled down her covers while she changed into pajamas. She crawled into bed, and I tucked her in.

"Hum, Daddy."

One corner of my mouth pulled up. I hadn't hummed to Zoe since before everything went to hell. One reason was that we'd had such full, tense days, she usually fell asleep immediately. The other was because I couldn't carry a tune to save my life. I never hummed anything in particular, I just let my voice go up and down, and somehow that was relaxing enough for Zoe that she'd fall asleep.

I began to hum, and Zoe closed her eyes. I don't know why I kept referring to this time as when the world went to hell. It had its good points. I got to spend all day with my daughter without worrying about work or bills, and I'd met Scarlet. Granted, there were frightening things beyond the perimeter of the ranch, but it could be much, much worse. Some days I thought it a fair trade.

Zoe's breath evened out, and I leaned down to kiss her button of a nose before heading up the stairs. Joey was at the top, sitting on the washing machine. "Scarlet made me a pallet in the living room. I'd feel weird sleeping down there with you guys."

"Okay," I said, shaking his hand once. "Sorry, man."

"No problem." He jumped off the washer and followed me into the living room. Covers and pillows were spread across the floor, and Scarlet was outside on the porch. Joey sat in the recliner.

I crossed my arms. "I want to go out there with her, but I feel like I crowd her. That's kind of her time, isn't it?" I asked.

Joey smiled. "I think she likes it when you're out there. Maybe that's one of the reasons she keeps going."

"No," I said, shaking my head. "She goes out there because she knows one of these days they'll come walking over the hill."

"You really think so, man? I don't know. It's been a while."

"It took me and Cooper all day to get here from Shallot, and we were trucking it. It's not flat ground. There are creeks, and rocks, and hills, and abandoned buildings, and old farm equipment . . . and zombies."

"Psh . . . ," Joey teased, waving me away. "You act like that's hard."

Scarlet came inside, her face white and her eyes full of tears, but she didn't look sad. I was stunned by her expression, and immediately thought it had something to do with the girls. She hadn't spent a fraction of the time she usually spent outside waiting.

"What is it?" I said quietly, taking a step toward her. I didn't want to alarm the pair in the doc's room.

Scarlet's jaws worked, and a tear spilled out over her cheek. "I'm going to kill that motherfucker."

She walked quickly across the room, grabbed her rifle, and before I could stop her, she barged through the French doors.

I began to yell for her to stop, but at the same time I saw her point the gun at the back of Kevin's head, I saw that he was in a totally inappropriate position, hovering over Elleny, without a shirt on.

Elleny was whimpering quietly. It still took me a moment to process what was going on, as if my brain didn't want to believe what my eyes had seen.

"Get up!" Scarlet yelled. "In the front room! *Now*!" Her voice broke when she screamed the last bit.

Kevin's bare, bony back was visible above the sheets as he lay frozen above the young girl.

Joey walked in behind me. "What the actual fuck?"

I stood in place, stunned, as Kevin jumped out of the bed with his hands up. He was completely nude. It was then that my stomach turned, threatening to expel my dinner right there on the floor.

Kevin scurried into the living room, and Scarlet followed him, her rifle pointed at his chest.

"You're a monster. Worse than those things out there. Get the fuck out so I don't have to clean your blood out of this carpet," Scarlet said.

"Was he . . . ?" Joey said, looking at Kevin, and then back toward the bedroom.

Miranda, Bryce, Cooper, and Ashley had wandered out of their bedrooms by that point, shocked by the noise and the scene in the living room.

"Whoa! What the hell is going on?" Bryce said.

"You don't wanna know," Joey said. "Shoot him, Scarlet."

"I'll leave!" Kevin said, his arms still high in the air.

"You're damn straight, you will."

Kevin glanced past Scarlet to the bedroom. "But I'm not leaving without my daughter."

"The fuck if you're not," Joey said. "She's safer with us than with you."

"Come on! At least let me get my clothes!" Kevin whined.

"Boohoo, you sick son-of-a-bitch," Scarlet said, incredulous. She cocked her gun, pressed the end of the barrel against Kevin's stomach, and pushed him backward out the door. She watched him for a moment, and then went into the bedroom. "Watch where he goes," she said to Joey.

Joey stood guard at the door.

Scarlet stood at the end of the bed. "Elleny, is that man your father?"

Elleny, clothed only in the sheet that she had pulled up to her neck, shook her head.

Scarlet nodded. "That's what I thought. I'll be right back."

"Scarlet," I warned.

She ignored me and walked to the front door, pausing in front of Joey.

"He's headed south," Joey reported.

Scarlet pushed out the door and we all looked at each other, unsure of what to do.

"Should I . . . follow her?" I asked, looking to Bryce and Joey. No one had an answer. It was difficult to even form words.

A scream echoed from the south, followed by a single gunshot. We all jumped at the noise. A few seconds later, another shot was fired.

I ran out the front door, followed by everyone else, stopping when Scarlet came into view.

She stopped, letting the barrel of her gun tilt toward the ground.

"You killed him?" Ashley said, her voice high and nervous.

Scarlet didn't flinch. "I wasn't going to let him walk away with my daughters out there." She stomped past all of us to the house, and slammed the door behind her.

After a few seconds of stunned silence, we all followed. Scarlet was inside the bedroom, talking to Elleny, whose whimpers turned into wails.

"What do we do?" Miranda said.

"Looks like it's taken care of," Bryce said. He tugged on her hand, and she followed him back to their bedroom.

Cooper and Ashley did the same, even though Ashley was still upset and asking questions.

Joey and I stood in the living room alone, listening to Scarlet speak calmly to Elleny. After an hour, she emerged from the bedroom.

"She's asleep."

"That was . . . I've never seen anything like that in my life, have you?" Joey said.

"No," I said, a little shocked that he'd even had to ask.

"They should all get the same end." Scarlet propped her rifle against the wall by the door, and then fell onto the couch, on top of her covers. "Better get some sleep. It's too late to bury him tonight, so we're going to have work to do in the morning."

"You shot twice," I said. "So did you make sure he wouldn't come back?"

Scarlet nodded. "I shot him in the dick, first."

Joey shook his head, satisfied. "Bastard. What did he do, take her in the chaos?"

Scarlet took a deep breath. "Her parents were killed. He lived down the street. She thought she had no other choice, even after he . . . she's safe now. She's going to be okay."

I kneeled beside her. "That is a freak occurrence. You know that, right? Andrew is with Halle and Jenna, and they're safe."

Scarlet nodded. "Everyone's a little safer now."

Chapter Twenty-One

Miranda

ELLENY FOLLOWED SCARLET AROUND LIKE A SCARED child, even after she helped bury Kevin's body. We were all stunned for days after. I wasn't sure if I was more shocked about what Kevin had done, what he was caught doing, or that Scarlet had killed him. The house didn't feel the same, and I wasn't sure if it was because of the new, awkward addition, or because we realized that it wasn't just teds that we had to fear.

Because Elleny stayed so close to Scarlet and so far from the rest of us, it was hard to get to know her. I didn't know how to talk to her, anyway. I'd never known anyone that had been through something like that. I didn't want to say the wrong thing, so I didn't say anything at all.

Nathan and Zoe had returned to the front bedroom, but Scarlet moved downstairs with Elleny, leaving Joey the couch. That made it easier for me to stay up and talk to him at night, and I felt more like we were just hanging out as friends instead of sneaking around in the basement like . . . nonfriends. I couldn't even say the word, that's how wrong it felt.

Whatever it was, I couldn't deny that I liked being around Joey. I more than liked it. Even if a moment had to be stolen when no one was looking. Bryce would get so angry to even see us chatting about nothing in particular, so I took what I could get because going too long without a moment with him made me feel like I was suffocating.

Everyone seemed to be suffocating. We were surviving, but every passing day felt less like living.

Every morning and night, Scarlet would stand out on the porch my father built and watch the red hill for her daughters. Nathan would wait with her, assuring her that they would come. Ashley pretended to be a teacher. The guys tried to keep themselves busy with upkeep of the house, and taking shifts to patrol the perimeter, and Joey and I pretended to ignore each other, but what was supposed to be our safe haven was beginning to feel like a prison.

Nathan, though, didn't seem to feel the weight like the rest of us. He and Scarlet would spend hours talking. Once, I walked by the door and saw them holding hands while they waited together on the porch. After that, they seemed to steal more moments alone, sharing secrets and whispering jokes that only the two of them found funny. Joey and I were sitting up late one night, talking in the darkness of the living room, and were both startled when the French doors opened, revealing Scarlet.

"Hi," she said, looking caught. "We were just talking."

I shrugged, and so did Joey. "So are we," I said.

Scarlet nodded before retreating downstairs to join Elleny.

Joey looked at me. I was barely able to see his eyebrow rise in the dim light. "Think they were . . ."

"No. Zoe's in there."

"So?"

"No," I said, shaking my head, disgusted in Zoe's honor. "I remember walking in on my parents, once. It scarred me for life."

"My parents split up when I was four," Joey said. "I don't remember what it's like to have them both in the house."

"Your mom never dated?"

"Once or twice. I did a pretty good job of scaring them off. I was a hateful little shit."

I smiled. "I can see that."

Nathan

I DIDN'T MEAN TO KEEP MAKING COMPARISONS, BUT AUbrey was the first woman I'd ever loved. So I had to wonder, now, feeling the way I did about Scarlet, if I just loved her differently than I ever had Aubrey, or if it meant I'd never really loved Aubrey at all.

My life went from one disappointing day to another, to keeping track of time by how much was spent with Scarlet, and how much time was spent between the moments I spent with her. We would sit on the porch and wait together, and she would tell me about her girls, how funny and smart and talented they were, and what it was like to bring them into this world. She talked about her marriage, and her decision to leave. I'd already thought she was maybe the strongest, bravest woman I'd met, but to listen to how alone she was in that decision, with no support, I couldn't help but be in awe of her.

Each night was a buildup to when I would finally have

enough balls to touch her. Sometimes I would play it off with a nudge, or a playful smack on her leg, and she wouldn't mind if I left it there. Childish, but she was nothing if not intimidating . . . and distractingly beautiful. I found it difficult not to stare at her, and was glad for the dim light after the sun went down, and that the darkness gave me an excuse to concentrate on her mouth while she spoke.

It felt strange—this happiness I'd found in such a dark time. But with Zoe content in our new home and the routine we'd found, and finding Scarlet, the only thing that bothered me was what life would have been like without death descending on the world. What did it mean that I'd had such good fortune when so many had lost everything?

Sitting on the top step of the porch next to Scarlet, it was easy to forget the nightmare that was just beyond that hill, and that she wasn't just outside spending time with me, but passing the time while waiting for her children, the true loves of her life.

"I'm still sweating," Scarlet said, letting go of my hand to lift the collar of her T-shirt to dab her forehead. "Summer must be in full swing."

The locust and crickets were taking over the symphony the birds had just ended. "It's going to be another hot one."

"Triple digits. Again. Probably." She reached over to lace her fingers in mine.

I lifted her fingers to my lips. I wanted so badly to just pull her into my lap and touch every part of her. It was a silly, but very real desire. Something I'd never felt with Aubrey.

"Were you in a relationship? Before?" Before was the general term we used for any time before the first day of the outbreak.

Scarlet shook her head. "No. I was enjoying being single."

"Oh."

She laughed and squeezed my hand. "Maybe I just hadn't met the right person, yet."

"Maybe not," I said, grinning like an idiot. Damn, I had it bad.

"Probably because the right person was married."

I frowned for just a second, but cleared my expression before she noticed. Technically, I wasn't single, and I worried that would make Scarlet think less of me.

"Does that bother you?"

Scarlet thought for a moment, and then shook her head. "The world is different, now. She left you a note saying that your marriage was over. I'd say in these times, that's as good as a divorce. I worry about Zoe, though, don't you?"

I loved her for that. "She doesn't know anything, yet."

"Oh, I think she knows more than you give her credit for."

"You think?"

"I know. My girls knew everything I didn't want them to. I think it's a female thing."

I smiled. "Good point." Scarlet looked up into my eyes, and I blinked, suddenly feeling how close we were. I leaned in just a fraction of an inch, my lips burning to touch hers.

Scarlet leaned her head against my shoulder. "I need my girls here."

I breathed out, her rejection deflating me. "I know."

"No. I mean . . . I need them here. Safe. It doesn't feel right to be happy otherwise."

I knew then what she meant, and for the first time, I realized that I had been fooling myself. There was no one that wasn't touched by the infection.

Miranda

BRYCE SAT ON THE FENCE, WATCHING BUTCH NOSE around in the dirt. We didn't have a lot to talk about anymore. I shared all of my thoughts and feelings with Joey, and Bryce had quit trying to get me to repeat them. It felt like a waste, anyway; redundant. My fourteen-year-old self wanted to hug him and assure him that I would always love him. My eighteen-year-old self wanted to apologize that he was stuck with someone who was so selfish, she couldn't see past her own impulsive wishes. I was too much of a coward to do either, so I just kept pretending—poorly—to Bryce that everything was fine, and sneaking around to spend time with Joey after dark.

Just as I could barely stand to look at myself, Scarlet could barely stand to look at the hill another day. The sight of it made her angry, and she began spending more and more time watching the same spot for signs of her children. Her moods shifted in an instant, and after a while, even Nathan's level head and smooth voice couldn't keep her calm.

She quit allowing him to wait with her, but he would wait on the arm of the couch, right next to the door, in case she would break down into tears, and occasionally she did.

After three weeks of watching Scarlet wait, I watched her walk in and grab her rifle and a backpack, filling it with ammo.

Nathan stood from his perch on the couch. "Scarlet?"

She shoved a few more boxes into the pack, a bag of chips, two bottles of water, and then zipped it up. "I just saw another ted heading south in the field."

"What are you going to do, chase it down? I thought we agreed that was an unnecessary risk."

Scarlet slid the pack over her shoulders, and then grabbed a hatchet from behind the front door. "My girls are out there, Nathan."

"Yes, but you don't know why they're not here yet, or when they'll show up."

"Maybe they can't get here. Maybe they're alone and are too scared to pass Shallot. I can't just sit here anymore."

Nathan sighed. "Okay. I understand that you're frustrated, but we need to talk about this."

Scarlet frowned. "What is there to talk about? I'm going."

"Okay, you're going, but we can't talk about it first? Get a plan together?"

Scarlet shrugged. "Walk the roads and shoot teds. What other plan do I need?"

"It's not safe to go alone."

Scarlet shook her head and reached for the door. "I'm not going to be responsible if something happens to you, Nathan. You have a daughter to take care of."

"You have two."

Scarlet looked around to the rest of us. "Will someone please tell Nathan this is a bad idea?"

"I'm going with you," Elleny said quietly.

Scarlet smiled and touched her cheek. "I need you to stay here where it's safe. I can't concentrate if I'm watching out for you, too. Got it?"

Elleny clearly didn't like it, but she nodded.

Joey stood up. "I'm going, too."

Scarlet held out her palm. "Now him I'll take. You," she said, pointing her palm at Nathan, "are staying here."

"Don't make me do this," Nathan said. He took the few steps to stand next to her, touched his fingers to her arm, and spoke with subdued desperation in her ear. He was becoming agitated, and that wasn't like him.

"Do what?" Scarlet said, instantly defensive.

"Choose between you and my daughter."

Scarlet was speechless, like the rest of us. Finally, she spoke, pulling away from him. "I would never ask you to do that. It's not a choice, Nathan." She began to open the door, and Nathan took her wrist in his hand. "Let go," she said calmly.

"Scarlet, I'm asking you. Don't do this."

"I'm not waiting for them anymore. I have to help them. This is the only way I know how."

"And what if you get yourself killed and they show up here? What am I supposed to tell them? That they came all the way here for nothing?"

Scarlet stared at Nathan, wriggled her wrist out of his grasp, and then looked to Joey. "Are you coming or not?"

"Right behind you." Joey began to follow Scarlet, but he stopped at the door. "I'll keep her safe, Nate."

Nathan nodded.

Bryce kissed my cheek. "I'm going, too."

"What?" I said. "*Why?*"

"I want to make sure she doesn't get herself killed before her kids get here. I've been watching her wait on that porch every morning for a month. I'll be damned if she doesn't get to see them because we didn't help her."

"Then I'm going, too," I said.

Bryce shook his head. "No, you and Ashley need to stay here with the girls. Coop?"

"Yeah," Cooper said, leaning over to kiss Ashley. Against Ashley's persistent pleas, he grabbed a baseball bat and followed Bryce out the door.

Once the door closed behind Cooper, the house was instantly and eerily quiet. Nathan took Zoe and Elleny to the table and began pulling out food for breakfast. Ashley stood at the door, watching Cooper walk down the road.

"You really think her kids are out there?" Ashley said, keeping her eye on the group. "You think they're still alive?"

"Yes," Nathan said from the kitchen.

"You shouldn't have let her go," I snapped. "Everyone we love is out there."

Nathan's worried eyes softened as he looked down at his daughter. "How could I argue with her when I would do the same?"

Scarlet

FOUR PAIRS OF SHOES ON DIRT AND GRAVEL WAS THE only sound. No one said a word as we walked east up the red dirt hill and back down, toward the intersection and then back north toward the cemetery at the next mile section. Bryce and Cooper trailed behind Joey and me by about ten feet—on purpose, I assumed.

Despite being determined not to, Nathan's pleas for me to stay kept entering my mind. I glanced over my shoulder, seeing Ashley at the door, wondering where Nathan was, if he was angry with me. If I had a type, Nathan was not it. I knew right away when he showed up in a loose tie and slacks. The day before our lives changed forever I would have appreciated his body for a few moments before dismissing him. Until I'd gotten to know Nathan, I thought a man that spent too much time in the gym was either vain or had self-esteem issues. I preferred men with dark hair, eyes that you couldn't look away from, and at least a head taller than me—even though I dwarfed Andrew when in heels. If Andrew had taught me anything, it was what I didn't want in a man. Sometimes I used my strict list of musts to push potential interests away. It worked for me. As a single mother, it was my job to be picky. After failing Jenna and Halle so many times, I owed them that.

Even after half or more of the population had been wiped out, it wasn't a good enough excuse to throw away the list—regardless of the strange excitement that I felt every time Nathan was in the same room.

We weren't a mile away from the entrance of the ranch when Joey tapped me on the shoulder and pointed to the field on our left. It probably wasn't the best idea, leaving that early in the morning with the sun in our eyes, but I could still see her, limping across the knee-high wheat stalks.

"Ted, ten o'clock," Joey said, alerting the others.

We approached her carefully. She'd noticed us right after we saw her, and instantly turned in our direction, her low moans signaling her excitement at the prospect of a meal. She reached for us as she walked, and I held the hatchet tightly in my hand as I charged her.

I lifted the wooden handle of the hatchet high in the air,

and just before I was within her grasp, I brought it down to her skull, letting the weight of it work with me. The steel pierced bone, and then slid easily into the softer part of her brain. She instantly froze, and then fell to the ground.

I bent over, steadying myself with my foot on her head, and then pulled, releasing the edge of the axe from her head. Joey, Cooper, and Bryce were all watching me, their expressions ranging from disgusted to awestruck.

"What?"

Joey glanced at the other boys and then back at me. "I'm not completely convinced at this point that you needed us with you for anything other than chitchat."

I laughed once, and continued on. "Come on. She isn't the ted I saw from the porch. There is another one out here. To the south."

We crossed the field in search of the large male I saw lumbering across the wheat. He met the same end as the previous ted, but then I wanted to return to the road. The girls only knew how to get to the ranch from Halle's song, so the roads were what needed to be cleared first.

We had eliminated a dozen or so teds by lunch time, when we stopped to rest and snack on the potato chips I'd stuck in my pack.

"So . . . Nathan . . . ," Cooper said with a smile.

"What about him?" I said, taking another gulp of water.

"He seemed really worried about you. You guys are getting along pretty well."

I wiped my mouth with the back of my hand, and then raised an eyebrow. "Are you really trying to play matchmaker right now?"

Cooper spit out the bite of sandwich in his mouth and laughed uncontrollably, and Bryce and Joey began to chuckle, too.

I rolled my eyes. "Stop it."

"It's okay, Scarlet. You don't have to be a badass all the time," Joey said.

"What is that supposed to mean?" I asked.

Bryce handed me his leftovers to put in my pack. "Nathan is a good guy. One of the best. Even before all this. You shouldn't be so hard on him."

"Am I?" I asked, a little offended. How was I being hard on him? Just because I wasn't throwing myself at him? Why I was even entertaining this conversation with a bunch of barely pubescent boys was a joke in itself.

Joey smiled. "There's nothing wrong with being happy, Scarlet."

"Are you happy, Joey?" As soon as the words passed my lips, I regretted them. The question wiped the smile off Joey's face, and the others fell silent. "I'm sorry. God, I am so sorry," I said.

"It's okay," Joey said, standing. "We better get going."

I stood and brushed the dead grass off my clothes. "I guess Nathan is okay."

Joey's small smile returned, and he closed one eye tight to help him look at me despite the sun. "You like him, then?"

"A little. I think."

"I think a lot," Cooper teased.

"Shut up," I replied.

"What if something happened to him?" Bryce asked.

I was quiet for a long time, and then finally said, "It would break me."

We continued until dinnertime. By the time we'd returned to the house, I had downed fourteen, and the boys had taken care of at least ten apiece. We'd stumbled on a herd just before we got to the highway, significantly upping our count for the day.

Ashley nearly tackled Cooper to the floor when we walked into the house, and the rest of us grabbed clean clothes and then found different places to wash up.

I was filthy, covered in sweat, dirt, and the thick, coagulated blood of shufflers. I went out the laundry-room door to the patio on the side of the house and pulled off my shirt, letting it slap to the ground. I used my foot to pull off one tennis shoe, and then did the same with the other before shimmying off my jeans. They were Leah's, and a bit tight, but my scrub pants weren't made for an apocalypse, and were shredded by week two.

I pulled the garden hose from its coil and twisted the water spigot. The water came out with a gush just as Nathan came outside. His eyes pored over my body. A month ago, it would have been embarrassing to be standing in front of someone in just a bra and panties, but we lived in a different world, now. In truth, I just felt like one of the guys.

The way Nathan was looking at me in that moment, though, was not like he was just looking at one of the guys. He took the hose from my hand and I bent over, letting him spray my back and hair.

"Looks like a productive trip," he said.

I stood up and scrubbed my face as he sprayed me with the water, and then used my hands to scrub my arms and legs. "Yep. We came across a herd. Not sure if I can beat my count tomorrow."

"Tomorrow? Scarlet . . ."

I turned to face him. "I understand that you don't want me to go, but I need to do this."

"I know," he said, taking a step toward me. He leaned over to pick up the stack of clean clothes off the rusted-out cooker beside the door where I'd tossed them, and handed them to me. "But I can't stand staying at the house while you're out there." He was just inches from me. Even though it was warm out, my skin was covered in goose bumps. He put one hand on my hip, and the other on my face.

His mouth was just inches from mine, but I put gentle pressure against his chest with my fingertips. "Did you love her?" The question was painfully out of place, but still needed to be asked. I may have far surpassed my days as an insecure adolescent, and we might have been the last of the few people left in the world, but it was still a valid worry to wonder if it was the situation that brought us together or his feelings were genuine. Maybe it didn't matter.

"Not for a long time, and never like the way I love you."

Even though I realized that I might feel the same, his words surprised me. He seemed to be waiting for me to return the sentiment, and when I didn't, he rushed to kiss me, covering the awkward silence in case it led to an awkward exit. I let him pull my bare skin against him. I parted my lips and he wasted no time slipping his tongue inside, searching every part of my mouth. I'd never thought about if he was a good kisser or not, but he was such a good kisser that it both surprised me and made me ache for more.

I walked backward to the back of the house, and he walked with me, never pulling his mouth from mine. He knotted his fingers in the dark, wet strands of my hair, as he pressed my back against the wooden slats of the house. There was no room between us, but I kept pulling him closer and closer to me. My thighs throbbed for the hardness behind his jeans.

I reached down and unbuckled his belt and then unbuttoned his pants, immediately pinching his zipper and tugging it down. Nathan let me go for just a second, took a quick glance around, and then put his thumbs into the waist of his jeans and pushed down just enough.

He reached down and pulled my knee up to his hip, and with the other hand slid over the small bit of fabric covering what he was after. The tip of his skin touched mine, and I instantly moaned in his mouth. I didn't realize how much I wanted him or how much I missed sex until just that moment.

He steadied himself and then rocked his hips up and forward, pressing himself inside of me. I moaned again. I wasn't sure if it was just because I'd been without sex in almost a year, or if he just felt that good.

Nathan pulled his mouth away from mine, and then hugged me to him, allowing him to go even deeper inside of me. The leg I stood on was burning, but I ignored it. Nathan slammed harder into me, making my ass bump into the wood behind me. He rocked into me over and over, in the most uncomfortable, amazing position. He licked and bit my earlobe, and I pressed my fingers into his back, and bit my lip to keep from screaming out just how amazing it felt. As my thigh began to feel numb and shake from exhaustion, Nathan pressed his face hard into my neck, and then groaned loudly, pressing into me a couple more times.

We stood still like that for a moment, and then we both let

our legs give way, falling gently to the ground. Nathan looked up at me, and I leaned down, kissing his lips, already red from how much he'd used them on my skin.

He smiled, and then slipped my panties down my legs.

"It's a little late for that, don't you think?" I said with a smirk.

He grabbed my hips and pulled me on top of him. I straddled his legs, leaned up, and then slowly, carefully, we fit perfectly together once again.

I was out of practice, but Nathan moved with me, slower this time. He pulled me down to kiss his lips, and then sucked my lower lip into his mouth, between his teeth, applying the smallest bit of pressure. I moved faster, and pressed against him harder, and then my whole body tensed, the orgasm holding on longer than I expected it to.

Finally, I collapsed against his chest, and he wrapped his arms around me.

"Does it make me crazy that I think the end of the world is the best thing to happen to me?" he said, touching my face.

I smiled, wishing I could say the same.

Chapter Twenty-Two

Miranda

IT WAS SITTING ON THE TABLE LIKE IT BELONGED THERE, like a flower vase, or a pen—or a toy. Zoe was playing Go Fish on the floor with Elleny, and there was a fully loaded 9mm Glock not five feet from them. I picked it up and checked that the safety was on—it wasn't.

"Are you f— whose is this?" I said, holding up the handgun. "What dumbass left a loaded gun without the safety on next to the kids?"

Nathan walked into the kitchen, likely just out of curiosity, because I knew he wouldn't be that stupid. Scarlet came in right after, followed by Joey.

"Oh. That's mine," Joey said. "Well, I brought it up from downstairs. I just had to take a leak. I was coming back to get it."

I made a show of pointing to the safety. "What if one of the kids had gotten ahold of this? You ought to have your ass whipped!"

"I'm sorry," he said, stunned at my anger. "I just put it down for a second. It won't happen again." He picked up the gun from the table, and went outside through the laundry room.

Scarlet and Nathan traded glances.

"Thanks for saving me the trouble of a lecture," Scarlet said. "You're becoming quite the mama bear."

"Yeah," I said, pissed off that I was still pissed off.

I went out the front door and stood on the porch, hoping some fresh air would help. It was getting hotter. Not only did being hot make me cranky, but it also reminded me of summers here with my dad. The dad I would never see again because his girlfriend ate him.

A gunshot rang out, and I caught Joey aiming at some cans on a fence from the corner of my eye. He shot a few more times and then walked to the fence to reset the cans.

I walked over to him. He didn't acknowledge me.

"I'm sorry," I said. "That was a little harsh."

"A little harsh? I half expected your head to start spinning around and pea soup to start spewing from your mouth."

"Don't be such a baby. It wasn't that bad. Are you telling me Dana never yelled at you?"

"No. As a matter of fact, she didn't. We got along really well."

"Well, you probably didn't leave firearms lying around when you were with Dana."

"Probably not. It was a stupid thing to do, I get it."

I glanced up at the sky, recoiling from the bright sun. I wasn't sure, but it had to be getting close to June, if it wasn't already. I could already feel beads of sweat forming along my hairline. God, I missed deodorant.

Joey lifted the Glock with both hands, aimed, and fired.

Bam, bam, bam, bam. Four cans in a row cartwheeled off the fence.

"Nicely done," I said, shading my eyes with my hand. "Can I try?"

"No. This gun is allergic to bitchiness."

"Are you calling me a bitch?"

"No, I said you're being bitchy. There is a difference."

"Not really." I took the gun from him and held it in front of me. I shot once, missed, and then hit the next three.

"Not bad," Joey said.

"I've been practicing with Bryce."

"I know. I've seen you."

"Oh yeah?"

"Yeah, you're getting pretty good."

"Thanks."

"You're welcome. You're still being bitchy."

I frowned. "You're still being a dumbass."

Joey frowned, too. His tan T-shirt was already soaked with sweat. His arm muscles strained and glided every time he moved them, and I couldn't help but wonder what the rest of him looked like.

"Why are you so mean all the time?" he asked, spitting on the ground next to him. "Is it because you're trying to hide that you want me?"

Ick. He was so arrogant. "I wouldn't want you if you were the last man on earth."

"That's just hateful." He was a little hurt. I could see it in his eyes, and to my surprise, that softened me up a little.

I sighed. "I just don't want you to know that I . . . I like you. A little. Not a lot."

"You like me," Joey said, more of a statement than a question.

"Not a lot," I qualified.

"Haven't you and Bryce been together since birth?"

"Close."

"He doesn't like me."

"Not really, no," I said, shaking my head.

"Is that why? Because he knows how you feel about me?"

"I don't know. I don't even know how I feel."

"You just said you like me."

I shrugged. "I like everyone."

"No you don't."

"That's true."

Joey put the gun on safety, showed me, and then took a step closer. He was so close that I could feel his breath on my face, and see the sweat glisten between the thick, dark whiskers of his five o'clock shadow. He was so unlike anyone I would normally be attracted to, but then again, I didn't know whom I would be attracted to because I'd been with Bryce for so long.

"I like you, too," he said. And then he walked away, leaving me in a puddle of holy shit and inappropriate thoughts.

After several moments, I walked to the porch and sat on the top step. The storm door opened and closed, but it wasn't until I saw two perfect legs that I knew who it was.

"Hey," Ashley said.

"Hey."

"You know what I miss?"

"Your flat iron?"

"Date night. You and me getting all dressed up and meeting Bryce and Coop somewhere fun. Just hanging out and talking about all the stupid stuff we used to do when we were kids."

I smiled. "Yeah, that was fun."

"You know what else I miss? Music."

"Cheeseburgers."

"Facebook."

"Movies On Demand."

Ashley laughed and shook her head. "I miss the mall."

"In about a week, we're going to miss toothpaste."

Ashley looked at me in horror. "Are you serious?"

I shrugged. "Dad had a few boxes, but between nine people . . . it's almost gone."

"You know what else I miss?" she asked. I waited. "You being in love with Bryce."

I craned my neck in her direction. She met my glare. "You don't know anything about anything, Ashley."

"I know what I saw in the field a minute ago. You better be careful. That guy in there loves you more than life itself. You don't want to mess that up."

"I'm not trying to."

"Then stop."

"You stop."

Ashley narrowed her eyes at me, and then shook her head. "We're all stuck here. No sense in everyone being miserable."

I picked at my nail. "No, just me, right?"

"Are you *miserable* with Bryce?"

"No."

"Okay, then." With that she stood up and went inside.

Movement just over the hill in the field caught my eye, and before I could yell to the others, Scarlet blew past me, a hatchet in her hand. She took care of the ted, and returned to the porch like she'd just picked a flower or something. She stood next to me, staring at the road. Since she was outside, anyway, she probably thought it was as good a time as any to wait for her girls.

"You still think they're coming?" I asked, feeling awful as soon as the words fell out of my mouth.

"Yes," she said without pause.

Nathan came out and stood beside her. Right at my eye level, I could see their fingers touch, and then intertwine.

"I guess I'll go in," I said to no one in particular.

I passed Joey and joined Bryce in the kitchen. He and Cooper were cooking with Zoe. That consisted of her sitting on the counter being entertained by Cooper while Bryce cooked.

I sat at the table and sighed.

"Bryce said you're feeling bitchy," Zoe said, matter-of-fact.

Bryce froze and looked back at me for a reaction. I peeked over at Joey, who chuckled to himself.

"I guess I am," I said, sighing again.

"Why?" Zoe asked.

"I don't know. My dad died. The world is over. We're stuck in this house together waiting for Scarlet to have a meltdown when she figures out her girls aren't coming . . ."

"You mean we're safe and we have each other?" Zoe said.

I looked up at her, feeling instantly guilty and yet cheered up by her sweet smile. "Yes. That's what I meant."

Scarlet

NATHAN WAITED FOR ZOE TO FALL ASLEEP, AND THEN he came to the laundry room with a smile and a wink. Elleny had just fallen asleep downstairs as well, and I was sitting on the dryer, waiting for him. He leaned in between my legs, kissing my lips.

"What is the plan?" I asked.

"I want to fall asleep with you."

"Is that all?" I smiled, and let him lead me to the front bedroom. He was so incredibly sweet. Knowing that made me wonder what kind of clueless moron he was married to. Zoe was snoring lightly through her nose as she lay on the far side of the king-size bed. Nathan crawled to the middle, and I lay next to him on my left side. His arms were wrapped around me, and his face was buried in my hair.

He took a deep breath. "I've been thinking about this all day."

I smiled. "Oh yeah? I've been thinking about yesterday all day."

"Don't remind me. I can't kidnap you to the backyard in the dark." He squeezed me, bringing our bodies closer together.

The conversation naturally fell silent, neither one of us feeling the need to fill it with nonsense that didn't matter. Quicker than I expected, Nathan's breathing evened out, and his arm relaxed. A few times, his hand would tense, and he'd grip my arm, or his whole body would jerk. It had been so long since I'd slept with someone else besides the girls, I'd forgotten adults did that, too.

The girls. It had been months since I'd seen them. Guilt washed over me for lying next to Nathan, happy, when they were probably huddled alone somewhere, scared to death.

Patrolling the road made me at least feel like I was doing something to help get them to Red Hill, but it wasn't enough. If they didn't get there, soon, I would have to go look for them.

I stood up, trying not to wake Nathan as I slipped out of the room. Just as I reached the kitchen, the French doors opened.

"Scarlet," Nathan whispered. He hadn't been asleep that long, but his eyes were heavy. "Everything okay?"

"Yeah, I'm just going to bed."

"You're not going to stay with me tonight?"

"I don't know that I should. It might upset Zoe."

He smiled. "That's really sweet of you to think of her, but I don't think that's it. Talk to me." He took a few steps into the living room.

"I'm going to take the boys into Shallot tomorrow. I just need a good night's rest. I'm not used to sleeping with you, yet. I have trouble falling asleep anyw—"

"Into Shallot? As in, you're going into the town of Shallot?" He shook his head, stepping closer to me. "But it's overrun."

"That's why we have to clear it out. What if Andrew takes the girls there for supplies, or looking for shelter?"

Nathan gently cupped my shoulders. "Scarlet, you haven't seen that place. The whole town was turned. That's at least three hundred infected."

"Teds."

"Whatever. You can't clear out that town. You'll get yourself killed."

I smiled and kissed his cheek. "Don't you know by now that I can take care of myself? You've heard the boys' stories at dinner."

"Yeah, and it scares the hell out of me. I have tried to understand, but I can't let you do this, Scarlet. It's reckless." For the first time, his tone was firm.

My face burned. "You don't get to tell me what to do just because we fucked in the yard."

He was surprised by my reaction, but the only thing he did in response was frown. "Don't do that."

That caught me off guard. Andrew had always been so quick to come back at me with angry words that I wasn't prepared to resume a fight picked with someone who stayed calm. "Then don't tell me what to do."

He gently grabbed my hand and kissed my palm. I tried to pull away, but he held on to it. "I can't begin to know what you go through every day waiting for your girls. I've never met them, and I'm worried sick about them. You can push me away all day long, but I'm in love with you. I *love* you, Scarlet, and it would destroy me if anything happened to you."

For just a moment, I let guilt seep in with his words. In that moment, I thought about staying there, with him, where it was safe. I thought about waiting for the girls, so I could be sure to be at the ranch waiting when they arrived. But then I thought about Jenna and Halle walking past Shallot, and running into a herd. Even a small one would be a death sentence. They were just little girls. I couldn't be sure that Andrew was with them to protect them or help them make decisions.

"I can't," I said, wriggling my hand free of his.

"You can't what?"

"Do this. It's breaking my focus."

He shook his head. "I don't know what you mean."

"I need to worry about *them,* Nathan. I need to stand outside and think about them and worry about them every second of the day, because I'm afraid if I don't something will happen to them."

He shook his head again. He was clearly confused by my babbling.

"I know it's irrational, okay? I can see it on your face and I can feel it everywhere but in my heart. Thinking about them keeps them alive."

"Okay. I get that, but worrying about them is one thing. Making dangerous choices is—"

"This is distracting me. You are distracting me. I don't think about them as much anymore. Sometimes I think about you, or Zoe or . . . I can't care about you. It makes me forget what I need to do to get Jenna and Halle home. I can't be responsible for your feelings. My children come first. They will *always* come first."

"Of course. They should, but—"

"So you understand that I can't do this. With you . . . I can't."

"Scarlet," he said, reaching out for me. His voice was tinged with desperation. "Just . . . let's think of another way. There has to be another way."

"But there isn't."

Nathan stood with his lips parted, breathing uneven, trying to think of something, anything to get me to change my mind, from both decisions. He looked down to the floor, searching the darkness for words. "I can't go with you. I have to stay with Zoe, I . . ."

"I know."

His eyes met mine. His desperation was discernible even in the dark. "I'll think about them with you."

Damn him. Damn him and his decency. It made me want to admit to loving him back, but I couldn't. Letting myself care about his feelings got in the way of what I knew I needed to do to get my girls safely to the ranch. "It's the last shred of sanity I have, Nathan. Don't take it from me."

I walked away from him quickly, and then jogged down the basement steps. I didn't know if he was still standing in the living room, stunned, pissed, confused, or disgusted. I didn't dare look back.

WE LEFT RED HILL AT FIRST LIGHT. WE WOULD SPEND all day in Shallot and still not make a dent in teds there, so I wanted to leave as soon as it was safe. Nathan jumped out of bed and waved good-bye as soon as he heard the front door open, but he didn't speak or kiss me good-bye.

We were to the highway within an hour, but getting to Shallot, clearing, and getting back before dark was going to take serious effort. I set the pace at a slow jog. After forty minutes, Cooper seemed to pick up the pace, but mine was more like a fast walk. We were all carrying packs, but Cooper was unfazed, which kind of pissed me off. I was in good shape for my age. I ran . . . sometimes. I walked all over the damn hospital, some days without a lunch or even sitting down. I figured the jaunt to Shallot would be work, but I was forcing myself to put one foot in front of the other, and we weren't halfway there yet.

"I've got to rest," I said, stopping.

"Whose idea was it to walk?" Joey smiled.

"We all agreed," I said. "We would only use the vehicles in case of an emergency exit."

"You look like an emergency to me," Joey said, still smiling.

I peered up at him with the threat of wrath in my eyes. "Shut up."

"We won't make it back by dark if we rest," Cooper called back.

"If we keep pushing like this, we'll all be too tired to clear," Bryce said. "We might just have to find somewhere to hole up for the night."

"In Shallot?" I said, grabbing my knees. I stood up and made myself take the first step. "Didn't you say some of your people got killed there?"

"Some of Nathan's people," Joey said.

I nodded, but didn't say anything else. We alternated walking and jogging, until finally I saw that damn car in the middle of the highway. The alarm had been silenced, or the car battery had died. The teds were gone.

The tire tracks from the Jeep were still rutted in the field on the other side. It seemed like a lifetime had passed since that day. "Come on," I said. "We'll go in slow. Stay together."

Chapter Twenty-Three

Nathan

BY LATE AFTERNOON, I CAUGHT MYSELF GLANCING AT the crest of the field or the road every time I passed the front door. By dinner, I had to work to conceal my worry. Ashley's anxious comments every five minutes didn't help anything, but when Zoe mentioned that it would be dark soon, truth began to creep in.

"They should be here by now," Elleny said in a quiet but anxious voice. "They wouldn't walk in the dark, w-would they? The sun has already set."

Ashley sat down at the table and closed her eyes. "They'll be back, Elleny, don't worry. They couldn't have all been hurt. If something happened, some of them would still come back. So you know what that means? They're *all* fine."

"They said they would come back tonight. If they don't come back, someone got hurt," Zoe said, oblivious to what her words would do to everyone else at the table.

Elleny puffed out a sob. Ashley covered her mouth with her hands.

"Everyone calm down," I said, on the verge of hysterics myself. "Shallot is almost fifteen miles away. It might have been too optimistic for them to think they could travel thirty miles in a day on foot *and* clear. That doesn't mean anything is wrong. That could just mean they're being smart and aren't risking traveling at night."

Elleny nodded. "Scarlet wouldn't do that. They'll be back in the morning." She took a small bite of mashed potatoes.

"Exactly," I said.

Ashley nodded. "Maybe they'll send Cooper back tonight to tell us. He can make it back faster than the rest of them."

"Maybe," Miranda said. "But don't freak out if he doesn't. Let's not worry until we have something to worry about."

Miranda's voice was calm, but the look she shot me said that she was only trying to help me keep the others calm. She didn't know if they would come back any more than we did.

Just as I took my first bite, the power went out. Zoe and Elleny screamed.

"Sssh!" I said. "We knew this was going to happen eventually, don't panic. Everyone sit tight."

I felt my way over to the cabinets and reached under the sink, grabbing two flashlights. I turned on one, and handed the other to Miranda.

"I'll get candles," she said. "Come with me, Elleny."

Ashley sat at the table with Zoe, holding her hand. I smiled at them. "This is no different than any other night. We always sleep with the lights out."

"But if we needed to turn them on, we could," Zoe said, shaken.

Ashley hugged Zoe to her side. "Don't worry. I'm right here with you."

"I'm here with you, too," Zoe said, patting Ashley's hand.

Scarlet

"IN HERE!" I SAID TO JOEY AND BRYCE, HOLDING OPEN the door. Cooper had led us to the house they'd stayed in before. It was already boarded up, and, according to the boys, was only a few houses away from another house full of guns and ammo.

Bryce and Joey had attracted the attention of a large group of teds to divert them away from the house, and then backtracked. Once they were inside, I tried to flip on the light. Nothing.

"Power's out?" Joey asked. He slipped off his pack and pulled out a small flashlight. "There's candles under the sink, but I don't have any matches."

"I do," I said, unzipping my pack.

We all sat on the floor in a circle, sipping our water and breathing hard. By the time we'd reached Shallot, we only had an hour to work with before we would need to head back. Shallot was so overrun, we all lost track of time, and then it was too late to even think about going home. We cleared until nearly dark, and even then we still had more than half to eliminate.

Joey didn't rest long before he stood up again. "I'm going to go check the windows and doors. Make sure all of our boards are holding up, and see if we still have a second exit."

Bryce rolled his eyes, and when Joey was out of sight, he grumbled under his breath. "G.I. Joe to the rescue."

"Hey," I said, taking a sip of water. "He saved our asses more than once today. Be nice."

Bryce rested his arms across the tops of his knees, unhappy.

"Uh . . . guys . . . ?" Joey said, walking into the room with his hands up. With only the candles to light the room, I could only make out Joey and the end of the rifle that was against his head.

Cooper, Bryce, and I all stood up quickly, pulling our guns. Joey stood in front of the man holding him hostage.

"Didn't your mothers teach you not to walk into someone's house without knocking?"

"I'm sorry," I said. "We'll leave."

"How did you get here?" he asked. "A car?"

"No, we walked," I said. "We're sorry. Just please let us leave." I lowered my weapon. "See? We don't want anyone to get hurt."

"Too late for that," the man said. Joey closed his eyes tight, but nothing happened. I grabbed my flashlight, and shined it in the man's eyes. He recoiled from the light. His hair was shaggy, his nails and fingers black with dirt, and his camouflage overalls and coat were stained with blood. He towered over Joey, and I wondered if we had a chance if we all charged him at once.

"Skeeter?" Bryce said.

The man struggled against the beam of my flashlight to see who called his name. "Who's that?"

"It's me, Bryce! Coop's here, too! I can't believe you made it!"

I lifted the flashlight so the light bounced off the ceiling and cast a dim glow over the entire room. Skeeter pulled his gun away from Joey and shook Bryce's and then Cooper's hands.

"Holy hell, boys!" Skeeter said, pulling his hat off his head.

"What are you doing here?" Cooper said, a wide grin on his face.

I was completely confused. Bryce and Cooper seemed to know this man, but Joey didn't.

"Skeeter McGee, nice to meet ya," he said, shaking Joey's hand. "Sorry 'bout that. I've had some run-ins with some assholes. You know how it is."

Joey shook his hand, bewildered.

"I knew the girls' old man's place was out this way. I thought I'd try to catch up to y'all, but I got stuck here. This place is crawlin' with creepers!"

"Creepers," Cooper said with a chuckle. "I like that."

"No," I said. "It's ted. Zoe wouldn't like it if we changed it."

Skeeter's face fell, and turned white. "What'd you say?"

I glanced around the room. No one else seemed to know why his mood had suddenly changed, either, and I worried the boys didn't know him as well as they thought. Whether the boys knew this man or not, we needed to protect everyone we left at home. "We just made a group decision on what to call those things. It's pretty silly, actually . . ."

"No, ma'am. You just said Zoe. Like little Zoe, 'bout yay high. Light brown hair?" he asked, karate chopping his chin to show the length.

"How do you know Zoe?" I said, instantly suspicious.

Skeeter ran over to me. "She's my niece. You've seen her? Where is she? Is she with her dad?"

"Your niece?" I said, wondering why Nathan had never said anything about a brother.

"Aubrey is my sister. Nathan's wife. Have you seen them?"

Nathan's wife. The words stung.

"Yes, we've seen them," Bryce said. "They're at Red Hill Ranch. They're safe."

Skeeter laughed once, and then stumbled backward, falling onto the couch. "Oh, thank God," he said, flattening the palm of his hand against the side of his face. After a moment, he covered his face in his hands, bent at the waist, and then the big, burly man began to cry.

We all traded glances, unsure of what to do. The one thing I was sure of was that as of that moment, there were ten of us.

"Skeeter?" I said. I touched his shoulder. "Skeeter. We're heading out tomorrow after we clear. You're welcome to come with us."

"Clear?"

"Yes. My daughters are meeting me at Red Hill, and we're making sure they don't run into trouble."

He nodded. "Then I'll help you."

THE NEXT DAY WAS HOTTER THAN THE DAY BEFORE. Two hours after sunrise, and it was already muggy. The hairs falling down from my bun were sticking to the back of my neck, and the waves of heat were dancing just above the asphalt. I didn't think it was possible, but the rising temperature made the pungent smell baked into our clothes waft into the air and blend to form a potpourri of rotten food and bad breath. I could barely stand to smell myself, so I tried to keep my distance from everyone else.

In Shallot, we each took down five teds apiece, and then began our trek back to the ranch. Skeeter told the story of how he made it through a herd of zombies until he got to his wife, who had turned, so that he could put her down so she didn't hurt anyone. The more Skeeter talked, the more I liked him, and I wondered if Aubrey was anything like her brother. It didn't feel so senseless now, telling Nathan that it was over between us. Now that Skeeter was moving in, it would have been weird, anyway. Suddenly the thought of being around Nathan without any prospect of fixing what I'd done was very depressing. The closer we got to the ranch, the sicker I felt.

"I can't believe you know Nate. That's just bizarre," Cooper said.

"It's funny y'all ran into him. You just missed him at the church," Skeeter said.

"He was at the church?" Bryce said, amused.

"Yep. He was. He left with Zoe the first chance he got because he knew it was only a matter of time before they got in."

"What church?" I asked, stopping in the middle of the road.

Skeeter grinned. "First Baptist Church of Fairview."

"Holy shit," I said, realizing that the people I saw running out of that church could have been Nathan and Zoe.

Skeeter nodded. "Holy shit, indeed."

We alternated jogging and walking. Cooper was anxious to get home to Ashley, concerned she would be sick with worry. When we reached the top of the hill, I glanced back, hoping my babies would be doing the same thing soon.

Ashley burst through the front door and ran down the drive, jumping into Cooper's arms. She began to cry immediately. Elleny jumped off the porch and hugged me, trying her best to keep her eyes dry. Nathan, Miranda, and Zoe were standing on the porch, confused at the sight of the gruff-looking fellow bringing up the rear.

"Skeeter?" Nathan said. By his words alone it was obvious

he couldn't believe what he was seeing, but he had the most disgusted look on his face.

"Uncle Skeeter!" Zoe yelled, running down the steps into his arms. The second he hugged her back, she wrinkled her nose. "You stink!"

Skeeter laughed. "I know! Yucky, huh?"

Nathan walked down the steps, and wrapped both of his arms around his brother-in-law. "I can't . . . I don't believe it."

The men hugged for a bit, and then we all hugged each other. When Nathan got to me, he held me tight, and then planted his lips on mine. After less than a second of shock, I let myself melt into him. His fingers dug into my back, and I pulled him close.

"I'm so sorry," I said against his lips.

He shook his head, keeping his eyes closed. "Don't. Don't say a word. Just let me hold you."

I buried my face into his neck, feeling safer than I had in weeks. Nathan loved me more than he should after what I'd said. Hopefully it wasn't too much to ask that God give me just one more miracle.

Bryce climbed the few steps to Miranda, and gave her a quick kiss on the cheek.

"Good God almighty," Skeeter said, his voice grave. "Y'all shoulda warned me."

"About what?" Bryce said.

"Two redheads in the house." He sighed. "I had better chances in Shallot."

Miranda narrowed her eyes at him, and I laughed. "You're probably right."

"I'm so glad you're back," Nathan said, hugging me again. He kissed my cheek before pulling me into the house by the hand. He left me long enough to show Skeeter the facilities, and get him some clean clothes, and then he returned. "I have some bad news. The electric is off. I've tried to flip the breaker, but it's . . . it's gone."

I nodded. "We knew it was temporary, right?"

Nathan nodded. "So, you met my brother-in-law? He's something else, isn't he?"

"Yes. Is this going to be . . . awkward for you?"

"No. Skeeter knows she left. He knew it was over a long time ago. Are you okay?"

"Yeah," I said, hugging him to me. I pressed my cheek against his shoulder, glad that he didn't take anything I'd said before seriously. "What I said before . . . I . . ."

Nathan shook his head. "No . . . forget about it. It's okay."

"No, it's not okay. That was a horrible thing to say, and I'm sorry. I wasn't good at this before the end of the world, and apparently I haven't gotten any better."

"Good at what?"

"Loving someone."

He raised an eyebrow, smiled, and then took me into his arms, planting a tender kiss on my lips. "I never asked for perfection."

I breathed out a small laugh.

"But I got it, anyway."

I touched each side of Nathan's face and pulled him toward me, kissing his lips. Only one thing could make my life better, and I ached for my girls to reach me so we could all be together. "It's not perfect. Not quite yet."

"But it will be," Nathan said, never missing a chance to reassure me.

"Uncle Skeeter, you should come meet Butch," Zoe said.

Skeeter had just emerged from the bathroom, his skin shiny and his hair wet. His face still looked a little dirty, but it was just the tan line around his eyes from his sunglasses.

"Who's Butch?" Skeeter said, fastening the last button of his clean shirt. He tugged at the fabric where it fit a big snug. The shirt looked expensive, white with horizontal pinstripes. It didn't look at all like something he would normally wear.

Zoe tugged on his hand, and he went along with her as if she were too strong to resist. "He's a cow!"

"You mean a bull?" Skeeter said, looking over at Nathan and feigning concern.

I laughed. "He seems like a good guy."

"He is." Nathan smiled, watching the two.

"Not at all like you've described Aubrey."

"He's nothing like her. But she wasn't that way at first, either."

Skeeter pretended to be too scared of Butch, and made a scene trying to break free of Zoe's grip.

"He's good with kids. Did he have any of his own?"

"Not yet," Nathan said, suddenly sad. "His wife was pregnant when this all went down." He looked at me. "Her name was Jill. She was the sweetest thing."

"I'm sorry," I said, kicking myself for bringing up the subject.

Nathan kissed my cheek. "We've all lost someone," he said. "It's just the way things are, now."

Cooper and Ashley came outside, hugged and kissed like they did every time he started his patrol. "See if you can't talk Nate into grilling chicken tonight." He winked at Nathan before slinging a rifle over his shoulder.

I patted Nathan's arm. "You are the best cook we've got."

"I love you!" Ashley called.

"I love you more!" Cooper called back, holding out both of his arms wide, and then jogging off to the east.

"Vomit," I said, teasing Ashley.

She stuck out her tongue. "Don't be jelly!"

"Jelly?" Nathan asked.

"Jealous," I said. "You'll learn all this when Zoe gets older.

He nodded, mouthing *Ah*.

Skeeter jogged up to us, breathing hard from playing with Zoe. "He's not all that scary. I think we should just cook him."

"That's not funny!" Ashley said, even though she was grinning. She turned to go inside. "He's a pet!"

Nathan elbowed his brother-in-law. "You talk awfully big when he's in a pen. Maybe we should let him out and see who wins?"

Skeeter sniffed. "I'd win."

We all laughed, and then Nathan held up his finger, leaning his ear over like he was listening for something. Then I heard it, too. Yelling. We all looked around, and then Nathan pointed, seeing Cooper sprinting at full speed, pointing and screaming. At first I couldn't make out what he was saying, and then Nathan froze.

His breath caught. "Oh my God. Zoe."

Nathan took off first, and then Skeeter and I followed behind. We ran south, the same direction as Cooper, even though the barn was obscuring our view. To my horror, I saw Zoe, her arms stretched out wide, turning in slow circles in the field, with a man limping toward her less than ten feet away.

Cooper yelled again. "Zoe! Behind you! Run!"

Zoe stopped turning, but her back was to the creature behind her.

"Zoe!" Nathan yelled as he ran. "Listen to me! Run to me, baby! Run to daddy as fast as you can!"

Zoe looked at her dad quizzically, and then turned around, seeing the infected approaching. She didn't move. Everything seemed to be in slow motion, like a dream. No matter how fast I ran, I couldn't get to her fast enough. My heart felt like it was about to explode, between the fear and me pushing my legs as fast as they could go.

I could hear the low groan, the sound they made when they were excited. The only thing they got excited about was satisfying their constant hunger. He reached out for her, but Zoe didn't move.

"Run, Zoe!" Nathan screamed, his voice breaking. I knew he was crying. I was, too.

Just as the creature bent down to grab at Zoe, Cooper used his entire body to tackle him to the ground. Zoe went with them.

Nathan screamed again, waving his arms, still a good twenty feet away. When we finally came upon them, Zoe was on her back, staring up at the sky, and Cooper was pummeling the infected's skull with the butt of his rifle.

Nathan stood Zoe up and checked her over. "Were you bitten?" he said, inspecting her arms and legs, and then lifting up her shirt to look at her back. He grabbed her jaw and turned her head from one side to the other, looking at her neck.

Zoe began bawling then, and Nathan took her into his arms. Skeeter and I slowed to a stop, just in time to see the mess Cooper had left. He met my eyes, and that was when I saw the bright-red blood on his shoulder.

Cooper looked at his wound, and then fell to the ground. I kneeled beside him to inspect the mangled mess of torn skin and muscle. A large gouge had been bitten from the front part of the shoulder, all the way to the bone.

Skeeter yanked his shirt over his head and wadded it up, handing it to me. I pressed down, hard, but I knew just like everyone else that it was just for show. Cooper winced from the pressure, and then his eyes met mine.

"Cooper?" Ashley called, still distant. Her voice had an edge of fear. She knew something was wrong.

Cooper looked at me. "Don't let her see."

I nodded, looking up to Skeeter. "Keep her away."

"Tell her I love her," Cooper said, his lip quivering.

My sight blurred as tears filled them. "She knows, Coop. You showed her every second of every day."

He smiled and nodded as Ashley yelled at Skeeter, cussing him for holding her back. "He'll be okay!" she yelled just out of sight. "Scarlet! He'll be okay! Don't hurt him!"

"She's going to hate me," I said.

Cooper leaned forward, touching his forehead to my face, hugging me the only way he could. "I don't want to risk turning and attacking any of you. Do it now."

Nathan lifted Zoe into his arms, and then wiped his eyes. "Thank you, Cooper. You saved my little girl."

Cooper nodded. "Keep Ashley safe, okay? Return the favor."

"With my life," Nathan said. "I owe you."

"Don't hurt him!" Ashley wailed. "Please!"

I leaned down to kiss his cheek, and then stood up, aimed my rifle at his temple, and pulled the trigger.

Chapter Twenty-Four

Miranda

WE GATHERED UNDER THE TREE AT SUNSET, NEXT TO the place my father and Leah were buried. This time, around a new mound of dirt. Ashley had made the cross herself, tying it together at the intersection of wood with twine, working wild flowers into the binding. She worked on it for hours, carving decoration and Stanley Leonard Cooper II into the wood. The only time she spoke to anyone was to tell them she would not allow a funeral until his cross was finished.

We never had time to bury Jill, and Scarlet had buried my dad before we got here, so it was our first funeral. I just couldn't believe it was for Cooper. He was the strongest and the kindest of us, it didn't seem right that he was gone.

Skeeter, Nathan, and Bryce were filthy from digging, and then carrying Cooper's body in from the field. I'd been inside consoling my nearly inconsolable sister. Once she finished the cross and the boys began digging Cooper's grave, it all hit her at once, and she'd been hysterical for the better part of the day.

Now that I'd coaxed her outside, she was silent. We all were. Finally, Nathan cleared his throat.

"Stanley Cooper was the best of us. We should strive every day to be as hard working, kind, and loving as he was. He was a good friend, and brother . . ."

"And husband," Ashley whispered. Her face crumpled, and her body shook with quiet sobs.

"And husband," Nathan repeated, his voice breaking. "He was a hero. He saved a life. And we should all strive to live the way he did so we can see him again in heaven.

"Cooper told me once about his little sister Savannah, how close they were, how much he loved her, and he also told me he worried daily if she and his mother were alive. If they're not, he's with them again. Maybe we can take comfort in that."

Bryce smiled. "I remember the first time I met Coop. It was in class, and he was staring at Ashley. Of course, I was dating the sister, so as soon as he heard that, he was automatically my best friend. Except, he didn't fake it just to be my friend, ya know? He was a good best friend. The best." He cleared his throat. "I'm going to miss him. The world isn't as good without him in it, but heaven is better off."

Scarlet smiled. "That was nice."

"Don't speak," Ashley said. "Don't talk here, Scarlet."

Nathan took a step toward Ashley, but she pulled away. "This isn't her fault, Ashley. She had to, you know that."

"It's okay," Scarlet said, motioning to Nathan. "She gets to be angry."

"Don't be nice to me," Ashley said, her emotional state quickly going downhill. "Don't fucking be nice, Scarlet. Just don't talk. I don't want to hear your voice, do you understand me?"

Scarlet looked down and nodded. Scarlet was one of the strongest women I knew, and she was letting Ashley talk to her that way in front of everyone. Even though we all knew Ashley didn't mean a word of it, I was still in awe of Scarlet's patience.

Nathan began to speak in Scarlet's defense again, but Scarlet touched his arm and shook her head.

We stood out there for half an hour, crying, telling stories, laughing, and remembering. Ashley began to weave back and forth, so emotionally exhausted she could barely stand. I took her inside, supporting her weight while we walked. She went straight to bed, and cried herself to sleep.

"Hey," Bryce said as I closed Ashley's door. I held up my finger to my mouth. Bryce nodded, and began to whisper, "How is she?"

"The same."

"How are you?"

"The same." Bryce put his arm around my shoulder and guided me to the empty living room. "Where is everyone?"

"Joey is on watch. Scarlet said it might be a good idea to get onto the roof, so Joey found a ladder and climbed up. He said he can see a lot farther. We'll have better warning this way."

I nodded.

"Nathan is with the girls. Skeeter and Scarlet went down the road."

"Clearing?" I asked.

Bryce nodded.

"Just the two of them? After what happened?"

"I'm going with them. I just wanted to make sure you were okay."

I took a deep breath. "I know Scarlet feels like she needs to do this, but I think it's time we accept that her girls aren't coming. It's been nearly four months now."

Bryce shrugged. "I don't know. It took Nate and Coop almost all day to cross fifteen miles. That's a long way for two little girls if they're on foot. I think if they don't make it by winter, we can call it."

"That's a long time to let her hope."

"Not long enough, if you ask me." He kissed my forehead. "See you soon."

"Be careful."

I watched Bryce leave, jogging to catch up to Scarlet and Skeeter, who were already out of sight down the road. My stomach felt like it dropped, and I wondered if it was a good idea for him to be alone at all, even for the few minutes it would take him to join Scarlet and Skeeter.

Once Bryce was over the hill, I pushed the door open, and noticed the ladder against the roof. One hand after another, I climbed to the top, seeing Joey sitting on the seam with a hunting rifle, a box of ammunition, and what I was sure was my father's best scope.

"Want some company?" I asked.

Joey looked up to the sun and squinted. "Always."

I sat down, but could see the bottom part of Cooper's grave, so I moved closer to the middle of the house. Nathan was by Butch's pen with the girls, watching them talk to the bull. He looked away only long enough to take a quick glance around, and then his eyes were on them again.

"Zoe seems okay. It's kind of weird," Joey said.

"I don't think she's like us."

"What do you mean?"

"I think she's a little different, that's all."

Joey nodded. "Nathan is a saint. I'm glad he and Scarlet have each other."

I smiled. "Me, too."

He glanced around, in every direction, and then pointed. "Look."

There was a single tree in the middle of the north field. A group of birds that were perched took off, all at once, from the branches. Joey looked through his scope and cocked his rifle. "There are four of them. You see?"

I narrowed my eyes; the wheat was now tall and golden, nearly ready for harvest. In the tall crop, it was easy to see a ted stumble through it. I looked at Joey. I could see three heads, and wheat moving around a shorter fourth. It was either a very petite person, or a child. "You can see them? They're teds, right, not humans?"

"Definitely teds."

"You got it?"

"I got it," he said, cocking his rifle.

One. *Reload.*

Two. *Reload.*

Three. *Reload.*

And after a pause, four.

Joey looked up from the scope, took another quick look through it at the area, and then put his rifle in his lap.

Nathan gathered the girls and yelled to Joey from the ground.

"Clear?"

"Clear," Joey called back.

"You see Scarlet?"

"No."

Nathan seemed frustrated. Cooper's death had been a reality check for us all. None of us could talk Scarlet out of clearing because there was no way to argue with her reasoning, but it was still a huge risk.

Joey wiped his forehead with a dirty rag. We were baking up there, even under the partial shade of the oak tree. Joey leaned back, supporting himself with his hands. His index finger brushed my pinky, and then he intertwined all of his fingers in mine. We didn't acknowledge it or talk; we just sat there, soaked with sweat and content that for a moment we didn't have to pretend.

Scarlet

"HEADS UP!" SKEETER YELLED.

We were downwind, and it was easy to smell the rotting corpses as they approached. This time, though, the smell was exceptionally bad. At first I thought it was because we were nearing the hottest part of summer, but then I saw them.

Skeeter laughed once. "Blackened and crispy fried. Like Nathan's fried chicken!"

"They don't smell like chicken," Bryce said, revolted.

We hadn't even reached the highway when we ran into a small herd. They were coming from the south, and as I was busy slamming down the hatchet into the tops of skulls and the sides of faces, I wondered why we were seeing so many more of them. We had been clearing for weeks; it didn't make sense for there to be more on the road, and that frustrated the hell out of me.

Skeeter and Bryce helped me pull the rotting bodies to the ditch. It was a rule I'd made when we started. It was too much work to bury them, and too risky to pile them and burn the bodies because of the heat, wind, and lack of rain in the last month. I just didn't want the girls to have to walk over them as they made their way to the ranch.

I stood up, breathing hard and wiping the dirt and sweat from my face. "I think they're coming from Shallot."

"I was thinkin' the same thing," Skeeter said. "These guys must have gotten too close to the gas station fire."

Bryce jerked his head to the south. "The fire must be out, and they don't have anything attracting them to town anymore."

"And they're starving," I said, nodding to another small herd trudging down the highway less than a quarter mile away. They were skin and bones. I wasn't sure if they actually needed to eat, or if it was just the natural state of decay, but they definitely looked starved. "Look at them. Maybe they'll eventually fall apart, or their bodies will give out from lack of nutrition."

"That's a promising thought," Skeeter said. "But I wouldn't count on it. Them ones we just cleared were burnt to a crisp. They were still walkin'."

"They're headed north," Bryce said. "Let's just let them pass."

I shook my head. "Maybe someone saw the one that got Cooper and let it pass. We're putting them all down. As many as we can."

Nathan

I PACED THE LIVING ROOM WHILE DINNER COOKED, checking the doorway every few seconds for any sign of them. My emotions bounced from worried, to angry, to frustrated, to panicked.

"They'll be back anytime now," Miranda assured me. "Dinner's burning."

I ran to the laundry room and out the side door to the grill. "Damn it!" I said, pulling the chicken off with my bare hands. I licked my burning fingers, and shook my hand, as if that would help.

Miranda stood at the doorway. "I know it's hard for you, watching her put herself in danger like this."

I took a quick glance around our surroundings. Looking over my shoulder was a habit I'd developed; I wasn't sure at what point I'd started doing it, but it happened every time I was outside, like a tick. "Bryce is out there, too . . . and Joey."

Miranda's cheeks flushed, and she looked behind her before coming all the way outside. "Is it that obvious?" I gave her a look, and her head fell in shame. "I didn't mean to. It just happened."

"It's a complicated situation," I said. "I'm in no position to judge you."

"I don't know what to do. I don't have anyone to talk to."

"You can talk to me. Not sure how much help I'll be, but I'll listen."

Miranda smiled, and leaned her temple across the doorjamb. "Thanks, Nate."

I brought in the plate of chicken, and looked at the three empty chairs with a sigh. Miranda left to get Ashley, but came back empty-handed.

"She doesn't feel like eating."

I nodded. "I'll give her a pass tonight, but she's going to have to start eating soon."

Miranda nodded.

We all sat down to eat. Elleny and Zoe discussed their day. They got along really well. Elleny didn't talk much, but she was a sweet girl. I'd tried to talk to her about her family, but she kept it all inside. Scarlet said she'd talked about her parents only once, but it was too difficult and she never tried again after that. I hoped after she healed from what that monster put her through, she might be able to talk to someone. That was too much pain for one little girl to hold inside.

"And then Butch went *mawwwwwwwwwwrrrr,*" Zoe said, giggling.

Elleny giggled, too, and pretty soon we were all laughing.

"Daddy!" Zoe said, sitting up on her knees. She pointed to the door as Bryce opened it.

Joey came in after him, and then Scarlet. I ran to her and took her into my arms. Those first few seconds when she returned from clearing always pulled a huge weight off my shoulders, letting me breathe again.

"I've got yuck on me!" she warned.

"I don't care," I said, squeezing her against me, and then kissing her lips.

Scarlet pulled away, lowering her chin. "They're leaving Shallot. Migrating."

"Looking for food," I said, thoughtful.

"If they're hunting, I've got to step up my efforts."

"Scarlet," I began, but she held up her hand and smiled. "I'm going to wash up. We'll talk later."

She walked away, and I sighed. She had already made up her mind.

During dinner, Scarlet explained the basics of her plan. After dinner, while we were lying in bed, she explained it in more depth to me. She was hoping I would agree that it was the right thing to do, but I was running out of reasons to support her daily trips into danger.

"For the next week," she whispered, "we'll concentrate on clearing the road, that way we don't miss any coming out of Shallot on this side. Then, we'll eventually make another trip to Shallot. I don't think they'll be that many left in town, do you?"

I shook my head. "It's hard to tell."

"I think it will be thinned out. We'll stay in Shallot until it's clear, and then we'll work on the road between Shallot and the other highway."

I sat up. "Have you told the guys this?"

"I mentioned it on the way home. Skeeter and Bryce are on board. I'll ask Joey if he wants to come."

"Jesus Christ, Scarlet, when will it stop? When will it be enough?"

"Keep your voice down."

"I'm trying. God knows I'm trying, but you have to tell me when this little project is going to be over."

"Little project?"

I frowned. "Do you have any idea what I go through every morning when you leave? What I go through all day until you come back?"

"Yeah. I have an idea," she said, crawling out of bed.

"God, Scarlet . . . ," I said, feeling terrible. "I'm sorry."

She left without saying a word, and I lay back against my pillow, looking up at the ceiling while I let myself drown in the guilt that washed over me.

Chapter Twenty-Five

Miranda

AFTER THE EIGHTH DAY IN A ROW OF CLEARING, SCARlet and the boys took a day off. We had all been looking forward to it. While they were gone, Nathan and I took turns keeping an eye out on the roof. It was so damn hot that—even guzzling water—we would be nearly sun sick by the time we climbed down. And then we had to keep an eye on the girls. It was exhausting. I couldn't imagine how the boys felt every day.

Ashley had been taking food into her bedroom, but today she decided to venture to the dining room. It was obvious we were trying to keep the conversation light. Ashley didn't eat or speak much, but it was a big step for her to come to the table with us, and we all knew it.

It was my turn to wash the dishes. Joey brought in a bucket of water from outside, and then stuck around to dry as I cleaned.

"I hope it rains soon," he said. "Not much water left in the basin."

We hadn't had any time alone together since the day we

were on the roof, and even though I played it off, and even though he'd come in with bad news, I was almost giddy when he offered to help.

"You're getting to be quite domestic," I teased. Joey elbowed me, and I giggled.

Bryce walked into the kitchen and grabbed a towel. "I'll do that," he said to Joey.

"We're almost done," I said, hoping I didn't sound like I just wanted to keep Joey in the kitchen with me—because that's exactly what I wanted.

Bryce looked at us both expectantly, and then Joey and I traded glances.

"I was going to get some target practice in, anyway." Joey and I used that to steal a few moments alone together a few weeks back, and I smiled, knowing it was an invitation.

"Better warn Skeeter," Bryce called. "Wouldn't want him to accidentally gun you down," he grumbled under his breath.

The second the storm door slammed, I tried to think of a reason to go outside with Joey. Bryce and I finished the dishes, and he was putting them away. Scarlet, Nathan, and Zoe were playing some kind of homemade board game in the middle of the living-room floor.

"Miranda, Ashley went outside earlier. I'm going to check on her when I'm finished," Bryce said, shutting a cabinet door.

"I'll do it," I said, trying not to sound as eager as I felt. My hands were shaking, thankful I had a reason, and excited that it was Bryce who had come up with one. That would mean fewer questions later. I tried to be nonchalant as I walked casually out the front door.

He wasn't at the back of the house, where we'd met the last

time. It didn't take long before I realized I didn't see Joey . . . or Ashley.

"Hey, Skeeter," I called, looking up to the roof. He poked his head over the edge. "You see Joey or Ashley?"

Skeeter pointed south, but didn't say a word.

I walked out to the barn, but Butch and I were the only two around.

Several emotions bubbled to the surface: confusion, worry, and even suspicion. Noises from behind the barn piqued my curiosity, so I peeked around the corner. Joey and Ashley were standing in the field together. She was holding the rifle, and he was trying to help her hold it correctly. He said something, making her drop the barrel toward the ground a bit. His hand was on her hip for a fraction of a second. They began to laugh, the ugly kind that produces tears. Joey even doubled over and steadied himself with his hands on his knees.

My face instantly flushed and my eyes filled with tears. At first I was angry with Ashley. She'd been walking around the house nearly comatose, not responding to anyone or anything. All she'd done for almost ten days was cry and sleep. Every time I tried to talk to her, she'd just get angry. But in the field with Joey, she was herself again. Laughing and joking like Cooper hadn't been shot in the face right in front of her less than two weeks before. Suddenly, alone with Joey, she was just fine.

I stifled back a sob, letting the jealousy, and then the guilt, swallow me whole. Of course Ashley deserved to do something other than be miserable. How could I say that I loved her and then be angry with her for having a moment of peace? I slowly let myself slide to the ground and sat in the dirt. Sweat was forming along my hairline, and a drop finally fell just in front of my ear. It was like an oven, even in the shade, but Ashley and Joey didn't notice they were baking with the sun shining straight down on them.

She was alone now, and so was Joey. They would talk about their loss, and find comfort in one another, and I would have to watch them because I had nowhere else to go. I closed my eyes and let my head fall back against the wall of the barn. God, I was a horrid, selfish bitch.

Joey's and Ashley's voices got louder, and I realized they were walking my way. I stayed very still and didn't dare breathe, afraid they would catch me eavesdropping and crying over them like a crazy person. I was convinced they would both know why if they saw me. Thankfully, they were too busy impressing each other to see me, and continued to the house. I finally took a deep breath and let out a quiet cry. I said once that I wouldn't want Joey if he were the last man on earth. Now I was just horrible enough to wish we were the last ones on earth so I could have him to myself.

That night at dinner, Ashley and Joey sat next to each other. They carried on about their afternoon and how awful a shot she was. For absolutely no reason at all, I was annoyed with Ashley's voice and the entire conversation. No one else was talking, just listening to them go on and on and on about how funny that was, and how hilarious this was, and bragging about how much help Ashley needed.

"We've decided she needs some serious help, and this should be a daily thing until she gets better."

"Sounds like a good idea," Nathan said, nodding.

"You've shot a gun before, Ashley. I don't understand how you'd be so bad at it," I said.

Ashley chuckled, and then when she realized I wasn't amused, she stopped altogether. "I haven't shot that much."

"As much as I have. The way you guys are talking, you were confused on how to hold the damn thing."

"Miranda," Nathan said in his infuriatingly smooth voice.

"I'm just curious." I tried a smile, hoping it would cover how crazy I felt, and how awful I was for being angry that my sister was happy.

Ashley looked down at the table, the light that had come back to her eyes snuffed out. "It was just never my thing."

The corners of her mouth evened out, and she rolled her food around on her plate with her fork, returning to the same lifeless vessel that she'd been since Cooper died.

Bryce shot me a look. I didn't have to ask him what he was thinking. I knew he was angry that I'd been so hard on her, and he should have been. I was angry with myself.

"I'm sorry, Ashley. I didn't mean—"

"It's fine," she said, her face devoid of emotion.

I sat back in my chair, feeling judgment from everyone at the table. I deserved it, so I sat there, letting them glare, stare, or shake their heads. I wasn't sure who was the angriest. I wasn't brave enough to look up from my plate.

AFTER THE LIGHTS WENT OUT, BRYCE TRIED TO TUG ME out of the recliner. "You coming?"

I nodded. "I'll be there in a bit. I'm not really tired."

He nodded back, resigned. After he disappeared in the hall and closed the door, I stood.

Joey was breathing hard but regular, facing the floor in the last half of a pushup. His face was red and moist, and as usual, he was without a shirt. The veins were bulging from his hands and arms.

Noticing my feet next to his face, Joey looked up at me.

"Can I talk to you outside for a minute?" I said, and then turned to go to the front porch. Joey came out, quietly shutting the door behind him.

Now that we were alone, and he was half naked, I fought to recall why I was angry in the first place.

"What's going on with you?" he asked.

"I saw you."

"Huh?"

"With Ashley. Earlier. What the hell do you think you're doing?"

Joey crossed his arms across his chest and shifted his weight nervously. "Um . . . teaching her to shoot?"

I laughed once without humor. "Oh, bullshit. You've taught me to shoot before. I don't remember your hands being all over me like that."

"My . . . *what?*"

"You heard me. I saw you!"

Joey's expression morphed from surprise to mild anger. "I didn't have my hands all over her, Miranda, you're being ridiculous. And you knew what you were doing pretty well before we went out because you've shot before."

"So has she!"

"Well, then she's not as good as you are."

"She is sad, Joey. Whatever you're thinking? Don't."

"Don't what? Maybe I'm stupid, so you'll have to tell me exactly what you're saying." He was getting defensive, which only made me angrier.

"I'm saying Ashley is my sister. I love her. She just lost the love of her life, and she's vulnerable. I don't know how much more clear I can be, so let me just say it: I don't want her to be taken advantage of."

"You don't *really* think I would do that," Joey said, seething. When I didn't answer, his expression changed again. "Do you really think so little of me that I would try to fly under the radar to get into her pants? While she's grieving?"

"No, that's not what I'm saying, I'm—"

"Good, because if you really think I'm that big of a piece of shit, what have we been doing?"

"We haven't done anything!"

"You know what I mean!"

"Wait, did you mean that when she's not grieving anymore you'll try to get in her pants?"

"*What?*" he said, clearly trying to remember when he'd said anything remotely close to that. He shook his head, completely flustered. "You have to know me better than that. You have to know how I feel about you. She's your sister. I would never . . ."

"Yes. I do know you, and I know you've lost someone, too, so I thought maybe you felt like you two had something in common."

"So it's not that you think I'd pull a dick move like that, but you wanted to warn me not to make a dick move like that."

"No! I don't think you're an asshole, I just think you're both . . . maybe not thinking about what it means if you get together just because you're alone."

"So you came down here to make sure I wasn't trying to get close with your sister because you didn't think I would try to get close with your sister?"

"Yes!"

"You're not making any sense!" He turned his back on me and walked a few steps in the other direction, and then turned to face me. "Or maybe you are."

I watched him for a long time. I wasn't sure if I was embarrassed or angry or both, but that smug smile that I hated and loved was spread wide across his face. I flipped my wrist and showed him my middle finger. "Maybe you *are* an asshole." I turned on my heels for the stairs, but Joey flipped me around and then his mouth was on mine. After the initial surprise, I gripped his skin and pulled him against me just as his tongue slid into my mouth. He smelled like two days of sweat and dirt, and I'm sure I did, too, but I couldn't get close enough to him. I wanted more of his mouth on mine, more of his arms around me, more of his hands on more of my skin, but he pulled away.

By the look on his face and the glimmer of sadness in his eyes, kissing me had brought back a memory. Maybe I deserved it, loving someone who loved someone else.

"Wow, I'm sorry," he whispered, stumbling backward. "I can't believe I just did that."

"It's okay," I said, reaching out for him, desperate to make him feel better.

"I can't do this to Dana."

My eyes filled with tears. "You're not doing anything wrong. I know you loved her, but Dana's not here."

"But Bryce is."

His words sliced through me like an axe. He wasn't doing anything wrong, but I was.

"We're going all the way to Shallot again," he said. "I've got an early morning and a long day, and when we get back, Skeeter wants to dig ditches around the perimeter. I need to rest."

I nodded, stepping backward a few times before finally opening the door. It would have been just my luck to run into someone, maybe even Bryce, as I retreated into the living room with wet cheeks. When I walked in, I was alone. Nathan and Zoe had more than likely heard us go outside, and probably heard us yelling. Everyone probably heard us yelling.

I wiped my eyes quickly, and took a few steps toward the laundry room. I could hear Scarlet's whisper in my mind. *I wouldn't.* If she were still married to Andrew and stuck in this house with him and Nathan, maybe she would.

I lost my nerve, and then crept back into my bedroom, took one look at Bryce sleeping on my side of the bed, and sat in the chair in the corner. He usually fell asleep fairly quickly after his head hit the pillow, so he did that when he was waiting for me to come to bed, knowing he would wake up when I pulled the covers back to crawl in to my side. I wasn't sure if I'd stayed with him so long because I loved him, or if I just didn't have a good enough reason to ask for an ending. Either way, I was crawling in bed with the man who loved me, wishing he was the man I loved.

Chapter Twenty-Six

Nathan

"NEED MORE WATER?" MIRANDA CALLED.

I poked my head over the edge. "Sure," I said. It was hard to guess on top of the roof, but I was willing to bet the temperature was easily over a hundred degrees.

Miranda climbed the ladder with another large glass, taking my nearly empty one.

"You know what I miss?" I said. "Ice."

Miranda smiled. "Oh my God. I do, too. But I'm sure we'll get some this winter, and then we won't miss it so much."

I laughed. "You're probably right."

Miranda climbed back down, and I squinted from the glare. Scarlet and the others had been clearing for three days, and I hoped they would be back soon. I'd seen a pillar of smoke earlier that morning in that direction, and I hoped it wasn't some sort of signal from them that they needed help. I didn't bother telling Miranda. We couldn't risk taking the girls, and it was too dangerous for one of us to go alone, anyway.

I ate lunch on the roof, and then climbed down, waiting to

make sure Miranda got situated up top before I went inside. Elleny was tidying up after lunch, and Zoe was coloring on the few nubs left of her crayons. I hoped that if Scarlet had time to stop at the store in Shallot, she would think to pick up Zoe some more—if they had any—and then I laughed at how oddly normal that thought was.

"Nathan! I see them!" Miranda yelled. Her voice was muffled, so I wanted to be sure I heard her right.

"You see them?" I said, stepping out onto the porch. She didn't answer, so I crawled up the ladder. She was looking through her scope, her lip quivering.

"What is it? What do you see?" Miranda looked at me then, her eyes red and threatening to fill with tears.

After they got a little closer, I squinted in their direction. "Don't panic," I said, realizing what had her so upset. "It might not be what you think."

I turned, watching the group cut across the yard. I crawled down the ladder, with Miranda right behind me, and met Scarlet just in front of the porch. It was obvious the news wasn't good.

"I'm sorry," she said, looking to Miranda. "I'm so sorry."

Miranda's hands shook as she covered her mouth. "No."

"We were pinned down. He was going to lead them away, but he never came back."

Miranda sucked in a breath. Elleny and Zoe came outside. Elleny hugged Scarlet tightly, and Zoe hugged Skeeter.

"Are you sure? Did you look for him?" I asked.

Skeeter nodded, his eyes sad. "I found him. I put him down."

Miranda fell on her knees and wailed, covering her face.

Ashley came outside wide-eyed, and kneeled beside her sister. "Are you okay?" she asked. She looked up at us. "Where's Joey?"

Bryce stared down at Miranda, blank-faced. "He didn't make it."

Miranda leaned forward and screamed, unable to conceal her pain. Ashley held her, glancing up at Bryce. He was tearing up, watching his girlfriend mourn Joey the way Ashley had mourned Cooper. Finally, it became too much, and he went into the house.

Skeeter looked over to me with a frown. "Am I the only one confused as hell?"

"Yes," I said, not knowing what else to say.

"Maybe it wasn't him," Miranda sniffed. Her eyes brightened with hope.

"It was him," Scarlet said. "I'm so sorry. This is my fault."

Miranda's face hardened, and she stood, pushing Ashley away. "You're goddamn right this is your fault. Everyone here thinks *I'm* the selfish bitch, but you take the cake, Scarlet! You got him killed! And for *what*? Your dead kids?"

"Miranda, that's enough!" I growled. My tone surprised even me.

Miranda sucked air in through her noise. Ashley reached for her again. "Get off me!" she cried, exhaling in tiny sobs. "Get off me." She climbed the ladder to the roof, crying alone.

Scarlet swallowed and looked up at me from beneath her brow. "Is she right?"

"No," I said simply, taking her into my arms. I kissed her hair, unsure of what else to say.

Scarlet

NONE OF US WERE IN THE MOOD TO EAT, SO I JUST MADE the girls a plate of peanut butter crackers and called it good. I sat on the couch, drinking water, trying to forget the way Joey looked before Skeeter put a bullet in his forehead.

He hadn't told Miranda the whole truth. Joey did lead the teds away from the safe house, and he didn't come back, but when we went looking for him at first light, I was the one who had found him. I just couldn't pull the trigger. Joey was stumbling toward me, his neck and arms chewed in parts to the bone. I knew it was my fault that he was dead, and I couldn't be the one responsible for his death a second time. Skeeter held me with one arm while he put Joey down.

I took another sip, and then went out to the porch to wait. I could hear Miranda on the roof. Even though I knew I was the last person she wanted to see, I decided to join her.

"Hey," I said when I reached the top rung.

Miranda didn't even bother to respond, she just laughed once, incredulous.

I sat down a few feet from her. We didn't speak; I just wanted to wait where I could see farther down the road. After about ten minutes, the sky turned, marking the beginning of sunset.

"You're doing this so I can see that you still think they're alive. So Joey didn't die for nothing."

"No, I'm just waiting for my girls."

"You have two inside."

I sighed. "I have two more inside, yes."

"You know what? It doesn't matter whether you think they're alive or not. Their lives are no more important than Joey's, or Bryce's, or Skeeter's . . . or Nathan's."

"Nathan's?"

"He will die if something happens to you. Do you see Ashley? Empty and hopeless? That will be Nathan one of these days after you get yourself killed."

The thought made me sick to my stomach, but didn't change my mind. "I take total responsibility for Joey. You're right. It's my fault. But I can't apologize for doing whatever I can to help my little girls get to me safely, and I won't turn down anyone that wants to help."

Miranda craned her neck at me. "No one else will say it, Scarlet, but I will: You can go fuck yourself and your stupid idea to clear the way for your girls. There are more infected out there than humans. You're never going to clear them all, and one of these days you're going to hack into one of their heads with your hatchet, and you're going to realize too late that it was Jenna or Halle. But it won't matter, anyway, because *they're fucking dead*!" With the last words, Miranda screamed, clenched her eyes shut, and shook her head, her hair sticking to the sweat on her face.

I closed my eyes, trying to stop her screams from forming pictures in my mind. "Miranda . . ."

"Will you admit it, then?" she said, her eyes both angry and desperate.

"I don't know. I don't know what will happen to me if I have to admit they're not coming."

"They're. Not. Coming."

A tear escaped my eye, and I quickly wiped it away. "I don't believe that."

"Scarlet!" Nathan screamed from the porch. He climbed the ladder, his eyes wide. "Are you looking?"

"What?"

"Look! Look at the hill!"

I narrowed my eyes to focus, seeing two small figures walking up the red hill. Skeeter was standing in the yard, yelling and waving his arms. The figures began to run, and it was then that I realized it was Halle and Jenna.

A sob exploded from my throat. "Oh my God!" I cried. "It's them! It's my babies!"

They were alone. I could barely process what that might mean, or what they'd gone through, but in that moment, the only thing I could do was scramble for the ladder.

Nathan climbed down a few rungs, and then jumped the rest of the way down, knowing I was in a hurry.

"Scarlet? Scarlet!" Miranda screamed.

I looked to her, and then to the field where she was pointing, seeing a herd of about two dozen infected limping and stumbling toward my daughters. "Oh, Jesus! No! No!" I began climbing down the ladder, but Nathan stopped me. "Stay on the roof! You're the best shot! I'll go get them!"

Reluctantly, I nodded and climbed back up to my perch on the roof. I knew he was right, and the best thing I could do for my daughters was to pick off the infected from high ground. Nathan, Skeeter, and Bryce, with various weapons in hand, ran off to reach my girls before anything else did.

Jenna and Halle were still running toward the house, but they would be cut off by the herd that was walking through the field toward them. They had no idea what was hiding behind the wheat, but they didn't stop running, even when I began to shoot into the field.

"Jesus! Jesus, Scarlet!" Miranda said. She scrambled to the ladder and then climbed down, sprinting at full speed toward the road, screaming for the girls to hurry.

Ashley chased after her a few steps before Miranda pointed back at her. "Stay with the kids, Ashley! Stay with the kids!"

Ashley tossed her sister a handgun, and then looked up at me. I pressed my cheek against the rifle, looking through the scope. I pulled the bolt handle, aimed, and pulled the trigger, taking out the first infected. I leaned my face away. "Run, Jenna! Run to the house! They're in the field! In the field!"

Jenna slowed down and looked around. She couldn't see them coming.

"Run!" I screamed.

Jenna looked behind her, took Halle's hand, and took off toward Nathan and Skeeter. I could hear the boys calling to my children, motioning for them to hurry. I could hear Halle's frightened cry carry across the muggy summer evening air.

I pulled the bolt handle again, aimed, and shot. Grabbing another bullet, I loaded it into the chamber, and then repeated the process. I'd had so much practice over the summer that I barely had to look to load the bullets, but the more shufflers I put down, the more there seemed to be.

The first of the infected emerged from the wheat. Jenna stopped and leaned back so hard she fell backward, taking Halle with her.

I kept shooting, and the boys and Miranda yelled to get the attention of the herd. A wall of bodies was created between my friends and my daughters, with infected fanning out in both directions.

The girls hugged each other and screamed. "Mommy!" Jenna cried. "Mommy!"

I swallowed back my fear and continued shooting, focusing on the walking dead that were reaching for my daughters. I was sure Nathan and the others were killing every undead thing in their path, but the girls were defenseless.

My hands shook as I reloaded, but I forced myself to stay focused, to put down anything that got too close to my kids. Suddenly, Nathan emerged from the opposite field and grabbed the girls. They screamed at first, and then Nathan pushed them behind him. I aimed at the infected closest to him and put it down, but there were three more behind it, and I couldn't reload fast enough.

Nathan shoved the closest one away, but as I was reloading a gunshot went off. The infected fell. Skeeter reloaded and shot again. Through my scope, I could see Nathan say something to the girls. They nodded, and then they disappeared into the north field.

My heart nearly exploded when I lost sight of them, but I continued to put down anything that tried to follow. A horrible, suffering scream made me search the area frantically through my scope. I settled on Bryce, fighting off shufflers in front of him, but being attacked from behind. From point-blank range, Miranda shot Bryce's attacker in the temple, and then fell with her boyfriend to the ground. I couldn't tell where he was wounded, but they were both covered in Bryce's blood.

I pulled my chin away from my rifle, and then forced myself

to reload and search for them again. Miranda was scooting backward, pulling Bryce with one hand, shooting with the other.

"No!" she cried, aiming at the shufflers closing in on her. "Help us!"

I shot one after another. Skeeter did, too, but Miranda only managed to get off two more shots before half a dozen monsters obscured her from view and then began to feed. When her screams of pure anguish filled the air, I closed my eyes tight. Skeeter's rifle popped. Even after Skeeter ended her suffering, the echoes of her screams lingered in the surrounding wheat fields for a few moments.

I looked up, seeing Nathan, Jenna, and Halle emerge from the field and then run across the road and toward the porch. I watched the girls until Ashley corralled them into the safety of the house, and then I looked through the scope again. Nathan ran toward the herd with my hatchet to help his brother-in-law. As much as I wanted to go inside the house and hug my babies, I knew none of us was safe until the last of the herd was taken down.

In one moment, it was as if they were endless, and in the next there were only a few left. I shot, Skeeter shot, and Nathan hurled the hatchet. Bodies lay all over the road and in the ditches. It looked like a scene out of a horror movie; a massacre. Nathan and Skeeter didn't return to the house, instead they stood over the bodies of Miranda and Bryce. They were lying together, chewed and bloody. Skeeter pulled out a handgun, and shot Bryce in the head. He'd already made sure Miranda wouldn't come back. Spending another bullet wasn't necessary.

I climbed down the ladder, and stood in shock as I watched

Jenna and Halle push through the screen door and bury their faces against me. I wasn't sure if I collapsed, or if they did, but all three of us were sitting in a sobbing mess on the porch.

Ashley stood over us for a moment, and then began running toward the road. Her wails were the background music to my reunion with my children. Elleny and Zoe stood in the doorway in shock, neither of them seeming to be able to make sense of what had just happened, nor of the scene on the porch. It seemed like everyone was crying, both happy and sad tears.

Night was falling, and Skeeter and Nathan guided Ashley back to the house. She was sobbing, fighting to stay with her sister. Skeeter had to force her the rest of the way into the house.

Nathan watched Ashley and Skeeter until they disappeared behind the door, and then looked down at my family, offering a small smile. "You have some incredible kids there."

"Miranda?" I asked, already knowing the answer.

He sighed. "Bryce was attacked. She tried to save him. I couldn't get to them in time."

Halle's face was buried under my arm, and her dirty fingernails dug into my skin. I kissed her head. "Come on, girls. I've got you. Let's go inside."

Nathan helped us up, and we walked inside together. The girls were filthy, and I couldn't be sure, but I thought they were still wearing the same clothes they put on the last morning I saw them.

I couldn't stop staring or smiling at them. It almost didn't seem real.

"We saw your message," Jenna said, trying not to cry.

I shook my head. "Where's your dad?"

"He was bit," Halle said in her small voice.

"He made us leave him," Jenna said, her voice quivering. "He made us."

"Ssh ssh," I said, hugging them both. "How long have you been alone?" I didn't know why I was asking. I wasn't sure I wanted to know, or that it mattered.

"I don't know," Jenna said. "A week? I think."

"Wow," Skeeter said. "Tough like their mama."

Jenna smiled and nodded, and leaned her head against my chest. "That's what Dad said, too, when we left him. He said we could do it because we were tough like you."

I looked at Nathan, who was holding Zoe and Elleny close. It made me sick to think my sweet little girls had been alone that long, and I wasn't sure I wanted to know what they had gone through during that time.

"If you hadn't cleared the way for them, it would have been tough for them to make it past Shallot alone, if not impossible," Nathan said. "You were right. It wasn't for nothing."

I nodded, and hugged my girls again. "Come on, babies. Let's get you cleaned up." Halle whined, but I kissed her hair. "You're safe now." I looked to Jenna. "When is the last time you've eaten? Or slept?"

Her eyebrows pulled in. "It's been a while."

I pulled her into my chest. "Okay. Okay, that's all over, now. Nathan?"

"I'm on it," he said, going straight into the kitchen.

I helped the girls wash, and brushed their hair. It was so surreal, doing something so mundane while listening to their terrifying journey. I sat with them at the table and watched them shovel food into their mouths, and once their bellies were full, I walked them into Bryce and Miranda's bedroom, and tucked them in.

In the other room, I could hear Nathan humming to Zoe and Elleny.

Halle gripped her fingers around my wrist, tight. "Don't leave, Mommy."

I shook my head, brought her hand to my mouth, and gave it a kiss. "We'll never be apart again."

"You promise?"

"I *promise*. You are so brave," I said, kissing Halle's forehead, and then looking into Jenna's eyes and touching her cheek. "So brave."

The girls settled in, and within ten minutes they were both in a deep sleep. Nathan came in and watched them for a moment with a smile. "They're beautiful."

"Thank you," I said, sucking in a sharp breath to hold back the sob in my throat.

"You're sleeping in here?" he asked.

I nodded. "In the chair. So I can be here when they wake up. They'll probably forget where they are."

Nathan kneeled down beside me and kissed the tender skin just below my ear.

I leaned into him. "Where is Ashley?"

"Skeeter is with her. She's feeling pretty alone."

"I imagine." I sighed.

"They've both lost the loves of their lives. They have that one awful thing in common, and they can help each other get through it."

We hugged for a while, watching my babies sleep. Jenna jerked a few times, unable to escape the struggle to survive, even in her sleep. I hoped that as time passed, she could rest easy again—that we all could.

"I can't stop staring at them," I whispered. "A part of me is afraid that if I look away or fall asleep that they'll disappear."

"Trust me, they're here. They're safe, and we'll keep them that way."

I looked to him, touched his face, and pressed my lips against his. "I didn't really understand when you said the end of the world was the best thing to have happened to you, and how it was so close to perfect. But now that everyone in our family is here . . . and safe . . . I get it."

"Our family, huh?" he smiled.

"They're finally here," I said, shaking my head in disbelief. I smirked when a random thought popped into my head. "Four girls. You're outnumbered."

"I think I can handle it."

I laughed once. "I love you."

His eyebrows pulled in, and he smiled like those words made him so happy that it hurt. "*Now* it's perfect."

Epilogue

Scarlet

JENNA WAS FOCUSED, IGNORING THE SWEAT DRIPPING into her big brown eyes. She rested the butt of the rifle against her shoulder. It was her fifteenth birthday, and Skeeter would call her at any moment to walk with him into the field. For whatever reason, he'd decided that on everyone's birthday, he would challenge them to a shoot-off. The winner would get a can of peaches, a delicacy we saved for special occasions. Somehow, even though Skeeter could beat any one of us on his birthday, he always seemed to lose by a hair on everybody else's.

"I'm going to beat him for real this year, Mom."

"Oh, yeah?" I said, glancing around the perimeter. It was my turn on watch, even though it had been over a year since the outbreak and the few teds that stumbled by were so far decayed that we didn't need to make much effort to put them down. Shoving them to the ground and stomping their heads usually did the trick. The act was a lot like crushing an empty soda can; their insides were mush. Even Elleny had put a few down that way.

We still took turns, though, on top of the roof of the farmhouse. A surprise attack was still dangerous, especially on a day like today when everyone would be running around, celebrating, forgetting to be careful.

I glanced down at the crosses under the oak tree. The soil on the graves now had grass growing from the settled mounds.

Ashley stepped off the porch and looked up at Jenna and me, holding her hand over her eyes to shield them from the glare. "Are you coming or what?" she said, smiling.

Jenna managed a half-smile. "Just getting my sights lined out."

"You're going to surprise him," I said, nudging her arm.

"I'm going to surprise everyone."

With that, Jenna crawled to the ladder carefully and climbed down to the porch. She caught up with Elleny, and they interlocked arms. Over the last year, they had bonded and become best friends, both bearing a truth no child their age should carry. Elleny, with the nightmares she endured from Kevin, and Jenna, with the guilt of leaving her father to die. Except for that first night, she didn't sleep through the night for months, tortured by the last moments she'd spent with her father. Elleny understood her pain in a way no one could, and they'd become inseparable.

"Mommy!" Halle called, pushing her glasses up the bridge of her nose. "You comin' down?"

"No, ma'am. I'm on watch."

"Aw," she whined, kicking at the dirt.

Nathan stepped off the porch carrying Zoe in one arm, and scooped up Halle with the other. He kissed Halle's cheek. "I'll walk you, baby doll." Nathan glanced up at me and winked, and then followed Elleny and Jenna to the open field.

I glanced around the perimeter, checking hard to see places through my scope, and then turned to watch my happy family marching to the place Skeeter had set up for the challenge.

Ashley had stayed behind, standing over the graves of her father, her sister, Bryce, and Cooper. She stared at the crosses she had painstakingly made for them, mouthing words I couldn't hear. Finally, the front door slammed and Skeeter appeared. He walked up behind Ashley and put his arm tenderly around her waist. They stood there for a moment, with Ashley leaning back against his chest. Skeeter leaned forward to kiss her cheek and then took her hand, leading her away.

Skeeter and Ashley had leaned on each other for support for a long time after we lost everyone. Their friendship turning into something more wasn't really a surprise, but it was interesting watching them love each other while still mourning and loving Jill and Cooper. We lived in a strange new world, where even relationships required a new understanding.

As everyone I loved walked hand in hand or in someone's arms, a familiar and yet strange sound echoed in the distance. As soon as I heard the sound, I knew what it was, but it had been so long since we'd heard or even seen an airplane, it was easy to believe it could be my imagination.

I stood up on the roof, trying to discern from which direction the muted, swirling sound of air was coming from. I turned, holding my hand over my eyes to block out the glaring sun. The sound of the planes' engines was present, but the planes themselves were not. Nathan, the girls, Ashley, and Skeeter stood in the field, every one of their faces tilted to the sky.

The sound grew closer, and just before it was on top of us, two fighter jets soared over side by side, heading northeast.

Instinctively, I called out to Jenna, and also instinctively, she pulled Halle from Nathan's arms and ran toward the house. Everyone hurried toward the porch, talking at the same time in excited tones.

"Where do you think they're going?" Ashley asked loudly, most likely directed at me.

"Wichita, looks like. It's about an hour and a half that way, right?" I answered.

Jenna encouraged Halle up the ladder, where they both sat close to me. The planes were out of sight, but we kept our eyes on the horizon.

Nathan set Zoe on her feet. "At those speeds, you'd think they'd be there by now."

Just as Nathan finished his sentence, a bright light outshone the sun, and then a mushroom cloud formed, climbing miles into the sky. Every one of us stared in disbelief. I remembered seeing mushroom clouds on television, but in person . . . it didn't seem real.

"What is that?" Halle asked, finally breaking the silence.

"Is that a nuclear bomb?" Ashley said, her tone signaling her impending panic.

"'Bout how far away are we from Wichita? In miles." Skeeter asked.

Nathan shrugged. "Right at seventy, I bet."

"We should get inside. I don't know what kind of bomb that is, but . . ."

"Oh my God," I said, seeing a wave of dust rising above the horizon. It was heading our way. "Go, Jenna! Go!"

Nathan and I helped the girls climb down the ladder, and I climbed down a few rungs, jumping the rest of the way when

I saw the cloud was coming up fast. "Get inside!" I screamed. I closed the door and ran to get towels to stuff under it. Ashley and Skeeter were pulling up the blankets we used to cover the windows at night, and Nathan was shoving towels under the back door.

We stood in the living room, panting and staring at each other. I shook my head at Nathan, at a loss for what else to do. A roar welled up outside. Jenna, Halle, and Elleny ran to me, and I hugged them all, watching Nathan do the same with Zoe.

Ashley ducked under Skeeter's arm and looked up at him. "What do we do?"

Skeeter scanned the room as the roaring got louder. "Everyone get down on the ground."

We huddled together, waiting until the wave was upon us. The wood frame of the farmhouse creaked against the blast, and the dirt popped against the outer north wall. The three windows on that side burst, throwing glass all over the dining room table and the floor. I kept the girls' heads down, praying that would be the extent of it.

As soon as the wave hit, it was gone. We all slowly looked up at one another, wondering what to do next.

Ashley sniffed. "Are we far enough away, if there's radiation?"

"I can't believe it," Nathan said. "I can't believe they bombed the city. A year after this all started? That doesn't make any sense."

"Maybe the cities are lost, and this is their way of cleanin' up?" Skeeter said. "They can eliminate a lot of teds that way."

"So does that mean there's not a cure?" Elleny said.

"We don't know anything, yet," I said. Halle was curled into a ball in my lap, shaking. "Sssh, baby. It's going to be all right."

"Will they bomb us?" Jenna asked.

"No," I said. "We're so far removed from everything—"

"But what about Shallot?" Elleny asked. "It was full of teds. What if they drop a bomb that close to us?"

I shook my head. "I don't think they will, honey. Most of the teds there have wandered off. Probably to Wichita."

"I hope there weren't any survivors left," Ashley said. "To make it this long and then have that happen. How awful."

"I don't think anyone would survive long in the cities," Skeeter said. "I think we should all stay inside for now. Wait till the air clears. We'll watch to see how Butch acts the next couple of days, watch for fallout. I don't see why they'd risk dropping a nuclear bomb. A regular one'd do the trick."

Nathan nodded. "I agree. No sense in getting all worked up."

"Okay," I said. I stood up and pulled the girls with me. "Did you hear that? Birthday party has been brought inside."

Jenna's mouth pulled to the side. I cupped her face in my hands. "First thing's first. There is a can of peaches with your name on it."

"Can I have one, Jenna? Pleeeeease?" Halle begged.

I left them for the basement, searching through the pantry. Nathan followed me down. I pulled the can off the shelf and looked up at him from under my brow. "We didn't make it this long just to die of radiation poisoning, right? You weren't just saying that to make us feel better?"

Nathan shook his head and pulled me into his arms. "No, love. Skeeter's right. What point would there be to using a radioactive bomb? Unless they had a specific reason to use it, I don't think it makes much sense."

"Really?"

"Really."

I took a deep breath and squeezed him tight, and then followed him up the stairs. Even with his promise, a suffocating sense of dread consumed me. Jenna and Elleny crawled to the window and pulled back the blanket.

"Mom! Is that snow?"

I stood up and walked over to the window, peeking through a crack between the boards. "No," I said softly, watching the fluffy, dark pieces float to the ground.

"That's fallout, ain't it?" Skeeter asked.

Nathan leaned down to get a better look through the largest crack. "Fallout isn't radioactive in itself. It could just be dust and debris from the blast that was shot into the air."

Everyone brought blankets and pillows to the basement that night, hoping that putting one more level between us and the ash covering the grass outside would provide a little more protection. By nightfall, enough of it had accumulated on the ground to look like a blanket of dirty wool.

After the children fell asleep, Skeeter and Nathan discussed what the fallout—radioactive or not—might do to our water supply, and other frightening things, until Ashley asked them to stop. It was too late, though; even after we settled in and tried to get some sleep, I found myself staring at the ceiling, worrying.

Nathan kissed my temple. "I think it's going to be okay, Scarlet. I really do."

"But what if it's not? How can I save our kids from this?"

Nathan didn't answer, which scared me even more.

My eyes were just getting heavy enough to stay closed when Skeeter scrambled over to one of the small windows that ran along the top of the east wall. He stood up on the tips of his toes, and could barely get a glimpse.

"I'll be damned," he said softly.

"What?" Nathan said. He wasn't as tall as Skeeter, so he jumped once. They traded glances.

"What do you see?" I said, sitting up on my elbows.

The men rushed to the stairs. Their footsteps only got faster when they crossed the kitchen and living room. I scrambled from my pallet and followed them, gasping when I caught sight of what had them so amazed. The ash was still falling from the sky, gray like a cloudy winter day.

"Is it going to storm?" I said.

"No," Nathan said, his eyes bouncing between the falling and accumulating ash. "The debris is in the atmosphere."

"How long will it stay this way?" I asked.

Nathan shook his head. "I don't know, honey." He looked to me, for the first time real worry in his voice. "I don't know."

Six days after the blast, we were all feeling the effects of being stuck inside. The kids were arguing, and the adults were quick to anger. Without being able to hunt, we were forced to make a significant dent in the precious few canned goods in the pantry.

I stood in the basement, holding three cans of black-eyed peas, and let the tears flow. Ashley took the cans from my arms and leaned her cheek against mine.

"It's going to be okay, right? You're just frustrated, but it's going to be okay."

I nodded and wiped my eyes, taking back the cans. "Yes. We're going to be fine."

"Good," Ashley said, breathing a sigh of relief. I wasn't exactly convincing, but she wanted to believe me, so she was easy to fool.

We walked upstairs together, greeting the kids who were already seated at the dining room table. Nathan took a second look at me, knowing right away I'd been upset. I pulled the can opener from a drawer and began spooning out the beans into everyone's bowls, noting the absence of our usual cheerful dinnertime discussion—or any discussion at all. The girls were staring down into their bowls, looking lost, but Skeeter and Nathan didn't have any more comforting words to offer.

"When it's clear outside, we're going to have to finish Jenna's birthday party," I said, joining everyone at the table. "She's been working really hard to beat you, Skeeter."

Skeeter forced a small smile. "Oh yeah, Jenna?"

Jenna didn't look up from her bowl. She didn't speak. The hopelessness on her face broke my heart.

"Baby?" I said quietly. Her doe eyes rose to meet mine. "This won't last forever. I promise."

Jenna slowly turned to the living room to look out the window. Her eyes widened, and she stood up. "Mom!"

For the first time in nearly a week, ashes weren't falling from the sky. I looked to Jenna, and then to Nathan. Everybody stood up at the same time and rushed to the window, and then sighs of relief and laughter filled the house.

Elleny put her hand on the door, but Nathan stopped her. "Not yet."

"What do you mean? Why not?" Jenna asked, her eyes instantly filling with tears.

Nathan began to answer her, but stopped. The pause that followed was filled with a distant, repetitive beat.

"What is that?" Ashley asked. She listened again. "Is that what I think it is?"

A black helicopter passed over, and then made a wide turn. We watched in awe as it returned, hovered over the road for a moment, and then lowered, landing just beyond the mouth of the drive. Four men with guns filed out, and suddenly I was more terrified of them than I was of the ash. They jogged across the lawn to the porch, and we all jerked at a banging on the door.

"Elleny, take the girls to the basement," I said, keeping my eyes on the door.

"But," she began.

The door opened, and Nathan stepped in front of me protectively.

The men weren't military. They looked more like SWAT, black from head to toe and helmets with large, clear facemasks. The man in front glanced back to his cronies, just as surprised to see us as we were to see them.

The helicopter's blades were still whirring, so the man in front spoke loudly. "My name is Corporal Riley Davis, sir! I'm looking for a Skeeter McGee!"

Ashley grabbed Skeeter's arm, her eyes wide.

"That's me," Skeeter said.

"I have a Ms. April Keeling in the helo. We picked her up from Fairview. She said there might be survivors here, including you, sir!" the corporal said. The corners of his mouth turned up. "Glad to see she was right!"

Skeeter turned to Ashley. "April! From the church!" He turned to the corporal. "Her kids?"

"All well, sir."

"The ash," Nathan said. "The blast. You know anything about it?"

"Yes, sir. The air force has been ordered to target the largest concentrations of infected, sir."

"But is it radioactive?" I asked.

"No, ma'am," the corporal said. "The fallout is just debris from the initial blast. They've been targeting all the major cities."

"So there's nothing left? Of anything?" I asked.

"The cities have been overrun, ma'am," Corporal Davis said. "They're torching everything. We're picking up survivors farther out, though."

I looked to Nathan, and then back to Corporal Davis. "Define everything? How far reaching is the outbreak?"

The corporal's face fell. "Everywhere, ma'am. It's everywhere."

Nathan shifted. "Will they bomb outside the cities?"

"They're leaving the countryside alone, don't you worry," the corporal said, tossing his gun onto his shoulder.

I blew out a sigh of relief, and looked back to the kitchen. The girls were peeking around the corner. I signaled to them that it was okay for them to join us. After a few moments of hesitation, one by one they scurried to my side.

The corporal glanced to the children. "We would have come for you days ago, but the ash clogs up the helos. I'm sorry, sir, but we don't have much time. Is this everyone in your camp? We've been instructed to collect all willing survivors and bring them to our compound."

Nathan looked at me, and then back to the corporal. "Compound? Where?"

"About seventy klicks south of our position, sir. McKinney hospital."

"That's not a compound," I said, my mind racing. We'd gone so long without seeing anyone; it was a lot to take in all at once.

The corporal smiled. "It is now. We've built walls and reinstated the running water. Working on electrical now."

Ashley turned to Skeeter, a wide grin on her face at the prospect of those luxuries.

"How many survivors so far?" Nathan asked.

The corporal's mouth pulled to the side. I could see he wanted to give us better news. "Not as many as we'd like, but new civilians come in every day. I'm sorry, sir, but we should get going. It'll be dark soon, and we're running low on fuel."

Nathan and Skeeter traded glances, and then Nathan turned to me. "What do you think?"

I shook my head. It was too big of a decision to make in that moment. We didn't know who these men were. We could get to McKinney and find it's more like a prison camp, or it could be sanctuary.

I looked to the girls. "They want to take us to someplace safe."

Jenna's eyebrows pulled in. "We're safe here."

Zoe looked up to Jenna, and then mirrored her expression. "And they probably won't let us take Butch."

I smiled, kissed their foreheads, and then turned to Nathan. He nodded, and looked to Skeeter and Ashley.

"We're staying?" Ashley asked. She searched everyone's faces, and then took a deep breath, a resolved smile on her face. She turned to the corporal. "We're staying."

"Sir?" the corporal said to Skeeter.

Skeeter squeezed Ashley to his side. "Let April know we appreciate her sending you boys after us, but we're doing just fine here."

The corporal looked back to his men, who all seemed baffled, and then back to us. "If you change your mind, anchor something bright like a blanket to the roof. We'll be making the rounds. Good luck to you, sir!"

The corporal held a small radio to his mouth. "Pedro to HQ, come in, over."

A man on the other end of the radio confirmed through a scratchy connection.

"Yeah, we're out here at Red Hill. The civilians have decided to sit tight, over."

After a short pause, the radio scratched again. "Roger that."

The corporal nodded to us, and the men returned to their helicopter. Within moments it was in the air and out of sight.

"There's people!" Zoe said, grinning. She clapped her hands together once and intertwined her fingers.

The sky was nearly clear, finally empty of the fallout from the blast. I climbed up the ladder, and one by one, everybody followed. We stood, able to see for miles in each direction. Over the past months, fewer walking dead could be seen. Before the blast, it had been nearly a month since the last of them had wandered too close to the ranch. We couldn't be sure why. Maybe they had all migrated to the city, or maybe others like us were eradicating more shufflers every day. Eventually, the earth would be rid of them. We wouldn't live in fear forever.

Nathan reached out for my hand and sighed, sharing my unspoken relief that we had made the right decision. At Red Hill, we made our own destiny; raising our children in the safest way we could, and protecting each other in a world made of nightmares and uncertainty. The eight of us had carved a place there, and we were more than surviving. We were living.

Zoe and Halle clung to my legs, taking in the otherworldly scene. The ranch and its surroundings were entirely covered in ash, dreary and monochrome, except for a small stretch of red dirt road that had been uncovered by the blustering blades of the helicopter. It was exactly the way the end of the world should look. I smiled, and squeezed Nathan's hand. If the last year had taught me anything, it was that the end only led to one thing—a beginning.

Acknowledgments

WRITING IS OFTEN A SOLITARY JOB, BUT NO AUTHOR does it alone. If I didn't have my manager, biggest cheerleader, and strongest supporter in my corner, the distractions of life wouldn't quiet down long enough for me to write a sentence, much less an entire novel. My husband is all of those things for me. Thank you for always calming the waters, love.

Thank you to Wes Hughes for always being kind. In 2008 you helped me, a struggling student, make ends meet, and in 2013 you let me, a struggling-to-meet-her-deadline author, stay in your guest house to finish *Red Hill*. Your smiling face and ever-encouraging words will forever stay with me.

Amy Tannenbaum, who rolls with whatever I throw her way, be it laughter in the morning or late-night, panicked texts. You are not only my super-editor-turned-agent, you're one of my most treasured friends. I've said before I wouldn't want to experience any part of this process without you, and it's still true. Your pep talks and constant voice of reason make me feel sorry for anyone who doesn't have you in their life. Also, enormous appreciation for the amazing Chris Prestia and all the folks at the Jane Rotrosen Agency for all you do.

Greer Hendricks came on as my editor in February of this year to replace Amy. Amy assured me Greer was perfect for me, and, as always, Amy was right. Greer has taken my writing to the next level, entertained my son in the backseat while stuck in traffic on the way to a book signing, and quite literally saved a manuscript for me—while on vacation, I might add. Thank you, Greer. I don't like change, but you've most graciously made this the most wonderful transition I could have hoped for.

After six novels, Nicole Lambert has been inexcusably overlooked when writing my acknowledgments. Nicole helped me set up my very first website back when I was posting one chapter at a time of *Providence,* before I discovered self-publishing. To add to my shame, she has never once reminded me of that fact. I love you, Nicole. You have been a fantastic friend.

A year ago I was in New York City meeting the geniuses at Atria Books. I was hugely pregnant, sweaty (it was August), and nervous as hell. Waiting for me in the lobby was Ariele Fredman, smiling and funny and oh-so-calming. I couldn't begin to list everything she does for me, but know that she is the best publicist an author could ask for. Thanks for being everything, Mermaid.

Enormous gratitude to my publisher, Judith Curr, who rules the world of Atria with an iron pillow. She is one of the most intelligent and intriguing people I've ever met, a force of nature, and yet she's a safe place to land when I need things to go right. Thank you, Judith. I wouldn't want anyone else to run my show!

A big thanks to my team at Atria! If I listed everyone who helped to mold this novel into its current state, I would need rolling credits, but I'll take this opportunity to sincerely thank a few: Isolde Sauer, Ben Lee, Sarah Cantin, Hillary Tisman, Jackie Jou, and Kimberly Goldstein.

I want to thank my assistant, Colton. I'm not sure how I managed my career—or my life—before he came along. Thank you for all you do! Here's to many more terrifying (but safe) plane rides together!

Dr. Ross Vanhooser is someone who has appeared in my acknowledgments time and time again. Had he not believed in me, and encouraged me in an environment where no one else did, my life and career would be in a much different place. This time around, he also assisted me with my medical research for *Red Hill*. You have always offered invaluable advice, benevolent help, and endless enthusiasm. Thank you so very much. I'll never forget your kindness.

I also wish to thank Sharon Ronck. When others asked her to not wave my flag quite so high, she proudly held up two. I'm honored to have fulfilled your predictions! We need more people in this world with a heart like yours.

To Leah, Miranda, and Ashley for the use of their names, and for allowing me to add fictional flair to their characters.

To authors Colleen Hoover, Karly Lane, Lani Wendt Young, Eyvonna Rains, and Tracey Garvis Graves for reading *Red Hill* and validating that I wasn't absolutely insane for going with my gut and in a completely different direction. I so appreciate your time and enthusiasm.

Finally, I wish to thank my daughters for having such big, amazing personalities and letting me write about them. I learned what all-consuming, unconditional love is when you came into my life. Since 1999, my heart has lived on the outside of my body. Since 2005, that joy, fear, and suspense has been doubled. I hope if you choose to become mothers, your children might give you half the joy you've gifted to me. Maybe then you'll understand why I look at you the way I do.

E, thanks for working on this with me, Taterbug. You are going to blow me out of the water someday very soon.

And to my little man: You are perfection. You are tied as one of the three best things I've ever done. It brings me so much joy that you'll never know what life was like before our dreams came true, and I'm so thankful that, thanks to my fans, I work from home so I can spend as much time with you as I possibly can, because I wouldn't want it any other way.

So much love to my readers! You've made the impossible possible for my family and me. A lost, small-town girl became a #1 *New York Times* bestselling author. If that's not a miracle, I don't know what is!